A VIAL
UPON THE
SUN

A VIAL
UPON THE
SUN

JAMES
CODLIN

with CRAIG CODLIN

And the fourth angel poured out his vial upon the sun; and power was given unto him to scorch men with fire. And men were scorched with great heat, and blasphemed the name of God, which hath powers over these plagues: and they repented not to give him glory.

—Revelation 16:8-9, King James Bible

CHAPTER ONE

Spain—1487

EVERY DAY IT surprised him how loudly a man could scream.

Though the cells were deep underground below a windowless and unremarkable building in Zaragoza, the cries pierced the morning calm, causing the man to look up from his documents. His hair and beard were gray, and his face was thin but not emaciated. His eyes were alert and intelligent, unmoving while reflecting, then animated while writing. The man's visage was pleasant and had none of the diabolical details depicted in the artists' renditions circulating throughout Europe. Though he was one of the most powerful men in Spain, his clothes were the humble raiment of the Dominican friars.

The priest scraped a knife over the point of his quill pen, which had been worn down by his energetic penmanship.

A new scream rang out, a woman's voice this time—high pitched and steady, then wavering, then roughened by hoarseness, and finally dying away. The man of God adjusted his sackcloth robe and turned back to his writing. After thirty minutes, he closed with a flourish of his pen:

> *Remember, Your Most Royal Highness, this is not just for our time on earth. This we do for one, ten, a hundred, or a thousand years, whatever is required to bring on the Millennium.*
>
> *Your faithful servant,*
>
> *Tomás de Torquemada*

Torquemada reread his writing. Then, not trusting the work to scribes, he wrote two identical originals—one to retain for himself, and the other two for the king. Each went by separate couriers to King Fernando II in Barcelona to ensure that at least one document would survive the vagaries of fifteenth-century delivery.

The first document went by horseman on the road through Lleida to Barcelona and was in the king's hands within four days. King Fernando II immediately convened the additional three members of the Council of the Supreme and General Inquisition. They reviewed Torquemada's document and called into their conference a minor official of the Royal Treasury. The accountant, a recent Jewish convert to Catholicism, listened to his liege lord and councilors, wrote detailed instructions to the Royal Treasury, and was put to death. His body was interred along with the corpses of the three council members, the dead courier rider, and the ashes of Torquemada's papers.

The second document went by boat down the Ebro River and into the Mediterranean, where a storm shipwrecked the vessel on the beach near Tarragona. An illiterate fisherman found the leather pouch containing the document washed up on the sand and was intrigued by the intricate wax seal on the papers. Two weeks later the fisherman's nephew breathlessly burst into the house, crying that armed men of the Holy Office of the Inquisition were smashing down doors and searching for lost documents. The terrified fisherman hid the papers, never speaking of them to anyone.

In 1720 the fisherman's long-abandoned house was being torn down to make way for the oceanfront home of a wealthy merchant. A minor municipal official saw a weathered leather pouch in the rubble and took it to his office. The archaic Spanish baffled him. He sent it to a cousin in Seville, suggesting that he take the documents to the royal repository.

In Seville a harried bureaucrat glanced at the seals on the papers, then sharply remonstrated the man, pointing out that his office filed documents pertaining to the House of Commerce and the imperial trade monopoly with the Indies, not the Holy Office. Disgusted, he snatched them from the ignorant commoner and threw them in a pile.

Weeks later, the pile of documents—which had grown with the arrival of a hundred other documents from Madrid and Spain's colonies in the

Indies—was tied into a bundle and tossed onto a dark shelf among thousands of similar bundles in an obscure Seville warehouse that sixty-five years later would come to be known as the Archive of the Indies.

CHAPTER TWO

"HAVE YOU SEEN your face on the newsstand?" Teodoro Lenin asked.

"Yes. Thirty of me spread over almost a whole wall in the airport bookstore. What a handsome bastard!"

Lenin laughed and walked across his study to a magazine rack. His age was hard to pinpoint, but definitely over sixty. His head was completely bald and highly polished. His eyes had heavy bags under them, but the rest of his face was surprisingly wrinkle-free. This was Miami in August, but Lenin wore a brown wool herringbone suit with vest, crisp white shirt, and a paisley bow tie. His wingtip shoes sparkled with a high gloss.

He threw a copy of *Vanity Fair* to the young man sitting on the sofa and said, "But I forgot, Martín—since you defected to technology you don't read analog publications anymore."

"Give me a break, Doc," Martín said. "I like to think of architecture as the convergence of the old and the new—art and science, joined as one."

Martín had to admit that he liked his picture on the cover of the magazine—full color and capturing his dark hair and eyes that contrasted with his light skin, reflecting a heritage that traced back to the north of Spain by way of Cuba. His hair was stylishly long and somewhat windblown, hanging over his ears and cascading down to his neck. It was a head and shoulders shot taken on the deck of his fifty-foot sailboat with the Miami skyline in the background. Yellow block letters read: MARTÍN IBARRA PAZ—THE CUBAN-AMERICAN MR. FIXIT.

"Ah, Mr. Fixit," Lenin said. "I don't want you to strain yourself, so I'll summarize it for you."

Lenin ignored Martín's exaggerated eye roll and clasped his hands behind his back, tilted his face up, and began pacing slowly back and forth in front of his antique Spanish trestle desk. The younger man, having spent many hours in Lenin's presence, recognized his former professor's lecture posture and sank back in his seat, knowing that there was nothing to do but listen.

"It traces your heritage back to the Ibarras of Zaragoza, Spain—several generations of goldsmiths. It even gets into that unsavory business in 1492 when your ancestors were asked by the Church, 'Don't you think you would be happier converting from Judaism to Catholicism?' To stay alive, your ancestors wisely accepted the Church's generous offer. But when the Inquisition began persecuting converted Jews, your great-great-great, et cetera grandfather decided it might be a good idea to make a fresh start in the New World. Off they went to Cuba, building a new life as artisans and merchants in Havana, until their neighbors became jealous of the Ibarra's success—fine clothes, nice home, and big parties—and began to gossip that the Ibarra family never ate pork. What could that mean?"

Lenin beamed at Martín with his best professorial smile—a smile signaling the rhetorical nature of the question. Any student so impudent to answer such questions from Lenin would be subjected to a barrage of savage sarcasm.

"Back in Spain everyone, especially the *conversos*, ate pork frequently and ostentatiously—if for no other reason than to prove that they were not Jews. But the Ibarra family of Havana—who went to the Catholic cathedral every Sunday, who fasted on Fridays, who fed half the town on Catholic saints' days, who raised a son who became archbishop of Cuba—didn't eat pork. What was a good Catholic to think?

"Fast forward to the 1950s and there is the Ibarra family, right hand to the dictator Fulgencio Batista. Enter, stage left, Fidel Castro. Batista bails, and the bearded one from the Sierra Maestra is in charge.

"The Ibarras are worried, thinking about the pogroms in the Soviet Union, but Fidel makes a remarkable announcement: he is proud of his *marrano* heritage—his ancestors were Jewish converts too! The Ibarras hang in there, now with *everyone* being discouraged from going to mass or temple or adhering to any organized religion, it being the opiate of the people and all.

"Then *Granma* runs a front-page piece about the Ibarras, claiming that they were found practicing Jewish rituals in their home. Fidel frowns—not because they are of the Chosen People but because he wants to maintain official state atheism and having such a prominent and politically connected family flaunt its religious practices is quite... problematic. Suddenly the Ibarras are in Miami and Fidel is quite upset that they left without saying good-bye to their old patron.

"Their youngest boy, Martín, their first child born in America, graduates as valedictorian from his Miami high school and gets a National Merit scholarship to the University of Miami, where he has the great fortune to study under the brilliant and witty professor Teodoro Lenin, who has recently arrived from the University of Buenos Aires. The professor does his best to teach this philistine the thinking man's history of the great world empires, but young Ibarra proves obstinate beyond all reason. During his third year, he shocks the academic world by transferring to Cornell to study—dare I say it out loud?—architecture.

"Ibarra goes on to graduate *magna cum laude*—blah, blah, blah— apprentices at a prestigious Coral Gables architecture firm—blah, blah, blah—wins awards for his work in North and South America—et cetera, et cetera—but there are also some odd gaps during his career where he apparently spent some time in Guatemalan jungles with shady Cuban exiles. Hmm, what could that be about?"

"Hey, let's not gloss over that part about the awards," Martín said. "Let's go over them in detail!"

"Oh, they did, ad nauseam, with photos and reproductions of your 'architect's renditions.' Next comes the explanation about the formation of the Latino Union—all the Latin American countries, tired of years of hyperinflation and existing essentially as raw materials colonies for the *norteamericanos*, form an economic confederation akin to the European Union. The new union has its problems but forges forward and realizes that in order to centralize its new government it needs a new and neutrally located capital city. They don't want to ruin their economies as Brazil did with Brasilia, so they form a team comprised of architects from all the LU countries to design a modest capital nestled among the foothills of the Ecuadorian Andes. They fight over the design, and time drags on with the project in limbo.

"In a panic because it doesn't want the stalled project to be branded as another exercise in Latino *mañana* escapism and bureaucratic bungling, the union casts its eyes around the world to find an architect who can make peace among a coalition of architectural prima donnas and get the project done. It seems, though, that the best person for the job is a *gringo*—oh, no! There is gnashing of teeth and rending of garments! But organizationally, there's none better. What to do, what to do? Aha! There is a technicality— the Gringo's parents are from Cuba, a non–Latino Union country—ergo, he is a Latino of neutral non-union heritage, so bring him in!

"Enter *deus ex machina* Martín Ibarra Paz, super architect, super organizer, 'Mr. Fixit.' He waves his magic wand and—shazam!—the project is completed on time and within budget.

"There you have it: the whole article in three and a half minutes. I have saved you hours of tedious labor."

The old professor finished his pacing and turned to face the younger man.

"One more thing, Martín," he said in English. "Guess who appears with you in one of the photos?"

Martín flipped open the magazine. There was a black and white photograph of his parents and older brothers and sisters on the porch of their grand house in Havana, and another in which he was wearing his mortarboard at his Cornell graduation. In a third shot, which was grainy and blurred but unmistakably him, he was wearing fatigues and crossed bandoleers loaded with bullets. There were several pages of pictures and sketches of his best buildings, and a photographic panorama of the partially finished Latino Union capital city, San Juan Diego, named for the full-blooded Chichimec Indian who had fought Spanish colonists for more than 40 years in the 16th century.

Next were photos of various Latin American leaders: Miguel Días-Canel, of course, along with Osvaldo de Valencia, president of Chile; Agustín Azul Cuahutemoc, president of Mexico; and Carlos VII, king of

Spain. Finally there was one showing Martín shaking hands with Takeshi Ishikawa, then-president of Brazil.

And there she was, on Martín's left arm.

A young woman—mid-twenties with long black hair, the elegant build of a ballet dancer, and a broad smile. Her eyes gave her a look of wisdom beyond her years, like a Tibetan monk, and her high cheekbones tapered down to a strong chin. She was Gina Ishikawa, the daughter of the Latino Union's president.

Both of Gina's parents were from the Japanese-Brazilian community in São Paulo, and Gina was a third-generation Brazilian. She looked and spoke Japanese and observed the traditional Japanese etiquette toward her parents, but her daily language, dress, and outlook away from home were 100% Brazilian.

Professor Lenin chuckled. "Still holding a torch for her? If you had gotten off your ass and done something about it, she wouldn't be engaged to that Japanese billionaire."

Martín closed the magazine and stared at his face on the cover. His good feelings about the day were gone. He looked up and saw that Lenin was behind his desk at a computer. He turned the monitor around so Martín could see.

"Have you used this yet?" Lenin asked. "Of course you haven't! You're an architect now—not the historian you should have been. Carlos VII will dedicate this project at the inauguration of San Juan Diego. It's an online tie-in to the Archive of the Indies in Sevilla to permit research among the millions of documents there. I remember when it was a dank old building with a few bare light bulbs hanging and they just dumped bundles of documents on your tiny table, allowing just anybody to paw through those magnificent papers. Bring your chair around and sit next to me!"

Lenin surged expertly through menu after menu until two documents filled the screen. The left side showed the paper in its current state—dark, blurred, stained, and torn—and on the right side a computer-enhanced version reduced the discoloration of the paper and enhanced the lettering that had been penned four centuries earlier.

"Look here," Lenin said, placing the cursor halfway down the page.

"This is a page from the passenger manifest, dated March 12, 1515, for the ship *Córdoba*. She sailed with the Indies Run spring fleet to Havana."

Martín squinted at the writing, a cursive called *procesal* in which letters and words were tied together with long chains of small arcs and flourishes. There was little punctuation or spacing, and the entire page seemed to be made up of a few long words.

The professor moved the cursor to an icon and clicked. The enhanced page on the right suddenly shifted from *procesal* into modern Spanish printing.

Martín scanned the page. "Sir Francisco de Ibarra and his woman, Gloria Cárdenas de Ibarra and their children Pedro, Maria... and Martín."

"Your venerated ancestors," Lenin said. "And look at this notation in the margin." There was a sketched cross followed by the words "*Buenos cristianos, limpios de sangre.*"

"'Good Christians, pure blood.'"

"No Jews, or even *conversos*, were allowed to go to the colonies," Lenin said. "Before the ships were cleared to sail from Sanlúcar de Barrameda, officers of the Inquisition boarded and went over the manifest and the papers of every soul on board—a final rigorous screening during which everyone had to prove the purity of their blood." He chuckled. "Your relatives must have had good false papers. The Holy Office blessed them, as it were, and they escaped to a new life."

Martín forgot the funk that had overtaken him since he had seen Gina's picture and stared at the screen. He tentatively reached out his finger, paused, and then gently touched the screen, stroking the names of his forebears.

*

Gina Ishikawa was out of breath as she walked into the Vatican press office. She had just sprinted from Saint Peter's Square to get a seat in the pressroom before the official announcement of the election of the new pope.

She went to sit down and froze when she saw Martín Ibarra's face staring up at her from the table. There was a yellow Post-it note affixed to the cover of the magazine, scrawled with the words "I see your ex made the big time." That could only be from Dennis Prinn.

She picked up the magazine, taking in every detail of Martín's face, and let out a long sigh. His face was more pinched than she remembered, and his features had hardened a bit. But his eyes still had that brightness that, when focused on hers, seemed to look inside her. In the photo, the hair that she used to stroke was flying in the wind as he stood among the rigging out on the deck of his boat where they had spent more than one wondrous night.

Doors crashed open and other journalists flooded into the room.

A hundred phones suddenly chirped, played tunes, rang, sang and buzzed in an electronic cacophony. The official announcement had arrived. A babel of languages filled the air as reporters barked into their phones, dictating their pieces while reading the source document.

Gina put aside the *Vanity Fair*, pulled out her phone, and clicked opened the Vatican release. The 267th pontiff—including the anti-popes—had been elected at conclave with the election signaled moments ago to the masses by the usual means, a puff of white smoke from the chimney of the Sistine Chapel. This new pope was from France, not Italy—the most common country of origin by far—or, following recent trends, a country that hadn't seen one of their countrymen elected before.

The new pope had started as parish priest in a small town near Lille. He was a Dominican, and he had been taught history in a Dominican school. His surname was Legendre and he came from a family of farmers at Nord-Pas-de-Calais. He had a long list of publications, served on courts to determine annulments of marriages, and was well versed in canon law.

Gina pulled out her tablet and began pecking out her story. She began with the sudden death of the incumbent pope, the rapid convening of the council of cardinals, and the unusually long time it took for them to decide who would become the new pope. She then started to type the summary of His Holiness's life story and career development, but then she stopped. She looked around at her competitors who were all frantically doing the same—churning out the same boilerplate stories off of the same release they had all just received. A release that was already available and being read around the world.

She closed the lid on her computer, put it back into its bag, and started for the door. Dennis Prinn called out to her from across the room, cutting through the noise with his broad Aussie accent.

"Yo, Gina, you wrote one fast bloody story!"

She stopped by his makeshift desk and glanced at the photograph of a pretty dark-haired woman he had taped to the lamp. The woman in the picture was beaming with unabashed pride and was gesturing dramatically toward a home with a blue tile roof and a statue of Pan near the front door. Gina recognized the architecture, placing it in one of the pristine new suburbs of San Juan Diego. It seemed that there were reminders of her father everywhere she looked these days.

"No, Dennis, I'm not going to do the usual born-raised-priest-bishop-archbishop-cardinal-pope story. They can get that generic shit from the wire services."

Dennis tugged on his gaudy clip-on tie which clashed with the pinstripes on his ill-fitting suit. "What other story is there?" Dennis grandly gestured around the room. "In a few minutes, once this lot realizes that no one is going to read their half-assed regurgitation of the press release, most of these guys are going to be begging me for the footage I've prepackaged and had ready to go for this very occasion. For the right price, I'll be able to make them look awfully good to their editors when they can run a slick, professionally produced video along with their written piece and deliver it to the masses—" He snapped his fingers. "That fast!"

Dennis was the best Gina knew at managing and facilitating television-computer-satellite-internet interfaces. For years he freelanced for the American and international networks. But in recent years, as the global reach and capacity of the mobile internet made worldwide video distribution easier than ever, his formerly steady stream of freelance work had begun to dry up. Gina felt sorry for him, but she couldn't let his unsubtle dig at old-school print journalism go unchallenged.

"I know, Dennis… but believe it or not, some people still read—and they want some depth and *real* reporting. So I need to come up with something better than thirty seconds of B-roll interspersed with meaningless sound bites."

Dennis feigned a hurt expression. "An obsolete and inefficient way of transmitting information." He crumpled up a sheet of paper and slam-dunked it into a wastebasket that he had commandeered for his own private use, dragging it over next to his desk. He had fashioned a backboard for the wastebasket—a poster board festooned with cutouts of various cardinals' faces, each with Vegas-style odds scrawled next to them. Legendre had been at 150-1 odds, and no one had placed any bets on him. Based on all the notations made next to the other presumed candidates, it was clear that Dennis had taken a fair amount of action on who the next pope would be. Gina felt oddly proud that her friend had already managed to make some decent money out of his trip.

"Since the 24-hour news cycle has perpetual deadlines of 'right-fucking-now,' I've got the means to help my clients meet them. But, of course, you being a president's daughter and a Sheila and all, I reckon your editor has to cut you some slack, right?"

"Doesn't matter how fast they get it if it's cookie cutter garbage," Gina said.

Dennis laughed. "Yeah, yeah, yeah. You keep servicing your wine and cheese crowd and I'll keep feeding the unwashed masses with my—wait for it—*sound and moving pictures*!"

Gina shook her head in good-natured indignation, winked at Dennis, and turned to walk away.

"But, hey! How 'bout old Marty?" Dennis asked. "See that *Vanity Fair* piece? That had depth and real reporting!"

Gina paused and started to say something, but found no words. Even for Dennis, that cut a little too close to the quick. She did her best to show no reaction other than to throw her head back in comically exaggerated mock exasperation, toss her hair, and walk out the door.

*

Martín placed a bag of groceries on the kitchen counter and pulled out his phone, starting his voicemail. The first message played on speaker as he methodically put his groceries away.

"Hey, Marty. Dave calling. I'm in Seville, man. Got some heavy legal work underway, but I wanted to let you know that I'll be finishing up in five or six days. I'm looking forward to getting back to Miami. I've got a ton of papers and books and stuff—I hope you can pick me up at the airport. I'll even buy you dinner if you do. Call me back when you can. Bye."

Martín smiled at hearing the voice of his old friend from college, now an attorney specializing in international law and living in the condo building next to Martín's on Key Biscayne. He was not a traditional lawyer—Dave scoffed at the "lawyer-bots" who lived their lives dressed in high-end conservative suits while toiling sixteen-hour days at urban law firms, trying to claw their way onto the partner track. Dave had long hair that he pulled back into a ponytail and wore only jeans or baggy cotton pants along with oversized oxford cloth shirts. And ties? Never.

Conventional wisdom would have dictated that Dave put in time at some well-heeled law firm to learn his craft and earn a name for himself. But Dave Broch refused to do so, choosing instead to go directly from his graduation ceremony to a container vessel sailing from New Jersey for Rotterdam. He worked his way across the ocean as a seaman, met a girl in Amsterdam, moved in with her, and waited tables at an Italian restaurant. When he had time off, he hopped the train to The Hague and sat in on sessions of the World Court.

A year and two girlfriends later, Dave was writing briefs for Dutch law firms. When the offers came, he refused to become a full-time employee. Instead he moved to Brussels and wrote briefs and published papers on sovereignty issues for the European Commission for the next three years. Eventually he found his way back to America, but he continued to freelance, preparing white papers for the U.S. Department of State and private law firms whenever there were questions of national sovereignty in government or private business dealings with emerging nations all over the world.

As usual, Dave's message had been supplemented by the raucous sounds of a party in the background. Dave worked hard, but the freelance lifestyle allowed him the flexibility to seek out the night culture wherever he found himself. At this point in Martín's life he grew exhausted just thinking about staying out past nine, but Dave still showed no signs of slowing down.

Martín put a six-pack of Red Stripe beer in the refrigerator as the next message started playing over his phone's speaker.

"Architect Ibarra, this is Dr. Herrera calling from San Juan Diego. Sir, I call on behalf of His Excellency, the president."

Martín froze, clutching a box of cereal that he had been about to put into a cabinet, and listened.

"We have a… problem. No, well, a… *potential* problem. His Excellency requests… no, requires… your presence. So, well, uh… please call me with your travel plans. We will expect for you to arrive here tomorrow. Call me on my personal phone. You have the number. Good-bye."

Martín slammed the cabinet door shut. During his tenure leading the architectural committee he had been subtly pressured to enter the political arena in the new union. When he resisted, the pressure became more overt. Still, Martín refused, pleading the necessity of returning to his firm in Miami. Once he had made his intentions explicitly clear, he had been assured that his further presence in San Juan Diego would not be required. Now he would have to go back and endure an awkward reunion with Gina's father. He snatched his phone from the countertop and pulled up his travel app.

*

Gina sat at a cubicle in the Vatican library, poring through the official data on the new pope. Father Guy Legendre had been named both a bishop and archbishop at a fairly young age, and she was surprised to learn that he had been a cardinal for only a little over a year. He had been selected as a cardinal *in pectore*, in secret, four years before ascending to the position. The internal politics of the Vatican were largely invisible to outsiders, but the election of such a young man seemed… out of character.

The sources in the library listed Legendre's good works—help for parishioners beyond the call of duty, educational awards, a stint in a Catholic hospital in India. All of these were laudable and demonstrated that as a churchman Legendre was well above average, but… papal material?

The librarian had referred Gina to some clips from the world press, both written and electronic, and additional Vatican internal published sources. There was also a list of magazine and internet articles from both Catholic and commercial sources.

Gina spent the rest of the day going through all of them.

CHAPTER THREE

Santo Toribio de Liébana, Spain—1515

THE ABBOT OF the monastery walked to the iron bars of the entrance gate where a man stood on the other side, shaking dust off his cape and stamping his boots. The abbot was accompanied by a monk carrying a torch. The man on the other side of the gate was the same height as the abbot but younger, perhaps thirty-five years old, well-dressed but somewhat gaunt. His hair was black and long and he had no facial hair. He kept a red broad-brimmed hat with a white plume in place and did not remove his gloves.

The abbot made the sign of the cross. "In the name of God, how may I help you, traveler, at this very late hour?"

"I am sorry to disturb you, Abbot, but my need is urgent." The man spoke with natural-sounding formality, and an air of sophistication surrounded him. He came across as a man of some importance, albeit in the secular world. "Brother Alonso Gomez of this order is my cousin, and I understand he is gravely ill."

"And you are…?"

"Don Diego Santiago of Valladolid."

"Then you have been on the road—"

"Three days. I came as quickly as I could."

There was a pregnant pause as the abbot considered his options. He did not relish letting in a stranger at this hour, no matter the reason.

Both the monk and the visitor looked at him expectantly. "You are a man of commerce?"

"Yes, Abbot."

"Then you must be the man with whom Brother Gomez corresponds so often."

"Yes, Abbot. We were very close when I was a child."

"I had understood he had no family."

"As I say, we are cousins—distant cousins."

"I see. Yes, Brother Gomez is quite ill. Frankly, we don't expect his time on earth to be much longer."

"Then, Abbot, may I see my cousin before he passes?"

Something felt oddly amiss to the abbot. The man's attitude seemed... off. He came across more like a man who was looking to finalize a business transaction than someone whose aim was to comfort a loved one in his final hours. The abbot, still uncertain, lamely offered, "This is very unusual, and the hour is late."

"Please, Abbot, I have traveled so far to have at least a little time with Alonso."

The abbot stood silently while the man stood patiently on the other side of the gate, watching the abbot deliberate. Finally, the abbot relented. "All right," the abbot said as he reached forward to unlatch the gate. "Brother Del Rio will accompany you to his cell."

The traveler followed the monk into the monastery and across a wide patio with a fountain gurgling in the darkness. They descended stairs to a long hallway with multiple doors on each side, eventually stopping at one of them. The monk opened the door and stepped in, holding the door open. The traveler entered and stood in the torchlight, regarding the old man on the pallet. The sick man stared back at him with rheumy eyes, laboring to focus.

"Brother Del Rio," the man said to the monk. "I have some very personal things to say to Brother Gomez. May we be alone?"

The monk nodded, relieved to be dismissed, and placed the torch in a sconce before retiring from the room. The man listened as the echoes of Brother Del Rio's footsteps receded. He knelt beside Gomez and removed his hat and one glove.

Gomez gripped the man's arm. "Brother Segovia, I recognize you with the scar on your right temple, your green eyes, and your missing thumb." His voice was hoarse and almost inaudible.

"And I recognize you from your cleft chin and wing-like ears," Segovia said with a slight smile.

"Your disguise is excellent. You look like a wealthy merchant—not a monk."

Segovia let the compliment settle for a moment, maintaining his smile. But now it was time to resolve matters. "Have you transferred the knowledge?" Segovia asked.

"Yes, Brother Alejandro Rojas met the requirements, has taken the blood oath, and received the instructions." With a palsied hand Gomez reached under his robe and withdrew a paper.

Brother Segovia, Benedictine monk of the Monastery of San Benito el Real, Valladolid, took it and held it up to the torchlight, reading the physical description of Brother Rojas. He then touched the paper to the flame. Ashes fell from his fingers as the paper disintegrated. He reached into his breast pocket and removed a small object.

"I will inform Burgos," Segovia said, holding up a glass ampoule. "You were the first man nominated for our responsibility. You have served the Guardians of the Fourth Angel well."

"As have you, Brother," Gomez replied. He nodded toward the ampoule and, using what little strength he had remaining, lifted his head slightly in expectation.

Segovia pulled the stopper from the ampoule and poured three drops of liquid into Gomez's mouth. Gomez settled back onto the pallet. Segovia gently took the hand of a man he had never met before in his life, but with whom he shared the deepest of bonds.

They recited in unison, "This we do for one, ten, a hundred, or a thousand years, whatever is required to bring on the Millennium."

Gomez closed his eyes and, within moments, stopped breathing.

CHAPTER FOUR

GINA ISHIKAWA HURRIED through the Brussels National Airport terminal. She carried only her briefcase and a small carry-on bag as she walked straight to the rental car counter. Fifteen minutes later she was driving west toward Lille, France, squinting through the windshield against the fierce August sun and mentally mapping out her piece on the new Pope Pius XIII. She skirted around Lille, continuing west, absently noticing signs for World War I battlegrounds before spotting a sign for Vincennes, the village she was looking for.

Much like other towns in Nord-Pas-de-Calais, Vincennes was tiny, neat, and agricultural. The church stood out among other buildings, and Gina was surprised to see how new it was compared to most small-town churches. In fact, the whole town seemed to have been recently built.

After parking the car, Gina took her Nikon camera out of her shoulder bag and snapped several pictures of the church where Guy Legendre had been a priest. She pushed open a rusted gate and stepped into the small cemetery. Looking around, she saw a few graves decorated with fresh flowers and one with a small French flag stuck in the turf. Gina walked among the weather-beaten and mossy tombstones, peering at the names.

In the northeast corner, she spied a tombstone with the engraving GASTON LEGENDRE, and next to it, LUCILLE LEGENDRE. The Holy Father's parents.

Gina checked the sun, moved to the proper position, changed lenses, and snapped five more photos.

A man called from behind her in French, "Hello, may I help you?"

Gina turned. A young man wearing stylishly baggy casual pants, a Nautique polo shirt, and round John Lennon sunglasses, stood looking at her with his hands in his pockets. When he saw her face, he said in Japanese, "May I help you?"

Gina, taken by surprise, answered in Japanese, "Please excuse me—I am studying the cemetery. I hope that is all right."

The man bowed, his arms down straight, hands close to his knees, and replied, "Sorry to interrupt you. You are most welcome. I am very honored to have a visitor from your country."

Gina was shocked. The man, a Caucasian, was speaking Japanese flawlessly, and even knew the culture's courtesies.

She returned the bow and said in Japanese, "Do you know this cemetery and this town? I have some questions."

He gave her an enigmatic smile. "I do know some things about it. But please, you are too warm out here in the sun. Would you care to have some cool tea?"

"If it will not take you out of your way," Gina replied. She followed him into the church. Once inside, she turned toward the altar and crossed herself. This time it was the young man's turn to wear a shocked expression.

"You are a Catholic?"

Gina looked at his serious young face and laughed. "Yes, and I'm afraid I have misled you. I am not Japanese, I am Brazilian."

He looked a bit flustered. "Proving again, one must never assume. I am sorry, I speak no Portuguese." He led her to a small kitchen, took a jug from a wheezing old refrigerator, poured tea into two glasses, and handed her one.

"And you," she asked, "do you live around here?"

The young man gave her his crooked smile again. "Yes… in the rectory. I am the priest."

Once more, it was Gina's turn to be surprised. "And your Japanese language?"

"Straight out of the seminary, I went to Japan for three years."

"I have never been there," Gina said. The words hung in the air for a moment before the young priest began to laugh. Thinking he was being impolite, he tried his best to stifle the laughter, but Gina joined him moments later as they both absorbed the irony.

"Well, then," he said as their laughter subsided, "what exactly are you doing here, in my little French village?"

She switched to French. "I'm not being fair to you. I went to school in Geneva. I'm a journalist and I'm trying to come up with an original story on Guy Legendre—excuse me, on His Holiness."

The priest grimaced. "I'm afraid I'll be overrun with the press. Also, tourists… priests… nuns—everyone will want to visit this place, now that it has suddenly become famous." His warm smile returned. "But you are the first. What do you want to know?"

Gina sipped her tea as she looked around at her relatively modern surroundings. She couldn't help but be a bit disappointed that the photos in her story would be of a 20th-century structure rather than one dating back hundreds of years. Still, she was glad that she was here and, at least for the time being, she had the resident priest all to herself. "I want to put together a complete story of his family, with photos of anything of interest related to his roots here."

"You found his parents' tombstones," he said, nodding toward the cemetery. "But you won't find his grandparents and great-grandparents, even though they were buried here. During World War I this village was in no man's land between the Allied and German trenches. It was pounded to rubble by artillery. A tragedy. The original church and cemetery dated back to the thirteenth century." The priest regarded her for a moment. "But once again, I've forgotten my manners. I'm Father Croix." He extended his hand.

"Gina Ishikawa."

Croix raised his eyebrows. "Same name as the president of the Latino Union?"

"My father," she heard herself say a little more curtly than she had intended. "Are there any surviving written records I could see? Something, anything, about his time here. Birth, baptism, christening… even from when he was a parish priest?"

Father Croix considered the question. "We keep Bibles for most families in the parish. And baptism records. Let's go to my office."

They went through the sanctuary and into a small, tidy room. One wall was occupied by shelves overstuffed with books of all kinds. Croix moved his finger along a long line of Bibles, coming to one with LEGENDRE printed in gold on the cover. He pulled it out and laid it on the desk. Inside the front cover was a family tree penned in variously colored inks and disparate handwriting.

Gina gently touched the facing pages with her fingertips. "Am I looking at history?"

Croix looked rueful. "I'm sorry—this is reconstructed, starting in 1920. When the church was destroyed, the original family Bibles were also."

Gina frowned. "What else do you have?"

For twenty minutes, Croix pulled more books off the shelf and rummaged through a battered metal file cabinet, emerging with a handful of additional papers. He sorted through them by hand, produced baptism and christening papers for Guy Legendre, and spread them on his desk. He also laid out a number of parish papers signed by the young priest.

Gina took photographs of the documents, but she wasn't satisfied. "Father Croix, is there any way I can reconstruct his lineage with original documents?"

The young priest put his hand on his chin. "Lille was the department seat for the church and wasn't hit as hard during the war. I think we can find documentation there."

Gina smiled. "We?"

"I like your project—it will result in something original. I want to help."

"Can you go now? I have a car."

They walked back outside. "Father," Gina said, "since you know the way, perhaps it would be easier if you drive."

The young man looked chagrined. "This will be a case of the priest confessing to the parishioner. I don't know how to drive."

Gina laughed. "How is that possible?"

"My parents were extremely strict, and very fearful of what troubles a young man could get into once he had access to a car." Father Croix chuckled. "I suppose it must have worked, given my choice of profession. Once I was at the seminary I never had time to learn. And it was too complicated to get a license in Japan... well, I've just never bothered. My passion is bicycling, and this is a small town, so... that's how I get around."

Gina shook her head and laughed again as they got into her rental car.

"Please do remember the centuries-old sanctity of the confessional," Father Croix said, smiling broadly. "You cannot tell anyone! No one in Vincennes knows of my disability."

*

Gina drove to Lille and parked at the cathedral where Father Croix whisked her past outer-office clerks and directly to the archives. There, they worked together to pull birth and death certificates as well as bishopric copies of baptism and christening records. Gina took notes and photos as they reconstructed the pope's family. Many documents were missing, but Father Croix proved to be resourceful. Using the information gleaned from what they found at the cathedral, they drove to three other nearby churches where their digging produced a few additional records. The new pope's grandparents were Guy and Nicole Legendre, and Jean and Nicolette Legendre were his great-grandparents. The Holy Father's great-great-grandparents were Christian and Marie Legendre, christened in 1825 and 1831. There they were, the four generations of the official biography. Gina spread the papers on the floor of the church and carefully took pictures of each one.

When Gina finished, she looked up to see that Father Croix had disappeared. She followed the sounds of cabinet doors opening and closing and found him shuffling carefully through a stack of papers. She looked over his shoulder as he knelt on the floor.

He held a stained piece of vellum inscribed with a church birth record of Antoine Legendre, dated 1791. He picked another sheet off the floor and held it beside the first, this one a marriage record for Antoine and Claire Legendre. It bore the year 1821. A badly worn third document showed Antoine's death in 1825.

"Five generations," Gina whispered. "You did it, Father. You went beyond what even the Vatican knew."

Father Croix looked pensive.

"What's wrong?" Gina asked.

Father Croix pulled several papers off a stack on the floor. "Look at these. Christening records for three children of Antoine and Claire. But all three are girls. I can't find any documents for Christian, the male child who carried the Legendre name forward."

"But Father, you said yourself records were not always made. And even then, there might not have been copies. The originals, if they existed, could have been destroyed in Vincennes."

"Yes, you are right, of course," he said, but the priest still seemed pre-occupied. He absently glanced at his watch and his face filled with alarm. "*Merde*!" Croix exclaimed. "I'm late for confessions!" He turned to Gina with a genuinely dejected expression. "I am afraid that my time as a gene-alogist has come to an end. As much as it pains for me to say so, I need you to take me back right away, if that is not asking too much."

The two drove back to Vincennes in silence, each in their own thoughts. When they stopped in front of the church, Croix hurriedly jumped from the car, but then paused before shutting the passenger door to ask, "Is there anything else I can do for you?"

Gina grinned with genuine affection. "You have done so much, Father. There is just one more thing. Can you tell me where the Legendre farm is?"

Despite his tardiness for confession, Father Croix gave her detailed instructions to a location a few kilometers away, and then turned with a warm wave goodbye and ran into the church.

Gina sat in the rental car and took a moment to soak in the late-after-noon sun. Then she pulled a pad of paper and her notes out of her brief-case. On the paper she drew lines for an ahnentafel and began filling in the names and dates she now knew:

Generation 1:
#1—Guy Legendre; born 1970

Generation 2 (parents):
#2—Gaston Legendre (father); born 1922, died 1994
#3—Lucille Legendre (mother); born 1928, died 1993

Generation 3 (grandparents):
#4 —Guy Legendre (father's father); born 1890, died 1936
#5 —Nicole Legendre (father's mother); born 1896, died 1933
#6—Name Unknown (mother's father)
#7—Name Unknown (mother's mother)

Generation 4 (great-grandparents):
#8—Jean Legendre (father of #4); born 1861, died 1916
#9—Nicolette Legendre (mother of #4); born 1871, died 1919
#10—Name Unknown (father of #5)

Gina impatiently scribbled "etc.," anxious to get on with the ones she knew.

Generation 5 (great-great-grandparents):
#16—Christian Legendre (father of #8); born 1825, died 1905
#17—Marie Legendre (mother of #8); born 1845, died 1910

Generation 6 (great-great-great-grandparents):
#32—Antoine Legendre (father of #16); born 1791, died 1825
#33—Claire Legendre (mother of #16); born 1795, died 1838

Gina studied her diagram, fixing the relative dates in her mind. After several minutes, she put the car in gear and headed out of town.

*

Gina pulled up in front of a farmhouse with a warm and textured facade of brown bricks and tan-colored natural stone. The shutters flanking each window were pleasantly silvered by weathering. Although it was getting late in the afternoon, the summer sun would be out for some time, giving Gina plenty of light for photographs. She went to the front door and dropped the heavy brass knocker twice but no one came to the door.

Gina drove back onto the road, continued for a minute, and then pulled off onto the grass. Emerging from the car, she could still see the house and outbuildings. She shouldered her camera bag and waded through waist-high golden grain toward the farm, taking photos as she walked.

She found her way to the side of the barn opposite from the farmhouse. There was a weathered wooden table under a copse of trees, some wooden chairs, and a bucolic stone bridge arching over a small brook. Gina knelt to change her lens. A shadow fell over her and she cried out and spun around, looking upward. A masculine figure stood over her, but the sun was directly behind him, so all she saw of his head and face was a fiery corona around a black void.

"Who are you?" a hoarse voice demanded.

"Gina Ishikawa… journalist." She dug into her camera bag and pulled out her press credentials.

"My God," the voice rasped. "Vietnamese?"

"Brazilian. But my grandparents were Japanese."

"Come closer," the voice demanded.

She moved so she could see the face. The man was easily more than eighty, with a craggy face as wizened and weathered as the stones of the nearby bridge. A week's worth of beard stubble dotted his face.

"You look Vietnamese," he insisted.

"No, sir." she said.

The man was suddenly taken by a coughing spell that doubled him over. Gina took his bony arm and led him to one of the wooden chairs. His face turned purple while he coughed and wheezed. Panting, he fumbled in his pocket for a cigarette, which he put in his mouth with trembling hands and lit with a disposable lighter.

"I still see Vietnamese every night," the old man said. He sat up a bit straighter as he exhaled smoke through his nose. "Foreign Legion. Dien Bien Phu."

"You were there, sir?"

"Yes. Damned near starved. Mortar barrages day and night. Viet Minh sappers inside the perimeter, killing us one at a time. Then prison in Hanoi. Months. Fish heads and rice. Are you Vietnamese?"

"No sir, Japanese."

"Just as bad. Yellow horde."

"Sir, I am a journalist." She hesitated. "The Legendre family. Are you of that family?"

"Legendre? Me? No."

"But this farm was theirs for many years."

The old man studied the cloud of smoke that billowed around his head. "Legendre?" He shook his head. "Debray, now. Before, Cartier... Bovier... I can't remember."

"And before them, the Legendres, yes? Do you know the pope?"

"The pope? Who is it now? John?"

Gina sighed. "Sir, did you ever know Guy Legendre? Parish priest here?"

"Legendre? Are you Vietnamese?"

"No, sir, Japanese."

"Same damned thing. Yellow bastards."

"Sir, Guy Legendre—the priest."

"Legendre? Just a kid, doesn't know shit. Why'd they make him the priest here? Where is Father Dubois?"

Gina realized it was hopeless—the man had no touch with reality. She took his hand. He looked up with terror in his eyes and jerked it away.

"You devil, you worshipper of Ho Chi Minh, damn you! Get away from me, leave my men alone—don't kill us! We're so hungry, so hungry—just some food, for the love of Christ!"

"Sir, may I help you back to the house?" Gina asked.

"You'll take me out there in that yard and shoot me, like you've done to the officers. Vietnamese bitch! Whore of Giap!"

Gina sighed, collected her camera gear, and started to walk away.

"Legendre?" the old man asked. She stopped. "Legendre?" he asked again. He waved his hand toward the hedgerow that came up to the trees. "That's where you'll find Legendre."

Gina squinted in the diminishing light. "Sir, what do you mean? Where is Legendre?"

The old man waved his hand again. She walked in that general direction, seeing only dense shrubs forming the hedgerow. He motioned her on. She got down on her knees and wriggled between two bushes, pushing branches out of her face. After three meters, she broke into a tiny clearing.

There were bumps in the thick thatch on the ground and she reached out to one of them. It was solid. She pulled at the grass, peeling it away to reveal a stone. In the dense vegetation there was no sunlight, so Gina pulled out her phone and thumbed her flashlight application. The limestone had eroded badly, but she could make out letters. She took a deep breath.

The name on the stone was Antoine Legendre.

She pulled the ahnentafel out of her pocket and checked it. The birth date, 1791 agreed with the stone. But the death date on the stone was 1815. The document at the church in Lille said he died in 1825, the same death date as had been reported by the Vatican.

Antoine had died ten years before the documented birth of his son, Christian Legendre.

CHAPTER FIVE

Valladolid, Spain—1610

BROTHER SEBASTIÁN CRUZ knocked twice on the abbot's door and waited. The animated men's voices inside the room were abruptly silenced by his knock. The door opened, and the abbot answering looked at him grimly.

"Come in, Brother Cruz," he said.

Cruz entered and saw a bishop, his rank indicated by his vestments, seated facing the chair that the abbot had vacated to answer the door.

"This is Bishop Sergio Cano, a judge from the Holy Office of the Inquisition here in Valladolid."

There was no greeting or offer of a hand from the visitor.

"He has spoken to me of troubling things, and I expect full coopera-tion from you and absolute truthfulness—with an eye to your eternal soul."

Brother Cruz said nothing.

Cano spoke for the first time. "A monk of the Monastery Santa Maria de la Vid has declared, under oath, that you serve the Holy Office."

Cruz knew that "under oath" meant that the declaration had come during torture. "Bishop, if that were true—which it is not—why would that demand your attention?"

"Because the Holy Office has crown-established rules, procedures, canon laws, and jurisdictions," Cano said. "You have been identified as a rogue member of the Holy Office who is operating outside the bounds of these laws and procedures, which were given to us by His Holiness the Pope Paul V and our king."

"Bishop Cano, may I know the name of the monk who made this claim?" Cruz asked.

"You may not."

"Then may I instead ask the bishop if the monk made a similar admission about himself?"

"It is irrelevant. You need only admit that the charge about you is true."

"In what capacity does this... admission... claim that I serve the Holy Office?" Cruz asked.

"You are presumptuous in asking these questions! I am asking the questions."

Cruz ignored the bishop's indignation and looked directly into his eyes. "Bishop, have you checked to see if my name is inscribed among the servants of the Holy Office?"

Cano reddened. "We looked but could find no such enrollment. But we—"

"And because of King Felipe III's stipulation that inquisitors must have studied law, you surely would have also looked to find my name among the law faculty graduates."

"We have searched all the law faculties and do not find that you were enrolled. However—"

"Bishop, you also know an inquisitor must be of the secular clergy— not a member of an order such as mine. The abbot will attest to my affiliation as an Augustinian for many years."

The abbot looked down at his desk. "Yes, I can confirm that," he said quietly.

"I only say that the monk in question is mistaken," Cruz said. "I am no more than what you see before you, a brother of the Augustinians. No law studies, no university education. I meet no prerequisites to be an inquisitor, and as such I cannot be an inquisitor."

"Your insolence violates the customary humility of your order," Cano protested. "Without those prerequisites you could be a lesser functionary of the Holy Office—"

"I can only state what is true, Bishop."

It was more than the bishop could bear. "Get out!" Cano shouted. "Get out of my sight!"

"As you wish, Bishop Cano. Abbot, may I be excused?"

The abbot nodded weakly. Cruz walked across the monastery and down the steps to his cell. He lit a candle, removed quill and ink from his small desk, and wrote a letter addressed to Brother Rodrigo Talamera at the Monastery of Santo Toribio de Liébana. The letter depicted at length the mundane and repetitive activities of a monk in a monastery, extensive observations about the spiritual results of daily prayer and meditation, the glories of living the ascetic life, and his efforts to help the poor and incapacitated of Burgos.

He wrote the letter using an extensive memorized transcription of every letter of every word that hid the true encoded text. The hidden text read:

Dear Brother Talamera:

Bishop Sergio Cano of the Holy Office tribunal in Valladolid is accusing me of being a functionary of the Holy Office. It appears that Brother Ferrer, for reasons I do not know, was taken and tortured, and he divulged some small bit of information about me. Brother Talamera, I applaud your efficacy years ago in removing my name from the rolls of the university in Valencia, the law faculty in Salamanca, and the rolls of the secular clergy. Having no proof, Cano failed to press his accusation. Brother, I call upon your specialized expertise to immediately locate and silence Brother Ferrer, if he is still alive, lest under further torture he confesses additional information. You must also silence anyone in whom Bishop Cano may have confided. I will handle the rest. I know I can count on your alacrity in addressing these threats to our sacred trust and to nominate a candidate in Burgos to take into our confidence to replace Brother Ferrer.

This we do for one, ten, a hundred, or a thousand years, whatever is required to bring on the Millennium.

Sebastián Cruz, Guardian of the Fourth Angel

Brother Cruz rolled up the parchment and placed it aside. He would set about the process of finding a reliable courier in the morning. In the meantime, there was some unpleasant work to be done. Given the lateness in the day, the bishop would be staying for dinner as a guest of the abbot and spend the night before making the short journey home at first light. That made things much easier, as Cruz would only have one location to visit tonight.

Cruz retrieved a key from underneath his simple cot and unlocked a drawer in his desk. He withdrew a dagger and unwrapped the cloth that bound it, admiring the ornate blade, but the weapon's unparalleled crafts-manship did not inspire its usual pleasure. It disheartened Cruz that the abbot was going to be an innocent victim of Brother Ferrer's inability to live up to his oath. The abbot was a kind man, and apolitical. All he had wanted for his simple life was to do God's work. Sadly, that work was about to end.

Cruz inspected the blade and found its sharpness satisfactory. He vowed to himself that he would make the abbot's exit from this world quick and painless. Bishop Cano, however, had been nothing but arrogant and rude. Most damning of all, the bishop had been complicit in the arrest and torture of one of Cruz's fellow Guardians.

Cruz slowly turned the dagger in his hand. The manner of Bishop Cano's death this evening would be unspeakable.

CHAPTER SIX

MARTÍN LOOKED AROUND the room he knew so well from his own sketches and blueprints. One entire wall was glass, and beyond it the Andes rose to snow-capped heights. The wall opposite the window was paneled with a rich dark red wood and highly polished. The far end of the room had a large stone hearth and chimney with a metal hood made from copper mined in Chile, smelted by native artisans, and hammered by hand into sheets. The carpeting was a rich beige, as was the leather furniture—comfortable and informal.

The door opened and Takeshi Ishikawa walked in. His build was slight, and he was dressed in a maroon V-neck sweater, a starched blue oxford cloth shirt open at the collar, and beige pants with sharp creases running down the legs. His full head of silver hair was carefully brushed. He had the same gentle and wise eyes as Gina, and his well-proportioned nose was also reflected in her face. He looked tired.

Martín bowed slightly. "Your Excellency, Mr. President."

The two men looked at each other for clues as to how this interaction would play out.

"Martín, thank you for coming. Please be seated. I trust that, as usual, we can put aside personal matters."

The younger man nodded.

"Martín, I do not have to recite for you the problems facing this office—you know them well." Martín nodded again, acknowledging the long list. It began with the Latin American countries themselves, each fiercely protective of its sovereignty, all with a history of warring against each other, and many still harboring both secret and overt agendas of revenge. Mexico still had not yet joined, hypersensitive about a history of interventions by their neighbor to the north. French-speaking French Guiana was a department of France, and Paris had not permitted it to join. There was also the tenuous financial situation of the union, which was short of cash because the member countries only grudgingly paid their dues—most of them well after the agreed-upon deadlines. Then there was the "*problema brasileño*"—the Brazilian problem. When English-speaking Guyana and Dutch-speaking Suriname had opted to join the union, but insisted upon recognition of their official languages, their relatively small populations and economic impact made it easy enough to accommodate them. But Brazil, whose customs and roots went back to Portugal, not Spain, was the most populated country with the largest economy, and its people feared they would gradually lose their unique language and culture.

The litany went on.

"The Americans, as a gesture of friendship to this office and to the union, are sharing some of their intelligence information with me," the president continued. He held out a small remote control and clicked a button. On the wall opposite the hearth a large screen television flipped from a BBC news feed to a high-resolution map depicting South and Central America. Dots of various colors were speckled throughout.

"What I am showing you is highly classified. I am counting on your discretion."

Martín nodded and the president continued, using an on-screen marker to highlight each of the countries as he discussed them.

"You know of the hostilities that are just under the surface in El Salvador and Honduras, where gangs can currently outgun the governments. In Guatemala, a strongman barely keeps a lid on revolutionaries in the rural areas. Though Colombia has largely stabilized, there are still powerful drug cartels there, and the cartels in Mexico, Venezuela, Ecuador, and Peru have taken advantage of the power vacuum. The Shining Path guerrillas have found new life using the existence of the LU as a foil. Radical Peronistas are still active in Argentina. Bolivia remains far to the left under Evo Morales.

"You know all this, of course. But there are new elements to the equation. The foreign nuclear experts who helped North Korea develop its program are now available for hire, and we have intelligence placing a number of them within the LU's borders. ISIS terrorists, fragmented now in the Middle East, are regrouping by redirecting some of their most radical followers to islands off the South American coasts. Even though we have done our best to watch for them, there are too many thousands of kilometers of unoccupied coasts, and they are now here with us."

Ishikawa clicked his remote, and the dots on the map sprouted arrows. Those from South American points of origin swept toward the north and those in Mexico and Central America extended south, through Panama, and then fanned out into Colombia and Venezuela.

"All the loose pieces are coming together," Martín said.

"Yes, though we do not know why. They pose not just a threat on their own but in how they might provoke the many restive militaries in our union. My own general staff in Brazil has warned me that if they determine a threat to Brazilian sovereignty, they will act to 'restore' it, as they say. I am sure the generals in other countries have said the same. That would, of course, be the end of the union—whose capital we will not even officially inaugurate for another week. And then what? Back to military rule? People disappearing during the night? Hyperinflation? I cannot allow that to happen, yet I do not have the assets or the political capital this early in the union's existence to deal with this."

Ishikawa stared at Martín for a long time. "In spite of what happened on a personal level, I want you to know that I believe you are an intelligent young man. You are Latino in language and personal philosophy. There are many here who would follow your leadership."

Martín shook his head. "Sir, we have already discussed this. I will not accept a political position."

Ishikawa's eyes narrowed. "I understand. But at this moment, I am referring to other leadership skills. Those that you learned in Guatemala. From the CIA."

Martín tried his best to maintain a neutral expression, but he was stunned. Though he'd known that the president was likely fully aware of the nature and scope of his flirtation with an Agency-sponsored career, for him to raise it now as part of a request for his continued involvement with the LU was an extraordinary leap of faith. What could possibly make Ishikawa think that he would consider this?

"You are probably not aware of the identity of the man who has emerged as the leader of this assemblage of terror," Ishikawa said. "He is from Cuba, a protégé of Fidel Castro, and a young trainee of Che Guevara. He attended the best revolutionary schools in Russia and China. He has admirers—and patrons—in Chechnya, Syria, Libya, the Philippines, Indonesia, Nigeria—everywhere that terror lives today. Though he is of an advanced age for a revolutionary, he has lost none of his zeal."

The president gazed out the window at the Andes, his arms crossed behind his back. "You have unique knowledge of this man." Without turning around, he clicked his remote again.

Martín froze as he stared at the portrait of a man whose heavy beard and long hair was graying, and whose face was dry and tight—an aged reflection of his own. The man was Nicolás Ibarra, his oldest brother.

*

Gina Ishikawa lay on the bed in her hotel room. Her mind spun with the irreconcilable dates of the birth records and the tombstone. And there was the paper that Father Croix found showing three girls born to Antoine and Claire Legendre, but no son. To distract herself she grabbed her phone and thumbed through her emails and saw that she had two voicemails. They had come in thirty minutes apart, with the most recent one recorded only ten minutes earlier while she had been in the shower trying to unwind from her day's work.

Both messages were from Dave Broch. She tapped the play icon and was unsurprised by the Brazilian music suddenly blaring from the phone's speaker. Laughter and boisterous conversation added to the background din.

"Hey, Gina." Dave's voice was loud and his speech was slowed by exaggerated enunciation. "I'm leaving Seville tomorrow afternoon to head back to the States, so I just wanted to give my favorite girl a call to say good-bye. Sorry we couldn't get together. I'll be back in Miami and Marty is meeting my flight... Look, I don't exactly know how things stand between you two right now, so… if there are any messages you want me to give him… wait a minute…"

There was a muffled sound over the samba music in the background and Dave, who had clearly put his hand over the mouthpiece, shouted to someone. Gina could just barely make out the words: "Yeah, Julio, I'll be there *en seguida*, okay? Tell Ray to hang on, *momentito*, keep his *pantalones* on!"

The music surged again as the hand came off the mouthpiece, and Dave resumed talking as though he was speaking to someone severely hard of hearing. "Gina? Sorry, what I was saying was if, you know, you want me to tell Marty anything… well, just let me know. You're the best. Bye."

Gina loved hearing from Dave, who had been a great friend while she and Martín were together, but her smile faded a bit as she thought about how much had changed. Now, it was… harder. She needed to close out that part of her life and move on to… well, what was expected of her. Gina sighed. Dave had called her several times while he was in Madrid and Seville, but they just couldn't seem to synch up with dates to see each other, and probably that was for the best.

The next message began. There was the party music again, but this time it was more distant, and Dave's voice sounded tense and guarded.

"Gina, Dave again. Look, I'm going to have Marty call you, and when he does, tell him exactly these words. I have—"

The message cut off. She dialed Dave's number, but there was no answer.

For a few minutes Gina stewed about the second message, and how serious Dave had sounded, but she decided that he was still trying to reestablish diplomatic relations between Gina and Martín. She knew that nothing would make Dave happier than to see them back together again. But it was simply out of the question.

Gina's mind wandered back to Martín, and she knew she was in danger of going into a funk if she didn't refocus her thoughts. Perhaps she could get in just a little more work before she allowed her mind and body to succumb to sleep. She dialed Father Croix's number at the rectory, and a man answered.

"Yes?"

Gina paused. "Father Croix?"

"Who is this?" the man demanded.

"Who are you?" Gina asked, somewhat indignantly.

"This is the rectory of Saint Jean Baptiste Church."

Her irritation grew, sharpened by her fatigue and souring mood. "I am calling for Father Croix."

"Who is calling for him?"

"I am… a friend. Is he there?"

"Where are you calling from?"

"Look, is Father Croix there, or not?" Gina asked.

"Are you the young woman who was with Father Croix earlier today? You must tell me who and where you are."

Gina felt a rush of anger and abruptly hung up. She didn't have time for games with an anonymous man at the rectory, and would try to reach Father Croix directly in the morning. She lay back on the bed, staring at the ceiling. Her mind still balked at the notion of shutting down for the night. She picked up the remote control from the nightstand and turned on the television. One of France's interminable talk shows was ending, followed by a series of commercials. Gina went to the sink and began brushing her teeth as the nightly local newscast began, which she absently watched in the mirror. She wondered whether there would be any more stories about Pope Pius XIII tonight, or if the news cycle had already moved on. Part of her worried that someone else would uncover the lineage discrepancies before she had gotten her arms around the potential story.

Gina was spitting into the sink when the announcer said, "Tonight in the town of Vincennes there was a tragic automobile accident involving a young priest from the local church."

Gina spun toward the television and saw an old Citroen upended beside the curve of a road. Smoke spilled out from the crumpled hood, and the roof of the car was completely crushed inward.

"Father Regis Croix, church priest for the past two years, and only twenty-eight years old, was involved in a one-car accident. He was apparently driving at an excessively high speed when he failed to control the car in a curve and ran off the road and into a tree, flipping the vehicle. Vincennes is mourning the loss of its priest."

Gina gawked at the television, her toothbrush still clutched in her hand. The next story was about fires—attributed by authorities to vandals or skinheads—in the offices of three parish churches in Lille. The announcer said that thousands of historical documents were destroyed in the blazes.

Gina picked up her phone and tapped Dave Broch's number. A recording said that the phone was either turned off or out of range, and she was not given the option to leave a voicemail.

There would be no sleep tonight. Gina threw her toiletries in her travel bag and rushed out the door.

*

Martín pulled his necktie knot tight against his shirt collar and stared into the mirror. He had tossed and turned all night thinking about the previous day's meeting with Ishikawa.

Nicolás's decision to stay in Cuba—made before Martín was even born—was a dark day in the family's history. When Martín's father finalized the arrangements for the family to escape to Miami, where they would be welcomed by the burgeoning Cuban population and would no longer have to conceal their religion, Nicolás announced that he believed in the Marxist revolution, condemned his parents' bourgeois mentality, hugged his younger brothers and sisters, and calmly left the house. They lived in terror for the next two days and nights, fearing that Nicolás would turn them in. But the police never arrived and the go-fast boat had met them at the rendezvous point on schedule.

Martín had met his brother only once, while attending a meeting of Latin American architects in San Jose, Costa Rica. One evening Martín returned to his hotel room and found Nicolás sitting on Martín's bed in the darkness. Though they had never met, Martín recognized him instantly. They embraced warmly, and through the night Martín talked at length about the rest of the family and their lives as Americans while Nicolás eagerly soaked in the news about the brothers and sisters he had known as children, but who were now grown.

As dawn broke, the brothers embraced again. "Please give all of my siblings my love," Nicolás said, "and tell them I miss them desperately. And you, *mi hermano menor*, I am so very glad that I have finally met you. I hope our paths cross again."

And then he was gone.

As yesterday's meeting with Takeshi Ishikawa had ended, the president had asked Martín to stay overnight and then meet with King Carlos VII, who had just arrived from Madrid in preparation for the inauguration ceremonies at the union capital. Adding to Martín's disquieted mind was the previous evening's odd sequence involving Dave Broch. Dave had emailed Martín his flight information, presuming that Martín would be able to meet his plane in Miami. Martín, realizing that he had completely forgotten to relay his change of situation to Dave, texted him immediately to tell him he was out of the country and wouldn't be able to pick him up. So far, there had been no reply. Martín tried calling as well, but Dave's voicemail didn't pick up.

Martín drove to the state guesthouse, parked, and went inside. Spanish soldiers checked his documents and admitted him to the royal chamber. The king was sitting with his back to the door and working on a desktop computer, casually but smartly dressed. Martín stood at the door looking at the monitor and saw the Archive of the Indies database that Lenin had shown him. The king, without turning around, raised one hand slightly to indicate to Martín that he knew he was there, but then continued to click and type without regard to the fact that Martín was waiting to be admitted.

After several minutes the king stood and walked quickly toward Martín with a warm smile on his face. Martín bowed from the waist. "Your Majesty."

"Architect Ibarra, it is a pleasure to meet you at last! I have heard great things about your work, and what I see here in San Juan Diego confirms it." Carlos VII gripped Martín's hand, shaking it vigorously while maintaining piercing eye contact. "Thank you for coming so we can get acquainted before the craziness of the formal ceremonies begins."

The king gestured back to the screen. "Isn't that database of the archives marvelous? It is one of my proudest achievements."

Martín regarded the king, who ushered him to a comfortable sofa. Carlos was only 32 years old, a young man who had been invested with the crown when the Bourbon king Felipe VI was felled by a brain aneurysm at the young age of 43. The cardinal of Valladolid heard Felipe's confession and received the dying man's last testament, which called for Carlos's ascension to the throne in place of his son. When the cardinal announced the death of the king and called for the investiture of Carlos that very day, a muffled shock rippled through Spain and all of Europe. Why hadn't Felipe's son inherited the throne? There was no explanation.

Martín had read extensively about this man. Carlos was young, well educated, energetic, and married to the beautiful daughter of an Austrian count. This had raised eyebrows in Spain, but she won over the public by speaking both perfect Castilian and Catalonian. She showed a deep knowledge and enthusiastic appreciation for the country for which she was now queen. The European nobility embraced this youthful and vibrant couple, elevating them to the most venerated royals on the continent. The Spanish public, skeptical at first and snubbed for years by the rest of Europe, now basked in the attention lavished on their royal family.

After his inauguration, the king had immediately scheduled a tour of Latin America. He and Queen Isabel were received by presidents looking to benefit politically from the enormous goodwill that the royal couple was receiving. Throughout the tour, Carlos and Isabel repeatedly ordered their motorcades to stop and emerged from their Rolls Royce to walk among the miserable, sewage-strewn *favelas* of Rio and São Paulo, and the *barrios* of Caracas, Bogotá, and Mexico City. In those places they openly wept as they embraced ragged, emaciated children. Announcements followed soon after each stop that a portion of the family's fortune would be donated to causes dedicated to improving living conditions in the area they had just visited.

The king's most sublime moment had been at the inauguration of Pope Pius XIII just a few days earlier. When the pope returned to Saint Peter's square to deliver his homily, Carlos rose from his chair and prostrated himself at the feet of the Holy Father. While church bells rang throughout Europe celebrating the new pontiff, the masses were abuzz about the king of Spain's incredible gesture of humility and obeisance.

Today, in this comfortable room, the most beloved Spanish king in centuries spoke easily to the commoner before him, asking intelligent questions about architecture and life among the Latino community in the United States. "Your sister Carmela certainly did well at Harvard. Her thesis on Spanish colonial capitalism was masterful. And your brother Roberto—I trust his work at Tesla is going well? You know," Carlos said, gesturing toward the computer, which now displayed a screensaver photograph of a billowing Spanish flag, "I cannot describe the sense of history that website gives me. I tell you Martín, it brings tears to my eyes. Words that flowed from the minds of Cortés, Isabel, Fernando, Carlos V, the Hapsburg kings—they go straight into my heart. I hear their voices across the centuries. I hear their wisdom and strength. I hear their call to serve our mother country.

"What a noble language we have! What a culture, from the Visigoths through an empire the likes of which the world has never seen before or since. Our philosophy, our sense of *pueblo*, worldwide. These are great times, Martín, and the future demands a realization of our destiny."

The king crossed the room and drew a book from the bookshelves. "*Don Quixote de la Mancha*, Miguel de Cervantes. What a treasure are the works of this man. And those after him in the *siglo de oro*, Martín. We are a people of arts and letters of the highest order."

"I also am a great reader of the generation of '98," Martín said. "Their expression of the pain of coming to grips with the reality of Spain's new world order in 1898 is stunning to me."

The expression of ecstasy faded from Carlos's young face. "Ninety-eight?" he asked quietly. "A time of decay and defeat for our country."

"But also a time of great introspection and realization—and acceptance of responsibility."

"Don't you find that period an aberration in the march of our history?"

"No, Your Majesty. I find it to be a shining moment of truth and redemption. I—"

"On another subject, Martín, I see you pulled off a little deception and got away with it." Carlos had a conspiratorial smile.

Martín looked back at him blankly. "Your Majesty?"

The king reached for the coffee table and turned over a copy of *Vanity Fair*. Martín looked down at his own face. Carlos nudged him in the ribs with his elbow.

"You know, that little sleight of hand that Francisco Ibarra pulled off in the 16th century. Having himself and his wife and children designated *'buenos cristianos.'"*

Martín laughed nervously. "Oh, yes, Your Majesty, that."

"And now, after all those years of hiding your Judaism, your family is once again living up to its covenant with the House of David." The king winked. "Well done, young Ibarra, well done."

There was a somewhat uncomfortable silence as Martín searched for a response. After a few moments, Carlos conspicuously looked at his watch.

Martín sprang to his feet. "Your Majesty, I am sorry to have taken up so much of your time. I know how busy you are."

"I am glad we have had this talk, and I am sure I can count on you as we fulfill our Spanish destiny."

Martín was puzzled by this repeated sentiment, but dutifully bowed. The king gave him a casual wave as he sat back down at his computer.

As Martín walked, he thought back to the king's screensaver. At first glance, Martín had merely registered the Spanish flag, with its horizontal red stripes at the top and bottom and gold field in the middle. But as he processed the photo he realized that under the flag's traditional Pillars of Hercules was written "S.C.C.R. Magestad."

Martín had not seen that phrase since his days at the University of Miami, when it had been a focus of his relentless history professor, Doctor Teodoro Lenin. It stood for *Sacra, Cesárea, Católica, Real Magestad*— Sacred, Caesar, Catholic, Royal Majesty.

It was the title conferred upon Carlos I in 1519 when the king of Spain had gained the additional moniker and title of Carlos V, Emperor of the Holy Roman Empire.

CHAPTER SEVEN

Madrid, Spain—1700

"WHY ARE YOU here?" Brother Mateo Velasco demanded. "We are never to meet in person."

Cardinal Álvaro Fonseca, seated on a bench in the monastery's orchard and watching his agitated colleague pace back and forth in front of him, replied evenly, "Yes, but there are imperatives."

"Tell me! What are the reasons! How can you betray more than two hundred years of secrecy?"

"You forget yourself, brother. You are speaking to a cardinal and the confessor to the king."

"And you forget that I am also one of the three Guardians of the Fourth Angel, so I am equal to you in this responsibility!" Velasco's eyes darted around the orchard from time to time, looking for peering eyes or listening ears. He wrung his hands.

"The Hapsburg line of succession is in danger of being broken. As will be made public shortly, Carlos II is dead. Once I knew the end was imminent, I sent for you. Since he has no living heirs, and he did not designate a successor in his final confession, we are in a very delicate situation."

"And what was His Majesty's... competence... toward the end?"

Fonseca snorted. "You're asking about the state of mind of a man who had his father's body exhumed, and spent time with the rotting remains, because an astrologist told him it would help produce an heir."

Velasco grimaced, and said, "I was afraid of that. People are referring to him as Carlos *el hechizado*."

"Bewitched is accurate, but charitable. Lately, Carlos had been nearly an idiot. Several years ago I tried to discuss the Fourth Angel knowledge with him, but I am sure he never understood it. Fortunately, I am equally sure that he never communicated it to anyone else. And even if he had, they likely would have taken it as the ramblings of an imbecile."

"What about Carlos's will?" Velasco asked.

"His will designates Felipe of Anjou."

"A Bourbon? And a boy of only 16 years!"

"It gets worse," Fonseca said. "The Holy Roman Emperor also plans to claim the Spanish throne."

Velasco paused in his pacing. "Well, at least he's a Hapsburg."

"Yes. And Carlos's father had stipulated in his will that the Spanish throne should be retained by the Hapsburgs by passing it to the Austrian branch. Torquemada assumed that the House of Hapsburgs would always rule Spain, but I am sure he intended for only men of the Flanders branch to do so."

Brother Velasco sat on the bench and exhaled. "So both men have a legal basis for their claims. Do we pass on the knowledge to both of them? Surely Torquemada's plans cannot die because an inbred dynasty collapsed due to lack of offspring!"

Cardinal Fonseca shook his head. "Too many would have the secret. Felipe is related to the king of France, and so England would not stand for his ascension. Carlos's claim would also be opposed—the great powers don't want all of Europe to be subject to the Holy Roman Emperor."

"What is the answer, then?" Velasco asked.

"We wait, and we temporize. I believe we must keep the knowledge among the three of us until someone emerges clearly victorious. We must continue to communicate by letter frequently, and yes, we may have to meet in person periodically."

"And the gold?"

"We leave it in the Fugger bank in Augsburg," Fonseca said. The cardinal paused to let his nervous counterpart absorb all the information that he had imparted. "Do I have your agreement on the handling of the knowledge and the funds?"

Brother Velasco mulled it over, then nodded. "I see no alternative if we are to carry out the Fourth Angel imperatives."

"There is another thing the three of us must do to prepare for either the Bourbons or the Hapsburg Austrians winning the throne. We must lay the groundwork to win it back. We must research every man, woman, and child in the Flanders-based Hapsburg branch lineage—rich or poor, legitimate issue and bastards, living and dead—every one of them in Flanders and Spain dating back to the time of Carlos I. And we must make certain that the Guardians continue documenting this information so they will be able to act when the time is right."

Velasco let out a long breath. "That will require extensive travel. How do I explain my absence to the abbot?"

"Leave that to me. I can truthfully tell him it is official business of the Holy Office of the Inquisition. No one would dare probe further into that explanation."

"You have convinced me. I will travel on to Toribio, seek Ribera's agreement, and have him conduct the same research so we can compare information."

Cardinal Fonseca stood. "Go with God, and safe travels."

Velasco gripped the cardinal's hands in his, and they recited together, "This we do for one, ten, a hundred, or a thousand years, whatever is required to bring on the Millennium."

CHAPTER EIGHT

GINA TOOK THE escalator steps two at a time, rushing from the customs and immigration area of the Miami airport to the main terminal. While waiting in line for a taxi she tapped Martín's number on her phone. When the call went to voicemail she hung up and dashed off a quick text to Martín—"Please call me ASAP"—and then placed another call.

"Gina!" Lenin exclaimed with genuine enthusiasm. "How good to hear from you. Are you here in Miami?"

"Yes, I just arrived. Professor, I… well… I'm not sure—"

"Something's wrong, Gina. I can hear it in your voice."

The young woman smiled at the genuine kindness and concern of her former professor. Doctor Lenin had dismissed most of the people taking his classes as uselessly occupying precious scholastic space. But he also identified the few who had a passion for learning and admitted them into his world. Gina and Martín were still part of this inner circle.

"Doctor…" She looked around and lowered her voice. "I can't talk about it. May I—"

"Come over."

She took a taxi and when the professor opened his front door he gave her an affectionate hug. "Where is your suitcase?" he asked.

"I don't have one—just this carry-on bag. I had to leave Europe in a hurry."

Lenin led her into his study. Gina looked around the familiar room that smelled of leather and lemon oil. The Spanish trestle desk was stacked with papers and books, but somehow still gave the impression of being neat and orderly. She pictured the room as she had always known it—filled with students sitting on the floor and sprawled on the sofa and chairs, sipping wine and debating points of history.

Gina realized Lenin was watching her closely but waiting patiently, allowing her privacy in her own thoughts. She gave him a tired smile and said, "Thanks for taking me in."

He waved his hand in dismissal.

She sank into a leather chair and Lenin sat on the sofa, leaning toward her. "I tried to call Martín," Gina said, "but he didn't take my call."

"He just went to San Juan Diego. Your father asked him to come."

"He did?" she asked, confused.

"I don't know what it was about. Are you going there to cover the arrival of the pope?"

"I was, but something else happened. Has Dave Broch called you?"

Dave had also been in their circle of "history groupies," as Lenin had called them.

"No," Lenin said. "Why do you ask?"

Gina took a deep breath and began the story.

After hearing Gina's tale, Lenin had brooded for several minutes. He had reached the same conclusion that she had—even though all of it was circumstantial, there were too many coincidences. And now Dave Broch was not responding to communications. He could have opted to stay in Spain for any number of reasons—Dave tended to do things impulsively— but they needed more information. He tried Martín's phone, but there was no answer.

*

Martín walked out of the CIA headquarters in Langley, Virginia, and got into his rented car. He put his hands on the steering wheel and took a deep breath. At President Ishikawa's request and with approval from the American president, the CIA had briefed Martín on the latest intelligence regarding the movement and possible intentions of the terrorists and guerrillas.

Martín had read through four white papers containing background materials on the various groups, each setting forth much of the same things that Ishikawa had told him in San Juan Diego. They showed him satellite photos of ships from various world registries discharging passengers and freight. There was a series of pictures of encampments masked by dense jungle canopy and covered with camouflage netting, but not quite well-hidden enough to escape the photo analysts employed to find such things.

When the contact points were superimposed over a map, they confirmed what Ishikawa had said: Central American groups were now in South America and starting to turn east, and groups from the south had moved north of the Amazon River. Nicolás Ibarra was likely in Venezuela, south of Maracaibo.

Martín started the car and drove to Dulles Airport. A Latino Union military plane was waiting for him, and he directed the pilots to take him to Miami. Once he landed, he would head straight to Little Havana. Martín glanced at his phone and saw that he had messages. A few from Dave, which he assumed were confirming his arrival in the United States and no doubt giving Martín a hard time for abandoning him at the airport. There was also one from Lenin and a text from—he did a double-take—Gina! A familiar cocktail of anguish and longing, along with a healthy dose of anger, flooded his synapses. What could she possibly want to talk about? Perhaps Dave had put her up to it. It would have to wait, though. He had a long series of grueling days ahead of him.

Martín strapped himself in as the military plane began to taxi toward the runway for takeoff. Within moments he had dozed off.

*

It was early evening when Waro Moto was admitted to President Ishikawa's study. Moto strode in with the swagger of a man who considered himself the most important person in any room. The two men bowed several times to each other, with Moto correctly acknowledging Ishikawa's technically higher social standing by bowing a little deeper. They then exchanged greetings and statements of respect in Japanese.

Over tea they traded questions about health, business, and politics. Eventually Moto asked with deference if he might inquire about a matter of mutual interest. Ishikawa nodded.

"Mr. President, I wish to report that the last of the communications satellites you ordered has been completed, and is being flown in from Japan today."

"And the plan is still to have the launch coincide with the inauguration of San Juan Diego?" Ishikawa asked.

"I spoke to Paris a half hour ago, and they assured me that everything is in order."

"The booster will be the new Ariane 6?" The president took a measure of pride in being able to name drop the state of the art European Space Agency rocket.

"Yes, Mr. President." The large man shifted in his chair. "There is another matter of great delicacy we must discuss." He looked around the room.

"I assure you, we are not being recorded."

"It will be best for you if we are not." Waro Moto's gaze, which had been directed generally at the floor, now locked onto the president's, and his stooped shoulders abruptly straightened. He smiled at Ishikawa with a tight mouth.

"The transfers to your party's bank account are being made today. My media experts will arrive within the hour. Your leadership will be unchallenged."

Ishikawa gave a single nod of his head and looked away.

"Oh, come now, Mr. President. Surely you are not having qualms? Remember, Ishikawa-san, your union needs your discipline and order. Years of *gaijin* running these countries into disaster after disaster have proven their unfitness to rule. Contrast that with the miracles Fujimori-san accomplished in Peru. Only the combined intelligence and discipline of the Japanese mind can accomplish these things."

Ishikawa sat in silence for a moment. He had heard this from Moto before and loathed it and its racist implications. More and more, he hated himself for getting involved with the Japanese billionaire, but the die had already been cast. "You forget—I am Brazilian, not Japanese," he said.

Moto gave a dismissive wave. "You were raised Japanese. Your parents did not forget themselves when they arrived here." Moto leaned forward. "It's the money that makes you uneasy, isn't it? Don't be stupid. Speak of your ideals to that mass of mongrels that make up this hemisphere. Don't think for even a moment that I will permit you to go weak on me now. Especially considering the size of the favor I am doing for you."

Ishikawa stiffened, shocked by Moto's gravely insulting breach of etiquette.

Moto sat up straighter, raising his head higher than the president's. "I have accepted a huge liability in taking your... damaged goods."

Ishikawa savagely sucked in air through the corners of his mouth. His face froze and his voice became hushed. "You are on very dangerous ground, Moto-san."

"I don't think so. Your daughter will now marry within our race, even though you let her go to local schools and American and European universities. Even though you gave her a *gaijin* name, not Japanese. And even though you allowed her to sleep with a *gaijin*—a Cuban-American Jew, no less."

Ishikawa was determined to keep face even if Moto was losing his by being blunt beyond all belief. It was unthinkable to speak of such things, particularly with the agreement having already been struck. He would have demanded instant satisfaction from this wealthy but barbarous man—except that he himself had to bear the shame of brokering the unconscionable deal.

Ishikawa desperately needed the money to grease the political machinery so that he could remain in power. To gain the certainty and stability that he needed to get the Latino Union on its feet, he had given Moto two things. First, he had ensured that the Union's full telecommunications contract—including the state-of-the-art mobile telephone and high-speed data network that was now fully operational in the capital—would be awarded to Moto Electric. Second, Ishikawa promised Moto his daughter in an arranged marriage, forging a bond between the billionaire and the Latino Union's political and social landscape that would persist even after Ishikawa stepped down.

When Ishikawa ordered Gina to end her relationship with Martín Ibarra and marry Waro Moto, he offered no explanation of why, and she didn't ask for one. Gina simply left the room and began packing to leave Brazil to be with Martín. Ishikawa reminded her of her traditional filial obligations to him, to her race, and to her culture. He left the room, fearing she was lost to him, along with the political ambitions he had for his country and continent.

Then a miracle had occurred. Gina came to him several hours later, her face an impassive mask, and announced that she would accept her obligations. She requested only that she be allowed to practice her university major, journalism, for a two-year period before she married Moto. Ishikawa feared this was a trap—that she would spend the two years with Ibarra, making it impossible for Moto to have her. But instead she had taken an assignment in Rome, and from all indications he believed that she would follow through on her word.

Sitting across from this foul, arrogant man, it broke his heart.

*

Martín startled as the Latino Union Air Force pilot shook him awake.

"Rise and shine, *dormilón*! You're home."

Martín took a few moments to shake the cobwebs out of his head and wipe the drool from his mouth. His body ached from the awkward position he'd slept in.

"It's 1900 hours right now," the airman said. "What time do you want to be wheels up tomorrow?"

"Uh, 1400 hours work for you?"

"Sure thing, *jefe*," the airman replied, and headed back toward the cockpit.

Martín checked his belongings and saw that Lenin had called twice more, leaving a voicemail. Unusual. Feeling a twinge of concern, he tapped the message.

"Martín, when you get this message, call me right away, day or night—"

The urgency in Lenin's voice was unmistakable, so Martín abandoned the message and called. "Doc? What's going on? I just got back to Miami and—"

"Have you heard anything from David Broch?"

"There are a few messages I haven't listened to yet. My flight just landed and I haven't had time—"

"Come over to my place right now."

"What? Look, I—"

"Just do it. I don't want to say more by phone."

The line went dead.

*

When Martín arrived at Lenin's house, the professor greeted him stiffly and with obvious distraction. Instead of leading him directly into his study, Lenin stood with Martín in the entry hall.

"What about the messages from Broch?" Lenin asked.

"After we got off the phone, I listened to them. They raise a lot of questions."

"I have a bad feeling," Lenin said. "And someone else needs our help too." With that he stood to one side and gestured toward the door to the study. Martín opened it and saw Gina sitting at the professor's desk. He froze just inside the doorway.

Martín's mind raced, shocked by her sudden reappearance in his life. The omnipresent dull ache that had been with him since their breakup rose to a roar. This surge of emotion was topped off with a dose of self-loathing—in this moment she clearly needed him, but he was making no move toward her.

Martín tried to speak, but his vocal chords weren't working. He cleared his throat and tried again. "You... look great."

Gina felt her resolve ebbing. Martín looked so surprised and vulnerable—even desperate. "You too," she said. The clock on the wall ticked noisily as they struggled for how to proceed. "Look, let's just agree to be civil and work together on this specific problem, okay?"

Martín nodded.

Lenin strode across the room purposefully, and sat down at his desk.

"Let's get to work," he said.

*

Martín listened carefully to Gina's voicemail recordings, hearing Dave's voice above the din of laughter and Brazilian music in the background.

Dave said he was planning to travel the next day, but was interrupted by someone in the background. They leaned in close to the phone's speaker.

"Yeah, Julio, I'll be there *en seguida*, okay? Tell Ray to hang on, *momentito*, keep his *pantalones* on!"

"Who are Julio and Ray?" Gina asked.

Martín shook his head. "Some friends he met in Europe, I guess."

They listened to the message fragment when Dave told Gina he had specific words for Martín before being cut off. Then Gina relayed the conversation she'd had with the man answering at the Vincennes rectory.

"I listened to Dave's messages on the way over," Martín said, "but I couldn't make any sense of them. Let's see if they somehow fit with the ones he left for you." He set his phone down on the desk in front of them, turned on his speaker, and played the voicemails.

The oldest message began with a flourish of guitar chords and the furious hammering *taconazo* of flamenco music. Dave's familiar voice came on, saying, "Marty, my main man! Sorry I had you on alert for my homecoming but bailed on you. Sounds like you're not around to pick me up anyway! Such a terrible, unreliable friend!"

Dave laughed heartily and then started to talk again, but the music and *taconazo* had risen to a thundering level, drowning out Dave's next words. Gina, Martín, and Lenin could hear a woman's voice shouting at Dave, "Come on, *cariño*, come back to the dance floor. Come now... please... I want to..." The next words were a breathy whisper that they couldn't understand because of the music. Then the woman's voice, audible again, "I'll dance without you until you come to your senses and get off the phone! You get to see for free what others have to pay for!"

Dave laughed again and then continued in a more serious tone, "Don't know how you feel... uh... about this, but I left a message for Gina yesterday. She's—" Wild applause and cheering drowned him out. Finally, he could be heard again, saying, "... hope we can catch up soon. Over and out." The time stamp put the call at yesterday evening at 8:20 p.m. Miami time, which would have been 1:20 a.m. in Madrid.

Dave's next message played. "Yo, Marty—just wanted to let you know that I'm going to hang out a while longer here. I'm rooting around in stuff C-R would love."

Martín and Gina couldn't help but laugh as Lenin looked at them with a raised eyebrow. Cr, the periodic chart identifier for the element chromium, was the students' name for their bald, shiny-headed professor.

"Look, I'm just going to check out Spain for a while. You won't be able to reach me, but I'll call in a few weeks. And, hey, Marty—remember our nine holes at Gables? The deal was twenty bucks a hole. We knotted the first three holes, you eagled four and birdied seven to win, but I birdied five and eagled six, winning those—you won with a bogey on eight, and we both parred nine. I owe you twenty and will pay you as soon as I can.

"And one last favor. Talk to Gina as soon as you can. It's important. Marty, you're a choice guy. Some other guys know that too, and they want to give you a Saint Benny. Gina's got more about that. I'm out of here."

The recording ended.

They listened to all the messages again. As Martín replayed Dave's last message, he shushed Lenin when the professor interrupted to ask what was so important about a golf game.

"I don't get why he said I wouldn't be able to reach him," Martín said. "He's in Spain, not Mongolia. And what bothers me even more was what we didn't hear."

"What are you talking about?" Gina asked. "We heard all of it—repeatedly."

"Yeah. But, I mean, you literally didn't hear it."

"Hear what?" Lenin asked with irritation.

"That last message. There was no party—no music."

CHAPTER NINE

Monastery Toribio de Liébana, Spain—1805

"BROTHER COBO, YOU'RE early," the Augustine monk said enthusiastically as he took the reins from the arriving man's horse and tied them to the hitching post.

Brother Cobo slid down from his saddle and stretched his cramped legs. "With all the uncertainties that these wars have brought upon the kingdom, I left very early—but even then, I had doubts that I would get here. I was shot at by both sides!"

"Yes," Brother Enríquez said. "First we invade France because they killed their king, and we fail. So it only makes sense that we would then fight the British alongside the French revolutionaries who started it all with their regicide!" He smiled and cast his arms outward to indicate the absurdity of it all.

Cobo, tired and stressed from his perilous journey, was unable to share in the humor. He looked back at the horizon, squinting to see if perhaps he could spot the third member of their elite cabal making his way up through the Cantabrian foothills. But he saw nothing but the road winding its way out of sight between lush green hills. "Perhaps Cardinal Gasco will be late for the same reason I was early," Cobo said, shaking his head.

They retired to Brother Enríquez's cell, and Cobo noted that they passed no one as they walked through the abbey. "There doesn't seem to be anyone here," Cobo commented.

"Yes, I'm alone for several days," Enríquez said. "I had to tell the abbot a white lie that I was sick and could not accompany the other monks on a nearby mission."

Cobo nodded, somewhat uncertainly. Though he was pleased that they could speak freely, it seemed impossible that the location of the *Lignum Crucis*, the greatest fragment of the Cross of Christ remaining in the world, would be left to the care of a solitary monk.

Enríquez read Cobo's dubious expression. "By 'alone,' Brother, I mean down here among our simple devotional spaces. I can assure you that your approach was monitored carefully from the bell tower by those whose job it is to ensure the security and tranquility of this sacred site."

Cobo relaxed a bit and sat down, accepting the cup of red wine that Enríquez poured for him. He sipped it, relished the robust flavor, and sighed. "Our meetings in person are occurring more and more frequently, against Guardian rules."

"It is regrettable," Enríquez agreed with a shrug. "But the uncertainty and instability of the world have forced our hands. Even the great Torquemada, when he penned the Guardian laws, could not have foreseen the turmoil of the last century." Enríquez tugged at his robe. "It is the changed world and its uncertainties that I want the three of us to discuss. Since you are here first, let's talk about it a bit before the cardinal arrives."

"It would be unusual to discuss Fourth Angel matters without all three of us being present."

Enríquez smiled. "You and I have been exchanging letters for many years. I feel that I know you better than the cardinal, and I feel I can speak more freely with you. I am concerned about the transfer of our gold to the Rothschild Bank in Frankfurt. They are Jews."

"That concerns me as well," Cobo said.

Enríquez visibly brightened at their shared prejudice. "I believe you and I have a common thought about this matter. I would like to add these additional points for you to consider. The British naval blockade is bankrupting the Spanish monarchy, which is borrowing heavily from the Rothschilds. What is to keep them from lending our assets to a king—a Bourbon king!—who has no possibility of repaying his loans? Or worse, what if the Rothschilds decide to foreclose on the entirety of the Fourth

Angel assets, keeping it all for themselves? You know the Jews—they only look out for themselves. We could lose the entire fortune!"

Cobo took a larger swig from his cup and sloshed the wine in his mouth, mulling Enríquez's concern. "I am uncertain as to what you are suggesting. Where else should we keep the fortune?"

Enríquez leaned toward Cobo, lowering his voice as a gleam of joyous menace crept into his eyes. "I say we take possession of it ourselves."

The words hung in the air. "You mean the Holy Office should take possession?" Cobo asked.

"No, I mean you and I will take possession."

Cobo shook his head. "Are you mad?"

Although the sardonic gleam remained in his eyes, Enríquez's expression flattened somewhat and he assumed a lecturing tone. "You need to be practical. The Hapsburgs are in decline, and their power in the Austro-Hungarian Empire is waning. Why should we continue to safeguard a fortune for them? Why should we risk the Bourbons, or the Jews—the people who murdered our Lord and Savior!—taking over the fortune?"

The lecturing tone gave way to passion and Enríquez's voice swelled. "And our Guardian cardinals in Valladolid? For all these years none of them, including Gasco, have been confessors to the Bourbon kings. We have had no inside knowledge for a hundred years—none! Their role within the Guardianship has been utterly useless."

Cobo straightened in his seat. "We are the latest in an unbroken line of more than 60 monks and cardinals who have taken the Fourth Angel oath, putting our eternal souls in jeopardy if we break it. I will not listen to this madness." Cobo stood and glared at the other monk. "You can be sure I will inform Cardinal Gasco of this blasphemy that you propose the moment he arrives."

Cobo turned, began to walk toward the door... and stumbled. His legs, already weary from the riding, had suddenly lost their strength. As he dropped to one knee, nausea swept through him, and he began to lose feeling in his hands. Cobo reached for the chair he had just vacated, hoping for some measure of support. As his fingertips brushed against the edge of the chair, it slid slowly away and out of his grasp, scraping against the stone floor with a sorrowful screech. Cobo looked up and saw the calm disappointment on Enríquez's face as he finished sliding the chair under the table.

Enríquez withdrew a small glass bottle with a cork stopper from his robe, and leaned over the weakening man. "My brother, you have reacted rather poorly to my proposal. As such, I am afraid that I must deny you the relief that this elixir would have provided you had you been more… receptive."

Cobo collapsed to the floor, his limp arms providing no buttress as he fell. He turned his head to look up at Enríquez, the cool stone against his cheek the only remaining tactile sensation of which he had any awareness. "How can you… why would you… you are damned," he said, and died.

Enríquez impassively placed the bottle back within his robes. When the cardinal arrived, it would have another opportunity to be utilized. Or perhaps not. Time would tell whether Enríquez would have a co-conspirator, or if he would be forced to work alone to get his hands on the Fourth Angel fortune. Until then, he had work to do. He would wait until the cover of darkness to dispose of the body in the nearby woods, where wild animals would make short work of it. He would also free Cobo's horse and encourage it back along the road from which it had come. The explanation of Cobo's predawn departure, should anyone bother to even ask, would be more than satisfactory.

The door swung open and Cardinal Gasco looked over the scene.

Enríquez instinctively backed away, startled. "Cardinal! Brother Cobo has had a seizure of some sort! Please, help me assist him!"

The cardinal stepped in, still blocking the small room's only exit, and removed a dagger from underneath his raiment. "It appears my arrival has come at an inconvenient moment for you, Brother Enríquez. It was clearly God's will that I would locate your cell in time to hear your unholy proposal to Brother Cobo. I am comforted that he will ascend to join our Holy Father as an innocent who gave his life in protection of his sacred duty. You, on the other hand… your treachery is disgraceful. I take pleasure in the fact that you will spend an eternity in hellfire for your actions."

Enríquez lunged forward in a desperate attempt to bull rush the larger man. The cardinal readied his dagger and braced for impact, but it never came. Enríquez's foot tripped over the lifeless, outstretched leg of Brother Cobo. His arms pinwheeled wildly and his mouth formed a surprised and horrified "O" as he grasped the fatal nature of this turn of events. The moment Enríquez's body smacked against the hard floor, the cardinal promptly straddled him and plunged his dagger into the base of Enríquez's skull.

*

Gasco disposed of the bodies and returned to the cathedral in Valladolid. He sat in his study, thinking of the future.

The cardinal reflected on how the original plan for three Guardians had been based on Torquemada's then-contemporary actuarial mortality estimates. He had taken into account accidents, plagues, murders, wars—all the possible ways that men could die in the 15th century. Now it was up to the cardinal to modernize these calculations to sustain the essence of Torquemada's master plan, even if it meant modifying the Inquisitor General's original instructions.

As for the current political climate, Gasco had to concede that Enríquez was right—the Hapsburgs had been out of power in Spain for more than one hundred years and were losing influence throughout Europe. But if he could tie the Spanish Hapsburgs, the papacy, and the Austrian Hapsburgs together some way…

Cardinal Gasco unlocked a drawer and withdrew the voluminous Flanders Hapsburg family research that had been completed by the Guardians eight decades earlier and meticulously updated by their successors. He turned to the first page: King Carlos I of Spain, also known as Carlos V, the Holy Roman Emperor.

CHAPTER TEN

LENIN PACED THE floor while Martín sprawled on a sofa and Gina hunched over Lenin's desk, continuing to replay the recording Dave had left for her. They had listened to each of the messages so many times that they could recite every word Dave had said.

Martín was adamant that the absence of background noise during Dave's last message meant that the call had been made under duress. Everything he said had to be a code, particularly since he and Dave hadn't played golf together in quite some time. He pulled up the Gables Golf Club's scorecard on his phone and wrote down each hole's par score on the front nine.

"Three, four, four, three, five, four, three, four, four," he read aloud as he wrote the numbers one through nine across the top of the sheet of paper over the par values. Under that he wrote the scores that Dave referred to, omitting the first three holes because he hadn't said what the scores were in relation to par.

1	2	3	4	5	6	7	8	9
			Eagle	Birdie	Eagle	Birdie	Bogey	Par
Par 3	Par 4	Par 4	Par 3	Par 5	Par 4	Par 3	Par 4	Par 4
–	–	–	1	4	2	2	5	4
			Marty	Dave	Dave	Marty	Marty	M + D

"So, the numbers he wants us to know are one, four, two, two, five, and four," Gina said. "We don't know what the first, second, and third holes are supposed to be."

"And we also don't know what 'choice guy' and 'Saint Benny' mean," Martín said.

They tried country and city telephone dialing codes, but none made any sense in this context. If the numbers corresponded to letters of the alphabet, they spelled A-D-B-B-E-B. Grid coordinates were a possibility, but only had meaning if they knew the map that they referred to.

The hour was late, and Lenin brought in three mugs of coffee before shocking Gina and Martín by removing his jacket. In all the years they had known the man, they had literally never seen him without one.

Lenin regarded their slackened jaws with a raised eyebrow, but refrained from making any sarcastic remarks. He was too exhausted to generate much wit, and his anxiety over Dave's fate was acute.

The three sipped their coffees in silence for a few minutes, lost in their individual thoughts.

"This is delicate, Martín," Lenin said. "I don't want you to compromise yourself, but could this in any way tie to your conversation with Takeshi Ishikawa? Don't answer out loud—just think about it."

Martín thought hard, but he could see no connection with the guerrillas and terrorists that President Ishikawa had discussed with him. He shook his head. "I also had a conversation with King Carlos. But there's no connection there either, of course."

For a moment the tension in Lenin's face melted and he looked pleasantly surprised. "You had an audience with the king? I'm impressed!"

Martín related the conversation with Carlos and Lenin nodded, remarking that he had heard that the king was a dedicated scholar of Spanish history.

"There was one thing that was odd, though," Martín said. "I noticed the king's screensaver. It was the Spanish flag, but it had the Hapsburg coat of arms, with the S.C.C.R. acronym."

Professor Lenin's eyes widened a bit and he scribbled something on the pad of paper in front of him. "Let's puzzle through the other recordings a bit more. Perhaps this chromium head of mine can come up with some ideas—even at this late hour." He looked down at his exposed dress shirt. "And in this obscene state of undress."

Gina and Martín exchanged a smile, prompting one from their former professor as well.

"Why was Dave in Sevilla?" Lenin asked.

"I don't know," Martín said.

"Hmm. All right, he's researching in Sevilla. No doubt it's a legal matter, and since David's specialty is national sovereignty, we can assume it has something to do with that. There are two named persons who may or may not have something to do with his research: Julio and Ray."

"Or they could just be fellow party animals," Martín said.

"Possibly. At the same time, Gina is in France researching Pope Pius's lineage, and she finds a discrepancy. There is an immediate reaction—the priest who helped her is murdered and the conspirators running the cover-up begin to seek out Gina as well.

"Dave finds himself in a situation of duress. He sends Martín a coded message—a series of numbers—and says that he is staying in Spain. It has something to do with Spanish history 'that Cr would love.'" He glared at his former students. "Plus, an admonition to talk to Gina. Any possible tie to what Gina uncovered? 'Choice,' 'Saint Benny.' Anything else?"

Gina chimed in. "We also know that whatever I was supposed to tell Martín was cut off in the message Dave tried to leave me. He must not have realized that the message didn't go through. Otherwise he would have tried again, given how important he made it sound."

Martín's phone rang. He fumbled the phone out of his pocket, then shook his head apologetically as he answered the call.

"Ibarra here," he said and listened silently for thirty seconds. He clicked the phone off.

"I have to go," he said.

"Let's take it up again tomorrow morning," Lenin said.

"Okay," Martín said. "But I have to leave for South America tomorrow afternoon. I'm sorry."

Gina grimaced, then stood. "I'll walk you to your car."

They went out the front door and across the lawn, Martín with his hands in his pockets, Gina with her arms crossed tightly across her chest. As they walked, Martín pulled a hand out of his pocket to put an arm around her shoulders, but stopped himself. When they got to the car they avoided eye contact.

Finally, Martín spoke. "I'm worried about you, Gina."

"So am I," she said. "Where are you off to?"

"I have to meet someone."

"Something about my father?"

Martín said nothing.

Gina turned to face him, looking directly up into his eyes. He saw genuine concern in her expression. "My father is almost messianic about his… mission, I guess you would call it. But at the same time, he's in a bad political spot. He's desperate, Martín. I'm afraid for you too, and what my father may want of you. He'll do anything to maintain what he believes will be his greatest legacy. I know this better than anyone, and I want you to think carefully before you do what he asks of you."

Martín felt a twinge of annoyance that Gina had turned the conversation around on him. She was the one who had recently escaped death, not him. His fatigue amplified his annoyance and he responded abruptly, and with a harsher, more condescending tone than he intended. "I'm going to be fine, Gina. As for you, I want you to just lay low with Cr and not go anywhere until—"

Her eyes flashed. "You want? You have no right to 'want' anything about *my* life. And lay low until what, Martín? Until this—whatever the hell it is—blows over? Or Dave comes back? Maybe if I hide for long enough I can write my big story about the pope without one shred of evidence to back it up and they'll hand me the Pulitzer! Don't tell me what you 'want,' Martín. Just go. I'm not your damsel in distress to protect."

Gina turned and stalked across the lawn to the house. Defeated and angry with himself, Martín opened the door to his car, started it, and drove away.

*

Martín drove slowly through Little Havana. Young dark-haired women in tube tops and form-fitting elastic shorts strolled the sidewalks arm in arm with young men in colorful shirts and tight pants. Cars with glossy paint jobs cruised by, seeming to float on cushions of delicate fluorescent lighting that reflected off the pavement. The cars throbbed with the deep bass beats of salsa and meringue music. Martín pulled to the curb, turning to look at the front of a cafe displaying glowing pink flamingos in the windows and a painted sign saying MANTANZAS CAFÉ COCINA CUBANA.

Martín walked inside and looked around. The café was narrow and dark, extending a long way toward the back. Jalousie windows at the front let in the humid evening breezes. On one side two old men rasped in Spanish while playing checkers. In a booth near them were three beautiful girls in bright-colored dresses, winding down after what looked to be an evening on the town. Everyone in the cafe gleamed with a sheen of perspiration. The radio blared a song by Orquesta Revé.

Martín slid into a booth with a hand-sawed plywood table covered in heavy coats of red paint. A flat-screen television with the sound turned off showed the lowlights of yet another Marlins loss. One of the girls from the front of the cafe slinked past him on her way to the restroom, giving him an inviting smile that changed to a pout when he looked away.

A waitress brought him a Cuban coffee, served steaming hot in a large glass tumbler. The liquid was light beige in color due to its heavy dilution with milk, and its consistency was sticky-sweet with sugar. Martín sipped it and watched the television as Giancarlo Stanton, a former Marlin now with the hated Yankees, thundered a home run into the second deck.

Martín was startled when a voice next to his ear said in Spanish, "Listen, architect—wait thirty seconds, then follow me."

After a few more sips of his *café con leche*, Martín stood and walked toward the kitchen doors. The girl came out of the women's bathroom, made eye contact with Martín, and formed another hopeful smile. Then she caught sight of the small man standing by the kitchen door and looked back at Martín with new respect. Her lips puckered into a kiss, and she headed toward the front of the restaurant.

Martín pushed through the swinging doors. The kitchen was steamy and smelled of spicy Cuban beans with rice. The man led Martín to a door that he knocked on twice, paused, and knocked once more.

Behind the door a man sat at a large, ornate desk. He had thick black hair that was combed into a 1940s-era pompadour. His face was puffy and his eyes were magnified to caricature proportions by thick glasses in Buddy Holly-style black frames.

The man wore a Bluetooth headset and was talking softly in Spanish. He held up his thumb pressed against his index finger toward Martín, talked for another minute, clicked off the phone, and stood, opening his arms broadly.

"*Martinito!*" he bellowed in a voice roughened by heavy smoking. Martín came forward, throwing his arms around the man, and they slapped each other's backs furiously in a Latino *abrazo*.

"Gallego," Martín said affectionately. No one in Martín's generation knew him by any other name. He had been given the nickname because he had gone to live with an uncle in the Galicia region of Spain after his parents had fled Cuba in 1962 and still affected the accent of that region.

Gallego came around the desk and plopped his massive frame into a chair beside Martín, gripping the young man's forearm tightly. He asked enthusiastically about each member of Martín's family, smiling broadly and nodding frequently as Martín answered. Martín reciprocated by asking Gallego about his wife, children, godchildren, and parents, and was genuinely saddened to hear of the passing of Gallego's father. They spoke of Cuban baseball and gossiped about Miami's Cuban-American community leaders.

Gallego moved easily within the Cuban community in America. And perhaps uniquely, he was also able to pass easily into and out of Cuba from the United States using clandestine means that baffled even those closest to him. He did favors for, and received favors from, Cubans on the island and overseas. He operated in the vague areas between the bombastic Marxist dictates of Cuba and the elaborate Anglo common law system in America, helping unofficially here, facilitating something there, and passing official and unofficial messages back and forth. He had brought together many family members divided by the isolation of Cuba from its large neighbor and had moved millions of dollars from prosperous Cuban-Americans to their destitute Cuban relatives.

After a half-hour and two Cuba Libre drinks each, Gallego got to the business at hand, using his curious Caribbean and Iberian blend of the mother tongue.

"So of course you come to Gallego for information about your brother. You will go to Caracas—the sooner the better—and check into the Reyes Católicos Hotel. Ask the night clerk for directions to Ranchito Fierabrás. But, please be careful in your work for Ishikawa." He waved off a weak denial by Martín. "Remember who you are talking to—I hear such things. Ishikawa is Latino in birth and citizenship, but his heart is Japanese and unknown to anyone but himself."

"Do you know what my brother is doing?" Martín asked. "This marshaling of various forces, and foreigners joining his movement?"

The large man shrugged. "Many things are heard. Perhaps a symbolic act for indigenous rights? A blow against the Latino Union to force continent-wide land reform? A demand for a homeland for those who feel excluded from the new Eurocentric culture? It is not clear who he considers good and who he considers bad in this matter."

"Drug trafficking?" Martín asked quietly.

"Impossible. Not your brother. He is a true ideologue—the purest Marxist remaining in the world. I am helping bring you two together because I believe in both of you. Something good will come of it."

"Ishikawa says he's a vicious terrorist."

Gallego considered this for a moment, and then shook his head. "Nico was trained that way. But today he is older and his temperament has mellowed."

Gallego rose, indicating the end of the meeting. He affectionately took Martín's elbow as he walked him to the door. They slapped another *abrazo*. "Be careful of who may follow you to Nicolás and what you tell Ishikawa after you meet your brother. And for you personally, be careful of priests."

"Priests?"

"They are everywhere in the Latino Union right now—going door to door, on TV, staging rallies, handing out crucifixes to everyone. I've never seen such things before. There are rumors that some may even have an interest in you. As I said, many things are heard. I would tell you more if I knew. An *abrazo* for my friend Teodoro, and a kiss on each cheek for Gina."

Martín started to tell Gallego that he and Gina were no longer an item, but was met with a knowing wink. "I think things are not over yet between you two."

With that, Gallego disappeared back into his office while Martín stood in the kitchen facing a closed door, wondering how Gallego knew so many things so quickly.

*

Lenin was up early the next morning studying the notes they had taken the previous night. Gina came into the kitchen cradling the mug of freshly brewed coffee that her mentor had delivered to her room. She wore a borrowed sweatsuit—far too large for her small frame—while her own few clothes were in the washing machine.

"I have called friends of mine at various Spanish universities," Lenin said without looking up. "Broch did some research at a law school in Madrid, at another in Zaragoza, and just in the last few days at another one in Sevilla. They are pulling up computer data on the nature of his research. I hope that will help."

Gina nodded, started to say something, but fell silent.

"Nothing yet from Martín," Lenin said, anticipating the question that she hadn't asked. He set the papers aside. "Will you go to San Juan Diego?"

Gina sipped her coffee and mulled the question. "I have press credentials to cover the pope's visit. I thought about it last night. Maybe I should just get on with my work despite my paranoia."

Lenin considered this. "Perhaps. But you are wise to play it safe."

"Will you go?" she asked.

"I have an invitation, and I made the flight reservations. Seems like I still have some stature in Latin America! I think yes."

Gina gestured at the papers "Have you come up with anything?"

"No. I haven't seen any patterns yet. I—" He looked over her shoulder and through the kitchen window into the yard outside. There was a pickup truck parked on the grass belonging to the house next door, and a man in a uniform stood in the bed of the truck checking the electrical service hookup.

Lenin turned back to Gina. "That phrase David used, 'You're choice.' Is that part of the current vernacular of you young people?"

Gina snorted. "I haven't seen it on Instagram yet, if that's what you mean." She saw his unsmiling reaction and revised her answer. "No, I haven't heard Dave use it before, and I don't know of anyone else who would say that."

Gina noticed that Lenin was looking past her again, and she glanced over her shoulder. The pickup was now parked by Lenin's kitchen window and the uniformed man was checking the wire connections to Lenin's house. He typed something into a handheld tablet and walked out of view.

"I've never heard my students use it," Lenin said. "I had a thought last night about choice, choices, chosen… possibly chosen people…"

Lenin was again staring at the truck by the window. His eyes opened wide and he lunged from the breakfast table, clamped his hand on Gina's wrist, and jerked her out of her chair. Gina's mug was flung from her startled grasp and shattered against the dishwasher, spraying coffee across the floor. She yelped in surprise as Lenin broke into a run, dragging her small body behind him like a kite as she struggled to maintain her footing. Lenin sprinted across the living room toward the closed sliding glass door that led out to the patio and swimming pool, gathered Gina close to his body, and threw his shoulder and back into the glass. Pellets of tempered glass flew in a sparkling shower as they smashed through it. They sailed across a few feet of brick paving and plunged over the pool's edge into the water. As they fell, a brilliant flash like a lightning bolt erupted with an ear-splitting whoosh.

*

Martín sat in the cockpit of his sailboat, which was moored in front of his condo building. The sun was just up and the air was damp, but not yet hot. He studied the Miami skyline, watching the sun glint off the glass skyscrapers.

Martín had gone home after the meeting with Gallego. He wanted to see Gina but didn't know what to say. Restless and unable to sleep, he had called the military crew of his union jet, telling them to move up the departure time to ten in the morning.

Martín thought back to what Gallego had said about working for Takeshi Ishikawa. If the Cuban knew about it, who else did too? And what were his brother and his guerrilla movement doing? And most perplexing, what did he have to fear from priests?

At the bottom of these swirling questions was Gina Ishikawa. He remembered the first time he saw her at the Miami Ballet, having been dragged there by a girl he was dating. He was stunned when he saw Gina on stage. The other dancers were good, but her grace stood out. He knew nothing of ballet, but her every move spoke to him.

A month later the new semester had started at the University of Miami. On the first day of Lenin's class for history majors, The European-Indigenous Clash: 1492, Gina strolled in wearing jeans and a white blouse. She made pointed eye contact with Martín, walked up, and sat beside him—challenging him with her eyes to make the next move. He had hesitated, intimidated by her good looks, grace, and sophistication, and waited until the third day of class before getting up the nerve to ask her out.

They moved quickly into a relationship that was both passionate and comfortable. Then he decided to transfer to Cornell and study architecture. When he told her that he was leaving Miami, she shocked him by urging him to do so. "You have to go in order to become the best," she said without the slightest hesitation.

Relieved that his revelation had not resulted in a tearful scene, but also feeling slightly wounded that it hadn't, Martín steered the conversation back to Gina's dancing, education, and dreams for the future. A few minutes later there was an awkward pause in the conversation, the perfect opportunity for him to tell her where he saw their relationship going. But he said nothing, hoping the situation would somehow resolve itself.

He moved to upstate New York and she traveled to Ithaca to see him during semester breaks, and he returned to Miami periodically. Each time, they easily picked up where they had left off, resuming the relationship with the ease and comfort of putting on a well-loved T-shirt. Neither of them knew whether the other was seeing people during their long periods apart, and neither asked.

When he graduated, Gina and Martín left his parents at their hotel and went back to his apartment. There she looked at him with those wise, expressive eyes and wordlessly posed a question: What now?

Once more Martín hesitated, saying only that he loved her, but nothing more. Gina, unfazed, enrolled in a language study program in Geneva and became a stringer for a newspaper. Martín went to work for a Coral

Gables architectural firm, and both he and Gina crossed the Atlantic regularly for joyous reunions, exchanging daily emails and texts in the interims.

Without his being consciously aware of it, Gina influenced Martín's design work—strong and resilient internal structures supporting graceful, dignified, and understated exteriors. He won several awards for office buildings he designed for the rising Miami skyline, and his career blossomed.

After finishing her studies in Geneva, Gina returned to São Paulo and was caught up in the dizzying world of politics during her father's campaign for the Brazilian presidency and subsequent electoral victory. A short time later he was named to head up the new Latino Union. In her telephone calls and emails to Martín she obliquely referred to the increasing pressures on her father, which seemed to be affecting her in unspoken ways. When Martín was brought in for the San Juan Diego project, he was able to spend more time with Gina and also came to know her father, as much as anyone could know such a distant and deep-thinking man. Martín quickly realized that the newly minted president had serious concerns about his daughter having a relationship outside of her race.

On his boat in the early Miami morning, Martín groaned out loud at the shame brought about by the memories of how things had culminated in San Juan Diego. He was preparing to leave for the airport to fly back to Miami when Gina called him. There was more tension in her voice than he had ever heard before. She told him that she was leaving home immediately and wanted to accompany him back to Miami. The woman who occupied his thoughts day and night, who flowed from his mind through his fingers to his conceptual drawings, was implicitly stating that she wanted to make him a permanent part of her life and that she wanted that life together to begin immediately. Something significant had clearly been the catalyst for her to reach out to him in that moment, over the phone rather than in person, but she didn't say what it was.

Again, Martín had hesitated.

For what seemed like the smallest measure of time he didn't respond. The pause likely didn't last the time to take a breath—hardly a heartbeat—but it was too long. Martín tried to recover, effusively expressing his love for her and his desire to take her with him, but that fatal silence had proclaimed his reluctance louder than any Wagnerian opera singer could have.

In a quiet voice Gina said that she understood his hesitation and told him that she would never want to push him into a commitment unless he was completely enthusiastic about it. With that, she hung up the phone.

Martín returned to Miami alone, and a few days later Dave Broch called to tell him that Gina had taken a job as a Rome-based reporter for a São Paulo newspaper. She had asked Dave not to give Martín her address or her new number. A few months later, Martín heard that she was inexplicably engaged to a powerful Japanese businessman—a pairing that made no sense at all for the woman he knew, and seemed to have her father's fingerprints all over it.

Last night at Professor Lenin's house, an unexpected chance to do something about Gina had again presented itself. And yet Martín, now seething with self-loathing at the fresh memory of lost opportunity, had hesitated yet again.

Martín looked up at the rising sun cresting over the Atlantic Ocean. The slight rocking of his boat, together with the pungent smell of saltwater and seaweed, heightened his awareness of his surroundings. He contemplated how every element of his life that mattered the most to him pivoted upon a single fulcrum: Gina Ishikawa. In the clear morning air this simple fact was so manifest and focused, he marveled at his past indecisions. It was as if a fog of madness had suddenly cleared. He was certain that he wanted to spend his life with Gina. And he also realized that some of the emotion driving him to this realization was his fear for her well-being.

The dead priest in France.

Dave Broch's disappearance.

Gallego's warning about priests.

Something was wrong, and there was no more time for hesitation. It was time to *move*—to take her irrevocably into his life and to confront this danger together.

Martín leaped from the cockpit and hopped onto the dock. He ran to the parking lot, jumped into his car, and spun the tires as he accelerated away from the marina. He raced through intersections, ignoring yellow and red lights, not wanting to waste a single moment more. He had wasted enough time already.

His car fishtailed wildly as he turned onto Lenin's street. He stomped on the brakes and whipped the steering wheel to the right, causing the car to career over the curb. There were two police cruisers blocking off the street, and he had nearly plowed into them.

Martín jumped out of his car and sprinted past the cruisers, ignoring the shouting of an officer ordering him to stop. He rounded a curve to see part of a concrete slab sitting next to a smoking crater. A blackened metal lump was all that was left of Lenin's Toyota that had been parked in his garage. A thick pile of debris floated on the surface of the swimming pool. There was not a single stick of Lenin's house still standing above ground.

Martín ran up to a fireman who was rolling up a length of hose. "What happened? What happened?"

"Can't say for sure yet," the fireman stammered. "But it went up quick. Probably a bomb. Forensics will confirm."

Martín looked wildly around the scene of ruin, spotting three ambulances parked just beyond the fire trucks.

"Survivors?" Martín asked.

"We haven't found anyone," the fireman said. "If anybody was in there, they didn't make it. We'll know more soon." Peering at Martín's stricken face, the fireman reached out to steady him. "I'm really sorry, buddy. Were you a relative of the homeowner? If so we can contact you if you give us your—"

Martín shook off the fireman's hand and stumbled back to his car.

CHAPTER ELEVEN

Barcelona, Spain—1917

THE HISPANO-SUIZA AUTOMOBILE drew stares as it parted the people on the street and pulled up in front of the Café Catalán. A man in a crisp navy suit and homburg hat seated at an outdoor table watched the priest step down from the vehicle and look around at his surroundings. He made eye contact with the man at the table and walked toward him, extending his hand.

"Accountant Las Casas?"

"Yes. Father Cisneros?"

"At your service."

They sat and the priest ordered coffee. For a half-hour they talked about inconsequential things—Las Casas asking about automobile travel from Burgos, Cisneros asking about the accountant's family.

"Never married, and no prospects for now," Las Casas said.

"You specialize in international banking, I understand."

"Father, you seem to know a lot about me. You contacted me. Tell me about yourself."

"Just an ordinary priest of the Augustine order," Cisneros said. "I serve in a monastery in Burgos, Santa Maria de la Vid. Do you know it?"

"No, I've never been to Burgos."

Cisneros shifted in his chair. "Allow me a personal question. How do you stand with God?"

Las Casas looked back steadily, mulling the impertinence of the question for a moment, but decided to go forward—business was business. "I am a good Catholic. I was educated in the Church. I attend mass regularly." Las Casas paused, tried to read the priest's expression, and found it inscrutable. "How did you find me and why are you so interested in me?"

"What about your parents and siblings?" the priest pressed.

Las Casas sighed, but decided to continue playing the priest's game a bit longer. "My parents died 11 years ago. My brother was killed fighting the Germans with the French."

"And what do you know about your ancestors?"

"My grandfather used to say we had Jews in our heritage, centuries ago."

"Hmm."

Las Casas laughed. "Does that matter? This is the twentieth century, you know. We Spaniards don't keep track of 'tainted blood' anymore."

Cisneros smiled. "No, of course it doesn't matter," he said, but he sounded unconvinced.

"We need to get to the point," Las Casas said. "Why are you here, and why am I meeting with you?"

"I need a banker I can completely trust," Cisneros said. He looked around to make sure that no one was listening. "Come to work for me and I can make you wealthy beyond your wildest dreams."

Las Casas laughed. "You're a priest—an Augustinian, no less. You've taken an oath of poverty."

"Do you know the Rothschild Bank in Frankfurt?"

"Of course. I communicate with them every day," Las Casas said.

"Do you know the Ono Osaka Bank?"

"Absolutely. Millions of marks and yen are exchanged each year between my bank and theirs."

"Before we say any more," Cisneros said, "I must take your confession and then I will require you to take both a blood oath and a brotherhood oath."

*

Las Casas and Cisneros sat across from each other in a small chapel, a crude wooden table between them. A week had passed since they met outside the café. Two days after that, Las Casas had punctured his own arm and dripped his blood into a chalice on the altar at Sagrada Familia in the middle of the night. Father Cisneros officiated, with no one else in the cavernous nave. Afterward, they each pricked a fingertip and mixed their blood while chanting in Latin.

"If I decide to work for you, must I resign my post at the bank?" Las Casas had asked before agreeing to the ceremony.

"No," Cisneros said. "It is important that you continue to work there. But you must understand that your first loyalties must be to God and to me."

"You have my oaths." Las Casas had been wired an enormous sum of money the previous day. For more of that, the banker was willing to give an oath swearing to just about anything the old priest asked of him.

"You have not spoken to anyone about this meeting, correct?" Cisneros asked.

"Correct."

"And you never will?"

"Never."

"You are the first outside of clergy and kings to receive the information I will impart to you now," Cisneros said. He set a stack of papers in front of the other man. "Please note the amount on deposit in this bank account."

Las Casas studied the account page from Rothschild Frankfort. "What currency is this?"

"German marks."

"Then there's an error in the placement of the decimal point."

"No. It is accurate."

The banker's eyes widened. "Impossible. This is larger than the gross domestic product of some countries!"

"What is important is that it is in a German bank. The war—it concerns me. What do you think will happen to Germany?"

"The Americans are in it now. I believe the Germans will lose."

"And what about the German economy?" Cisneros asked.

"France and Britain will demand very large reparations," Las Casas said. "The Germans will face the demobilization of millions of soldiers.

I believe there will be serious inflation, possibly even hyperinflation. The mark will become essentially worthless."

"Exactly my opinion. In addition, this fortune has grown to an unwieldy size, calling for a need to diversify. I want you to move the assets in the account I just showed you to the banks on this list." Cisneros slid a piece of paper over to the banker, who eyed it warily.

"When?"

"Immediately."

Las Casas chuckled wryly and turned his attention back to the account statements. After a few moments, he looked up, removed his glasses, and polished them with a handkerchief. "Gold bullion, German marks, British pounds sterling, American dollars, yen... this portfolio is unbelievable." Las Casas nodded down toward the list of destination banks sitting on the table. "Most of this makes sense to me—Switzerland, London, Royal Bank of Canada—but why Japan?"

"You could call it a hedge against the turmoil in Europe. They have assisted in the war against Germany and being on the winning side will open up economic opportunities throughout the West. I believe they will become a major force in the world, which suits my purposes."

"Okay. But why not America? They're helping the war effort as well. Personally, I see them as a major growth opportunity."

Cisneros gave a dismissive wave. "Their government has proven in the last decade that they are inclined to freeze the assets of any entity they consider undesirable."

"Does this account—" Las Casas gestured toward the documents— "belong to the Catholic Church? I can't see the United States deciding to freeze—"

"It is far more complicated than that," Cisneros said, his voice rising slightly with impatience. "I will tell you more as we go forward. For now, I need you to follow my instructions exactly."

"All right, all right," Las Casas said. "I accept your commission."

Cisneros sank back in his chair. "Excellent. In addition to the amounts you have already received, here is your retainer for the services you will provide. The documents in your hand will give you all of the details you need for the transfers." Cisneros slid an envelope across the table. Las Casas peeked inside and his eyes widened at the quantity of currency he saw. "We shall meet here every Wednesday night at 11 so that you can update me."

*

Several months later, Las Casas sat down for their weekly appointment with a smirk of self-satisfaction. "It took longer than I expected, but everything is completed. Here are the bills of exchange, letters of credit, and transport receipts. The bullion going overseas departed the port of Barcelona this morning, and the rest is going by rail. These are your marine bills of lading, insurance certificates, and certificates of purity. I engaged security guards who will accompany the cargo all the way to its destinations—they have been well compensated."

Cisneros spent two full hours meticulously reviewing every document. At last he pushed his chair back, straightened the thick sheath of papers, and placed them carefully into a leather briefcase.

"You have not spoken to anyone about me or about the nature of these transactions, correct?"

"You made that clear from the beginning. I have handled everything personally, without involving any of my associates."

"You have done well, Accountant Las Casas. You have been honest and efficient in carrying out God's work. He will approve of your service to Him when you appear before Him for judgment."

"If I have earned your trust and confidence," Las Casas said, "then, as you promised, please tell me what this account is about. To what purpose will it be employed?"

"Trust, yes. But neither God nor I can forgive your tainted blood."

Las Casas stared back in confusion.

"This I do for one, ten, a hundred or a thousand years," Cisneros said, "whatever is required to bring on the Millennium." He withdrew a small silenced pistol from his black coat and shot Las Casas through the heart.

CHAPTER TWELVE

THEIR LUNGS WERE burning from a lack of air as Lenin and Gina surfaced through the shattered planks and chunks of wallboard floating in the pool.

"Air and then back down," Lenin said.

Gina gulped air and ducked back underwater. She saw Lenin swim to a side of the pool away from the house. He reached up and came back down with a rubber tube. A snorkel, she realized. Lenin swam back to Gina and handed her the snorkel. She bobbed up near the surface and breathed deeply, then passed the tube to him. They traded it back and forth for what seemed to be a very long time.

Finally, Lenin passed the snorkel to Gina and eased himself toward the surface, clearing a small opening through the debris. He slowly broke through the surface of the water and turned a full circle before waving her over.

"We've got to get out of here fast," Lenin said, pulling himself out of the pool.

"But the police—"

"We want whomever did this to think that we're dead. I think it's safe to say that your trip to rural France was more fruitful than you could have imagined. Let's go."

They heard the wail of a police siren as they hoisted themselves out of the pool. Gina was barefoot, and hesitated when she looked at the field of burning wood, nails, and broken glass all around her. Lenin, reading the situation, swept her up in his arms and quickly carried her through the wreckage. He made his way behind a neighboring house where they were shielded from view and the ground was no longer piled with debris. As the bawling of fire engine sirens grew louder, Lenin knelt, lifted a brick in the small flowerbed, and picked up a key, which he used to unlock the back door.

Lenin shrugged. "Snowbirds. Friends of mine. I water their plants while they are away."

They made their way to the garage, where Lenin looked through a now-vacant window frame. The glass that had been blown inward by the concussion from the blast crunched underneath Lenin's shoes. Gina gingerly poked around the garage. She was pleased to find a pair of men's work boots. They were oversized for her, but she was able to lace them tightly onto her feet.

Lenin turned from the window and threw back a tarp to reveal a lime-green Kawasaki motorcycle. "We've got to get going while they're still focused on the fire," he said. "Do you know how to drive one of these things?"

Gina smirked and went to the bike. She took the handle bar grips in her hands, and threw her leg over. She worked the choke, turned the key, and kicked the starter pedal. The engine caught immediately, sounding a throaty purr.

Lenin tentatively took his place behind her. He leaned forward, and she heard the nervousness in his voice as he said, "Little Havana."

Gina nodded, put the motorcycle in gear, and released the clutch. She eased the bike through the garage's side door and around to the front of the house. Then she slowly motored along the sidewalk for a block before driving into the street. Lenin wrapped his arms tightly around her waist as she began to accelerate away from the neighborhood.

Once they were on the interstate, Gina drove south toward central Miami. She crossed the river and took an exit leading to Little Havana, then pulled to the curb of a side street. She looked back to see her former professor smiling despite himself.

"I'm sure glad you know how to operate this… vehicle," Lenin said. "It's quite exhilarating, really! My suit is nearly dry!"

Gina laughed. In his windblown and grungy suit, it was the most disheveled she had ever seen him.

"Where to now?" she asked.

"Ah, yes. Go right, eight blocks up, and look for a pool hall called 'Ruben Dario's.'"

Gina gunned the high, whiny engine and spun the rear tire. The bike lurched forward as Lenin clutched her waist.

*

Lenin and Gina waited on a bench inside Ruben Dario's main room, watching as a small group smoked and shot pool while giving the odd, bedraggled pair curious glances from time to time. Finally, a short, skinny man approached and motioned for them to follow. They went out the back door of the pool hall and down an alley. At the far end was a mobile construction office up on jacks. The guide opened the door and they climbed the two steps and entered.

Gallego stood up from a chair behind a card table, and Lenin and the Cuban embraced.

"Please meet Gina Ishikawa," Lenin said.

Gallego's face lit up. He gripped Gina's sooty hand and shook it warmly. "The daughter of the president, here in my humble office! And more beautiful in person than in any of the pictures I have seen. I am honored."

Gina snorted with laughter at the gushing compliment, given her current appearance. The Cuban feigned a wounded expression, but the spark didn't fade from his eyes. "You do not believe my sincerity? I know that you have been through a great deal today. Perhaps this will help a little bit."

Gallego lifted a cardboard box off his cluttered desk and handed it to Gina. She opened it to see neatly arranged khaki slacks, an emerald green polo shirt, two large towels, and shoes. There was a hairbrush, bath soap, and shampoo. Tucked beneath the towels Gina spied a La Perla bag. Eyebrows raised, she opened it and found a lacy bra and panties in shimmering blue.

Gina looked at Gallego reproachfully, and he smiled broadly. "Please allow one indulgence for a fat old man. Going there for shopping is the only sexy thing I can do anymore."

Gina slipped into the trailer's tiny bathroom and was reminded of the cramped shower on board Martín's sailboat. By now, he likely believed that she was dead. Somberly, she turned on the shower and scrubbed off the multiple coats of grime that caked her body.

When Gina emerged from the bathroom Lenin and Gallego were huddled together, talking quietly. Gallego looked up at her and smiled. "*Señorita* Ishikawa, you look wonderful! But I must apologize. Those clothes I gave you are not fit for a president's daughter, I am afraid."

"This hasn't been a day fit for a president's daughter," she said. "But thank you, *Señor* Gallego. The shower and clean clothes make me feel like royalty."

Gallego beamed at her graciousness, but noted her formality. "Please, let's use *tu*," he said, insisting on the familiar pronoun. "Today you are an honorary Cuban. You are family." He turned to Lenin. "And when you see Martín, I want you to give him a swift kick in the ass. Actually, make it two. I can't believe he let this one slip away." Lenin nodded in return with a wan smile and Gallego's attention turned back to Gina. "As I was saying to Teodoro," Gallego began, lighting a cigar, "there are logistical matters we have to discuss. You will need anonymity where you are going if you want to let others think you are dead."

"Yes, that's critical," Lenin said.

"I've arranged a flight with Brothers to the Rescue later tonight from an airfield near Orlando. They can get you into Venezuela undetected. From there you will go to this address on the beach near Maiquetía." He handed Lenin a typewritten note. "It's a condo that belongs to a friend of mine. You can stay there as long as you need to—no one will ask questions. There is a car there, and its keys are in a drawer in the kitchen."

Gallego handed Lenin a thick envelope from a briefcase on the floor. "That should be enough cash to get you to San Juan Diego. There I assume that you will be able to resume your real identities but remain outside of the public eye until you can be seen alive again."

Lenin looked inside the envelope and silently tallied the bills inside. "This looks like around ten thousand dollars. I can repay you before we leave."

Gallego dismissively waved his hand. "Authorities—and who knows who else—will know if you try to access your money now. This is my gift to the two of you. And you will find more cash in the condo. Use it." He stood and took Gina's hands, kissing her on each cheek. "My best to your father."

Gina's eyes widened. "He knows you?"

"He is in a difficult place at a difficult time. I wish him the best. Go with God."

Gina and Lenin left the construction trailer, then walked back through the pool hall and out onto the street.

"Ready for the drive?" Gina said. "I could get us there in about three hours, except that I suppose it's not safe to speed."

"I'm done riding motorcycles," Lenin said. "Gallego arranged for something more suitable while you were in the shower. But we have an errand to attend to before the airport."

A Ford Taurus stopped at the curb in front of them. The driver got out, leaving the engine running, and walked across the street without looking back. The professor and his former student climbed into the car and headed for the turnpike.

*

Martín sat on the bed in his hotel room in Maiquetía, Venezuela, and stared at the wall. There would be time for mourning, but for now he needed to think clearly.

At 4 p.m. he took the elevator down to the lobby. He went to the desk and asked for the night clerk. A young man came out, and Martín asked him for directions to Ranchito Fierabrás. The clerk nodded, saying Martín should go back to his room and await a call.

At 4:15 the phone rang and an electronically distorted voice told Martín to go jogging from the hotel at 5:15 the next morning. The voice dictated the route that he should follow, which Martín scrawled down on hotel stationary. He hung up and restlessly passed the hours playing solitaire on his laptop. Sleep was not an option.

*

The Church of All Saints in Orlando was a splinter organization that had broken off from the Mormon Church 22 years earlier. The church had prospered in Central Florida and its membership grew rapidly. It maintained their Mormon-based belief that when anyone joined their congregation, his or her ancestors were also sealed within the church for eternity, and upon death members would join their deceased relatives. When separating from the Mormon Church, their IT department copied the Mormons' extensive electronic genealogical files onto portable media. Put another way, they ripped off the data.

Lenin's friend Efraín Bertrán, a member of the Church of All Saints after converting from Catholicism, warmly greeted Gina and his former professor upon their arrival. The trio stood in a section of the main church's complex that was open to the public for genealogical research. Around them towered shelves of books, most of which looked fresh und unworn.

"So, Teodoro, what do you think of my humble operation?" Efraín asked.

"I still think you made a big mistake forsaking history for computer science."

Efraín laughed. "Well, that was the first important conversion in my life. This is the second!" He gently elbowed Lenin in the ribs. "When am I going to get you converted, you old lapsed Catholic?"

"The day I hear Gabriel's horn blowing, I suppose."

Efraín smiled. "So how can I help the two of you today?"

"How many people do you track here?" Gina asked.

"We have more than 150 million families in our database. We can go back as far as the 15th century. Of course, many of the names have changed by emigration, misspellings, changed spellings, and changed names. Then there are common surnames that trace back to many different origins. A blacksmith who was known by his trade in a small village in Germany might have completely different ancestors than the blacksmith from a small village in Denmark, for example, but both their surnames were dubbed 'Smith' in English when they came to this country. We have to do intensive research to make these distinctions."

Efraín led them to his office, which was spacious and well-lit with a view of the church grounds. The sun was setting and a golden hue sparkled across the underside of the scattered clouds. Efraín pulled up chairs so that Lenin and Gina could see the screen clearly.

"I already have your trace on file, Teodoro, in case I can finally convince you to join," Efraín said.

Lenin smiled. "Not what interests me today, thank you very much." He pulled out papers that he and Gina had recreated from memory in the car and laid one of them in front of Efraín. The Argentine's eyebrows rose.

"Do you expect this man to convert anytime soon?" Efraín asked.

"It's probably best if you don't ask too many questions," Lenin said. "And please remember—Gina and I were never here, and you certainly weren't doing any research on His Holiness."

"Only God, and those in this room, shall know of this visit and inquiry," Efraín said as he started typing.

*

The sackcloth robes of the men in the room contrasted sharply with the modern equipment around them. Rows of consoles shimmered with glowing displays while the monks seated at each of them spoke softly into microphones on their headsets. The holy men frequently referred to manuals as they adjusted data flows rushing in from the antenna array outside of Burgos to the Cray supercomputer housed in the room behind them.

The monks were running calibrations and tests on data arriving from new systems installed in churches and cathedrals throughout Latin America. As data-gathering equipment in the ecclesiastic installations came on line, sample runs were collected from the audio and video being transmitted from confessionals, as well as from the smartphones of churchgoers who had been encouraged by their priests to download the new official app of the Roman Catholic Church to their phones. This app, written by a small team of coders hired by Moto Electric, sunk its virtual tendrils into their electronic devices, siphoning their personal data and granting live access to their phone's camera and audio. The Cray computer in Burgos operated at a fraction of its capacity as it took the audio and video files, scanned them, sorted them according to keywords and images, and printed them for review by Inquisition authorities.

Selected priests in Latin America were being trained to utilize more probing lines of questioning within their confessionals in order to solicit verbal admissions of misconduct and wrongful thoughts. These priests, ignorant of the Inquisition's new surveillance methods, were told that it was for a new initiative by the pope to do a more thorough job of understanding people's sins so that the priests could better assist in the process of cleansing their souls. Confessionals were equipped with state-of-the-art audio and video equipment transmitting the facial expressions, body language, and intonations of people confessing. Crucifixes distributed to parishioners to hold while they confessed were embedded with microtransmitters that recorded body temperatures, heart rates, perspiration quantities, and salinity while also taking fingerprints. Lie detection and voice stress analysis subroutines scanned all incoming voice data to establish files of truths and lies confessed by the faithful. Cameras embedded within crucifixes hanging in people's homes recorded sex acts and other misdeeds.

A portion of the vast fund founded by King Fernando II at the urging of Tomás de Torquemada, and guarded for more than 500 years by the Guardians of the Fourth Angel, was finally being wielded to ensure that the 21st-century Inquisition would not fail as an instrument of ecclesiastic and political control.

*

It was dark in Orlando when Gina pushed back from Efraín's desk. She stared out at the shrubbery beyond the glass. The three of them had checked and rechecked Guy Legendre's genealogical data, which extended back to his great-great-grandparents birth, marriage, and death certificates, as well as his extended family's records.

Gina gave Efraín the additional names of Antoine and Claire Legendre, and the birth and death years she had found with Father Croix. There was no match for that combination of names and dates in that location. They tried again with the same birth year but this time with the tombstone date of 1815. Nothing was found. Efraín expanded the geographical data to the northern half of France, but no match was found. Then he increased it to all of France.

Nothing.

"Vincennes is just a kilometer or two from the Belgian border," Gina said. "Try there."

Efraín clicked away on his keyboard. Still nothing was found. The three sat for a few moments, at a loss as to how to proceed.

"Of course, I'm an idiot," Lenin mumbled to himself. "Use Flanders as the location, and 'Burgundy' for the name."

Lines of data began to trace across the monitor. "How did you think of that?" Efraín asked.

Before Lenin was able to respond, the screen went blank. Efraín frowned. After some furious typing the data flow resumed, but after a few moments the display once again went blank.

"This is very troubling," Efraín said. "I never designed blocks like these into this system."

"Would your church do that?" Gina asked.

"There's no one here who has enough knowledge to keep me out. No, this was done by someone outside who somehow got access."

"There's nothing more you can do?" Lenin asked.

Efraín scoffed with indignation. "I was always a bit worried that the Church of Latter-day Saints would realize that we had replicated their data and come after us. It wouldn't be very Christian-like behavior, but sometimes even the most righteous can get a bee in their bonnet. I installed some fail-safes to ensure that we never lost it—I can access the data through one of those channels. Just give me a few minutes."

Efraín resumed typing, and eventually the screen lit up again with the information they were seeking:

LEGENDRE, ANTOINE. BORN 3 JAN 1795
BAPTIZED 13 JAN 1795
MARRIED: RENARD, MARIE 12 MAR 1815
DIED: 29 AUG 1815
BURIAL SITE: TERRE BONNE, FLANDERS
DATES: DOCUMENTED C, M, BG(0)
LINEAGE: Y/N

"What does 'Documented C, M, BG' mean?" Gina asked.

"One of the responsibilities of our missionaries in every country is to verify and validate our genealogical data," Efraín said. "In this case they confirmed the birth, marriage, and death dates of Antoine Legendre in C—church documents or the family Bible—and M—municipal documents, birth, and death certificates, the like. BG is an additional confirmation we seek: burial grounds. But in this case, there is a zero after it, indicating that a search was attempted, but nothing was found."

Lenin looked up from his phone. "Terre Bonne is also on the border, just over three kilometers from Vincennes."

A genealogical chart filled the screen. The branches went back six generations, but with notations indicating that with each additional generation the data was increasingly unreliable. This was typical, Efraín explained. There had been three previous generations in Terre Bonne from 1710 to 1795, and before that the carriers of the family name had resided in Mechelen, Flanders, for at least four generations.

"Where is Mechelen?" Efraín asked.

"Near Brussels," Lenin said. On a pad of paper he copied from the screen several surnames that were different from, and predated, Legendre but were confirmed to be in the lineage.

Efraín commanded the program to go forward in generations, and after a pause, another genealogical chart formed on screen. One name stood out without a successive generation: Legendre, Guy Pierre.

Efraín blinked. "There must be some mistake," he said.

"No, that's what I expected," Lenin replied. "Somebody has cooked the books."

*

At a small airport near Orlando a Piper Comanche airplane with no lights illuminated and no markings waited in the dark at the far end of an uncontrolled airfield. Gina drove their Ford Taurus up to the airplane, where two men stood beside it. The men used small flashlights to check the faces of the Gina and Lenin. Then one man opened the cabin door, helping them step into the passenger seats while the other drove the Taurus away.

The pilot started the engines, did a run up, and took off, all without any radio transmissions. Hours later they landed at a small airstrip near Maiquetía, Venezuela, where a taxi was waiting for them.

Martín Ibarra was out of bed before five and in the hotel lobby in his running shorts, shoes, and T-shirt 10 minutes later. It was still dark but the morning air was dank with humidity. His run took him downhill from the hotel past large homes belonging to the wealthiest of Caracas—small fortresses behind high walls and barbed wire.

At first Martín glanced around in anticipation. Who was he supposed to be looking for? How would the rendezvous transpire? But it wasn't long before his mind wandered. He was still numb from the disaster at Lenin's house and hadn't slept. All the way to the Miami airport and during the flight on the Latino Union's military Gulfstream aircraft he tried to make sense of what had happened.

Martín increased his pace in an attempt to banish Gina and Lenin from his thoughts, but their faces swam before him and he ran faster. A sense that he could have done something—moved sooner, told Gina that he loved her before leaving that night—gripped him. He was sprinting now, his heart pounding.

Caught up in his misery, Martín failed to notice a panel van pulling up beside him and matching his speed. He only realized that something was amiss when the sliding door of the van opened. Before he could react, a man grabbed his arm and jerked him into the vehicle. The door slammed shut, and the van accelerated. A knee to his back pinned him to the floor as tape was clapped over his eyes and mouth and zip ties bound his wrists and ankles.

*

Gina and Lenin let themselves into the beachfront condo. It was beautifully furnished and had a balcony facing the Caribbean. There they sat at a small table overlooking the water. Lenin wrote furiously for several minutes, then laid his tablet of paper on the table.

"I see a pattern that unfortunately eluded me when we were with Efraín last night. With a phone call, I can put him to work either proving or disproving my idea. Claire and Antoine Legendre were from Terre Bonne, a small village near Vincennes. The generation before Claire and

Antoine lived in Mechelen. The seat of the House of Burgundy, one of the strongest branches of the Hapsburgs."

"I don't understand what you're getting at," Gina said.

"The new pope's lineage comes from a line that, years ago, was spliced into a French family line that wasn't his. His true ancestors were bastards from suppressed and unrecognized branches of the family. But with his family's altered lineage, he is a full-blown, legitimate member of the Hapsburg family line. I believe when we examine King Carlos VII's background we will find the same tampering. In the eyes of anyone who would care about such things, he, and if I am correct, the new king of Spain are the most prominent and powerful members of a line that for hundreds of years was the most influential and formidable family on earth. We are witnessing the attempted restoration of Hapsburg rule in Spain with the backing of the Catholic Church."

"That is a… remarkable conclusion."

Lenin smiled. "Come now. When you did research for me, you didn't treat me like an old man whose mutterings you tolerated just to avoid an unpleasant scene. You attacked, challenged, and proposed alternatives. Don't back off now."

"Fine!" Gina said. "It's crazy! What are you thinking? In the first place, why the Hapsburgs? They haven't mattered since World War I. And who cares about bloodlines these days?"

Lenin looked out at the whitecaps and a passing sailboat, sails billowing in the breeze. Finally, he turned back. "Let me ask you that same question. Why indeed the Hapsburgs?"

As if she was back in Lenin's classroom, Gina fielded the Socratic volley. "Well, they were among the earliest to establish monarchical power after the chaos of the fall of the Roman Empire and the Dark Ages. Eventually Charles V ruled more of the planet than anyone else has before or since. Spain, the Holy Roman Empire, the Netherlands, Peru…"

"But then…?" Lenin asked.

"They collapsed from inbreeding and were swept out of power."

"That would have left a lot of disappointed and unemployed Hapsburgs scattered around a large part of Europe, don't you think? Not to mention those Spaniards still yearning to restore Spain's fabled *siglo de oro*."

"Yes," Gina said. "But how could people with meaningless noble titles do anything about it now?"

"What would you do if you were one of them?"

Gina was silent for a long moment. "Me? I'd become a journalist. But if I was some conspirator wanting to usurp power, I guess I'd start conspiring."

"You're getting warmer," Lenin said.

Gina shook her head. "I can't take it any further. It would require too many people and a lot of money, influence, and political upheaval to make any power transfer happen in Spain. Even if the Spanish people were willing, the rest of the EU—"

"The European Union is distracted right now by the departure of the United Kingdom as well as the populist movement sweeping through the continent. Add in the vitriol happening in the United States and now would seem like the time to strike. I don't think this is only about Spain and the Vatican. I believe that Austria and many other nations will become involved. The Hapsburgs had their fingers in pies from Mexico to Eastern Europe."

Gina stared back at him. "How can you reach that conclusion? There's been nothing in the news that points to a conspiracy on that scale."

"I know. If one of my students had advanced this idea I would have immediately given her an F, dropped her from my course, and signed her up for a creative writing class. But consider what has happened to you in France and now to both of us in Florida. Put that together with David Broch's disappearance, along with the pope's family anomalies."

Lenin took a sip of his lime spritzer. "Two months ago I attended a history symposium in Vienna. I ran into a colleague of mine, the head of the European history department at Corvinus University in Budapest. We had dinner together and a few too many whiskies afterward. He told me he was a colonel in the Hungarian army reserve and was still active with military exercises, and that he had many friends in the officer corps."

"I don't see how this applies," Gina said.

"Bear with me, I have a point. The Austro-Hungarian Empire collapsed during World War I. Emperor Carlos and Empress Zita fled to Switzerland. As we had another round of drinks my friend became... wistful, nostalgic.

He looked around to be sure no one was listening, and said that he and many other officers in both the Austrian and Hungarian armies had taken secret loyalty oaths to Zita before her death. By the time she died in exile, never having been permitted to return to Austria, those officers had become high-ranking generals in the military commands of both countries, or had retired but retained commands in the army reserves. My friend spoke in reverential terms of the possibility of an era of Hapsburg rule in a restored Austro-Hungarian monarchical state. A month later I happened to see a small news item that he and 10 other reserve officers had been arrested. They were found to be buying arms from dealers in Brussels and smuggling them into a warehouse in Vienna."

Gina was silent for a long time. She rose from her chair and leaned against the balcony, staring out at the sea.

Lenin laid a comforting hand on her shoulder. "There is, I am afraid, one more part of my hypothesis. It is personal. We know from Martín that the king of Spain was recently in the Latino Union, speaking with your father."

Gina's voice rose sharply. "You know as well as I do that there is no way in hell—"

"I am not suggesting for a moment that your father is part of the conspiracy that I have laid out. Please hear me. For the first time in history Latin America has joined together. But you and I both know that the bond is not a solid one, and your father is using all the political capital he has to keep it all together. As such, he has reached out to not only the extremely popular king of Spain to bolster the star power at his upcoming inauguration in San Juan Diego, but also the head of the church that three-quarters of his new constituents belong to. All of those countries, many of which were once ruled by the Hapsburgs, are about to be consolidated under one legal authority. If I am correct, your father has unwittingly invited the foxes into the henhouse."

"But how would they instigate such a massive transfer of power? The constitution allows for member countries to drop out at any time."

"I agree. But what if the pope and the king pledged a massive influx of funds—for infrastructure, social safety nets, and investments in the economies of the member countries? A chicken in every LU constituent's pot, as it were. Wouldn't that potentially tip the scales? Wouldn't most of the Latino Union's tax-weary and debt-ridden members be willing to trade some portion of their autonomy to potentially solve many of their social ills?"

Gina was incredulous. "To undertake what you are describing would require a fortune!"

"I agree, Gina, and I haven't figured that out yet. But don't forget the resources of the Catholic Church, now controlled by a man whose lineage was tampered with to make him a pure Hapsburg."

"You know that's not enough. Otherwise there wouldn't be any poor Catholics any longer."

Lenin laughed wryly. "You have more faith in organized religion than I do, Gina. You don't control people by giving them enough support to dig themselves out of poverty. You do it by dangling just enough that they believe that they will do so, and that the entity reaching out that helping hand—the one that isn't quite long enough to pull you from the dregs—is your salvation."

Gina nodded as she took the point. "Still…"

Lenin patted Gina on the back. "I don't mean to mock you, Gina. I do agree with your underlying point. There would have to be enough money somewhere to at least make such claims somewhat credible. Enough to get the ball rolling, as it were. And for that, I have no answers right now."

Gina paused, taking it all in. There were so many variables—so much complexity. She wanted to get to the bottom-line.

"Professor," she said, taking the older man's hands in hers and looking him in the eyes. "Tell me in a single sentence what your overarching hypothesis is. Give me your elevator pitch."

"What I'm talking about is a grand scheme to bring about the restoration of the Holy Roman Empire, with the Hapsburgs once again at the helm."

CHAPTER THIRTEEN

Tokyo, Japan—2001

WARO MOTO STARED across the conference room at the odd pair in front of him. Outwardly, he projected the calm and confidence of a man in complete control, but inside he seethed. The very fact that he was having to consider the terms that had been presented to him was shameful.

Moto had built his telecom company by leveraging his personal fortune, which grew dramatically throughout the Nineties as Moto correctly anticipated and exploited the internet explosion. But investing in winners among the dot-coms was merely a means to funnel more and more money into his true enterprise, Moto Electric. Moto saw the internet companies that he bought and sold as vastly inferior—devoid of assets and run by children, they were the antithesis of the global telecommunications network that he dreamed of creating. All around the world Moto Electric purchased the only meaningful real estate left on the planet—wireless spectrum. Moto knew that wireless telecommunication was the future, and he ordered his chief financial officer to borrow as much as he possibly could in order to finance the spectrum purchases. Interest rates were low, as were the network infrastructure build-out costs—vendors were practically paying the telecom companies to take their equipment. When Moto Electric's level of debt became toxic, Moto collateralized his personal holdings and borrowed more.

And then, last year, the dot-com bubble burst.

The same bankers who had bought him $5,000 bottles of wine as they patted him on the back and called him a visionary now came hunting. They sent him default letters and sought to tear Moto Electric and his personal assets to pieces and sell them to the highest bidders. Moto looked for partners in other Japanese industries, but those he spoke to either were feeling the financial pinch themselves or were salivating at the opportunity to cripple him. At his lowest point Moto had even entertained allowing Russian money into his company, but a single meeting in Moscow made it clear that the moment he got into bed with these men, he'd be stripped of any power other than to rubber-stamp whatever potentially criminal enterprise the Russians put in front of him. He was too proud to let that happen.

What frustrated him the most was that he knew with 100% certainty that his long-term vision was still the path to fortune and enormous power. But without the capital to bail himself out, he had no means to pursue it. Worse, if Moto Electric collapsed, he would watch helplessly as others without his foresight and business acumen profited enormously after getting his valuable assets for pennies on the dollar.

Then an unanticipated call had come, and now Moto was listening to a banker's pitch while the man's client sat silently across from him.

"So, you can see the broad strokes up here on the screen. Moto Electric will get a one-time capital infusion that it will use to retire all of its existing debt, including all of the default premiums and fees. In return, we will get a 49% interest in Moto Electric with the veto rights described in this slide here."

The Japanese banker waited for any indication of assent or understanding from the CEO, and got none. He paused, uncertain as to whether he should continue, and looked over to his client for some guidance. The Spaniard twirled his hand in an impatient gesture to keep the presentation going, and the banker clicked on to the next slide.

"As you can see here, Phase Two of the investment by Guardians Capital will come in the form of loans to Moto Electric. From this day forward, Guardians Capital will be your sole source of debt or equity funding, and all proceeds will come with strict covenants as to how they can be used—as such, Guardians Capital will have sole veto power over all Moto Electric budgets, as well as any acquisitions or expenditures in excess of one million United States dollars."

"That's outrageous," Moto growled. "I won't be able to buy toilet paper for my workers to wipe their asses without coming to you to seek permission!"

For the first time since they had entered the conference room, the Spaniard spoke. There was no trace of anger or irritation in his voice. "If there is a better deal out there for you, Moto-san, I encourage you to take it. We're offering you a chance to remain the majority shareholder as well as the face of the company. I would also note for you that the interest rates on these loans are well below market rates. Market rates for a *healthy* company. In your current state you wouldn't be able to get the *yakuza* to lend you money."

Moto scowled.

"Please don't think of us as adversaries, Moto-san. We want to help you carry out exactly what you had planned—a dominant global telecommunications company with unparalleled reach and scope. Our goal is only to ensure that certain aspects of that plan are prioritized above others. At the end of the day, you will find that the financial restrictions we are imposing are only there to ensure that you do not take advantage of our generosity."

"Like an electric collar on a dog," Moto said.

"Whatever metaphor suits you, Moto-san. I think you'll find that we are excellent partners to work with, and that you will have a great deal of flexibility—again, so long as certain priorities are adhered to."

"Excellent partners? And what track record am I to base that on? I've had my people digging around since you first called and no one has heard of you. You have no standing in the private equity community, and no portfolio of companies. Do you have any idea the massive amount of funding it will take to finance my vision for this company going forward? Your initial investments would be just a drop in the ocean."

The Spaniard gave an almost imperceptible nod to the Japanese banker, who clicked through to the next slide. "Here are our projections for the capitalization of Moto Electric to be provided by Guardians Capital for the next 10 years. Does this comport with your estimates?"

For the first time in his life, Moto was truly stunned. No private equity firm on earth would be able to fund these amounts. "Impossible," Moto said. "And even if it was, the dilution I would experience…"

"There will be zero dilution beyond your fifty-one percent holding,

Moto-san. You will remain the majority holder and face of the company at all times."

Again, the Spaniard nodded at his banker, who responded by reaching into his briefcase and producing a stack of papers. He slid them across the conference table to Moto.

"The documents Fujita-san has just passed to you show the current Guardians Capital cash, currency, and precious metal holdings here in Japan. I trust you recognize the names of the signatories attesting to each of these accounts? They are, after all, some of your largest creditors."

Moto flipped through the documents. This was not just impossible. It was completely insane. It was a joke that he would be expected to believe that these were legitimate numbers.

The Spaniard relished the moment, waiting until Moto had leafed through the entirety of the papers before speaking. "Impressive, no? And those are just our domestic holdings here in Japan. Moto-san, it is with deepest respect and admiration that I submit that you will not in your lifetime, no matter the state of your company, find a better proposition than what we are offering here to you today. My lawyers will send you the paperwork tomorrow. You will not try to negotiate a single word or comma within those documents. If, by Friday, we have not received your signature on them, the offer will be removed and we will go elsewhere to invest our holdings. Please take careful note of the confidentiality provisions. Guardians Capital requires the highest level of secrecy from those that we deign to do business with. You will find that any violation of these provisions will result in consequences that are quite… draconian."

Fujita nodded toward the stack of papers still in front of Moto, who dutifully slid them across the table. The banker neatly restacked them and slid them back into his briefcase.

The Spaniard rose from his seat, and he and his banker bowed. Moto could have sworn that beneath the man's exquisitely knotted tie he saw the distinctive white of a clerical collar. It was just another preposterous detail in a day full of absurdities.

Thirty-six hours later, Moto signed all of the documents.

Forty-eight hours later, the first wire from Guardians Capital hit Moto Electric's accounts.

CHAPTER FOURTEEN

THERE WAS NOTHING Martín could do but sit quietly and wait.

The van he had been hauled into had been in stop-and-go urban traffic for some time, then picked up speed as it left the city. An hour or so later it turned on to what sounded like a gravel road.

When it stopped, Martín was lifted out of the van, carried a hundred meters, and dumped on the ground. The sound of boots on grass receded. Martín listened for several minutes to the insects buzzing around him. He didn't hear anyone approaching, so he was startled when someone ripped off the tape around his eyes and mouth. The dazzling sun blinded him as the zip-ties binding his arms and ankles were cut, freeing his hands to rub his burning eyes.

When at last his eyes focused he saw his brother Nicolás squatting in front of him. His eyes bore into Martín's.

"Three good people, dead because of you," he said.

Martín dully returned his brother's gaze.

"Three?"

"Lenin. Ishikawa. De Valencia."

Martín's mind whirled, but came up blank. "I don't know a de Valencia," he said.

"Yes, I am afraid you did. You knew him as Gallego."

*

Lenin called the United States on the disposable mobile phone he had purchased in a neighboring hotel's gift shop. He used the office extension number Efraín Bertrán had given him in case further questions arose. It went to voicemail.

Lenin hung up and thought for a moment. He turned Bertrán's business card over and read a number written in pencil on the back. He entered the digits, and Efraín's voice answered, "Hello."

"Efraín? Teodoro Lenin, calling from Caracas."

"Teodoro, good to hear from you," he said. "What can I do for you?"

"Are you on speakerphone?" Lenin asked.

"Yes. I'm on I-4 heading for Tampa. Programming meeting in Saint Pete. Beautiful day here in Florida! What can I do for you?"

"Just a moment, I'm going to turn on the speakerphone too. I have Gina here with me." He tapped the icon and laid the phone on the table between them.

"Good morning, Efraín," Gina said.

"I had some additional thoughts last night," Lenin said. "It's about Carlos—"

"Teodoro, hang on a minute," Efraín interrupted. There's an officer waving me off to a detour. Okay, you mean Carlos, the king of Spain?"

"Yes. We need his full lineage—as far back as you can go, please."

Efraín let out a long whistle. "First the pope, now the king? What's going on?"

"I don't know yet," Lenin said. "I'll explain when I can."

"Got it. I won't be able to get to it for two days because of this conference. If you're in a hurry, one of our missionaries in Maracay can help. Hold on." After a moment, he recited the number. "Name's Scott Westfield. Just tell him you're on a project with me and—sorry, there's someone trying to pass me. They're right on my tail, driving erratically—drunk or something. Hold on."

Through the tinny speaker, Gina and Lenin heard a sudden crash followed by a popping noise.

"Oh, God! Oh, God!"

There was the brutal crunch of metal on metal, a series of loud thumps and grunts, and then the continuous bleating of a car horn. "Efraín! Efraín!" Gina shouted. Lenin and Gina looked at each other in horror. A long groan issued from the telephone, and then stopped, along with the horn.

A man's harsh voice growled in Castilian Spanish, "You son of a bitch. Time to talk."

A high-pitched scream blasted from the small speaker.

"I'll do it again unless you talk to me," the voice said. "Who asked you to research the pope?"

Efraín screamed again.

"I know you didn't just do it on your own. Who wanted it?"

After a pause, there was another scream, and fast panting.

"Please… no more. Len."

"Who?"

"Len."

"Lenin? Teodoro Lenin? You're lying, he's dead."

"Lenin."

"If you're lying, what I've done so far will be insignificant compared to what's to come."

"Lenin."

"Was there a woman, too? Looks like a Jap?"

"No." A sharp yelp of pain. "Yes… woman."

"What did you do for them? What did you tell them?"

A pause, another scream, and racking sobs.

"Pope… Pius. Parents."

Another scream.

"Grandparents… everything… all the way back… Flanders."

A scream ripped from the telephone, a flurry of popping sounded again, and then there was silence.

*

Gina drove west on the highway to Maracay. The horror of Efraín Bertrán's torture and murder rode with them in the car, silencing them.

When they arrived in Maracay, Lenin tapped his phone. A man answered on the first ring. "Hola?"

"Is this Scott Westfield?" Lenin asked in English.

"Yes. Who's calling?"

"My name is… Ted Espinosa. I'm visiting from the States. I… uh… know Efraín Bertrán… of your church. He said to look you up while I'm in Venezuela."

"Oh, I see—Ted, was it? Are you staying for a while?"

"No, actually, just today. Would it be possible for me to come by right now?"

"Well, I was heading out," Westfield said.

"It's quite important that I see you… I need to use your computer."

"My computer? May I ask why?"

"Yes," Lenin said. "You see, I'm a professor doing some research. Efraín helped me earlier this week but he isn't available today and he said you could work with me. Just an hour or so."

"Well, all right. Let me give you directions."

Lenin took them down on a notepad and hung up. They decided that Gina shouldn't come along. She was famous enough that her failure to be dead might raise uncomfortable questions. She put on a floppy hat and sunglasses and Lenin dropped her off at a dingy and poorly lit café.

Westfield was staying in a tiny house in Maracay. It was humble, but freshly painted and neatly kept. As they sat on a sofa in the front room, Lenin noticed a newspaper on the end table. He could only see the right-hand side of the front page, but the last word of the headline said "*Asesinata!*" There was a photograph of Gina.

"I am a professor of history at the University of… Florida," Lenin said. "I've been doing some genealogical research on Spanish kings. Efraín helped me research some names in the Flanders Hapsburg branch, and now I need some background on the Spanish branch. Can you help me?"

"Do you have a specific name?"

"Yes, the current king. Carlos Juan Pablo Paredes Duarte."

Scott opened his laptop. Lenin turned to the newspaper. The headline read LATINO UNION PRESIDENT'S DAUGHTER MURDERED! Lenin's heart skipped when he looked further down and saw a small photo of himself. Fortunately, the paper's printing was poor, and the picture was very dark.

"Listen," Lenin said, "I know you have things to do."

"Actually, yes. There is a family we're welcoming into the church. I'm going through the catechism with them."

"Oh, that is important. Any chance you could just let me mess around with this for a while? Efraín showed me the basics of the software, so I can find my way around the database. No need for you to babysit an old man on a computer, as hard to believe as that might be."

Westfield looked dubious. But it was very much in Efraín's nature to send unannounced visitors to mutual friends.

"I'll even lock up when I leave," Lenin said.

"Okay, no problem. Just close the barred door behind you—I have the key."

"Thanks, Scott. This will really help my research." The young man shook Lenin's hand and left, pedaling away on a bicycle. Lenin finally relaxed.

He typed, "Carlos I," the name of the first Hapsburg king of Spain.

*

"Gallego?" Martín asked.

"You were seen visiting Takeshi Ishikawa," Nicolás said. Then at Langley. Then three people die. You set them up, and then the CIA took them out."

"You can't think I would kill them! They were my friends!"

"Spare me the innocence routine. It took pros to get to Gallego. He had years of experience protecting himself from both the left and the right."

"I did see Ishikawa. He asked me to find out what you're up to. The CIA briefed me about the movements of your… band of merry men, I guess, whatever you call them. They knew you were in Venezuela and they knew you left your camp to come to Caracas two days ago. That's all they told me. Nico, I swear on… anything you want me to, I didn't… I *could not*, do anything to harm Gallego or Teodoro or—" His voice caught in his throat. "Or Gina."

Nicolás stared at his brother for a long time in silence. "I think I believe you, but that means you unwittingly led someone else to them. If it wasn't the CIA, then perhaps Ishikawa's men."

"Ishikawa's a cold, calculating politician. No one knows that better than I do. But he couldn't kill his daughter. And why would the CIA want to kill Gallego? Gallego *helped* the government."

"The CIA wants to get to me," Nicolás said. "It's their old battle that started with Fidel and even after his death it has never really ended."

Martín shook his head. "Killing Gallego severs the link. If they were behind this they would have kidnapped him and waterboarded him until he gave up your location. I'd think a terrorist, trained by the best, could figure this out by himself."

Nicolás brightened. "I did train with some of the best." He pushed aside some brush to reveal a round metal hatch. "My brother the expert, what do you think of our 'architecture'? That's the main entrance to four kilometers of tunnels. A kitchen, a hospital, schools, armories. An example of me being trained by the best—I worked with Hamas to build tunnels in the Gaza Strip."

"So Ishikawa's right," Martín said. "You're leading a revolutionary force."

"The main force isn't here anymore, they've moved south to—" Nicolás stopped short and smiled conspiratorially. "But I can't tell you that, can I? You're the enemy."

"The Latino Union is determined to stop you," Martín said. "Previously, you were a nuisance. But now you're somebody they can no longer ignore."

Nicolás shrugged. "You might be their newly trained dog, but I've been in this game for a while. They've been after me for longer than you'd think, and I'll be gone in a few hours."

"This 'game' ended decades ago. You're not fighting over the fate of civilization—you've aligned with monsters who are trying to destroy it."

"It's time to burn everything down and start over."

"Oh, please, you sound like a high school stoner. The Soviet Union's dead, Mao's dead. And now in a final attempt at glory, you've gotten in way over your head."

Nicolás bristled visibly. If any man who was not his flesh and blood had uttered those words, he would have killed him on the spot. "Cuba remains a socialist fortress."

"If I ever need a 1950s Ford I'll move to Havana," Martín said. "Or maybe North Korea if I want to starve to death while getting whipped."

"So you want to get fat lapping up the scraps from a fascist like Ishikawa?" Nicolás asked. "Is that the modern way, my brother?"

The wheel on top of the hatch turned and a woman in faded baggy fatigues climbed up the ladder from the tunnel entrance. She looked to be in her thirties and was lean and hard. She carried a small plastic bag, which she dropped in Nicolás's lap. He looked up at her fondly and took her hand.

"She is the best thing that has happened in my life," he said to Martín. "Carolina is the right hand of our movement—a dedicated revolutionary with the best credentials in the business. A Basque by birth, she grew up in the ETA until their cowardly ceasefire with Madrid. I was becoming a burned-out shell until I met this woman. She ignited my fire again, both as a revolutionary and as a man." He took her hand and kissed it. She smiled thinly, but made no move or sound.

Nicolás opened the bag in his lap and pulled out a large green leaf. He ripped off a chunk with his teeth and began to chew it.

"Coca leaves?" Martín asked. "Seriously?"

Nicolás chuckled. "You are naive about so many things. Politics here in Latin America, for example. Ishikawa and his cohorts are all piranhas. They would kill any of their own just to stay in power. Look at Mexico, Colombia, Chile, Nicaragua, Panama."

"And North Korea is any better?" Martín protested. "Kim murdered his own brother. The Soviet Union, North Korea, the so called 'Peoples' Republic of China. Every one of them developed an elite class, and those elite then murdered the proletariat and sold them out just to stay in power."

Nicolás seemed to deflate a bit. "You do speak some truth, *mi hermano*. Shit, even Fidel finally went to France, put on a navy-blue suit, and got drunk with the bourgeoisie. Our 'glorious' revolution has been hijacked by capitalism around the world." He chewed some more coca and stared into the distance.

"I'm old now, Martín. My dreams are further away from reality than they were in 1962." He was lost in thought for a moment, and then continued, "I remember the year I spent with Che. Day and night, drunk or sober, he talked of revolution. He *lived* revolution every minute of every day. I was with him in Bolivia when he was killed. Did you know that?"

"No."

"They cut off his hands off and sent them to Fidel to prove he was dead. Back in Cuba, we paraded around chanting 'We will be like Che,' pretending we could sustain his revolutionary spirit. Pretending that we could really be like him. Did you know that in Cuba schoolchildren chanted that slogan at the beginning of every day? But we were never like him. Not anything like him."

Nicolás stared ahead for a long time, slowly patting the hand of the woman standing next to him. Then he shook off the reverie of his revolutionary long march and turned, looking almost surprised to see his brother still standing there. His weathered face had softened while he was reliving the past. Now it became hard again. His eyes were dilated from the coca.

"Listen, Martín, I believe you when you say you didn't know that anyone would die through your actions."

Carolina looked at Nicolás sharply. She dragged him several paces away and they hissed back and forth at each other with increasing animation. Finally, Carolina stormed away and retreated back down the hole in the ground, slamming the hatch closed behind her.

"She's right, you know," Nicolás said. "I don't know whether I'm talking to my brother or a direct conduit to the CIA and the Latino Union."

"Ishikawa did send me to find out what you are doing," Martín said. "That's all. No orders to kill you or stop you. And you know in your heart that I could have never accepted such an assignment. The only reason I visited the CIA was to get their opinion about what they thought you were doing."

"Then you were duped, little brother," Nicolás slurred. "Someone was following you. Letting you lead them to people, and killing everyone you contacted. Maybe Ishikawa, maybe somebody else. I've heard something about priests, but I don't believe it."

"Priests?" Martín asked. "Gallego told me to watch out for priests."

Nicolás's glassy eyes locked on Martín's as he processed this. He laughed. "You will be stuck, you know. Caught between your loyalty to me as your brother and your loyalty to Ishikawa and the Latino Union—and

Gina's memory. You know that betraying me will ensure my death. But if you don't have me killed, a whole city's going to die."

"A city? What—"

Nicolás clapped his young brother on the shoulder. "We're headed east, to the coast—a coalition of all the old revolutionaries for Latin America, and some new foreign muscle, as well. But this time with a common purpose—something big. No more bullshit, no more rhetoric, no more dogma. Did you know you can hire a North Korean rocket scientist for 10,000 US dollars? An Iraqi nuclear physicist for 12? A Russian inertial guidance engineer for 8? Do you know how easy it is to buy nuclear materials? Not just raw materials, but warheads: targeted, guided, ready to plug into a missile. Just make the right contacts in Brussels, Karachi, Kabul, Cairo, Damascus, and they make a few calls to Russia. The goods are shipped from Saint Petersburg."

Martín was shocked. Was his brother asking to be betrayed and killed? Why else could he be telling him all of this? Maybe it was the coca talking, or some sort of desperate need to impress. "Nico, surely you can't believe that obtaining nuclear experts and supplies is 'easy' for a career revolutionary encamped in the middle of the jungle."

Nicolás shook his head. "So naive. Things have come together very quickly over the past months. I have new… benefactors… who are as alarmed as I am by the rise of the fascist Latino Union."

"You're the one who's naive! You blow up a city, and then what? The world gets uglier, governments clamp down on their populaces and blow up Arabian wedding parties with their drones. And whoever's supplying you with these nukes will kill you and everyone in your faction to cover their tracks."

Nicolás stared for a long time. When he began to speak, his voice rose with revolutionary fervor, casting aside the doubts his brother was trying to sow. "No more demonstrating. No more strikes. No more kidnappings and assassinations of a few fat plutocrats. I have been doing this a long time, my brother—long enough to know that all of these things are too small. Pinpricks and paper cuts. All bullshit—all for nothing. This time we will finally go for the ultimate terror, the one the whole world fears. At last I will have the full attention, and respect, of the rich and powerful. And I will use that attention and respect to further the cause of the people—*my* people—no matter what anyone who arranged this may want."

Nicolás emphatically spat out another chewed clump of coca leaves, and Martín fell silent. In the heat, with only the drone of insects buzzing around them, the Ibarra brothers searched each other's eyes, looking for the truth.

*

Lenin browsed the database for more than an hour. He was astounded by its chronological detail. He had gone forward from the time of Carlos I, pursuing the known figures of the family whose lines had died out in the 18th and 19th centuries. He went back and found two bastard sons. They had been born in Mechelen, Flanders—just like the pope—when the House of Burgundy had its seat there. Their line went forward carrying the Hapsburg genes, if not the legitimacy and name.

He traced the line through the 17th then 18th centuries. The line started by one of the two bastards continued long after the official one died out. It ended with the marriage between Carlos VII and Isabel in Luxembourg, a quiet restoration of the Hapsburg's Flemish and Austrian branches.

Lenin looked at his watch. It would be very important to have this evidence on hand when he had to present proof. He found a sheet of paper and scribbled a note: "I hope you will forgive me, and please accept my word that I am working on an extremely important project. One that Efraín Bertrán considered vital—and for which he gave his life. I am taking your computer with me, but I swear that I will make restitution to you some day. Please accept my apology. T. Espinosa." He left $2,000 in cash next to the note.

Lenin shut the laptop and carried it to his car. As he drove away, he thought about the kings' and queens' names in the database. The rest of the world believed that the Bourbons continued to rule Spain. But in actuality the Hapsburgs were back in power there and at the Vatican. How much further could they go?

*

As Nicolás chewed on his coca leaves, a sound interrupted the low buzz of the jungle—a whistle that grew to a throbbing roar. Something skimmed over the canopy and then crashed to the ground just a few meters from the two men. A cloud of white powder filled the air. Nicolás stared up at the sky, his jaw slack.

"What have you done?" Nicolás asked. His knees buckled and he collapsed. Martín pulled his handkerchief from his back pocket and clamped it over his mouth. He felt his leg muscles spasm and used his last available strength to twist open the hatch and shove his vomiting brother down the shaft.

Martín's nose, throat, and mouth burned. He fought through his disorientation to close the hatch, cover it with deadwood, and crawl as far away as he could. He felt his sphincter and bladder muscles go slack and he started to cry with shame and anger as he soiled himself.

*

Lenin had once again outdone himself, chartering a flight to a private airstrip an hour's drive from San Juan Diego in a small plane piloted by Benjamín Álvarez, a retired air force colonel who had studied under Lenin in Argentina. When Gina joked that Lenin's loyal base of students across the Americas constituted his own private mafia, Álvarez turned around with a smile and gently corrected her with one word, "*Familia.*" Lenin grinned proudly as Gina shook her head in amazement.

Waiting at the airstrip was a taxi Álvarez had arranged. The cabbie was more than willing to take them into San Juan Diego for a handsome fare that he wouldn't have to report to his employer. As the taxi wound its way toward the new capital city, Gina and Lenin sat in silence taking in the beauty of their surroundings. The sun had begun to set behind Chimborazo, the snowcapped volcano to the west of San Juan Diego, and the waning rays of sun elongated the shadows of a herd of alpacas grazing in the plains on the outskirts of the city. Ahead of them shimmered the lights of the new federal district, with a skyline dotted with towering cranes.

The cab made its way into the city proper and dropped Gina and Lenin in front of a small, cheap hotel that had been hastily built for the army of workers that had descended upon the city during the most labor-intensive phases of its construction. Most of the workers had moved on to new projects, and as Gina predicted, a moderate tip forestalled any requests from the desk clerk for passports or paperwork.

They booked adjoining rooms. Lenin opened his stolen laptop, connecting it to the hotel's Wi-Fi. This was the first time in 24 hours that they were alone and could talk openly.

"Before my house was… vaporized… you may recall that I had called a couple of colleagues in Spain to see if they could find out anything about what David was researching. Before we left Venezuela I reached out to one of them to see if he had found anything."

Gina looked at Lenin in shock and dismay. "One of your colleagues now knows that you are alive?"

Lenin looked somewhat chagrined but pressed his point. "In order to stay alive and get to the bottom of what's going on, we'll need to reach out to people we can trust. I give you my word that I trust this man. And though he was admittedly a bit dumbstruck to hear that I was still alive, he gave me his sworn word to keep our conversation a secret. I told him that it was imperative not just for my safety, but for his."

Gina shook her head. "We need to be making these decisions together. Both of our necks are on the line, and we need the list of people who know we're alive to be as short as possible."

"You're right, of course. It won't happen again." He studied Gina's face for a moment to make sure that he didn't need to apologize any further and, sensing that he was okay to proceed, he gestured at a sheet of paper on the coffee table between them. "In Zaragoza David was apparently studying the Spanish *fueros*—special rights that various regions and cities in Spain had been granted by the crown. He looked up the viceregal seats of Mexico City, Lima, and Buenos Aires to see whether they had *fueros* that would have given them any special status with respect to the crown."

"Did someone ask him to do this?" Gina asked.

"I'm afraid I have no idea. All I can say is that he moved on to Sevilla to pore through the Archive of the Indies."

"That doesn't tell us much," Gina said. "They span hundreds of years and dozens of countries."

"I suppose you're right," Lenin said. He turned on the television, and after flipping through the channels for a few minutes, he stumbled upon a joint interview with the pope and the king of Spain. Carlos was dressed in a dark, conservative suit and the pontiff in white papal garb with gold trim.

They were being asked about the roles of temporal and spiritual leadership, and Pius answered that there was a need worldwide for a spiritual aspect to every temporal decision. Carlos added that he saw not only a need for a spiritual basis for every decision leaders make, but also believed the two concepts, spirituality and temporal rule, were inextricably tied. Both should be present in equal measure in all political leaders, he offered.

"I see a future when we live in a world community under the dominion of Christianity," Carlos said.

The pope gave the king a look. "Not just Christianity."

"Of course, Your Holiness," Carlos said. "All the great religions of the world will be stewards of our future."

"He's talking about Carlos V," Lenin said. "After he was elected Holy Roman Emperor, he saw the pope as a kind of co-ruler. With a united Christianity, he wanted to resume the Crusades and finally conquer the Holy Land."

"The West has already conquered Jerusalem," Gina said.

"They've persecuted the Jews many times before. And with a global reach, they can do the same to the Muslims, the Hindus, the Daoists, the Sikhs—"

Lenin was interrupted by a loud roar coming from both the television and outside their hotel as Pius and Carlos passed a pair of Swiss papal guards in traditional uniforms and stepped out onto a balcony overlooking the Plaza de Santo Narcisa de Jesús Martillo-Morán. The plaza was teeming with people chanting "PI-US, CAR-LOS, PI-US, CAR-LOS…" They unfurled banners depicting a king's crown with a Christian cross standing in the center of it and the legend ONE WORLD, ONE GOVERNMENT, ONE GOD.

"Oh, my God," Lenin said. He grabbed the papers they had been working with and quickly shuffled through them, discarding many to the floor.

"Where?… Where?" he mumbled to himself. He found a paper and held it up.

"What is it?" Gina asked.

"I know who David Broch was working for. Look at this." It was from their transcripts of the various voicemail messages. "When Broch said he was coming back, someone named Julio interrupted. And Broch said that they were going to see Ray. That's not a name. He meant 'rey' with an 'E.' This Julio was taking him to see the king. And that's who commissioned this research about legal sovereignty in the Latin American countries. And once the work was wrapping up, I'll bet he was the person to ensure that David Broch…"

He trailed off and Gina looked back at the television. As she watched the throngs of people chanting the king's name in near-hysteria, Gina felt a chill sweep over her.

CHAPTER 15

One Year Ago

IT WAS WELL past midnight. Harsh sodium vapor lights blazed inside the Basilica Cathedral of Lima. Had anyone tried the doors, they would have found them tightly barred. Work on the massive structure had begun in the 16th century, built on the site of two humbler churches, the first of which had seen the conquistador Francisco Pizzaro plant the ceremonial first log. In the august presence of the old stones and ornate altar of the Spanish Colonial cathedral, workers in spotless coveralls worked silently and efficiently. Had anyone seen them, they would have been struck by the fact that every single one of the workers was Asian. This was not totally out of place in a country with a small but influential Japanese-Peruvian community—one that had produced a Peruvian president. But these men, when they exchanged an occasional word, spoke Japanese, not Spanish, and the blueprints and technical documents to which they referred were written entirely in Japanese.

Some of the men operated laser cutters, burning long grooves into the stone floor, while others pulled cables through discrete openings in the confessionals and pews. An expert on such things would have recognized the high-end fiber optic cables. Another crew wearing night-vision goggles labored up in the old bell tower in complete darkness. They had meticulously cleansed the tower of centuries' worth of soot and bird droppings, and were connecting cables coming up from below to a metal box the size of a steamer trunk. Within the metal box was a wireless telecommunications microcell that could transmit reams of data at lightning speeds on spectrum that had been exclusively licensed by the Peruvian government to a subsidiary of Moto Electric. In exchange for having this massive virtual data pipeline all to itself, Moto Electric's local subsidiary paid the Peruvian government eye-watering fees, with kickbacks finding their way into offshore bank accounts belonging to high-ranking government officials.

This activity was not unique to the cathedral. Every night for the past six months the same activities had been taking place in great cathedrals and parish churches from Guatemala to Tierra del Fuego—any church with an average daily attendance of at least one hundred parishioners.

But the work was only done under the cover of darkness. By daybreak, there would not be any trace of the previous night's activities.

*

The two men sat facing each other across a large ornate desk. The Vatican City office was sumptuous, with soft velvet drapes, rich hand-woven carpeting, and gold-trimmed Italian Renaissance chairs. The man behind the desk wore the red cassock and skullcap of a cardinal. The other man was dressed in a simple black jacket with dress pants, well-shined black shoes, a black smock, and a crisp white clerical collar. His full head of black but graying hair was stylishly long.

The cardinal was accustomed to visitors being awed by the rich furnishings, high ceilings, and his own scarlet vestments. Subordinates usually sat in nervous silence looking at the floor until he addressed them. But after kissing the cardinal's ring, the priest looked him directly in the eyes.

Wanting to make the older man sweat a bit, the young cardinal opened a file that lay before him on a clean desk and scanned several pages. At last he looked up and reestablished eye contact. The delay had not induced the slightest anxiety in the priest.

"Do you know why you are here?" the cardinal asked.

"I do not, Your Eminence," the priest replied.

"Your stewardship of the work to modernize the electronic infrastructure and data collection capabilities throughout Latin America has been exemplary, and is being completed ahead of time and at minimal cost.

Thanks to you the data processing center in Burgos is fully functional with the supercomputer already receiving enormous flows of data. You have done well."

"Thank you, Your Eminence. I trust His Holiness is satisfied as well."

"*I* am most pleased, and that is what matters."

The priest's gaze remained steady. The cardinal was satisfied, and he congratulated himself for finding the right man for this assignment.

"We are now moving into new areas of investigation that will require the highest level of secrecy and loyalty from you."

"This has been revealed to me as God's will," the priest said.

"You will now be required to reaffirm your vows to God and the Holy Catholic Church. You will then take further blood oaths of secrecy, loyalty, and brotherhood to me personally and the responsibility that has been bestowed upon me. Do you require time to pray and to contemplate before making these affirmations?"

"No, Your Eminence, I am prepared to do so now."

"In addition, you will also be required to assume a completely new identity. The person you were, and the relationships you have as of today, will simply cease to exist. Are you prepared to make that sacrifice?"

"Yes, Your Eminence."

"Then let us repair to my private chapel."

*

The sun was rising over Rome as the two men of God sat in their respective chairs, reflecting upon the last 12 hours of discussion.

"The knowledge I have just imparted to you has been passed in an unbroken chain from Tomás de Torquemada to me and now to you," the cardinal said. "I trust you feel the full weight and gravity of more than five centuries of holy dedication."

"I do, Your Eminence. I am humbled by the faith you have put in me," the priest said, though without a trace of humility.

"You will answer to me and only to me. No one else, including His Holiness."

"I understand."

"You will continue with your work reestablishing the power of the

Holy Office under your new identity and with a new chain of command. I have handpicked your new subordinates and advised them of your imminent arrival. With this team, you will carry out one of the most crucial undertakings since the founding of the Fourth Angel initiative more than 500 years ago. Here is your first assignment toward attaining this goal."

The cardinal removed a sheet of paper from a folder and handed it to the priest. He scanned it quickly, noting that it listed the names of more than 100 current cardinals. It did not pass his notice that none of the cardinals listed were over the age of eighty, the maximum age for participation in a papal election.

"Beginning immediately, you will prepare dossiers on every one of these princes of the Church. I want to know every detail from birth to the current day. Most especially, I want full information and proof of any deviations from church doctrine. This includes any lapses in moral character such as violations of celibacy, financial improprieties, or child molestation. Anything that would blemish the record of these cardinals in the eyes of God and the Holy Office."

"This will require additional resources," the priest said.

"Through me you shall have any resources you need. A technician at Moto Electric has been assigned to provide you with exclusive use of any data-harvesting technology and equipment you require. A special server at the data center in Burgos is yours exclusively. If you need to hire specialized talent such as private investigators, do so, but with this proviso: upon completion of their work they will be silenced. Am I clear?"

"Yes, Eminence."

The cardinal reached into a desk drawer and removed a leather pouch, sliding it across the desk.

"This contains a universal letter of introduction and an unlimited letter of credit valid for drawing on any bank in the world. Your transactions shall all be in cash—no credit cards. There is also an encrypted phone that will serve as your direct line to me. You can reach me any time, day or night. A jet now waiting at Fiumicino Airport will be available for your exclusive use. You will also find inside your new church credentials, national identity cards, and a passport. From now on, you will be known as Father Luis Serrano. Any questions?"

"What is my timeframe for accomplishing this work?"

"A year and two days from today, at noon Greenwich time."

"If I may speak freely, it is apparent that this is in preparation to influence the next conclave of cardinals voting for a new pope."

"Correct," the cardinal said.

"How will you know with such precision the date on which a new pope will be required?"

The cardinal withdrew something from a drawer. He opened his closed hand, disclosing a small glass ampoule for a moment, and then placed it back in the drawer, which he slid closed.

Father Serrano nodded. "I see." He rose, took the cardinal's hand, and kissed his sacred ring. "This we do for one, ten, a hundred, or a thousand years, whatever is required to bring on the Millennium."

"Go with God," the cardinal said.

"Yes, Your Eminence, Cardinal Legendre."

CHAPTER SIXTEEN

FRENCH GUIANA IS located on the northeast coast of South America, sharing borders with Suriname and Brazil. Attempts to colonize it began in 1608 with the Tuscans, and after being driven out by the indigenous peoples several times, the Europeans exerted their control and then squabbled over the territory for several centuries before it finally rested permanently in the hands of the French in 1814. From 1852 through 1951 its infamy was that of a brutal penal colony for undesirables banished from France, most of whom quickly starved to death or perished from disease.

After a legacy of slavery and punitive barbarity, a new industry came to French Guiana in 1980. Capitalizing on French Guiana's location close to the equator and away from population centers, France built a spaceport and launched rockets carrying communications satellites into orbit in competition with the American NASA and SpaceX launch systems.

Although the French government had prohibited French Guiana from joining the Latino Union, the LU chose Arianespace to be its launch contractor for a communications satellite arriving from Japan. The 35 Moto Electric engineers and technicians who had traveled on the plane with the satellite now swarmed over their masterpiece of Japanese technology. Around the clock they unpacked, inspected, calibrated, and installed the satellite that would tie the countries comprising the new union together with telecommunications services, television, internet, weather reconnaissance, and ecological and resource-development surveillance.

The French engineers at the launch complex were at first amused by their total exclusion from these activities, but with time they became annoyed that they were not permitted to see the payload, even from a distance. The Japanese were courteous and quickly forthcoming with any technical data needed by the French rocket booster team, but inspection of the satellite was politely but firmly refused. They insisted that their company had committed to a very tight delivery schedule to make the launch part of the inauguration festivities for the capital of the Latino Union. They were solely responsible for this deadline, and they requested, please, that everyone else stay out of their way.

*

Martín hovered in a state of half-consciousness and delirium. As he tried to take in his new surroundings, he wasn't sure whether hours, minutes, or seconds passed. He had a dreamlike memory that he had been with his brother, but that had all ended abruptly and violently with a poisoning or illness.

He was in a sparkling clean room, covered in bleached white sheets. On the wall facing him was a crucifix showing the suffering of Christ on the cross in excruciating detail. Martín was dressed only in baggy white boxer shorts, and an elastic band was wrapped tightly around his chest. A doctor in a white coat stood at the foot of his bed looking at a clipboard.

Martín tested his throat and mouth several times, finally asking, in a rasping, trembling voice, "Where am I?"

The doctor looked up from the clipboard. "Our Lady of the Angels Hospital."

"But where?"

The doctor looked back down at his clipboard, made several notations, and then left without a word. Nurses came in on several occasions—nuns in modern habits—all of them aloof and businesslike as they carried out their duties.

All, that is, but one. She was young, pretty, and enthusiastically started conversations. When he asked her where he was, she avoided answering by mentioning how hot it had been the past few days. But it was at least something for him to build upon.

Eventually Martín felt well enough to have something to eat. He discerned from the selection of food delivered to him—some fruit and an arepa—that it was still morning, although he wasn't certain whether only one day or more had passed.

While he was eating, a priest came in. The man was dressed in black pants and a matching coat, as well as a black smock with a white clerical collar. He was middle-aged with a craggy face, sunken eyes, and a strong jaw. He had a full head of hair that was just beginning the relentless change from black to gray. His body appeared robust and athletic.

"I am Father Serrano," he said. The priest offered a hand. Martín took it, and Serrano gave him a firm grip.

"It looks like you're back with the living," Serrano said. "How do you feel?"

"Okay. A little shaky, but as you say, back among the living. What happened to me?"

"You were brought here yesterday afternoon."

"From where?" Martín asked.

"Some distance away."

"What was wrong with me?"

"You were incapacitated by a poison."

"What kind of poison? How was I poisoned?"

"What do you remember happening to you?" Serrano asked.

Martín considered the question. Both Gallego and Nicolás had warned him to beware of priests. "I know this sounds strange, Father, but I don't remember."

The priest regarded him closely. "Why did you come to Venezuela?"

"Business."

"I thought your work with the Latino Union was finished."

Martín gave Serrano the broadest smile he could muster. "The work is never finished, is it? Always some loose end—some detail."

"I suppose. But you were an awfully long way from the LU's capital city to be tying up loose ends." The priest let this hang in the air for a moment, and then continued when Martín failed to offer up any additional explanation. "You were in Caracas, is that correct?"

Martín wondered if the priest knew, or if he was fishing. "In transit, yes. Father, where am I now?"

"You're still in Venezuela."

"But where, and how did I get here?"

"The proper authorities brought you in. You really need to rest and regain your strength. I'll leave you for now." Serrano turned toward the door.

"Wait, Father. I need to get to Caracas right away."

The priest paused, his interest visibly piqued. "Is someone expecting you there?"

"Yes. I must get to San Juan Diego. I have very urgent business there. The inauguration of the capital, you know."

"Yes, I am aware of that event. Who is waiting for you in Caracas?"

"As I said, it's official Latino Union business."

The priest gave him a cold smile. "Just tell me who and how to reach them."

"That's a kind offer, but I must make the contacts myself. And I have to leave immediately."

Serrano held out his arms, palms-up, in a signal of resigned powerlessness. "Your release depends upon the doctors."

Martín tried to sit up but found himself restrained by the harness affixed around his chest. His eyes followed the wires that protruded from the harness over to a heart and respiration monitor beside the bed.

"Would you please send in the doctor so I can talk to him? And is there a phone I can use? There are several urgent calls I must make."

Father Serrano was already at the door, his hand on the latch. "I'll see what I can do about the doctor. You must rest."

He disappeared out the door, locking it behind him.

*

Martín was sweating through his sheets as he waited for the doctor to arrive. Somehow he had to get word to Takeshi Ishikawa that the guerrillas were heading east to the coast where they had plans involving nuclear weapons. Even if those nuclear weapons were just a coca leaf dream of Nicolás and the other revolutionaries, the potential threat had to be taken seriously.

He sat up and craned his neck, looking at the window. The room was above ground level, and the window was a contemporary sliding glass type. There was a latch with a small lock.

When the door finally opened, the young nun entered. She turned and looked up and down the hall, then pushed the door shut. Once inside, she looked shyly at Martín, as if unable to decide what to do next.

Martín turned up his charm. "I have been so rude not to have asked before, but what is your name, Sister?"

Her face lit up with a radiant smile. "Sister Trinidad. And I've heard your name is Ibarra."

"Yes, Sister. But you can call me Martín. I'm so glad you came in. I was getting lonely. Recovery is such a dull business."

"Yes. Sister Juana—" She scrunched her face into a sour expression that was unmistakably a caricature of one of the older nurses who had regularly attended to Martín — "doesn't want anyone visiting you, including the doctors. Orders from Father Serrano. And some other visiting priests."

"Well, how about that? I wonder why. I am only an architect who lost his way and had an unfortunate incident yesterday. But I certainly don't pose a threat to anyone—I haven't bitten anyone in years!"

She laughed easily and smiled back at him.

"Where is this hospital?" Martín asked.

This time there was no hesitation, although her eyes did dart momentarily to the window in the door. "We're in Caracas."

"And what happened to my clothes?"

"I think they had to be burned. They had some kind of chemical on them."

"And my wallet, phone, and passport?"

She thought about that. "I think I saw them in a plastic bag, but I don't know where they are now."

That was unfortunate, but it was clear that the nun wanted to be helpful. "Sister Trinidad, I really need some clothes. And I need that bag. I have very important matters that I must attend to immediately." He looked at her with plaintive eyes.

The young nun looked down at her shoes. Sister Trinidad's expressive face searched for a way out of the discomfort she was feeling. "I need to leave, or Sister Juana will be angry. I hope you understand."

Martín nodded and forced back a smile, fighting the urge to press Sister Trinidad further. He recognized that he had pushed her as far as she would go—for now. Instead, he watched in silence as Sister Trinidad slipped out the door and closed it behind her.

*

Sister Trinidad was putting surgical instruments into an autoclave when she heard a door open in the next room. She immediately recognized the voices of Sister Juana and the visiting priest, Father Serrano.

"I want that man out of my hospital," Sister Juana said.

Serrano laughed. "Oh, come now, Sister. A little compassion toward a man in need of our charity and care."

"He's a Jew. Chavez did well in driving most of his kind out of the country. Take him to another hospital."

"I cannot do that," Serrano said, his voice lowering and becoming stern.

"I'm calling the bishop. If you won't remove that man, the bishop will."

Sister Trinidad crossed herself and closed her eyes. She knew it was a sin for her to be eavesdropping on this private conversation, but she was curious about the pleasant young man who had been brought into their care without any explanation. And why was he being detained? She wanted to know that there was a good reason for doing so. It would put her mind at ease, and perhaps she would even be able to reassure Martín that he was safe.

"I feel exactly the same as you, Sister!" Serrano barked. "But I have important plans for Ibarra—plans appropriate for a man whose people killed Jesus Christ."

Sister Trinidad instantly forgot her concerns about sinning. She moved closer to the wall and listened intently.

"And that is?" Sister Juana asked.

"You cannot say anything of what I am about to tell you to anyone. Do you swear it?"

"Yes," Juana said after a pause.

"An *auto-de-fé*. We'll burn him at the stake for his heresy… and in full view of the world."

Sister Trinidad jammed her fist into her mouth to stifle a gasp.

There was another long silence, and then Sister Trinidad heard Sister Juana's voice again, this time meek and uncertain. "I don't really understand exactly what you are doing… but I am not sure that—"

Father Serrano cut her off. "Oh, come on now. Are you suddenly feeling sympathy for the man you just dismissed moments ago as a Jew unworthy of taking up a precious bed in your hospital?"

"It's just that what you are…" Sister Juana's voice was trembling now, and Sister Trinidad could sense her deepening fear. There was a sharp cry of pain from the older nun, followed by a thud against the wall.

Father Serrano's voice was steady, even, and menacing. "I can see that I made a mistake confiding in you, Sister. I thought you could see the path to righteousness as clearly as I do, but your vision remains clouded by unwarranted pity for those who are beneath us and unworthy in God's eyes. Damnation will be arriving very soon for those without the purity of the soul to follow God's will. I will pray for you, Sister. And you will say nothing. Otherwise you will join Martín Ibarra at the stake."

Sister Trinidad heard soft sobs from the other side of the wall, and could not keep her composure any longer. Tears rolled down her face as she sprinted out of the autoclave room and down the hall, hoping to reach the bathroom before she threw up.

*

Martín looked up as Sister Trinidad slipped into the room. He smiled.

"Sister, I apologize. I had no right to ask you to—wait, have you been crying?"

She wiped her eyes with the sleeve of her habit. "You said you had something important to do, right?"

"Yes, I have very important business that will benefit many people. But I don't want to get you into trouble."

"The others don't want you to leave. Father Serrano said we should watch you, and always keep the door locked."

"Am I a prisoner here?"

Sister Trinidad started crying again.

"What is it, Sister?"

She glanced at the door before taking his hand in both of hers and staring into his eyes for a long time. She took more deep breaths and then spoke again, this time with more firmness and certainty. "I will help you. Let me see what I can do about clothes."

"Thank you. And I need access to a phone. A pay phone, an office phone, a mobile—anything."

Sister Trinidad looked back at him with determination. "I will do all I can," she said. "Pray for me."

And then she was gone.

*

Martín had been dozing when the sound of the door opening awakened him. Sister Trinidad entered, unlocked his harness, and then handed him a tightly rolled janitor's jumpsuit.

"Don't detach the wires until you're ready to flee," she said. "It will set off alarms and they'll be in here quickly."

He was surprised at the weight of the bundle. When he unrolled the jumpsuit, a cell phone and a plastic bag spilled out. The plastic bag contained his wallet and passport.

Martín's eyes widened in amazement and gratitude. "Is this your phone?" he asked.

Sister Trinidad's face went serious. "I am quite sure God wants me to help you. It's a small sacrifice to do His work."

With that pronouncement she went to the door and slipped out of the room.

Careful not to disturb the biomedical monitors attached to the band around his chest, Martín slipped out of bed and craned his neck out the window. He couldn't tell how far he was above the ground, but there was a tree with branches that looked sturdy enough to support his weight within leaping distance.

Martín looked around the room for something to jimmy the lock. Nothing. He sat back down on the bed and carefully wriggled halfway into his jumpsuit, filling its pockets with Sister Trinidad's phone and his wallet and passport. He looked down at his bare feet and cursed his lack of shoes, but he didn't have the time or inclination to send Sister Trinidad on another errand. It was time to go.

Martín wrapped the top and fitted sheets around his right forearm. After taking a deep breath, he lunged toward the window and hammered at the seam connecting the two windowpanes, forcing the cheap lock to give way and shattering the glass. He expended a few precious seconds sweeping the windowsill clean, and then ripped the monitor wires from his chest before crawling onto the ledge.

He was about 10 meters above the ground, and a closer look made him doubt that the branches would hold his weight. The fall was going to be brutal, but he was pretty sure that whatever Serrano had in mind for him would be worse.

Martín gathered his courage and leaped for the thickest branch within reach, grasping it with both hands. It immediately snapped, and his ailing body tumbled through the ones below until he landed hard on the grass below, forcing the air from his lungs as the pain spread throughout his body. He gasped, feeling the panic of being unable to breathe, but also gratitude for being alive. Slowly he staggered to his feet. The right side of his ribcage burned and there was a sudden sharp pain from his foot that caused him to collapse back down to the ground. Cursing, he pulled a shard of glass out of his heel.

Martín stood back up and retched from the pain. There was a parking lot to his left with cars and ambulances parked in it. To the right, there was an expanse of grass going down a hill that terminated in a stone wall, with small houses crowded together beyond it. He pulled the mobile phone out of his pocket and keyed a number. His pilot answered.

"Pedro," he whispered, "this is Martín. Get the plane ready to fly. I'll be there as soon as I can."

"What? Martín? Where are you? We've been—"

"No time. Just prep the plane." He hung up.

After a moment's hesitation, Martín cautiously edged toward the parking lot, though he didn't know how to hotwire a car. He stayed low and ran in a crouch to the rows of cars, keeping them between himself and the hospital. None of the cars had keys in their ignitions and he couldn't risk setting off an alarm by shattering one of their windows. He turned to search for a way to make his escape on foot and saw a rack of bicycles at the edge of the parking lot. It was completely out in the open, and Martín had to assume that the bicycles would be locked. But with a little bit of luck…

There!

A doctor in scrubs and a backpack was pedaling on an expensive-looking mountain bike toward the bike rack, slowing as he approached. Martín looked back at the hospital entrance, saw no one, and dashed forward. Just as the doctor began to dismount his bike, blissfully unaware of the man sprinting toward him from his blind side, Martín planted his remaining healthy foot and lunged forward, lowering his shoulder. As Martín's body plowed into the unsuspecting doctor there was a surprised and frightened grunt. The two men's bodies spilled onto the sidewalk, with the doctor letting out a dismayed "Ooof!" has he landed. Martín scrambled to his feet, lifted the toppled bike from the ground, and jumped into the seat. The bike wobbled beneath Martín as he realized that the seat's height was extremely low, but he managed to start awkwardly peddling toward the parking lot's exit. In Martín's peripheral vision he saw the hospital's automatic doors slide open and a group of men emerge. Shouts erupted as they spotted Martín. The road dropped down a steep hill, and in a short distance Martín was increasing speed. He shifted to a higher gear, pedaled hard, and was soon flying down the incline. Behind him, he heard engines starting. He turned to see two ambulances surging forward.

The road was now winding among the shanties of one of Caracas's *barrios*. He slowed at an intersection, weaving to avoid cars and trucks, and then pedaled hard again once he had cleared the traffic. There was a blur to his left, and a quick glance confirmed that one of the ambulances was already right beside him. Father Serrano was in the passenger seat, barking something at the driver. Any words Martín might have picked up were drowned out as the ambulance's siren roared to life.

Martín pedaled frantically, pulling ahead. The ambulance matched his acceleration, moving toward the shoulder and crowding him. But it stopped short of running him over. They clearly wanted him alive.

At the next intersection Martín didn't slow down, swerving violently to avoid a bus and a heavy truck that were crossing the intersection perpendicular to his path. He heard the screech of rubber on pavement and he anticipated the crunch of metal impacting metal, but was not rewarded. Instead he heard the bleating of the electronic siren closing the distance.

His legs were tiring. The ambulance came alongside him again, trying to force him off the road. "Stop, Ibarra, stop!" Serrano yelled.

Martín willed his burning legs to push harder, but the ambulance pulled slightly ahead, and he saw the priest aiming a gun. *A bluff,* he thought to himself, and turned the handlebars hard to the right, swerving off the pavement. He heard loud cursing behind him as he crossed the dirt shoulder and zipped into a narrow gap between two shacks.

Martín followed the dirt path as it turned to the left and pitched downhill into a slum. A man too well dressed to be from this part of town dashed on foot from an intersecting path and dropped to one knee. He had a gun and looked as if he fully intended to use it. Suddenly Martín was no longer certain that they intended to keep him alive if the alternative was his escape. The man shouted for him to stop, but Martín raced forward. Two bullets snapped past his ear. He bore down on the shooter, who dove to one side and rolled while Martín's mountain bike streaked past.

The garbage-strewn path curved to the right, taking Martín out of sight of his pursuers. As he was gaining speed, a small naked child darted out in front of him. Martín braked and turned, crashing into a wall of sheet metal, knocking him from his seat and onto the ground where the bike fell on top of him, followed by the sheet metal. Dogs barked somewhere in the shacks above him.

Martín struggled to free himself as his battered body shrieked in pain, but he was somehow able to stand back up. He was mounting the bike when he felt something hard pressed against the base of his skull.

"Don't move," a voice said behind him. Then, much louder, "Down here!"

Martín heard a sound like a ripe melon being thumped hard, and felt a bulk pitch against his back, then slump to the ground. He turned to see the gunman face down in the dirt. A ragged young man stood over him, holding a length of pipe.

"Fucking cops," he said. He gestured at Martín's torn and dirty coveralls. "Me and you, we're just shit that these guys scrape off their shoes. Get moving, we'll take care of the other assholes."

Martín stood in stunned disbelief as he saw other men appearing from the shadows, armed with rocks and steel bars. He nodded at the man in thanks, got on the bike, and headed downhill.

CHAPTER SEVENTEEN

GINA LOOKED UP at Lenin with a grin. "Patricia!" she exclaimed.

Gina and Lenin had spent the morning debating who they could contact to help them gain an audience with her father without revealing that they were still alive. Gina

had contemplated simply calling his personal line, but she knew that her call would be screened and monitored. This inconvenience extended to her mother as well. She had

always wondered whether this was a necessity of the office, or a choice her parents had made to avoid being bothered by personal matters.

Then it had hit her.

"I don't follow," Lenin said, searching his memory for a member of the president's staff with that name and coming up empty.

Gina smiled, grabbed the hotel room's phone, and dialed.

Patricia was a maid who had taken care of Gina since she was an infant. After Gina left home for college, Patricia stayed on, practically a member of the family by that

point, and accompanied the president and his wife when they moved from Brasília to San Juan Diego.

When Gina called, the poor woman broke into hysterical tears. After a lengthy process of relating incidents from her childhood that only Gina and her nanny would

know, the woman accepted that Gina was either still alive or she had returned from the dead—a possibility not completely excluded due to her *crenças supersticiosas*.

Gina asked Patricia if she could manage to get her and Lenin into the presidential residence without being noticed by security. The answer was an enthusiastic *"sim!"*

True to her word, Patricia proved to be remarkably resourceful, occupying the security men and women on fools' errands while furtively bringing Teodoro and Gina inside from their taxi.

After a brief private reunion with her mother, Gina led Lenin to her father's study. Gina knocked softly, then opened the door. Her father was sitting behind his desk. He glanced toward the door, did a double take, and shot to his feet. Gina said something softly in Japanese and closed the door behind her.

Lenin waited outside, letting the father and daughter have a few moments alone. When Lenin was eventually admitted to the study, the three of them sat around a coffee table.

"Professor Lenin, I am greatly in debt to you for saving my daughter's life," Takeshi Ishikawa said.

"Mr. President, I just happened to be at the right place at the right time. Your daughter is a very strong and resourceful person who would have done just as well without me."

Ishikawa nodded. "My daughter tells me you have information about troubling things."

"Mr. President, I have deductions, inferences, and hypotheses based on my knowledge of history. What I do not have is proof."

"Tell me quickly, then—important points only."

"Sir, I believe there is a conspiracy in Europe to restore old power structures." Lenin spoke awkwardly from his seated position on the sofa. After several false starts he stood, walked to the center of the room, and began to pace with his hands locked behind his back. The professorial stance relaxed him, and his thoughts began to flow.

"Item: The king of Spain is suddenly stricken. Behind closed doors, in the presence of only a cardinal, he changes his will and the succession to his throne. We have traced his successor, the current king, to a line of the Hapsburgs.

"Item: A year after the change of Spanish succession, the pope dies suddenly, the College of Cardinals meets, and after an unusually long deliberation, they elect a young and obscure priest from France. We have also traced his lineage to the Hapsburgs.

"Item: Carlos's wife of three years is from Austria. Her lineage is that of nobility, but vague. I have traced her to the Hapsburgs."

"Professor, what are you suggesting?" Ishikawa asked.

Lenin stopped pacing and faced Ishikawa. "Mr. President, I am suggesting that the Hapsburgs are engineering a return to power in Spain, Austria, and other countries. They intend to reinstate the Holy Roman Empire."

Ishikawa was expressionless and did not move for several seconds. "Doctor Lenin, what you propose is preposterous. And even if it were true, that would be a political problem for Europe, not the Latino Union. I must focus on our own problems here—not be concerned about some political abstraction overseas."

Lenin nodded. "In the absence of proof, I agree. It does sound ridiculous. But I'd hesitate to say that it doesn't involve the fate of this union. The Hapsburgs once called these lands their own as well. A colleague of ours, an expert in international law, was retained by King Carlos to research legal issues regarding Spain's sovereignty over its Latin American colonies. It stands to reason that a similar study of the legalities of the colonial relationship between Brazil and Portugal has been done."

Ishikawa frowned.

"Mr. President, I believe King Carlos intends not only to restore the Holy Roman Empire in Europe, but also to restore all of our countries to Spanish rule. This is a plan to turn the clock back five centuries and make things as they were then. The king intends to once again rule the Spanish overseas empire."

Lenin paused, looked up at the president, and waited to see if he would be thrown out of the room.

Instead, the president's phone rang.

Ishikawa answered it curtly, but then a look of surprise crossed his face. He put the caller on hold and said to Gina and Lenin, "If you will excuse me."

Gina felt a flash of anger. She started to speak, but he chopped at the air with his hand dismissively—a gesture she recognized all too well from a childhood spent trying to get her father's attention. Defeated, she went with Lenin into the corridor, closing the door behind them.

*

Martín peered out from the alley. He had ridden his stolen bicycle to the main entrance of Francisco Medina Army Airfield, but one of the ambulances from the hospital was parked across the street. He saw two men inside the cab, and Father Serrano standing on the curb. Some of their faces were swollen, and one of the men in the ambulance repeatedly wiped blood from his face as it poured from a scalp wound. All of them looked royally pissed off.

The rumble of a diesel engine grew louder. Martín looked to his right and saw an approaching flatbed tractor-trailer that was carrying an armored personnel carrier. It was time to do something brilliant, or fatally stupid.

As the truck began to rumble past the alley, Martín pedaled until he was between the enormous truck's tires and grabbed its undercarriage. His back and stomach burned as he bounced between the pavement and the driveshaft.

After an eternity of several minutes, the tractor-trailer stopped. Martín rolled back out and stood up to find himself staring directly into the muzzle of a soldier's rifle.

"Don't shoot!" Martín shouted. "I'm here to see Major Valencia!"

The guard kept his rifle aimed, cocking his head at this stowaway in a torn and scuffed janitor's coverall. He nodded at another soldier, who trotted off purposefully.

"So… who's your side?" Martín asked to pass the time.

The soldier smirked, still aiming his rifle at Martín's face.

"For me it's Corinthians. My father got to see Pelé, but Tevez wasn't a bad—"

The soldier's smirk turned into a smile, showing his teeth. "Liar. Your Spanish might be good, but I know a gringo when I see one. You support Madrid, or Barcelona, or both."

"At ease, soldier!" Valencia shouted. "I can vouch for this man. He's an official of the Latino Union."

The young soldier lowered his rifle and winked. "Good luck, gringo. Maybe when you get back to America you can buy yourself some shoes."

The pilot and architect rapidly boarded the plane as Martín asked, "Are you ready to go?"

"Where did you have in mind?" Valencia asked.

"San Juan Diego."

"I'll get clearance in the air." Valencia looked Martín up and down. "I imagine you've got one hell of a story. Would love to hear it some time." With that, he spun on his heel and entered the cockpit.

Martín pulled out Sister Trinidad's battered phone and placed a call to the Latino Union military communications center, connecting directly with the president's residence. Ishikawa's secretary came on the line, and Martín said, "This is a priority communication from One-Five India for the President."

"I'll put you through," the woman said.

There was a series of clicks, and then, "Ishikawa here."

"Sir, this is Martín Ibarra."

The president sounded startled. "Yes? Hold for a moment, please."

Martín waited, and 30 seconds later the president was back on the line.

"Where have you been? We have heard nothing from you for some time."

"First, Mr. President, let me express my most heartfelt condolences about Gina. I am so very sorry about what happened to her, and for your terrible loss." His voice caught in his throat. "I would have done anything, anything, to prevent her…" He couldn't finish.

Ishikawa was silent for a time. "Well, we must all bear our burdens. Please, hold the line." Even for a man who almost never displayed his emotions, the president's response came across as incredibly callous to Martín. Taken aback, Ibarra waited.

The president came back on. "What have you learned?"

"Mr. President, my brother Nicolás is leading a force to the eastern coast of South America. My best guess is that they are heading to French Guiana with the intention of taking over the spaceport. Nicolás insinuated that he has retained foreign nuclear scientists and experts, essentially implying that he has nuclear capability. Although he didn't spell it out for me, it would make sense that his plan would be to try and modify the LU's Ariane 6 from its current communications satellite configuration to carry a nuclear warhead instead. I don't know any of the details about what their specific demands or objectives will be."

Ishikawa said nothing for a long time. "Of course. A very smart move on their part, putting our union in a very embarrassing position with respect to Europe. It's unstable right now in Guiana, with a strong independence movement. I am sure they will get support from the locals. We were all fixated on anticipating the targets within the union and didn't consider the non-union countries."

"Mr. President, since the launch is scheduled to take place in two days, they must already be close by."

Ishikawa considered this. "I understand. Trust me, I do understand. Please hold the line again."

Martín once again thought about Ishikawa's lack of reaction to his expression of condolence and it angered him. Did he care so little about his daughter?

Takeshi Ishikawa came back on and said, "Martín, right now you are close to French Guiana, and your relationship to the rebel leader gives you insights others will not have. You have the latest information on the rebels' intentions. You are a foreigner, not a citizen of the Latino Union, so I cannot order you to do anything. However, I am asking, on the basis of our past... association, that you go there and improvise a defense. Do your best to protect your brother and stop this mad plan of his. We will arrange to get you directly into French Guiana on a non-official basis via an airstrip just over the border in Brazil. The French will meet you there."

"Sir," Martín said, "I'm sure it occurred to you, and that your military staff will consider it, but the fastest way to end this is an immediate air strike on the rocket."

"You are right, Martín. However, that is not something we want to do prematurely. There are Japanese technicians currently working there along with other foreign nationals, and it is French territory. We have those lives and French sovereignty to consider."

"Mr. President, then I urge you to warn the French and the ESA and get them to take immediate action. My brother and his entire movement will no longer have an objective if the rocket is removed from the equation. Otherwise, the security of any possible target city—"

"You are presumptuous. Do you think for a moment that I don't understand my responsibilities! There are complicated issues that you do not understand. There is a small military airfield in Cunani. You will be met by someone who can get you into French Guiana and Kourou. Keep me updated at all times."

The encrypted telephone circuit broke.

Martín turned and saw that the pilots were eyeing him. He shrugged. "We're going to Cunani," he told them.

*

Lenin and Gina quickly worked their way back to her mother's personal office, where they entered and, finding it empty, closed and locked the door behind them.

"That… was not ideal," Lenin said.

Gina laughed mirthlessly. "You're telling me. He looked at us like we were telling him we were time travelers from the future sent back to save the world."

"Then what is there left for us to do here? It seems unlikely that we will get any meaningful uninterrupted time with your father, who doesn't seem inclined to listen in any case."

Gina shook her head. "Why does he have to be so goddamned stubborn? And don't get me started on how rude it was for him to take a call while we were trying to have a conversation with him! It's just like when I was in school and…"

She looked up at Lenin, who was smiling down at her patiently. She grimaced. "I suppose this isn't the time to resolve decades-old family dynamics."

"It's quite alright. I completely understand. I think, sometimes, when we are in the presence of our parents, no matter the situation, we regress a bit. I suggest we get back to our hotel room and regroup… try to brainstorm other ways to convince your father of the truth of what we are saying. Or maybe even take a completely different approach."

Gina picked up the phone that sat on her mother's desk. "I agree. But we should be discrete with our departure. I don't really trust that everyone in this building will be happy to hear that we are still alive—and the fewer people that know that, the better."

As she dialed, a man in a crisp LU army uniform sat on the other side of the immense government complex, listening intently to the live feed streaming from the bug implanted inside the office. After a minute the man removed his earpiece. Quickly, he dialed his mobile phone. When the party on the other end answered, he summarized the conversation he had just heard and then went quiet as he received instructions.

"Yes, General Mello," he said once his orders had been received. "I will make sure that they do not leave the building."

*

It was the middle of the night in Tokyo when Waro Moto was awakened by an aide. He walked into his living room wrapped in a robe. An executive from his company waited for him.

"We have a recently recorded a call that triggered several keyword search alerts," the aide said. He handed a phone to Moto, who listened to a recording of the conversation between Martín Ibarra and Takeshi Ishikawa.

"Did General Mello check with Burgos?" Moto asked.

"Yes, sir. Burgos advised him that they will take possession of Ibarra at a small Brazilian airfield near the Guiana border. Mello also told them that Gina Ishikawa and Teodoro Lenin are alive."

Moto raised an eyebrow. "That's an unexpected loose end."

*

The Latino Union military Gulfstream landed at the Cunani airstrip, which was no more than a slash in the coastal mangrove forest. Valencia brought the aircraft to a stop just short of the end of the asphalt, turned, and taxied the jet over to a twin-engine turboprop plane that sat waiting for them.

"There's your ride," the pilot said.

Martín dropped the fold-down steps and descended. As Martín emerged, the idling turboprop engaged the right-hand engine, raising a cloud of red dust. Martín bounded up the stairs into the open door. A man in a military-style jacket and aviator sunglasses shook Martín's hand and in a smooth motion pressed a gun to Martín's ribs.

"Wave to the pilots so they know everything is just fine."

Deflated, Martín obediently stuck his head out the door and waved. Valencia and Lieutenant Vazquez gave him a thumbs-up, spooled up their engines, and started their takeoff roll. Martín watched forlornly as the LU jet accelerated down the runway and lifted into the air.

The man closed the door and used the gun to direct Martín through a curtain and into the passenger area. There sat Father Serrano, who gestured at the seat facing him.

"Have a seat, Architect Ibarra," the priest said. "This is a flight to your destiny."

Martín felt the sting of a syringe in his arm.

CHAPTER EIGHTEEN

AFTER A METALLIC click in the lock, the office door swung open, revealing a small Asian woman with Gina's build and facial features and a look of exasperated disapproval on her face. Before Gina or Lenin could speak, the woman pivoted away from them while giving an impatient gesture for them to follow. Sayoko Ishikawa led them down a side hallway and into a small room devoid of anything other than a plain, empty desk and one chair. She shut the door behind them.

The older woman looked her daughter up and down, frowned, and hissed some words in Japanese. After an extremely tense exchange, Gina fell silent.

Lenin felt invisible and watched in mute fascination until the small woman, arms still akimbo, turned her scowling glare from her daughter to him. She barked at him in English, "You are Doctor Lenin?"

"Yes, uh, ma'am," he said, uncertain of the correct form of address to the first lady. Lenin felt very much the student instead of the professor.

"Thank you for saving my daughter's life," she said.

"Oh, well, she is actually very self-sufficient." Lenin felt awkward as he towered over the diminutive woman. Her eyes remained locked on his. "I'm sorry, Madam, but there is very little time. There is a crisis unfolding—"

"Of course there is a crisis! Do you think I am blind and stupid? What do we have to do to stop it?"

"We?" Lenin asked.

"Yes, we. The two of you weren't accomplishing anything in here by yourselves."

"Madam, there is a military emergency developing in Guiana. The president—"

"I can assure you that the president is not controlling these events—others are. What can I do?"

"Well, for starters, get us out of here," Lenin said. "And no one can see—"

"Obviously no one can see you leave," Sayoko said, shaking her head as though she was addressing a dullard. The first lady pulled out her phone and scrolled through her list of contacts and then clicked on one. As she waited, she continued to glare up at Lenin, and then she began speaking rapidly in Japanese.

Gina listened for a moment and then whispered to Lenin, "My mother is calling the landscapers who constructed the garden behind this building. They're Japanese-Brazilians she's known for many years. She's ordering an immediate removal of a half-dozen small trees from the grounds, to be relocated and planted in the park downtown. She requested that it be done immediately, and included in her request a code indicating that this is a discrete favor."

Lenin nodded back at Gina as if he understood.

A few hours later Teodoro Lenin and Gina Ishikawa rolled out of the official residence's garage riding in a panel truck, sitting among a small, displaced grove of trees.

*

Martín woke up feeling better and more well-rested than he had in what seemed like weeks. Then with a start he remembered that he'd been abducted.

He looked around and took in his new surroundings. His room was a simple space with whitewashed stone walls and high ceiling arches. He was lying on a steel-framed bed that was positioned along one wall. There was a wooden chair next to the bed, and a gold crucifix hanging above the metal headboard. Other than those items, the room was barren. The only exit from the room was through a heavy wooden door.

Martín's peripheral vision caught a reflective glint—a small video camera peering at him from high above, mounted on the ceiling. He got up and walked around the small room, noting that the coveralls that he had worn during his escape from the hospital in Caracas had been substituted with white cotton pants and a white T-shirt. The grime had been rinsed from his body, and Martín noted that his sweat and body odor had been replaced with a hint of lavender. The oil and grime in his hair were gone as well. For whatever reason, his captors wanted him presentable.

The lock in the door rattled and the door swung open. Father Serrano, dressed in a black friar's cassock, walked in carrying a Bible.

"I'm pleased to see you looking well, Architect."

"Yes. Your drug of choice was quite benign—I'd love to get some from you for those nights I find it hard to sleep. But then again, it's not often I feel the need to be unconscious enough to be hauled off a plane, hosed down, and scrubbed without ever waking up. And who knows what sort of nasty secondary purpose the drug may have. Tell me, Father, did I have a lot to say?"

Serrano smiled and made a dismissive gesture as he sat down and crossed his legs.

"You've seen too many spy movies. We already have all the information we need."

"I suppose I shouldn't bother to ask where I am."

"Your same question as in Caracas. My answer is the same as the one I gave you then: the exact location is not important."

"Can I ask who exactly is 'we'? The 'we' who have all the information on me, I mean."

"That will soon be obvious to you," Serrano said.

"And why the makeover?" Martín asked. "You even gave me a manicure."

"The last time we had to intervene with chemicals, you were not particularly photogenic afterward."

Martín looked surprised, and the priest smiled.

"Yes, in Venezuela. You thought it was the CIA or U.S. military, of course. That is certainly what your brother thought. It will make it much more difficult for them to work with Nicolás on any basis."

"What organization are you with?" Martín asked. "And why would you go to so much trouble to capture me of all people?"

Serrano stood. "Whatever Sister Trinidad told you is already more than you need to know. I will impress upon her the need for more discretion. Now follow me—it's time for your arraignment."

The legal term jarred Martín, as did the reference to the young woman who had helped him in the hospital.

Serrano rose from the chair and knocked on the door, which swung open. He motioned for Martín to follow him, and led him out of the cell into a courtyard. At first Martín thought it was an overcast day, but then he realized that there was an opaque plastic canopy above him. A guard stepped up and locked leg irons around Martín's ankles and clapped heavy handcuffs onto his wrists. Martín looked around and saw a line of identical cell doors at the base of a high wall. The cell he had emerged from was in the middle, with 10 identical doors on each side. He could hear the muffled noise of diesel engines and the horns of cars and trucks from somewhere beyond the walls. To Martín's surprise, he was not socked away in some remote hideaway. The cacophony of urban life was being generated mere meters away from where he stood. They were somewhere within a major city, surrounded by busy streets.

They crossed the patio of a three-story Spanish colonial townhouse. The corridors of each of the floors looked out on the patio and were semi-enclosed by graceful arches and delicate columns.

Martín hobbled behind Serrano up a flight of stairs and down a corridor. The priest opened a heavy door, holding it open for Martín to follow. Along one side of the high-ceilinged room they entered were large floor-to-ceiling windows. They had been painted gray, but still glowed from the sunlight.

As Father Serrano spoke in a low voice to another priest, Martín looked around the room. Getting out into the city and among the public seemed to be his only means of escape. He glanced at the windows. He could only guess as to the thickness of the glass. A few millimeters either way could be the difference between the glass shattering harmlessly or cutting him to shreds as he passed through it. Still, he really didn't like the sound of an arraignment.

Martín broke for the windows.

The leg irons clanged loudly on the wooden floor as he frantically pumped his legs in mincing steps, slowly gaining momentum. Ibarra didn't look to see his captors' reactions or whether they were already in pursuit. Instead, he kept his focus forward on the windows. After a few more steps, Martín pivoted, turning his left shoulder toward the glass, and lunged the remaining distance, his body bracing for the impact. He felt a surge of elation as it gave, shattering and exploding outward as his body passed through. Martín rolled in the air, and for the first time he considered the possibility that he was about to plunge into the middle of a street teeming with traffic.

And then, far too quickly, his back slammed into solid stone. His vision went white as a shock of pain went through him. He slid down into a sitting position. After blinking several times he saw that he was now propped against a wall at the edge of a balcony located just outside the now-shattered window. Wheezing, he tried to stand, but between the restraints and his injuries he just rolled impotently onto his side. Martín could hear the traffic jam of cars below him, and he tried to scream, but the lack of air in his lungs betrayed him. Only a hoarse whisper escaped his mouth.

Father Serrano stood over him with a pistol held against his ear.

"I will give you credit, Mr. Ibarra. You are a fish that keeps trying to wriggle itself off the hook. But while I admire your tenacity, this game has grown tiresome. It's a shame too. I really did want you to be at your most photogenic."

Serrano nodded at a wide, squat man with enormous arms and stood back, making way for him. The man pulled a blackjack from his belt and smashed it into the side of Martín's head.

*

When Gina and Teodoro opened the door leading into their hotel room, they had expected to find that it had been ransacked and their possessions seized. To their relief, the room was undisturbed.

The two of them spent the night laboriously reviewing their notes.

"Our only chance is to produce some meaningful evidence backing my hypothesis," Lenin said. "Even if your father won't listen, there are many leaders here for the inauguration. Perhaps we can find one who will listen to us." He rubbed his red eyes.

Lenin logged into the genealogy database maintained by the Church of All Saints and returned to the record for Carlos I of Spain and worked his way forward as the family diagrams bifurcated for each successive generation of legitimate and bastard children. He downloaded records that brought him as close to Carlos VII as he could.

The professor went to the websites of the various libraries that his friend in Spain had indicated David Broch had visited. There was something about the nature of the libraries and the works they housed that bothered Lenin, but he was exhausted and couldn't bring any conclusion to the fore of his consciousness. He looked his watch, but his vision was blurred by hours of concentration, stress, and lack of sleep. On the armchair next to the desk, Gina had already dozed off.

Lenin put his head down on his arms, vowing to rest his eyes for only a moment.

*

King Carlos's chamberlain appeared with a mobile phone on a silver tray. "Majesty, Mr. Waro Moto requests that you call him at your earliest convenience."

The king dismissed the chamberlain, tapped Moto's number, and checked the screen to ensure that the encryption was enabled.

"Please excuse me for disturbing you, Your Majesty," Moto said in English, "but a clarification is required. Martín Ibarra was briefly out of our control. I was not aware of this."

The king considered this for a moment. "Yes. Unfortunately, he briefly escaped while he was being detained in Venezuela."

"I see. Did he contact Gina Ishikawa or Teodoro Lenin?"

"I thought they were dead."

"It seems not," Moto said. There was silence, and then Moto continued. "Your Majesty, it would have been better if I had known earlier about Ibarra."

"I understand. There were legitimate reasons for maintaining silence on the matter for the time being."

"I see. Well, Serrano and his group have him again. President Ishikawa—"

"The president's role is not important to you, Mr. Moto."

"Your Majesty, judging from the communications I am hearing, he has been increasingly… ambivalent. I just want to be certain that we are all moving in the same direction, and that there are not loose ends that could harm us. Particularly since Lenin and the president's daughter have shown up again."

"Do not concern yourself, Mr. Moto," the king said sharply. "President Ishikawa will be controlled. And what Ibarra knows or doesn't will not matter for much longer."

The king broke the connection, and Moto quietly fumed.

*

"Translator!" Lenin exclaimed as he sat up abruptly. He looked around and saw sunlight flooding the room.

Gina was still slumped over the armchair when she was startled awake by Lenin's shout. "What?" she asked.

Lenin rubbed his face with the palms of his hands. "Broch's Spanish was execrable. Good enough for ordering a drink at a nightclub, perhaps, but not for antiquated legal works. What was that name David mentioned during his voicemail?"

"You're right!" she said. "Someone must have been working with him. Those recordings he made on my voicemail…" She flipped through the pages of notes on the table. "Julio. That was the name."

"When David called you while you were in Rome, did he mention anyone named Julio?"

"No, I don't think so."

"Then I will make some calls."

Lenin called the main research libraries in Zaragoza, Salamanca, Madrid, and Seville. In each case, the librarians said they remembered the American David Broch, but they had not seen any man with him. Nor did they recognize the name Julio.

Finally, Lenin called the Archive of the Indies. He talked to the director, a jovial and helpful man whom he knew from several stints of historical research that he had conducted at the Archives in person. The director, thrilled to hear that Lenin was still alive, said that he had signed a permit to allow Broch access to certain records, but had not met him in person.

"Would the librarian on duty know anything about his visits?" Lenin asked.

"Possibly. I'll connect you now. Good luck, Teodoro, with whatever you are trying to find."

There were a series of clicks and beeps.

"Hello?"

"This is Doctor Teodoro Lenin calling from South America. I understand that you may have met the American David Broch while he was doing some research."

"Yes, I did, but please hold on a moment." Lenin heard the clicking of a keyboard, and heard the librarian whispering, "*Cero, cero, cero, uno, cinco, tres, dos, siete, nueve.*"

"What?" Lenin asked.

"What?" the librarian parroted back to him.

"Were those numbers for me?"

The librarian said, "Oh. No, I was just entering a file number I was working on before I closed out of the program. Sorry, I was talking to myself, not you. Now, what can I do for you?"

"Was there a man with David Broch? Someone named Julio?"

"A man? No. There was always a young woman, but no, never another man."

"A woman? Tell me about her!" Lenin laid the phone down and put on the speaker.

"She was a *mamacita*, if you understand my meaning."

"Oh, yes, I do indeed," Lenin said, and gave Gina an embarrassed eyeroll. "Um, did you by any chance learn her name?"

"She seemed just as interested in the American as in their research."

"Really? Is that so?" Lenin looked up at Gina with a combination of amusement and exasperation. "And so, what was her name?"

"They couldn't seem to keep their hands off each other!"

"How interesting," Lenin said, maintaining a neutral tone while he threw out his arms and looked at Gina with amazement and dismay. "Lucky man. What was her name, please?"

"Name? I don't know."

Lenin banged the palm of his hand into his forehead.

"All I can tell you is that she sometimes wore T-shirts with '*Universidad de Zaragoza Derecho*' printed on it." The man laughed. "Stuck in my mind because they were always at least a size too small."

Gina gestured to Lenin, who said, "Hold on a moment, will you?" before muting the phone.

"Remember the phone message David left with the flamenco music playing in the background?" Gina asked. "There was a woman's voice."

"Right! Maybe that was her. She had asked him to come back to the dance floor and then what had she said?"

Gina consulted their notes. "You get to see for free what others have to pay for."

Lenin snapped his fingers. "A flamenco dancer, perhaps?" Lenin unmuted the phone. "Did she have to show an ID card to get into the library?"

"A very good thought, sir, but no," the librarian said. "Since Mr. Broch had proper authorization from the director himself, she was admitted as his assistant without having to present identification."

"Is it possible she signed for any of the records he checked out?"

"Hmm. No, that would not have been possible. Documents can only be signed out to the person named on the research permit."

Gina punched the mute button impatiently. "Ask him what she looked like! Hair color, eye color, height, frame."

Lenin did as he was instructed and Gina scribbled down the responses. "Thank you, sir," he said. He exchanged a few pleasantries and the librarian hung up.

"Now we just need to canvass the flamenco clubs in Zaragoza," Lenin said. He started typing.

*

The satellite systems operator at Moto Electric's headquarters in Tokyo answered the call from the company's Network Operations Center in Spain the moment it flashed on his console.

"Tokyo," he said into his headset.

"Seville, here," was the response in Japanese.

"Yes?" the operator asked.

"In accordance with Moto-san's instructions, we have been monitoring commercial traffic originating in San Juan Diego for unusual patterns. In the last few minutes we have several… unusual calls. There were a series of calls from a hotel in San Juan Diego to various research libraries in Spain, and then the Archive of the Indies here in Seville. Since that original call, there has been another call made from that same number in San Juan Diego to a number in Zaragoza. That call destination is… unique."

"How so?"

"It is a flamenco club, very unusual in northern Spain." Sensing impatience and irritation at the other end of the line, the Seville NOC technician continued quickly. "We were ordered to report anything unusual. Calls to libraries and a historic archive in Spain followed by a call to an ethnic dance club seemed—"

"Stand by," the operator said. He keyed his console, connecting the man with his supervisor.

*

Waro Moto was perspiring heavily as he stepped off the treadmill. A young man handed a towel to Moto, who wiped his face with it. The young man bowed, handing him a phone. Moto pressed it to his ear and listened for a time.

"Yes. Yes, I agree. Very unusual. You were right to contact me. Please dispatch a team immediately to the origination point and the final termination point."

He hung up the phone and turned to his assistant. "Tell the NOC in Spain to continuously monitor all traffic coming from the identified origination point in San Juan Diego. There seems to be yet another loose end."

CHAPTER NINETEEN

LENIN'S CALL WAS to a cabaret called La Morería just south of the Ebro River. The man answering immediately became defensive when Lenin asked about an English-speaking dancer matching the description that he had been given.

"Who wants to know?"

"My name is Teodoro Lenin. I am a professor of history at an American university."

"You talk like an Argentine."

"I am one. Very astute of you. And I have researched in Spain. I can give you references."

The voice on the other end laughed wryly. "References. If you want to talk to her, come here and pay the cover fee like everyone else."

"Please. She knows a friend of mine, David Broch, an American who is in peril. Just say his name and she'll want to help."

"Call me back in ten minutes." The line went dead.

Lenin and Gina sat in silence, waiting for the allotted ten minutes to tick away. Finally Lenin gave her a "here goes nothing" shrug and dialed the phone, clicking on the speaker so that Gina could hear as well. The phone rang four times, and Lenin's heart began to sink. They were going to be ignored.

But on the fifth ring, the phone was answered.

The voice on the other end was still cool, but Gina thought she heard a bit of genuine concern. "I want to know what this is about."

"Is she there with you right now?" Lenin asked.

There was no answer.

"Ask her if she has heard of me."

"She's already said that she has."

"And she must have told you I am truly a friend to the American. Please, it's most urgent that I talk to her. Lives are in danger."

"So I hear. Hold on a second."

Lenin and Gina heard the muffled, indistinguishable sound of voices as the mouthpiece of the phone on the other end was covered. Then there was heavy, feminine breathing coming through the line.

"Miss? This is Teodoro Lenin. We have a mutual friend, David Broch. He—"

Lenin heard what sounded like a cough, and then soft sniffling.

"They killed him. They killed him." The woman had the accent of Aragón and a trace of the Caló inflection that was heard among the Romani people of Spain known as *gitanos*.

Gina's eyes widened, and she covered her mouth with her hand. Lenin's heart dropped, as well, but he steeled himself and tried his best to maintain his composure. He took a deep breath. The woman needed to hear a calm voice or they risked losing her to her fears.

"Miss, listen to me, please. I'm trying to help. I know there's nothing I can do now for Mr. Broch, but there are others who are also in danger. Please, I need your help."

The sniffling continued, but it was the only response.

"First, what is your name, Miss?" Lenin asked.

She hesitated, then said, "Alejandra."

"Thank you. Alejandra of whom?"

Another hesitation.

"Please. This is very important. Much as you trusted Mr. Broch, I need you to trust me."

"Rojas. Rojas Deza."

"Miss Rojas, do you know who retained David Broch to do the research?"

"I… I never knew their names. But David said it was to legitimize something that someone wanted to do."

"Legitimize? What do you mean?"

"Just what the word means," Rojas said. Her voice seemed to sharpen.

Lenin softened his voice and tried to take on the most comforting tone possible. "You are clearly someone very intelligent, and I think that you must be a law student. Otherwise you could never have helped David accurately translate all the very technical legal language in those documents."

There was an extended silence.

"Please," Lenin urged. "I'm trying very hard to understand about what happened to David Broch, and the specifics of the work he was doing."

She responded, but with exasperation in her voice. "David was preparing a defense of what he called the status quo ante. It was to proclaim the Latin American declarations of independence and constitutions null and void and to restore the legitimacy of crown rule. David despised the premise, but he figured it was only a hypothetical exercise—that there was no way that anyone could actually act on what he was putting together. And he said the money was very good, and was reliably paid on time." She paused for a moment, then let out a small, humorless laugh. "He thought the whole thing was ludicrous."

"Miss, what you have just told me is very important. Do you have any of David's papers—drafts or copies of the work he did? Anything at all that confirms what you just said, and that might include the names of whoever employed him?"

"Yes… there are some things—papers, flash drives. When…" Rojas took in a sharp breath. "When they… took him they also took his laptop and notes. I thought that everything was gone. But that night, I came back to my apartment and found a package with my name on it under my pillow. I haven't gone through them yet."

"Miss Rojas, I need to ask you to send as many pages and files as you can to me. Are the documents in electronic form?"

"The files are on a flash drive… maybe I can email them to you."

Gina muted the phone. "I'll set up a new account," she said.

Lenin nodded. Gina got to work, and Lenin unmuted the phone. "I am going to set up a new email account online so that you can send them over. As for the hard copies…"

"I don't have access to a scanner…"

"What about a fax?"

"Perhaps," she said, seeming to mull it over. "But there are a lot of pages. I'd need to send them from a copy store. I don't have access to a fax machine at the school."

Lenin muted the phone and said to Gina, "Where is the contact information your mother gave to us?"

Gina, still typing on the computer, gestured at the pile of papers and notes that she and Lenin had been working on in the hotel room, and Lenin began to rummage through them. Lenin unmuted the phone.

"I will give you a fax number in just a few moments." He paused for a moment, considering his options. "And a way to pay for the transmission and other costs."

Gina heard him and paused her typing, giving him a questioning glance that said "really?" Lenin motioned impatiently for her to continue, and she did so, but not before giving him an arched brow.

"Alright," said Rojas on the phone.

Buying some time while Gina set up the email, Lenin asked, "Miss, do you happen to know who 'Julio' is?"

Alejandra's tone changed in an instant to seething anger. "Bastard! Son of a whore!"

"Was he the one who killed David?" he asked.

"No, but he may as well have. He was the Judas. A poor little rich boy. He became David's friend and then he sold him to them for pieces of silver."

"And who are 'them'?"

"I saw a man—just once, in the street. A priest. In a very expensive German car. He—"

She was interrupted by a loud thud and a crash. The telephone banged on something hard and Rojas screamed. The bartender shrieked a slur, and then the line went dead.

Gina and Lenin sat in stunned silence. "I had the proof," Lenin said. "It was there, almost in my hands. But someone has denied it to me again."

"Who?"

"Based on the bartender's unfortunate choice of words, they were

Chinese. Though I'm not sure I'd trust a club owner to distinguish one East Asian nationality from another."

"What about my father?" Gina asked. "Could he be behind this?"

"Perhaps," Lenin said, "but I don't think his arm is long enough. It's a miracle that he was able to cobble together the consensus he needed to get the military resources he has, and even those are far from fully adequate. But whomever it is seems to know our every move. How? It's as though they have ears everywhere."

Gina bent over and pressed her head between her hands. "Moto," she said. "He won the San Juan Diego telecommunications contracts, both civilian and governmental. He's the only one who could be tracking us so easily."

Lenin stared at her. "I killed that poor girl."

Gina stood. "And we're next unless we get moving right now."

They snatched up their notes and the laptop and scrambled down the stairs. As they raced into the lobby, they saw a taxi stop just outside the glass door. An Asian man in a black suit got out, staring at the hotel entrance. Lenin and Gina darted into a hallway that led out to a patio area. As they ran toward the street a bullet snapped past Lenin's head.

Horns blew and people shouted curses as Lenin and Gina sprinted between the cars. They crouched beside a battered convertible, and the driver bellowed at them to get away from his car. The convertible's windshield spiderwebbed as three bullets smacked through the glass. The driver yelped and punched the accelerator, smashing into the car in front of him. Undeterred, he floored the pedal, spinning his tires and slowly propelling the car he hit into the one in front of it. Horns blew again, and men jumped out of their cars, looking around and shouting.

Gina and Lenin stayed in a crouch and scrambled into a storefront. Lenin glanced behind and saw their pursuer retreating into the alleyway as approaching police sirens blared in the distance.

*

Nicolás Ibarra drummed his fingers on a rough tabletop. It was oppressively hot in the warehouse, the humid air pressing down on him like a blanket that had marinated for years in the odors of the diverse goods that had been stored there. There was an echoing cacophony from the hundreds of men and women billeted in the cavernous building as they talked, shouted, sang, argued, and fought—anything to release the tension of weeks of inactivity.

None of these things bothered him. He had learned from his years as a revolutionary to be patient. His mind and body were indifferent to pain, discomfort, and even stultifying boredom. Nicolás was accustomed to the habits and needs of both experienced and first-time warriors.

Over a period of months small squads of his forces had gradually moved their assets south to Ciudad Bolívar on the Orinoco River. Then he had dispersed them onto rusted barges, tramp steamers, riverboats, and even canoes to head east to the coast and then southeasterly to Albina, Suriname. Now the army awaited further orders to move into French Guiana and engage. Nicolás had argued fervently against an overland attack, as it would be a logistical nightmare to move an army through the most dense and extensive jungles of South America. But the revolutionary council, and most specifically its advisors from the Middle East, had overruled him, ordering him to attack French Guiana from the west. And worse, they had dictated that the forces would not mobilize down the main coastal road into the French department, but rather through the jungle further south. They insisted that, like the Japanese attacking Singapore through Malaya in World War II, the French would never expect an attack from the forests.

Nicolás's best arguments had failed. He had never anticipated that his life as a revolutionary leader would entail waiting to execute the ridiculous and ill-conceived orders of others, and yet here he was. But the possibility of bringing the establishment cowering to its knees—even if only for a brief time—was worth swallowing his pride and doing what he was told for now. Once he held the rocket, all of the power would shift, and the eyes of the entire world would be on him. All he had to do was wait just a bit longer.

*

Lenin and Gina sat with their backs against a concrete wall. The building was still under construction, with the steel frame in place and tilt-up walls being positioned.

Lenin looked around to confirm that they were screened from the street.

"Now what?" Gina asked.

"I suppose you don't know any other world leaders to go to," Lenin said with a grim smile. "What about your colleagues in the press corps?"

"That's it! Dennis Prinn, a television guy. I can trust him."

"Where's he staying?"

"He doesn't stay in hotels. His equipment trailer is self-contained. But there was a photo on his desk of a girl and a new house in the Palos District. He's probably camped there—unless he's already screwed things up with the girl… always a possibility."

They stood and hurried around the corner to face the street. Lenin waved frantically to a cab going by, but the driver ignored him. It was followed by a long stream of private vehicles.

"Too bad we can't call an Uber," Gina muttered. "We won't last long out here."

On cue, the tires of a Lexus headed the opposite way screeched as the driver hit the brakes. The horn of the car behind it blared. Heavy traffic in the next lane blocked the Lexus from turning.

Another cab was coming fast, the driver trying to avoid eye contact. Lenin jumped from the curb into its oncoming path and the cabbie was forced to lock up his brakes. The car went into a skid, rotating slowly as it veered toward Lenin. The historian dove onto the hood, sprawling with his face against the windshield and hanging desperately on to the wipers. The car slammed into the curb, rocking crazily as it stopped.

"You crazy son of a bitch!" the driver screamed, opening his door. "What the hell—"

Lenin scrambled off the hood, opened the back door, and slid into the back seat. Gina dove in beside him. The driver, enraged, yelled, "Get the fuck out of my cab! I ain't taking—"

A bullet shattered the passenger-side window, and the driver shrieked.

"Get this car moving or we're all dead!" Lenin shouted.

The driver slammed the accelerator, lurching the car onto the sidewalk. Pedestrians dove for the street or back into storefront doors as the cab smashed into a food stall, spinning the small wooden shack and showering the street with skewers of meat and corn. A bullet slammed into the trunk lid, ripping it open and bending it upward. "*Jesús, Maria, San Cristóbal!*" the cabbie yelled.

A bullet ripped through the rear window, exploding the plastic crucifix hanging from the rear-view mirror and shattering the windshield. The car roared down the sidewalk then bounced off the curb into an intersection, where it made a fish-tailing right turn onto the cross street.

Lenin threw an American hundred-dollar bill on the front seat and barked, "Lose that guy and take us to Palos."

"What about all this goddamned damage to my cab?"

Lenin dumped two more hundreds on the front seat.

"It's going to cost a lot more than that!"

"Bullshit! Insurance will cover it. The money's for you. Just keep driving!"

The cabbie took another look in the rear-view mirror, executed a series of fast turns, and then headed toward the Palos district of San Juan Diego.

*

Carolina watched Nicolás from where she sat at a table scattered with papers on the other side of the warehouse. She felt a surge of irritation at his ability to sit and do nothing while she managed all of the logistics. But there was one clear benefit to Nico's laziness—it gave her the freedom to make some decisions on her own.

Her phone rumbled, and she answered it immediately. Instinctually she spun away from Nicolás despite him being a good 50 meters away.

"The last forces arrived during the night. We are fully in place."

"Good, I'm making a note of it." She scribbled on a computer-produced Gantt chart, noting the date on a bar entitled MAIN ATTACK FORCE—NIEUW AMSTERDAM, SURINAME "The transports are scheduled to arrive tomorrow. Have everyone ready to deploy."

"Of course, commander. I will advise you of the embarkation."

Glancing up, Carolina was startled to see Nicolás approaching. She hung up and put a pad of paper over the Gantt charts. She picked up a fax and pretended to study it.

Nicolás put a hand on her shoulder. "What are all those papers?"

She ignored him and began to write rapidly. A fax machine on the table bleeped, screeched, and disgorged more sheets of paper.

"What would Che Guevara think of planning a revolution using Gantt charts and critical path analyses, communicating by mobile phone, and putting armies on the march using faxes?" He watched her face. She continued frowning in concentration, her eyes scanning the text line by line, her left hand making neat notations on a yellow legal pad.

"Hey," he said gently, "I'm talking to you."

"We need to arrange the television coverage," she said. "It has to be in place in Kourou within the next forty-eight hours."

"The container—"

"Arrived from Charleston yesterday. It's offshore at this moment. But we need the technician… otherwise we've just got a bunch of useless gear."

Nicolás dropped his rucksack on the table.

"My flight leaves Paramaribo in an hour and a half. I'll get him."

He reached down and took her hand. She looked up at him, frowning.

"Why don't you come with me?" he asked.

"You make it sound like you're going on vacation," she said.

"It is, in a way. We've been so focused on arrangements here in camp, a change will do us both good."

She eyed him closely. "What is with you?" she asked.

He laughed. "I think I'm beginning to get old. In some ways the feel of a young woman next to me in a hotel bed is as good a prospect as the national liberation of French Guiana."

She pulled her hand free. "Get yourself a whore in San Juan Diego, then. I don't have time."

Nicolás grabbed her arm. "You have a younger, better prospect here?" he demanded, gesturing toward the many men lying on cots and walking around in various stages of undress.

"Don't go bourgeois on me. Everything we've been working toward depends on the next few days. I need to be here. You have your tasks. I have mine."

Nicolás released her arm, and she turned her back to him. As she resumed writing, he shrugged, picked up his rucksack, and headed for the bathroom to prepare his travel disguise. Carolina stole a glance at the relic television mounted on the nearby wall, with aluminum foil wrapped around its antenna rods. The faded screen showed yet another talk show featuring King Carlos VII. The background roar of noise in the warehouse made it impossible to hear, but the closed captioning was on. The king was, as always, going on and on about the need to combine political and spiritual power and his fervent hopes for the return of Christ to rule the world.

Carolina's ETA combat years had taken place during the reign of the previous king, but she despised this *nuevo* royal just as fiercely. She had robbed banks, placed explosives in public places, and kidnapped men, women, and children until she was caught by the Guardia Civil. In prison she was beaten, raped, starved, and tortured. Years of suffering had sharpened her hatred for those who had been handed their privilege, money, and power to a fine, needle-sharp point. She could now focus that hatred on this king.

CHAPTER TWENTY

DENNIS PRINN RUBBED his temple and popped three Advils as he scrolled through his messages from the night before. Mostly texts from other media people, all asking him to come join them at such-and-such bar and they'd buy him a drink. Based on his pounding head, Dennis thought it was likely he met up with all of them. Then there were a few texts from early in the morning, mostly of the "hey, did you get home ok?" variety. He texted back to those who asked, letting them know he was home, but definitely worse for wear.

Dennis groaned. He was getting too old for this lifestyle, but it wasn't often that almost all his client base converged into one place at one time unless there had been some sort of disaster or terrorist attack, in which case partying wasn't an option. But an inauguration? Well, that allowed everyone plenty of time to get into town and let it all hang loose. He wondered, though, how much of his partying was an effort to dull the ache that he still felt over the loss of Gina. His friend and colleague should've been there. She wouldn't have been pounding drinks like the rest of them, but her acerbic humor and dignified presence always enhanced gatherings. How her father could go on with the inauguration was beyond his comprehension.

Dennis lay back on the sofa cushions and listened to Paula puttering in the kitchen. Making a fresh pot of coffee, Dennis hoped. He opened his Twitter app and mindlessly scrolled through his feed.

There was a noise outside the front door and Paula walked over, opened the door, and peered out. She pulled her head back inside and quickly shut the door. She turned toward Dennis, her eyes wide, and whispered, "There are two people hiding in my garden." She ran toward the back of the house.

Dennis reached into a drawer in the coffee table, withdrew a revolver, pulled on his girlfriend's bathrobe, and headed for the door.

*

As soon as the taxi entered the Palos suburb, the driver pulled to the curb. Sensing that they had pushed the driver as far as they could, Gina and Lenin climbed out.

All of San Juan Diego was new, and this neighborhood had just been completed eight months before. Grass had been laid down, but the trees were all new plantings. The walls in front of each house still lacked the vines and vegetation common to most middle-class neighborhoods in Latin American cities. As the two looked for the house that Gina had seen in the photograph, they shrunk against the nearest wall each time a car passed, averting their faces.

Finally, Gina saw a house with an eight-foot fence in front, a blue tile roof, and a statue of Pan near the front door. She looked up the street and saw a dark blue Lexus turning the corner. She nudged Lenin, who turned his head, then looked frantically for cover. There was none. Gina enlaced her fingers and held them out to Lenin at knee level. Lenin shook his head, but Gina urgently nodded toward the approaching Lexus. Unable to think of any other options, Lenin relented. He shoved his briefcase through the bars and put his shoe into Gina's hands. He transferred his weight and pulled on the wrought iron with his hands, then threw a leg over it and jumped down into the patio area.

Lenin was on his knees and collecting himself to stand when he saw a blur outside the iron gate. In a fluid movement Gina flew to the top, swung her legs over the wall, and gently dropped to the ground. They both fell to a prone position behind some leafy garden plants, listening as the car slowly drove past.

Behind them they could hear the house's front door open. Gina looked over her shoulder and made eye contact with a woman in a negligée peering out the door. The woman's eyes widened with alarm and she disappeared, slamming the door behind her.

Gina and Lenin exchanged glances, wondering what to do next. Before they could act, Dennis Prinn swaggered out of the house carrying a pistol and wearing a woman's bathrobe that barely reached his thighs. He squinted at the two on their knees.

"Jesus Christ!" he exclaimed. "Gina, it's you!"

Gina grabbed Dennis's arm, turning him around and leading him back toward his open front door with Lenin trailing awkwardly behind.

As the trio entered the home, Dennis said, "You're being pursued? By who? The terrorists? Is that why you're hiding?" Dennis's mind, already dulled by the hangover, was now tossing around, completely unmoored by this sudden chain of events. He slumped back onto his couch and stared up at Gina and the vaguely familiar-looking bald man.

"I promise, you'll get the whole story," Gina said. "By the way, this is Professor Teodoro Lenin. It was his house that was destroyed by the bomb."

Lenin reached out to shake Dennis's hand, but the Australian technician remained motionless and slack-jawed. Lenin let his arm hang in the air a few moments, and then slowly let it drop to his side.

"How did you know about...?" He gestured to the room.

"The picture you had on your desk in Rome," Gina said. "I know this will sound bizarre, but the king of Spain is plotting to reestablish Spain's rule over its former colonies, including the entire Latino Union."

"Whoa, whoa, whoa!" Dennis said. "Have some mercy on me. I have a raging hangover and one of my friends just rose from the dead!"

"We also think the pope is involved," Lenin said.

Dennis looked back and forth between their pinched faces. "I partied hard last night, and I must have gotten drunker than I thought." He rubbed his eyes. "You guys, I'm really glad to find out you're both alive. Good on ya! But you've got kangaroos loose in the top paddock. You're saying things that don't make any sense."

Lenin banged his briefcase on the coffee table and pulled out the computer and papers. "Read," he ordered in his best professorial voice.

*

Martín Ibarra awakened to the sound of heavy doors opening somewhere near the room where he was lying. He opened his eyes and sat up, letting out a hiss as searing pain jabbed at his torso.

He saw only a dark gray blur before him, as if he were engulfed in dense fog. He looked straight up, and the fog was a lighter gray. He rolled his eyes left, and everything was darker.

The images of crashing through the glass came back, as well as his last moments of consciousness as the stocky man beat him with the blackjack while Father Serrano watched with his hands on his hips.

Panic enveloped him as his stomach heaved. He lunged from the bed and crashed to a rough cement floor. He blinked wildly but his vision would not clear. He felt something smooth under him and grabbed it with his hands—a plastic shrink-wrapped package of some kind, soft and pliable to the touch.

Martín dropped the package and sat up. He felt iron against his back—the bed frame, he realized—and turned around to grip the frame, squeezing it with his hands. A sob ripped from his chest. Bizarre, disjointed thoughts from his period of waking-sleep began to fill his head as he tried to clear his mind.

Father Serrano. What did he want? A religious fanatic who was out of control? Lay vigilantes and a rogue priest? A cult and a defrocked monk? Ultra-conservative church militants? Avengers of the death of Christ?

Takeshi Ishikawa. Was he working with the dark priest? Why? How?

Martín shook his head violently and rubbed his eyes. Still, he found only the same gray gloom.

Martín heard the rattle of a key in the door's lock and the cell door banged open. There was the shuffling sound of multiple people entered and he was hauled to his feet. His wrists were pulled together and clamped with handcuffs.

"Martín Ibarra Flores, you are hereby ordered to appear this day before the court of the Holy Office of the Inquisition to answer charges of heresy. May God have mercy on your immortal soul."

*

Dennis Prinn ended the call. His face was white and waxy and glistening with perspiration.

"Not good," Lenin surmised.

Dennis grabbed a crumpled soft pack from the coffee table. The cigarette that went into his lips was bent, and his hands shook as he lit it.

"Ben Moody. A national security staffer who's been a great source for me. He said he knows something about your story of a coalition of guerrilla forces gathering in South America and swinging east."

"See—" Gina began.

"Moody says they are *possibly* joining up, and are *tending* to move in an easterly direction. And *if* they combine their forces, they *probably* have the capability to launch a limited offensive action against a soft target. There are *unconfirmed* indications they are led by Nicolás Ibarra, and the rocket being prepared for launch at Kourou could *potentially*, with *sufficient time and expertise*, be modified for an alternative payload. And on and on."

"So, that confirms—" Lenin began.

"That confirms shit," Dennis growled, rising and pacing. "Your papers are like a horoscope—vague and could apply to anyone to predict anything on any day. The Security Council strings together more qualifiers than a barrister—tending, probably, potentially, unconfirmed—sorry, Professor, but you don't have bugger all."

Lenin looked at Dennis's shaking hand. "Oh? Why the anxiety then, Mr. Prinn?"

Dennis made a face at Lenin and took a deep drag.

Gina reached out and held Dennis's arm. "You and I have known each other a while," Gina said. "You think I'd concoct some crazy story?"

Dennis gave a vague gesture with his hand that signified he gave her some credence.

"I swear to God, if we go out on that street, we will be gunned down. If we hole up here and do nothing, or if we're killed, something terrible is going to happen."

Dennis stood in his undersized woman's bathrobe, smoking his crooked cigarette and looking sick. He ran his hand through his hair several times, took two deep draws on his cigarette, and stubbed it out in a glass bowl.

"Fuck it," he said. "Want to learn about the television broadcast business?"

*

Dennis Prinn drove his rental van across town with Lenin and Gina in the back, sitting among piles of newspapers. His head still throbbed uncomfortably, but getting dressed and heading out with a sense of purpose, no matter how bizarre, made him feel marginally better.

"So where are we going?" Gina asked.

"What's the best way to hide something?" Dennis asked over his shoulder. "Put it right in front of whoever's searching."

He stopped the car and shut off the engine. "Hang tight, mates, I'll be right back."

In a few minutes the side door slid open. Dennis gestured for them to get out. "Follow me. Don't stop, don't look around."

Gina went first, and Lenin followed. They had the sensation of going through a kind of hatch and then they emerged into a room. It was cold, lighted by fluorescent tubes, and animated by a bank of thirty small television monitors above a console covered with toggles, sliding switches, and a computer keyboard. The television monitors displayed shots of San Juan Diego, but some seemed to be showing television studios and outdoor scenes located in other countries throughout the world.

There was a clang behind them, and they turned to see Dennis closing a metal door behind him.

Dennis gestured around him and said, "Welcome to my world. We're in the parking lot just outside the LU palace complex." Gina and Teodoro flinched, but Dennis held out his hands in a placating gesture. "No worries, you're okay. No one will look for you here."

Dennis sat at the console and put on a headset. His fingers flew furiously over the keyboard. The small screens above flashed with new vistas—some of them in daytime, some night. Talking heads silently moved their mouths.

Dennis slipped one earphone off his ear and, while simultaneously watching the monitors and moving sliding switches with his hands, said, "I freelance for networks all over the world. Right out of university I scraped some money together and built two of these communications rigs into shipping containers." He waved a hand at their surroundings. "All the latest link-up gear for any type of satellite and ground station. Fully self-contained. Gas turbine generator, bedroom, loo, water, galley. Have a look around."

Dennis slipped his headset back on and spoke into his microphone. Gina and Lenin cautiously opened a door and found a galley similar to that of a sailboat's, with a refrigerator, a microwave oven, and a sink. Beyond that was another door. Inside they found a tiny bedroom with a surprisingly large bed and an adjoining small bathroom. Above the bed was a flat-screen monitor. The opposite side of the container held a small studio with video cameras, a blue wall, and a desk with three chairs.

"I can be in place and set up about two hours after my container hits a port of entry," Dennis said. "I've got friends in customs in most countries, and they clear me quickly."

While Lenin dumped a can of can of chili in a plastic bowl and heated it up in the microwave, Gina sat beside Dennis at the control console. They were monitoring the two Latino Union television stations and 35 private and governmental stations from each of the member countries. Many were showing footage of the king and queen of Spain visiting the miserable and the homeless. The young royal couple was often accompanied by Pope Pius, who blessed the poor and held the ragged children to his chest.

There were also interviews with Takeshi Ishikawa, who looked cool and stately as he discoursed on Latin American politics and his vision for the new union of Latino countries. He spoke of important developments coming soon, and proclaimed that everyone needed to prepare for changes— changes that were designed to distance the nascent union from the last three hundred years of corruption, incompetence, and social injustice. "A new day is coming," he said.

In panel discussions suited talking heads enthusiastically discussed the advantages President Ishikawa's administration were bringing to Latin America as well as the challenges he would face. There were interviews with people on the street who praised Ishikawa's intelligence, foresight, and boldness, as well as the new sense of morality and responsibility that the Spanish king and the new pontiff were bringing to Latin America.

Although decades of working in the media had made him a cynic, Dennis was struck by the blatancy of the propaganda. Almost all of the stations were carrying prepackaged pieces of incredible similarity. Entire passages were repeated as the announcers urged their viewers to follow in the footsteps of the Holy Father and rededicate themselves to God. There were reviews of rituals of the mass, communion, baptism, and confession—purportedly so that no one needed to feel awkward or embarrassed by not having been to church in many years. He turned around to comment on this to Gina and Lenin, but didn't see them. He got up and walked to the back of his container and was not surprised to find that they were both sound asleep on the bed in his tiny bedroom. Crazy story or not, they had both been obviously stressed and exhausted.

After eating a few bites of lukewarm chili, Dennis signed off with his client networks, put his equipment on standby, and powered down his mobile television center so it would appear unoccupied. He scribbled a note for his guests to let them know that he would return shortly and politely asked that they not touch any of his electronics. Then he drove off in his rental van to see whether life on the streets matched what he had seen on television.

*

Dennis stopped at a security checkpoint and showed his press pass. Once cleared, he drove through, turning into the parking lot where his container was set up. He parked the van twenty meters from the steel box, grabbed his briefcase, and walked among the parked vehicles toward it. Dennis turned the combination lock and pulled down the hasp. Then he felt something hard press against his spine.

"Open the door slowly and let's get inside," a man said in Spanish-accented English.

Dennis eased the door open as the pressure on his back increased. They walked inside. Dennis heard the door slam shut behind him and the lock bolt slide home. The gunman patted Dennis down and then asked him to turn around.

"What do you want?" Dennis murmured, hoping not to wake Gina and Lenin.

"You and I are taking a trip."

"Where? And why?"

"Your expertise is needed for an important cause."

"And when do we leave?" Dennis asked.

"Now."

"If I do, an alarm will go out right away. I'm expected to be manning my station in five minutes and there are a dozen news producers who will lose their collective shit wondering where the fuck I am if I'm not in that chair doing my job when the time comes. Word will get out quickly that I am missing."

The man grimaced. "How much time do you need?"

"No more than two hours. After that, you'll have my full cooperation."

"Do it."

The gunman gestured at the chair in front of the bank of televisions, and Dennis slowly sat down. Dennis groped for the master switch on the console and flipped it. There was a whine as the gas turbine engine spooled up. The florescent lights and television monitors flickered to life. Dennis donned his headphones. He had bought himself two hours, but he hadn't been lying. He was going to have to think through his options while working his ass off doing his day job.

Dennis glanced up at a blank monitor reflecting his assailant. The man was tall and thin, wearing a floppy cloth hat pulled low on his forehead. He wore glasses and sported a bushy mustache and goatee.

On the main monitors directly in front of Dennis were live shots of various reporters standing around San Juan Diego, ready to go. Once each of them went live he would perform his magic, matching their reports with shots he had collected from seven camera crews here in San Juan Diego, as well as live static shots of the presidential mansion. For the next ten minutes he was occupied by frantic news directors from three networks, lashing together a complicated timeline so that each of them would have their own window of exclusivity.

*

Martín blinked, trying his best to focus as he was led into a small room. Someone unlocked and removed his handcuffs and then shoved a folded item of clothing into his arms.

"Put it on, my son," the man said. His voice was empathetic—almost sorrowful.

"Father? I... I don't understand."

"Please. It's important that you follow instructions. Your immortal soul is at stake."

Martín began to ask another question, but was elbowed sharply in the ribs by one of the guards. Already disoriented, his head swam with waves of agony and he doubled over, clutching his ribcage. He dropped the garment onto the floor.

"Gentlemen!" the priest said. "Even the damned deserve our pity and compassion." He leaned down and whispered into Martín's ear. "I will help you with this if you can just stand up straight for a moment."

Martín did as he was asked, and felt the weight of the garment as it was lifted over his head and onto his shoulders. He then felt something get placed onto his head. Some sort of hat, he thought, although it was larger and more ungainly than anything he had worn before.

"Peace be with you, my son," the priest said, and the guards pushed Martín forward. Fearing the infliction of more pain, he stumbled into a much larger room. He flinched at the bright lights bearing down on him.

"Can you move him a little bit more to the right?" a woman asked. The guards nudged Martín again, and he shuffled his feet obediently.

"Okay, that's good. Mr. Ibarra? Can you hear me?"

Martín nodded.

"Good. We need you to stand perfectly still, okay? Otherwise, things will get unfriendly again."

Beyond the woman's voice, Martín heard the sounds of electrical machinery and men and women moving about, speaking Spanish. Martín tried to listen to what they were saying, which consisted of familiar-sounding jargon, but his dulled mind was unable to process and decode it.

"Mr. Ibarra?" came the voice again, this time in a scolding tone. There was the sound of fingers being snapped just in front of his face. "Are you listening? We don't have time for nonsense. Nod *now* if you understood me!"

Martín nodded again.

"Good," said the voice. "Everyone! Let's get started! Places!"

For a few seconds the din around him increased as he sensed people scurrying around and taking their assigned positions. Then all was quiet.

The woman's voice began counting down from ten. When it reached three, she stopped counting and silence descended upon the room. A few moments later, a man's voice from directly in front of Martín began a prayer. The prayer called for God's enlightenment, leading to His mercy and justice in the proceedings that were about to follow.

The voice was unmistakable. It belonged to Father Serrano.

*

During a lull between the live remotes, Dennis glanced at the unused monitors again and saw the gunman staring fixedly at a screen on the top row. Dennis followed the gunman's gaze and saw footage of a figure in a white-hooded robe facing the camera, seated at a long table covered with white linen. To either side of the figure in white sat two figures in black, their faces hidden by the hoods of their cloaks.

The man in white facing the camera spoke, although no sound could be heard. Occasionally, the man standing with his back to the camera turned his head, showing a momentary profile of his face.

The intruder behind him put a hand on Dennis's shoulder. "What is this we're seeing?"

Dennis looked at his console, clicked a series of keys on his keyboard, and squinted at his computer monitor. "It's a raw feed from a Latino Union satellite."

"Where is it originating from?"

"I don't know."

"What's it for?"

"Unsure, but it looks like it's a live feed that is being downlinked to television stations for later broadcast."

"Can you get the sound?"

Dennis reset some switches. "I've got it." He listened for a few moments as the feed's sound played in his headphones and shrugged. "It's in Spanish. I can't understand most of it."

The gunman roughly yanked the headset off Dennis's head and

clamped one of the earpieces to his ear. Dennis noted that he had dropped his gun to his side.

"Can you pause this—what'd you call it?—feed?"

Dennis looked around. "Well, I can't stop the downlink. But if you're asking if I can stop the image, yeah, my system is automatically recording it. I can freeze the preview any time. Just tell me when."

The gunman stared at the screen, waited a few moments, and then barked out, "Now!"

Prinn clicked his mouse and the image froze on a shot of the man standing before the table. But even with the frozen high-definition image, the face was too small for the man's features to be distinguishable.

"Can you zoom in on the face?"

Dennis clicked more switches and the face grew to fill the screen. The gunman was so engrossed in the television that he seemed to have forgotten where he was. He said something out loud in Spanish, and after thinking for a moment, Dennis recognized the words.

"*Mi hermano,*" the gunman had said. "My brother."

CHAPTER TWENTY-ONE

AN ATTRACTIVE YOUNG woman in a brightly colored silk blouse stood in the queue leading to the passport control officers at Barajas Airport in Madrid. Using the country code from a fax number that she had been provided, she had tried to book a flight to San Juan Diego. She had been told multiple times that due to the upcoming inauguration and resulting celebrations, all flights to San Juan Diego out of Madrid—and for that matter out of Spain—were completely booked. Finally, a helpful service agent suggested that she could fly to Bogotá, Colombia. There were much more frequent flights from there to nearby San Juan Diego. Her odds of getting a flight would be greatly improved. The young woman had concurred with the logic, and purchased the one-way ticket to Bogotá.

When she arrived at the front of the line, she bent forward to expose her orange lace bra as she handed over her passport. The officer opened the passport and flicked his eyes from her cleavage to the open pages and handed it back to her with a wink.

She winked back, and put away the passport belonging to her sister-in-law, who was twenty years older and twenty pounds heavier. She had the next nine hours to consider whether the same ruse would work upon her arrival in Colombia.

*

Gina and Lenin lay on the floor in the narrow space between the bed and the wall, concealed under a blanket. They had hurriedly constructed the makeshift hideout when they had heard the container door open and multiple voices in the control room. When the gas turbine generator started, the voices were lost in the noise.

Eventually, Lenin peeled back the blanket. He crawled on his hands and knees to the door, carefully placing his ear against it. Gina took the remote control for the television and turned it on. There was a momentary blast of sound before Gina frantically hit mute.

The gunman winced when the blare from the bedroom's television ripped through the earphones he was wearing. "What was that?" he demanded.

Dennis slammed his palm against the console. "Sorry, I hit the wrong button."

The gunman looked around suspiciously and went to the studio door, opened it, turned the lights on, and looked around the small chamber. Finding nothing, he came back, sat down, and fixed his eyes back on the screen.

*

Father Serrano finished the prayer, cited the Holy Tribunal's jurisdiction, and announced that the court was in session to adjudicate the case of the apostate Martín Ibarra Paz.

A canon lawyer addressed the court from somewhere behind Martín, speaking with humility and great deference to Father Serrano. He gave a detailed rundown of conversations he'd had with the defendant just before the proceedings, including those confirming the crypto-Judaism of Martín's parents in Cuba. He revealed Martín's description of a silver menorah dating back to the time of his great-great-great-grandparents, offering it as presumptive evidence.

The lawyer called upon Father Serrano and the tribunal to accept Martín's heartfelt apology for his heresy, and pleaded on behalf of his client for the opportunity to publicly beg for God's infinite mercy and forgiveness, repent, and to be allowed back into the fold of His congregation.

*

Gina studied the remote control and carefully flipped from one channel to the next. Many displayed live footage from around San Juan Diego.

Lenin abandoned his attempt to listen through the door and turned to the television. When Gina changed the channel again and the screen displayed a man in a white-hooded robe seated at a white linen-draped table, Lenin whispered, "Leave it there."

Intense white light cascaded downward from directly above, shadowing the man's face under the hood. The camera panned out, revealing a man standing before the hooded figure with his back to the camera. He wore a large pointed hat and a yellow scapular that formed a long rectangle on his back. Red stripes ran from each corner of the rectangle, crossing in the middle. Graffiti-like writing was scrawled across the yellow material between the stripes.

A man appeared on screen dressed in a contemporary suit. He bowed, conveying with his body language a great deference to the hooded man seated at the table.

The man in the scapular turned toward the camera. His face, illuminated in bas relief by the bright overhead lights, filled the screen with an image like that of an Edvard Munch painting—rage stretching the mouth, bulging the eyes, engorging the veins, and cording the neck muscles.

At the same instant that Lenin realized who he was seeing, he heard a cry from behind him.

*

The gunman had just pulled the headset off his ears to tell Dennis to pause the video again when he heard a woman cry out in surprise from beyond the door to his left. He remained motionless for an instant, his eyes narrowing and locking on Dennis's, and then he sprang from his chair toward the door. Dennis reflexively reached out and grabbed the back of the gunman's shirt, and the man spun, jamming the gun barrel against Dennis's cheek. Dennis threw up his arms in immediate surrender. The gunman grabbed him by the collar and dragged Dennis toward the door, throwing it open and pushing Dennis into the bedroom. A young woman was sitting in the center of the bed with her eyes glued to the television screen. On the floor next to her stood an older bald man.

"All of you, against the wall!" the gunman shouted. Lenin put his hands up in immediate surrender and started edging back toward the far wall, but Gina remained on the bed, still looking up at the television.

"Get with the others—now!"

Gina tore her eyes from the TV, stared at the gunman's face, and slipped her legs over the edge of the bed.

"Nico," she said quietly.

"You know him?" Dennis asked.

Gina gestured at the television. "So, Nico. Where are you keeping your brother?"

*

Father Serrano requested the list of secret witnesses and read their testimonies of Martín Ibarra's heresy.

Martín experienced a floating sensation as if time were warping between the past and future. This was an ancient rite surreally taking place in a modern television studio. It was a relic of history predating his lifetime by centuries, and yet his life was now immersed in it.

He listened to the testimonies against him and wondered who, if anyone, might have made them. Some sounded eerily familiar—things he had heard said by family, friends, coworkers, interviewers—but phrases had been pulled from contexts he only vaguely remembered. He was jarred by one quotation that was unmistakably from a telephone conversation he'd had with Gina Ishikawa.

How long had these people been keeping him under constant surveillance? How could they know many of the things they seemed to know?

His mind hovered just beyond the ability to cognize what was happening to him. He had no meaningful vision, and the things he was hearing were impossible to fathom. All he wanted to do was to lie down and sleep, uninterrupted, until the pain throughout his body was gone. Even if that meant never waking up again.

*

"You've taken him," Gina said.

Nicolás nodded toward the television as he aimed his gun at Dennis.

"Are you blind? That's not my revolution! That's the bullshit I fight every day."

"He's right, Gina," Lenin said. "Those aren't communists."

"You I don't know," Nicolás growled. He swung his gun from Dennis to Lenin. "Who are you?"

"Doctor Teodoro Lenin."

"The historian?" Nicolás asked.

"The same." Lenin's mouth curled into a hint of a smile. He was always pleased when someone recognized him.

"You don't know shit about history, Lenin. Your bourgeois mentality saturates everything you do."

Lenin's slight smile melted into indignation. "My monograph on Marx remains one of the standards throughout Latin America, especially among the *educated* leftists."

"The limousine leftists," Nicolás retorted.

"At least I'm not some play actor prancing around, trying to pretend he's Che Guevara."

"Capitalist swill from a pampered, soft-handed dilettante. You wouldn't know—"

"What's happening to Martín?" Gina demanded.

Lenin and Nicolás glared at each other.

"Tell her," Nicolás said. "You may be a capitalist stooge, but I think even you have figured this one out."

Lenin nodded. "It seems that he is being tried by the Spanish Inquisition."

Nicolás turned the gun back on Dennis. "You said that this is happening right now, but that it isn't airing anywhere yet. Why?"

"No idea," Dennis said. "I guess they're saving it for later. Maybe it will be simulcast by a bunch of stations at some point. Hey, could you do me a favor and stop pointing that goddamn gun at me?" He gestured with his head at Gina and Lenin. "Seems like you're mates here. Maybe we can all relax a bit."

"His eyes," Gina murmured. "There's something wrong with his eyes."

Lenin and Nicolás both stared at the monitor.

Martín's eyes looked completely vacant and unseeing.

Nicolás sat with his back against the inside of the only door leading out of the container, caressing his pistol.

The video feed had ended with Martín being remanded to his cell to reflect and consider how he would plead for clemency before the court. Specifically, he was ordered to prepare a statement accepting the one true church into his life and asking for God's mercy that the purifying flame of the Fourth Angel might save his eternal soul.

Lenin, Gina, and Dennis sat in quiet contemplation. Finally, Dennis broke the silence. "You know," he said. "What we just saw on the telly kind of jibes with what I saw on the outside." He looked at Nicolás. "My shout for some grog?"

Nicolás gave him a resigned nod, and Dennis pulled a bottle of expensive cognac from a cabinet. He set four snifters on the table and began to pour.

"It's really something out there," Dennis said. "Everything is calm and pretty much normal. You know, going to work, kids in school, shopping in the markets. But the LU parliament is locked down, and there are—what would you call them?—monks, I guess is the best word, spreading out all over town. Rich neighborhoods, poor neighborhoods, middle-class areas. And I swear, they look like Friar Tuck right out of a bloody Robin Hood movie: shaved heads, sackcloth robes, sandals on their feet, the long cord at the waist."

"Do you know which religious order?" Lenin asked.

"Well, my Spanish isn't too hot, but I'd guess they're Dominicans—that's what I think I heard, anyway. But get this. With each of these monastic platoons that goes house to house encouraging people to go back to church is a guy in a black outfit with a truckload of attitude. If anybody blows off the happy fat guys during their pitch, ninja padre 'explains' things so they can understand it."

"And people are going to church?" Nicolás asked.

"Believe it. I don't know what those guys in black are telling everyone, but every church in the city is chockablock. There's three-hour queues to get into the confession booths. Masses run around the clock. And they've got capital. They're handing out crucifixes—heavy, ornate brass ones, telling people to hang them over their beds as a daily reminder of Christ in their lives. I talked to a guy from a newspaper in Santiago, and it's the same story there."

"These men in black, did anyone say anything about who they were?" Nicolás asked. "You said you thought they were Dominicans, but what's their authority?"

Dennis pulled out his phone and opened a file full of audio recordings. He clicked on one and they heard Dennis asking, "Look, these guys in black, uh, *hombres negro vestido*, who are they… *quien es?*"

The answer in Spanish came in a hurried and hushed staccato. "*Quienes son? Mira, gringo, guardas tu alma, y guardas tu culo. Son el Gestapo de Díos. Son de la Santa Oficina.*"

Dennis shrugged. "I have to admit I didn't really get all of that."

Gina spoke, translating. "Who are they? Look, stranger, watch out for your soul, and watch out for your ass. They're the Gestapo of God. They're the Holy Office."

Lenin sighed. "Nicolás, I fear that even the extremity of your paranoia might not have done justice to what the right-wing factions in Latin America have planned. The Church and the Spanish crown are set on a *reconquista* of their former colonies. If you'll let me open my email account, maybe I can prove it."

Nicolás took his last swig of cognac and waved the empty glass at his three captives. "Fine. But on the big screen, so I can see it."

With a few strokes, Dennis brought up a computer screen onto the television. He handed the keyboard to Gina, who pulled up the Quickmail web portal and then entered the new email account and password.

The mailbox popped up, and there were two emails. The first was a welcome message from Quickmail. But the second was from the email address abogadaflamenco@quickmail.com. Gina clicked on the email, and Alejandra's words filled the screen.

I have the documents and I am coming to you. Iberia Flight 004 to Bogotá. Trying to connect there to San Juan Diego. Will follow up with my next flight's information as soon as I have it. Please confirm that you have received this and will meet me at the airport.

"She got away!" Lenin exclaimed. "And she has my proof! Dennis, is there any way we can get someone you trust to meet her in Bogotá? The sooner she has an escort, the better."

Nicolás sat upright, his eyes narrowing. His right hand seemed to suddenly remember that it possessed a firearm, and it sprang upward and pointed the gun at Lenin. "You have forgotten yourself! We will not be contacting *anyone* outside of this container!"

Dennis held up his hands. "Let's all slow down here and take one thing at a time. First, Nicolás, can Gina send an email back to Alejandra that just says 'confirmed'? No codes, no distress call, just 'confirmed.'"

Nicolás thought for a moment, then reluctantly nodded.

Gina typed in the one-word response and sent the email while Nicolás watched.

"Good," Prinn continued, "Now before we make the next decision, I am going to write down the email address and the flight number so that we have it, and then you can delete the email from Alejandra as well as the one you just sent to her. Everything apples?"

Everyone else in the container nodded back at Dennis.

"Excellent. Then I am going to write everything down." Dennis picked up a sheet of scrap paper and a felt-tipped pen, looked up at the screen, and read out the information as he wrote it down. "Abogadaflamenco at Quickmail dot-com, and Iberia flight naught-naught-four."

Gina and Lenin locked eyes.

"Naught," Lenin said.

"Knotted," Gina said.

"Tied up," Lenin said.

"Zero," Gina finished.

Nicolás jumped to his feet, waving his gun. "What is all that?" he demanded. "It's some kind of code!"

"No, nothing like that," Lenin said. "Well, it *is* a code, but it has nothing to do with you."

"It may be the key to all of this," Gina said.

Nicolás began pacing in front of the exit door, looking like a cornered animal, wild in the eyes. "What are these tricks? Enough with the foolishness and games!"

"Nico, please listen," Gina said. "A friend of Martín's was doing legal research for someone in Spain. Something happened, and he had to get a message out to us. He left a coded message on Martín's voicemail. We think we finally just figured it out. If we have, we may be able to help your brother."

"Show me what you have," Nicolás said, lowering his gun.

Gina went into the bedroom and returned with the satchel full of documents and the stolen laptop. She rummaged through the papers, found one, and showed Nicolás a matrix written in pencil:

1	2	3	4	5	6	7	8	9
			Eagle	*Birdie*	*Eagle*	*Birdie*	*Bogey*	*Par*
Par 3	Par 4	Par 4	Par 3	Par 5	Par 4	Par 3	Par 4	Par 4
–	–	–	1	4	2	2	5	4
			Marty	Dave	Dave	Marty	Marty	M + D

Lenin took Dennis's felt-tip pen and leaned over, writing zeroes where the dashes had been, making the number 0-0-0-1-4-2-2-5-4.

"We think this is a code for a document that came from the research our friend David did in Spain with the girl who is now on the flight to Bogotá," Gina said.

"I think I know exactly which document this refers to," Lenin said, "but I need to go online."

Nicolás glared at him but waved with the barrel of the gun for Lenin to sit down at the console. "I'll be watching everything you do, and if you do anything I don't like, you're dead."

Lenin entered the URL, and the homepage for the Archive of the Indies came up on the screen. He clicked on the search function, entered 0-0-0-1-4-2-2-5-4, and waited.

*

Waro Moto sat crossed-legged at a low table. He was considering the balance of the character he had just brushed onto rice paper when an assistant discretely entered the office. On a signal from Moto the young man carefully placed a message in front of the magnate.

Failed to acquire asset in Zaragoza. Residence searched: no package. Reestablished contact: MAD. Asset confirmed Iberia 004 / Bogotá, Colombia. Probability package is with asset: extremely high.

Waro Moto looked up. "Notify our security team in San Juan Diego that they will be meeting a flight in Bogotá."

*

Lenin brought up a standardized research form. There were no cross-references cited, and the document had only been accessed one time previously. One name was next to the entry: David Broch. As Lenin had expected, the text was written in *procesal*.

"Who can read that shit?" Nicolás asked.

Gina also shook her head, recognizing only a date for the year 1487. The rest of the text was incomprehensible to her.

Lenin said nothing as he downloaded the document.

*

Nicolás had returned to his seat on the floor with his back against the entrance door while Lenin sat across from him, writing furiously as he translated the document from *procesal* to modern Spanish. He hadn't said a word for more than an hour. Finally he removed his glasses, carefully put them on the pile of papers, and rubbed his eyes.

"For years there were rumors of the existence of this document," he said. "Rumors at monasteries, whisperings in the royal courts, innuendoes from audits of the royal treasury."

He paused, seeming to savor the moment.

"It's all here," he said in a quiet, awed voice. "Lost all these centuries because it was supposed to have been destroyed. But someone put it in a file where it didn't belong."

He put his glasses back on and picked up the first page.

"This document was written by the notorious inquisitor Tomás de Torquemada. There is no telling what series of events brought it to the Archive of the Indies, which was for documents about colonial trade and governmental matters, not the Inquisition. Somehow David Broch found this, probably by accident. If you want, you can read it for yourself."

"Just give us the gist," Nicolás said.

"All right. The document is entitled 'The Fourth Angel,' referring to the book of Revelation in the Bible and the seven angels carrying the seven last plagues that would be turned loose on the world to prepare for the Second Coming of Christ. Torquemada fervently believed that the Spanish crown and church could, by joint action, bring about the millennium of rule by Christ by carrying out the steps set forth in Revelation.

"Each angel carries what the Bible calls a vial containing the wrath of God. The first angel's vial brought festering sores to those wearing the mark of the beast. The second turned the seas to blood, killing everything in them. The third angel turned the waters of rivers to blood.

"The fifth angel poured blood upon the throne of the beast, and the beast's kingdom was consumed by darkness. The sixth angel poured his vial on the Euphrates River, which dried it up. And the seventh angel emptied his vial into the air, an act that was followed by thunder, lightning, and the strongest earthquake the world had ever seen.

"But it was the fourth angel that had special meaning to the Inquisition. This angel poured his vial on the sun, and was given the power to scorch men with fire. Torquemada understood this passage to be justification for the Inquisition to burn heretics—to purify them. He and his fellow inquisitors believed that by burning people at the stake they were helping to bring on the rule of Christ.

"The Torquemada letter is addressed to King Fernando II to advise him to make plans for a time in the future when Spain would have rights and obligations beyond the peninsula—an empire, in other words. That was a remarkable prediction. Spain was still four years from forcing the Moors to surrender at Granada, and the country remained completely introverted, consumed by its own passion to eject Muslims and embroiled in fighting among its own regions. Spanish dominion over Sicily, Naples, Milan, and Flanders were more than 30 years in the future.

"But although Torquemada believed that Spain was destined to spread Christian sovereignty all over Europe and the world, he also warned Fernando II that they had to learn from past great civilizations—the Carthaginians, the Greeks, the Romans and so on. The eventual Spanish empire would likely also collapse and have to be rebuilt.

"Torquemada urged Fernando not just to think of his own reign, but to build a secret edifice that would stand for however many centuries it took to bring about the rule of Christ on earth. He counseled Fernando to take the largest sum of gold he could get from the royal treasury and from the *cortes*, the ruling councils of the regions and major cities, spirit it out of Spain, and place the treasure in an interest-bearing account in the free imperial city of Augsburg, convinced that the Germans would be more tight-lipped than the more famous bankers in Genoa and Florence.

"Torquemada's plan was to grow the initial capital and add frequent contributions that would be made through secret automatic transfers from the royal treasury. He also devised a detailed method of accounting that Fernando could use to hide the transfers of money from his own financial chancellors and the auditors from the *cortes*. As the crown became more and more impoverished, auditors checked more and more frequently how their king was spending public money.

"In the document Torquemada writes over and over again how vital it is that an absolute minimum number of clergymen know about the fortune, but at the same time, he had to make sure its existence would not be lost if some of those men died. The information had to be carried forward as kings and clerics were succeeded or died, and at the same time absolute secrecy had to be maintained. Anyone suspected of having seen this document who was not needed for the stratagem was to be killed. The couriers who carried the message, the accountant who set up the accounts—even the other members of the governing council of the Inquisition—were to be killed.

"This was to be a secret not only from the councils of the Spanish royal government, but also from the papacy in Rome. Torquemada arranged for three monks at three monasteries in Valladolid, Burgos, and Toribio de Liébana to be bound by a secret blood oath to never reveal the secret fund to anyone outside of their group. The monks were to always be men who had no other living family members and who were fanatically supportive of the doctrines of the Inquisition."

"Preposterous," Nicolás said. "You're suggesting they received a constant return on their deposits for more than 500 years? Capitalism is far too unstable. They would have been wiped out during the Thirty Years' War or in the aftermaths of the world wars. And if they weren't, you think these German bankers would release this immense fortune known only to them and a few murderous priests?"

"Maybe they diversified," Gina murmured.

"They figured something out, *vaquero*," Dennis said. "Their minions are swarming from Juárez to Tierra del Fuego."

"Anyway," Lenin said, annoyed to be interrupted in the middle of his lecture, "Torquemada referred to these 'murderous priests' as the Guardians of the Fourth Angel. The Guardians were prohibited from meeting in person, but each would receive detailed physical descriptions of the others, and they had to exchange letters every 15 days to keep the others informed that they were still alive. The contents of the letters were coded using a transposition of letters—"

"Enough," Nicolás said. "Get to the point."

Lenin took a deep breath. "I have to make some assumptions."

"Bullshit!" Nicolás shouted. "You told me this would absolutely prove your fairy tales."

"It's not a fairy tale," Lenin said. "I have strong evidence that both the Spanish king and the pope were appointed as a result of fraudulent machinations to restore the Hapsburgs to power. Now we also know that the Inquisition has returned. All so they can usher in Christ's return."

"Fairy tales," Nicolás repeated. "Three monks from Spain taking over the world."

"Three monks, the pope, the Spanish king, and billions—if not trillions—of dollars. And, by the way, a Japanese CEO who controls the entirety of the Latino Union's communications networks. Once they decided to strike, they were going to land a heavy blow."

"And why single out my brother?" Nicolás asked.

"He's the principal architect of the Latino Union capital and the ancestor of a famous Jewish family. Some interpretations of the book of Revelation say the conversion of Jews to Christianity is one of the preconditions to Christ's return."

"And if he converts, they'll let him go?" Gina asked.

Lenin looked at Gina and then dropped his eyes apologetically. "As they see it, Martín is stained by his family's false conversion to Christianity. Once he's said what they want—under duress of torture—they will show him 'mercy' by burning him alive at the stake. A cleansing by the Fourth Angel."

CHAPTER TWENTY-TWO

PROFESSOR OHI, AN expert in classical Spanish from the University of Tokyo, arrived at Moto Electric headquarters by helicopter. Thirty minutes earlier a company computer technician had broken the simple encryption of the document that had been transferred from the Archive of the Indies website to a computer in San Juan Diego, but the *procesal* that appeared on-screen baffled the company's translation staff.

The professor arrived wearing his pajamas and bathrobe, having been awakened in the middle of the night by a call from the university's president ordering him to board the helicopter that was inbound to the professor's house and lend all necessary assistance. In return, he would be paid a stipend for his "trouble." When the lifetime academic heard the amount of his stipend, all thoughts of protesting this sudden and unexpected reassignment vanished. On the other end of the line, the president thanked Ohi for his cooperation and hung up the phone. For his own "troubles" he was about to be granted a new state-of-the-art wing for the school of physics.

Professor Ohi was taken to a large office containing a bookcase stuffed with Spanish dictionaries that spanned an entire wall. He stared at them, taking them all in, and realized that the dictionaries covered all of the eras and dialects that Ohi could possibly name. This library of dictionaries was supplemented by a computer with bookmarks for a large and diverse repository of online Spanish language resources. Curious, he typed in the URL for Google, then YouTube, and concluded that he had been blocked from the rest of the internet.

Ohi looked around at his surroundings—opulent beyond his wildest dreams—and let out a short breath of disbelief and wonder. He put his hands on the keyboard, brought up the first page of the document, and squinted at the first line of curling cursive. On a yellow pad of paper, he carefully penned the Japanese characters for "The Fourth Angel."

*

"Mr. Ibarra—" Lenin started to say, but Nicolás cut him off.

"Everyone—even capitalists—calls me Nico."

"Okay then, Nico. There are two things we have to do, and fast. One, we have to meet the young woman flying into Bogotá in a few hours, and two, we have to figure out where Martín is—before the Inquisition makes an example of him."

Lenin expected Nicolás to vehemently protest. Instead he just sat in his chair and stared into space.

"Did you hear me?" Lenin asked. "We have to act now to get the proof of this conspiracy." Lenin's voice softened as he realized that Nicolás's face was contorted with anguish. "What is it, Nico? What's troubling you?"

The gray-haired man looked up at Lenin. "I'm not saying I believe anything you've said, but in this scenario of yours, do you see any reason for the new Inquisition to… manipulate my revolution?"

Lenin thought for a moment. "As Orwell wrote, totalitarian governments seek to unite their subjects via a common enemy."

"Before I left camp, my co-leader in the movement was acting strangely—always going off by herself. At this moment she is in complete charge of the army I left behind. And now you are telling me, professor, that the communist revolutionary force I spent my lifetime building and guiding may be taking orders from a theocracy funded by the fortunes of kings."

Lenin remained silent. Nicolás balled his fists in rage.

*

Three Lexus automobiles stopped at a Mitsubishi Emerald corporate jet at the San Juan Diego airport, and eight Japanese men and one woman got out and walked quickly up the passenger stairs into the airplane. As the last of the passengers disappeared into the fuselage, the stairs folded up automatically, and the door was closed and sealed. The pilot immediately called ground control to get clearance to depart for Bogotá's El Dorado Airport.

*

After gaining Nicolás's permission, Lenin used Dennis's computer to Google that day's flights from San Juan Diego to Bogotá.

"There's a flight leaving San Juan Diego in an hour and a half, and it will arrive before the Iberia flight touches down. To get on it, I have to leave right now. There won't be another flight for five hours."

Nicolás stared at the tabletop as he clicked the safety of his gun on and off.

"Nico, did you hear what I said? I have to go *now*."

Nicolás set the pistol down. "They're going to make me a martyr—a perversion of the legacy of Che Guevara." He slumped in his chair, pointedly looking away from Lenin. "They've stolen my revolution out from under me, but perhaps I can save my brother. Doctor Lenin, you are not going anywhere. Prinn, we have to make a recording."

*

Nicolás dialed the number Gina had given him. Dennis had taken several countermeasures in order to minimize the risk that the device's location would be traceable by the call's recipient, but he fidgeted nervously nonetheless.

"Hello?" a man answered.

"President Ishikawa, this is Nicolás Ibarra. I will be brief. I know your daughter is still alive and I have her. My revolution demands an act of submission to our authority, or many innocent people will die. Iberia Airlines Flight 004 is two hours out of its destination, Bogotá. You will divert that flight to San Juan Diego immediately or else a bomb that has been placed on the plane will be detonated, killing all on board. At the same time, your daughter will be executed and her body publicly displayed. A video has been delivered to the San Juan Diego studios of the Latino Union's state television network. It will authenticate that I have Gina. It will also give you additional instructions. I am monitoring communications to and from the airliner. Goodbye."

Nicolás ended the call just as the man on the other end let out a distressed cry.

"Well, professor," Nicolás said, "the die has been cast."

*

Takeshi Ishikawa sat in front of the television in his private office. This was the third time he had watched the video.

Nicolás Ibarra did indeed have Gina, and in a quiet, reasonable voice Nicolás had ordered the LU president to divert the Iberia 747 to San Juan Diego where it was to land and then park on a taxiway just off of runway 18 right, which abutted a forest. The moment the aircraft stopped the doors were to be opened and the inflatable slides deployed. All passengers were to be quickly evacuated and ordered to run into the forest, not stopping until they could no longer see the airplane. If any soldiers were spotted anywhere at the airport or in the forest, Nicolás insisted that the bomb would be detonated before the passengers were evacuated. He also stated that if there were any aircraft overhead within fifty nautical miles of the airport, the plane and passengers would be destroyed. One by one Nicolás identified and forbade any possible methods of intervention.

Ishikawa's chief of military staff reluctantly concurred with the president that there was no option but to comply and to deploy troops into the forest to hunt down Nicolás and any others who might be with him. Ishikawa asked about the probabilities of success, and his advisers conceded that they were slim.

Ishikawa picked up his phone and made two calls. First he ordered the LU television network to run a specific ten-second clip of one of his speeches to the LU congress during the on-the-hour newscast. This was the signal that Nicolás had required for the president to acknowledge that he was complying with the revolutionary's demands.

Next the president called his military command center, which then patched the president via the Iberia Airlines company to the pilot of Flight 004.

Alejandra Rojas looked up when the plane's intercom clicked on.

"Ladies and gentlemen," the pilot said, "a minor technical situation has arisen, and we are diverting to San Juan Diego as a precaution. There is absolutely no cause for alarm, although I apologize for the inconvenience. As we approach the airport, your flight attendants will give you additional information and instructions."

Alejandra gnawed her knuckle as she felt the aircraft bank into a turn.

Dennis made a call to Switzerland.

"Colsen Transport Services."

"I want to leave a message for Captain Dubronski. Notify him immediately that a caller has said 'Bugle.' I'll wait on the line for a reply."

"Bugle," a man said two minutes later.

"Four niner," Dennis said, "break, one, zero, zero, break, four, break, break, five, six, two, five, break, null, break, null."

"Standby." Ten seconds passed, and then came the response, "One six."

Dennis hung up the phone without another word.

"We've got transport," he told Nicolás. "Four hours from now." Dennis began bustling around the container securing items, disconnecting cables, and locking cabinet doors.

"How are we traveling?" Gina asked.

Dennis paused to smirk at her and give her a conspiratorial wink. "Believe me, it'll be big. You and Lenin just stay put. You'll feel some thumping and bumping when the container is picked up, and it'll be delivered to the airport and loaded into an aircraft. Don't worry about it, just sit tight and Bob's your uncle."

Gina spontaneously gave Dennis a bear hug. He blushed.

"What the hell is that for?"

"I know what abandoning your post is going to do to your business, Dennis. The networks are going to be furious, and I know that your unblemished record of reliability is your biggest point of pride. It... it means a lot to me."

"Ah, hell, Gina. The way I see it is that once Nico got here I was heading out of San Juan Diego one way or another. At least this way it's on the right side of the ledger." In a clumsy effort to diffuse the emotional moment, Dennis reached out and mussed the top of Gina's hair. "We all knew that this tin can's days were numbered. Hell, people can do live reporting from their bloody phones these days! Maybe it's the kick in the arse I needed. I do feel bad about letting down the networks, though."

There was a pregnant pause as both Gina and Dennis processed the fact that he was sabotaging the only career he had ever known.

Dennis suddenly brightened. "Course, it helps that most of those guys are total wankers! I wish I could see some of their faces when they get on the horn and can't find me anywhere!"

Gina laughed, gave Dennis another hug, and let him get on with the business of packing up his rig.

*

"What does this woman look like?" Nicolás asked. "How will she be dressed? Anything that would help us identify her."

"I've never seen her," Lenin said. He coughed. "All I really know is that she's a flamenco dancer. Based on the amount she charged to my credit card, I would bet she's in first class. That would mean she should be exiting from one of the slides at the front of the aircraft."

Nicolás thought for a moment. "Dennis, do you have a portable amplifier?"

Dennis pulled open a large box and began rummaging. After some muttered curse words, he extracted an electric megaphone. "I can charge it on the drive."

Nicolás nodded in satisfaction. "When the time comes, I'll need your phone."

Dennis grinned. "You bet. Alright, my revolutionary *compadre,* time's a-wasting! Let's go." He pulled the final circuit breaker, blacking out the container, and closed the door behind him as he and Nicolás departed.

*

Waro Moto burst into the room filled with young men working at a conference table that was buried beneath stacks of papers. He ordered all of them out except for his chief of staff.

"What do you know about this diversion of the Iberia flight?" he demanded.

"President Ishikawa ordered it, talking to the pilot himself. He said there is a bomb on board."

"Who controls the bomb?" Moto asked.

"Nicolás Ibarra, according to the president."

Moto made a deep growling sound in his throat. "And do I understand correctly that there was a phone call placed that was routed through the same IP address of the computer that downloaded the Archive document?"

"Yes, sir. We were able to isolate the audio. It was Dennis Prinn."

"Of course it was Prinn. What did he *say*?"

The young assistant withered under Moto's glare. "A series of numbers, sir. A code. We don't know what it means."

"You say he called a transport company in Switzerland?"

"Yes, sir. In Geneva. They broker heavy cargo lifts, chartering specialized aircraft. Lockheed Hercules, the cargo version of the 747, and the Russian AN 124. He told the receptionist to contact a Captain—" He consulted a note— "Dubronski. He used the word 'Bugle.'"

Moto frowned. "More code."

"We are working on it, sir, and finding out who Dubronski is."

"I want men watching that container every minute. It's the key to all of this." Moto looked up at the ceiling and frowned, pondering for a few moments. Then he looked back at his chief of staff, who was anxiously awaiting Moto's next words.

"What has Professor Ohi turned up?" Moto asked.

"He has almost completed the translation. The document was written by Tomás de Torquemada. He was the—"

"I know who he was."

"Yes, sir. The document is called 'The Fourth Angel' and it is a detailed plan to build a vast fortune to be used to reinstate the Inquisition, and to build a Hapsburg dynasty. Very intricate, and—"

"Have him complete the translation, and then kill him," Moto said.

The subordinate bowed deeply. "Yes, sir."

*

Gina was almost asleep in the bed when she heard a diesel engine approaching. There were a series of noises outside, and the container started to move. One end tilted up, and after a brief cacophony of metal screeching on metal, the box returned to a stable, horizontal position. Gina and Lenin felt acceleration beneath them as the truck they had just been loaded onto departed.

CHAPTER TWENTY-THREE

TAKESHI ISHIKAWA PICKED up the phone on the first ring.

Without salutation Waro Moto said, "Events are getting out of control."

Anger welled up in Ishikawa, but he suppressed it. "No," the president said calmly. "I am in control."

"Why did you order the plane to San Juan Diego?" Moto asked.

"If I refused, Nicolás Ibarra says he has the means to blow it up."

"So what? The blame would fall on terrorists."

"There are over three hundred passengers, Moto-san. And he has threatened to kill my daughter. He has her. I have seen video of her being held by him."

"Ishikawa, you seem unable to grasp the obvious here. I don't yet know the specifics about how this came to be, but Nicolás Ibarra is now working with Lenin to get to a Spanish passenger on the flight that you have so kindly diverted at Ibarra's command. I believe that this Spanish woman has information that will be extremely damaging to our cause. And if Lenin is there in San Juan Diego, then your daughter is also. In case you have forgotten, she has suspicions of your involvement in all of this."

"And yours, too," the president said. Moto had shown no surprise upon hearing that Gina was still alive. Ishikawa mentally bookmarked this fact, but did not raise it.

"My companies and I will survive. You will not survive politically. In any case, Gina is not a hostage—she's part of their plan."

Upon hearing it expressed bluntly, Ishikawa realized this had to be true. Before he could conjure up a response, Moto said, "Get Ibarra on the phone."

"I have no way of doing so."

"Is he monitoring the aircraft radio frequencies?"

"Of course."

"Call the pilot and order him to Bogotá. If Ibarra blows it up—and I do not believe that he has the capability to do so—we will have our scapegoat. If this was a bluff, we will have called it and the woman will land many miles from Ibarra's grasp."

Ishikawa said nothing.

"Do it now," Moto barked. "I want to listen while you make the call, Ishikawa-*kun*." Moto put a sneering emphasis on the honorific of inferiority.

Takeshi Ishikawa sat motionless, stewing in his hatred for the monstrous man on the other end of the line and cursing himself for his involvement with him. His mind raced through the possible scenarios: this Spanish woman reaching Nicolás Ibarra and somehow teaming up with Teodoro Lenin and his own daughter, exposing the financial connection between himself and Waro Moto. The Latino Union would be destroyed, and all the member countries destabilized. Governments could fall, riots would break out, and thousands would die. This, in sharp contrast to the lives of a few hundred on the airliner.

Potential lives, he reminded himself. Although Ishikawa had no doubt that Ibarra had the means to carry out such an attack, particularly given his new connections within the global terrorist community, there was at least a chance that this was a bluff.

But what if it wasn't? Ishikawa weighed the outcomes. A momentary tragedy forgotten within a few months, or years of anarchy? Political expediency for the benefit of millions, or humanitarian morality, unrewarded and soon forgotten, for a few hundred? He knew that there was only one choice.

He slowly picked up another phone and told the military command center to patch him to the Iberia plane. In a moment, he heard the pilot say, "Yes, Mr. President?"

"Captain Santiago, there has been a change. You are ordered to continue on to Bogotá."

"What, Mr. President? Say again?"

"I said continue your flight to Bogotá. Ibarra has changed his orders. If you land in San Juan Diego, he will destroy the aircraft."

The pilot's voice rose several octaves. "Mr. President, I don't have enough fuel to reach Bogotá now. We burned too much diverting to San Juan Diego. Ibarra, I know you are monitoring this channel—you have to understand it is not possible for me to break off this landing and make it to Bogotá! Please, I beg you, let me land!"

*

From their makeshift dugout bunker in the forest that ran alongside Runway One-Eight's Echo taxiway, Nicolás Ibarra and Dennis Prinn peered through the canopy, anxiously awaiting the Iberia 747. Nicolás's portable radio was lying on the ground between the two men, and he grimaced with intensity as he listened through earbuds. Dennis looked back and forth from the sky to Nicolás's face, trying to read the situation as it developed. Nicolás spat out a curse and grabbed his radio out of the dirt. He quickly changed the radio to the approach control frequency, hearing the controller acknowledging that Iberia 004 was over the outer marker, inbound, and nine miles from touchdown. Nicolás clicked back to the Iberia company channel, put the radio to his mouth, and keyed the microphone.

"Iberia 004, this is Nico Ibarra. I don't know what President Ishikawa is trying to pull, but I have not changed my orders. You are to land at San Juan Diego. I say again, land at San Juan Diego or I will blow up the plane."

"Captain Santiago," Ishikawa responded, "I order you to ignore that impostor on the radio and continue to your original destination."

"Goddamn it, what the hell is going on?" Captain Santiago shouted. "I must continue the approach, Mr. President. We are out of options!"

Nicolás keyed his microphone again. "Do it, Santiago. Land at San Juan Diego, or I'll blow it."

There was a pause, and Nicolás listened to the crackle of dead air, waiting. It was Ishikawa's voice that came next, measured and severe.

"Captain Santiago, I'm ordering an LU fighter to intercept you. If you try to land, you will be destroyed."

"What?" Santiago shouted. "You'll be doing the work of the terrorists! I have to land *now!*"

*

Sweat poured down Captain Raúl Santiago's face as he looked desperately at his first officer, José Dominguez.

An F-35 streaked across the 747's nose, shaking the airliner with its jet wash. From behind the pilots, cries of alarm and terror emanated from the passenger cabin. Dominguez reached over with his left hand and shoved the throttles forward. The previously idling engines rumbled back to life.

"Iberia 004 executing a missed approach!" he transmitted to approach control.

Santiago reached over and slapped away the first officer's hand, slamming the throttles back to partial power. Dominguez jerked on the control yoke, and Santiago fought desperately to offset the first officer's control inputs.

Santiago keyed his microphone using the button on the yoke. "San Juan Diego approach, disregard that last message—Iberia 004 is continuing the approach!"

Just behind the battling captain and first officer, sitting in the 747 cabin's jump seat, was a third pilot. Sergio Gómez had boarded Iberia's Flight 004 looking forward to a relaxing trip as he deadheaded his way back to Bogotá, where his home and family awaited. He knew the two men in command of the aircraft well, and once the flight was airborne and at cruising altitude the men had chatted amicably. Eventually Gómez had left the cockpit, stretching his legs for a bit during the 12-hour flight. He had even been able to nap for a while in the crew compartment.

When Gómez returned to the cockpit to check in with his colleagues, everything had changed. He donned a headset, listening with growing alarm and dismay to the improbable series of radio calls pinging back and forth on the company's channel.

Why this flight? Gomez thought. *Why now?*

And then things had gotten immeasurably worse as the two men in front of him began wrestling for control of the 400-ton aircraft.

Gómez's eyes frantically flicked back and forth between the two pilots. He reached a decision.

From his flight bag he pulled a long socket wrench and swung it as hard as he could.

*

Nicolás was shouting into his radio. He had run to the edge of the forest with Dennis on his heels and locked his binoculars onto the distant landing lights of the 747. The lights veered left and right, then up and down. It was buzzed by what looked to be an American-made F-35, a late-stage capitalism boondoggle of a fighter plane fully idealizing the bourgeois pretensions of the Latino Union.

With a thundering roar the F-35 shot across the nose from the other direction. The airliner's nose dropped, came up again, and leveled. As Nicolás watched, it seemed to stabilize on the glide slope, and the engines wound up to a steady whine. He adjusted the binoculars slightly and saw the fighter rolling in behind the Iberia plane.

"The bastard's actually going to shoot them down!"

*

Pilot Jorge Chavez was monitoring all the radio chatter from the cockpit of his F-35 when the call came in.

"Shoot it down," he was told. The passenger plane had been seized by a terrorist and needed to be destroyed before it could endanger civilian lives. The LU's president did not want another 9/11 on his hands.

Jorge protested, noting that the 747 was clearly on final approach to the San Juan Diego airport. In fact, other than a few seconds where the plane had jerked wildly in the sky, the approach had been textbook and the pilots had followed approach control's instructions to the letter.

"You have your orders, Lieutenant!" barked his commanding officer. "This is way above your pay grade. Do it!"

Chavez swung the fighter around and leveled it on the jumbo jet's six o'clock. In front of him, the enormous civilian passenger jet's landing gear sprouted from its undercarriage, just as it should.

Madness. This was absolute madness. He suspected that his military career was over no matter what his decision was—either as the scapegoat for a downed civilian aircraft, or the man who disobeyed direct orders from the president of the LU.

He decided that he could live with one of those outcomes.

Fuck it, he thought. *Let's at least make it a damned good show.*

Chavez clicked some softkeys on the weapons computer, keyed his joystick, and let the missiles fly.

*

The airliner's landing lights gleamed less than a mile from the end of the runway, and close to the ground. The navigation lights on the fighter were behind it and coming up fast. Nicolás saw a flash as two air-to-air missiles ignited on the rails under the fighter's wing.

Nicolás dropped his arms in despair and disbelief. There was no point in transmitting anything to the doomed 747 pilots now. He watched the missiles' smoky trails track toward the giant airliner, and he braced for the enormous explosion that was about to occur in the sky above him.

And then the missiles streaked past the Iberia jetliner and raced onward, undetonated. The lumbering behemoth airliner, still intact, continued its steady descent toward the runway. The missiles, now clear of their assumed target, raced forward and for a terrible moment Nicolás thought that he and Prinn had been duped. He looked on helplessly, waiting for the missiles to alter their trajectories and arc toward the edge of the forest where he and Prinn now stood. There would be no time for them to react if that happened, and this is where it would all end for him.

Obliterated into nothingness because of an old professor's crazy theories, he thought.

But as the missiles reached the threshold of the runway, they leveled off about 15 meters above the ground, rocketed on for another moment, and then violently dipped in near-perfect unison, impacting the runway simultaneously with flaming explosions that rose up together in a glowing cloud. A split-second later Nicolás and Dennis winced as they felt a wave of dissipating heat reach them.

Nicolás looked up and saw the 747 jerk uncertainly from side to side as it approached the threshold. Nicolás wasn't a pilot, but based upon the rate of descent, the giant plane looked like it had no choice but to land.

Nicolás heard the engine power throttle back and watched the 747's landing lights plunge toward the ground. A shower of sparks glittered in the night as the landing gear ripped through the high-intensity approach lights aligned on the runway's threshold. The fighter screamed over the top of the airliner and then shot almost straight upward, pulling away from the carnage.

The Iberia jumbo jet dumped onto the runway, the tires shrieking as they slammed into the concrete. Two tires had been punctured by the approach lights and flapped wildly as they spun. The plane thundered down the tarmac toward the smoldering hole.

"Come on, Prinn," Nicolás yelled. "We've got to be there when it stops!"

The two men sprinted down the taxiway.

*

Captain Santiago desperately worked the rudder, trying to steer the 747 around the crater where the missiles had exploded in front of him. How he and the other souls on board this flight were still alive, and not vaporized, he had no idea, but he had no time to ruminate on it as the plane's enormous size and momentum propelled it relentlessly down the runway. As the brakes smoked in protest, Santiago managed to pivot the plane just enough so that the nose gear missed the hole. For an instant, Santiago thought perhaps he'd managed to successfully clear the ruined portion of the tarmac, but then he felt the plane lurch to the left as his landing gear caught the edge of the crater and smashed through it.

Santiago was sure that the gear had been ripped off as the wing dipped downward and made contact with the runway, spewing sparks as passengers shrieked. He glanced to the right, seeing Dominguez's blood drying on the windscreen from when Gómez had brought his wrench crashing down on the first officer's head.

Santiago tried the nose wheel steering, but knew it was useless at this point. The giant plane was skidding off the left side of the runway and into the grass, portions of which had already ignited into small patches of flame from the missile blast. He glimpsed a line of flashing lights as emergency vehicles emerged onto the taxiway, rushing toward the distressed aircraft. The nose slowly pivoted to the left until the plane was facing directly east, perpendicular to the runway.

Finally, it stopped.

The captain's training kicked in and he instinctively followed procedure and punched a switch to pop all the doors open and deploy the inflatable slides.

*

Nicolás and Dennis raced up to the airliner that loomed above them in the darkness. It was completely off the runway, into the grass, and listing heavily to the left. Emergency vehicles honked and shrieked, their spotlights flashing back and forth along the fuselage. Nicolás ran toward the front of the plane where a slide now stretched from the open door. A flight attendant stood in the door, calling instructions on a bullhorn. A large, balding man in a business suit was the first to jump onto the slide. Because the plane lay on its left wing instead of standing upright on the landing gear, the slide was at a shallow slope, and the businessman scooted slowly and awkwardly down its length. A woman jumped into it next, slender but older than Nicolás was looking for.

He glanced around as three men in firefighter uniforms rushed up, their attention focused on the aircraft and the passengers spilling to the ground from each of the five emergency exits. Nicolás, in an effort to blend in and secure Alejandra, helped the woman from the slide. Another woman followed her onto the slide, much younger this time, but in a conservative suit.

Nicolás looked around and saw there were more than 50 passengers already on the ground, milling around the base of the slides. An officer of the emergency crew was shouting through a bullhorn, ordering the passengers to move well away from the airliner and into the wooded area next to the runway. They looked around in confusion, reluctant to move toward the woods and into the darkness.

Nicolás began to panic. What if she went out a different exit? How would he find her among all these people? A man was now on the first-class slide with two more men waiting at the door for their turn. Nicolás looked around again at the forming crowd and stopped abruptly when he saw four Japanese men come into the lighted perimeter of the rescue effort. They were peering into the faces of the female passengers on the ground, grabbing them and roughly turning their faces into bright flashlights. It was clear that they didn't know exactly what Alejandra looked like either, as he noted that they were demanding to see the passport of each young woman they found.

Nicolás grabbed the bullhorn out of Dennis's hands and slapped Dennis's chest with his other hand, feeling for his phone in his breast pocket. He yanked it out, pressed the voice recognition button on the search engine, and spoke into the mic. The phone chirped, then located what Nicolás was looking for. From the phone's speaker came a few tentative guitar chords, and a tapping of heels. The guitar increased in intensity, and Nicolás clicked on the bullhorn and held the phone next to it. The strains of "La Malagüeña" blared forth, cutting through the sirens and shouts.

The guitar swelled, and the furious *taconazo* thundered. Nicolás weaved between the passengers, turning his head away when he bumped into one of the Japanese men, who stopped and briefly stared quizzically at the man wandering around with his phone pressed to a bullhorn.

A tall woman with black hair down to her waist wearing an orange silk blouse and a yellow and green cotton skirt whipped her head around. Nicolás saw her reaction and hurried over.

"Alejandra?"

She nodded.

"Come with me now! I am with the professor."

Nicolás grabbed her hand and made for the woods. Dennis scrambled after them.

"*Yameru!*" someone shouted, and broke into a run.

"Are you Nicolás Ibarra?" Alejandra asked as they headed away from the plane and into the darkness.

"You know me?"

"I have a poster of you in my dorm room." She smiled as she effortlessly sprinted next to the revolutionary. "My roommate hates it!"

They ran across the grass separating the runway from the taxiway. Nicolás checked over his shoulder for the Japanese men, who were about 200 meters behind them. Branches whipped their faces as they entered the forest. Nicolás took a step that failed to find the ground and he pitched headlong into a shallow ravine. Alejandra and Dennis tumbled down after him. When they came to rest Nicolás put his index finger to his lips, and they both nodded.

In the distance he could still hear the bawling sirens of the rescue vehicles. Much closer, he heard men thrashing in the forest. Nicolás rose to a crouch and headed down the ravine, motioning for Alejandra and Dennis to follow. Blinding searchlight beams sliced through the blackness from helicopters above, hunting relentlessly for the three figures below.

*

Waro Moto knelt at a tiny table in front of him, carefully penning Japanese characters on rice paper, using the calligraphy taught to him by a master of the art. His eyebrow went up slightly when he heard a sound emanating from beyond the paper sliding door that served as the entryway to his room. He made a small grunt, and the door slid open less than an inch.

"Please excuse me, sir. Prinn's container has been picked up from the presidential compound. A drayage company called Sanchez Hermanos collected it 20 minutes ago. The bill of lading presented to the security guard said it is being taken to the San Juan Diego airport for air transport."

"To what destination?"

"Manila."

Moto carefully penned another character. "Have our research department prepare a briefing paper within the next half-hour on anything that might be relevant in the Philippines right now. Also, have our people call you as soon as the container arrives at the airport."

"Yes, sir."

*

Lenin and Gina sat in the blackness of the windowless container.

"Is there any hope for Martín?" Gina asked.

"It's a foregone conclusion that he will be found guilty. Then—and I think it's a good bet they will remain true to history—they'll stage an *auto-de-fé*."

"But where?"

"If I wanted to make a historical comeback have maximum effect on the population of the Latino Union and the uncommitted countries," Lenin said, "I would do it in accordance with historical precedent."

"Mexico City," Gina whispered in the darkness.

"Yes," the professor of history said.

They both held their breaths as they heard the distant whining of jet aircraft engines.

*

The Antonov An-124 is the largest cargo aircraft in the world. It was a product of the Antonov Design Bureau, part of the Soviet government, and went into service in 1985 with the NATO designation of "Condor." After the breakup of the Soviet Union, a cash-hungry government made the military transports, complete with crews of up to 20 men, available for charter by freight brokers specializing in heavy cargo airlift.

Dennis Prinn had chartered 124s several times to fly his containerized television ground station to various points of the world. He had chartered through Colsen Transport Services of Zurich several years earlier, shipping his container to Hargeysa, Somalia, to set up a television relay station under the employ of networks in Europe and North America who were fearful of sending their own employees into the war-torn country.

The aircraft's commander was Captain Dubronski. After landing at the Somali airstrip, Dennis had found antipersonnel mines stowed in large crates of powdered milk. When he accused Dubronski of using the humanitarian mission as an excuse to engage in arms smuggling, Dubronski ordered his crew to load the pallets back on the plane. When a Russian civilian tried to stop them, Dubronski smashed his meaty fist into the man's jaw and left him lying on the tarmac.

As he had flexed his bruised hand, Dubronski thanked Dennis for making the discovery and insisted from that day on that if Dennis ever needed help without any explanation, he should call Colsen Transport and simply utter the word "Bugle."

"Bugle?" Dennis had asked.

"*Da.* We're on the damned horn of Africa."

*

At the San Juan Diego airport, Dubronski took the packet of shipping documents from the drayage driver. He sat on the end of the cargo ramp with his legs dangling, reading through the stamped papers. The enclosed bill of lading, cargo insurance policy, packing slip, and invoice all said that the communications center was to be airlifted by Colsen Transport to Manila, Philippines. Dubronski tore open another sealed envelope and found a handwritten note.

> *Bugle:*
> *No questions, no lies. See you soon.*
> *Dennis*

Dubronski's crew efficiently pushed the container off the carrier and rolled it toward the front of the plane where the entire cockpit area yawned open at a 90-degree angle from the ground, revealing the enormous cargo compartment inside.

Four Latino Union customs officials came on board before the container was tied down. Looking frequently at their clipboards, they thumped the metal sides of the container with their fists. When one of them came to the door, he motioned for Dubronski to open it. The Russian used his key from the envelope on the padlock, opened the door, and the inspector stepped inside, turning on his flashlight.

The inspector played his light beam on the console for several seconds. He turned right and tried the door. It opened, and he stepped in and looked around the tiny studio with its blue wall. Dubronski stood beside him and casually said, "General Velasco sends his regards."

The inspector regarded him for a moment. "My uncle. You know him?"

The pilot twisted his index and middle finger together.

The inspector returned to the control room, walked across to the other side, and stood with his hand on the door to the bedroom. He opened it, made a show of turning off his flashlight as he pointed it around the room, snapped it back on, and closed the door.

The inspector came out of the container, followed by Dubronski. "I'll give your regards to my uncle," the inspector said, and they were gone.

Dubronski turned toward the flight deck ladder but was blocked by two muscular Japanese men wearing suits. One of them bowed slightly. "Excuse, please. Where will you be taking the container of Prinn?"

Dubronski chuckled. "There's a flight plan on file, gentlemen."

"Ah, yes. Manila," the slightly taller of the two men said. The shorter of the two men produced a pistol from inside his suit jacket and pointed it at Dubronski. The Russian glanced over his shoulder and saw six more Japanese men standing in the cargo compartment with machine pistols aimed at the other Russian crewmembers.

"We will accompany you to Manila," the taller man said. He reached into his suit jacket and produced a manifest confirming them as employees of a Japanese textile company and official passengers of the flight.

Dubronski looked over the manifest and gave the spokesman a sardonic smile. "Looks like everything's in order, gentlemen. Now, if you'd excuse me and my crew, we have a plane to fly."

"To Manila," the spokesman said levelly.

"*Da*, to Manila," Dubronski answered with exasperation. "Where else?"

Dubronski ordered his men to their crew positions, and they went through the engine start checklist as the Japanese men shadowed them, their weapons still drawn. One of them slipped on a headset and took a position in the rear of the cockpit. "I am monitoring everything," he said in passable Russian, "and one of my team members will be in the jump seat. He is a pilot and is certified on five models of transport aircraft, including this one. Do not try anything."

Lieutenant Zharinov, the copilot, exchanged a glance with Dubronski and radioed ground control. The response came, "Colsen One One, runway heading, San Juan Diego two departure, climb and maintain flight level four-four-zero, squawk two-four-five-one, contact Departure on one-two-five point three."

Zharinov radioed back, repeating the instructions that he had just written on a paper on his kneeboard. He heavily underlined the altitude of 44,000 feet, glancing at the Japanese man in the jump seat and eyeballing Dubronski, who momentarily met his eyes and then looked away.

*

When the enormous aircraft had finished lumbering through the taxiways and onto the runway, the tower cleared the Antonov for takeoff. Dubronski pushed the throttles forward until the columns of engine instruments indicated the correct power settings and the cargo plane slowly, almost reluctantly, began rolling forward. As it gained momentum, the Japanese man in the jump seat sat with his eyes glued on the instruments, watching for anything out of the ordinary. The aircraft's speed continued to increase, and after hearing Zharinov call out "rotation," Dubronski gently pulled back on the yoke, lifting the giant plane off the runway. Departure control instructed them to turn to the south, and the Japanese pilot scanned the engine and flight instruments as they complied with the instructions. The cargo plane climbed steadily, received a new vector toward the west, and continued flying over the coast.

Zharinov signed off with departure control and dialed the radio knobs to tune in the regional air traffic control center that they had been assigned to.

"Colsen One One, Lima Center," the radio squealed. "Heading two seven zero, passing one zero thousand for flight level four four zero, squawk one-eight-zero-zero, resume normal navigation, good evening."

"Good evening," Dubronski replied and then clicked off the radio. He glanced back at his captor, who was still sitting rigidly in the jump seat, gun drawn and eyes fixed on the navigational instruments. Dubronski rolled his eyes, yawned, and made a show of leafing through his checklist book. "Crew, pilot, cruise altitude oxygen check in two minutes," he said over the intercom in a bored voice.

Zharinov looked over at his captain, who was removing his oxygen mask from its hook on the back of his seat, slipping the band over his head, and placing the rubber cone over his mouth and nose. The copilot and the flight engineer did the same. The Japanese pilot in the jump seat eyed the pilots warily, but said nothing.

"Navigator, Pilot, visual check on flight crew and report," Dubronski said.

Lieutenant Vilov, the navigator, sat motionless for a moment, then unstrapped from his seat and headed for the ladder to the cargo compartment. One of the Japanese men on the flight deck made a show of cocking his pistol and followed him.

Vilov climbed down and walked around the cargo compartment. The Russian crewmen and the Japanese watched him closely. The chief loadmaster donned his oxygen mask, and the navigator gave a slight nod. The deadhead crewmen did the same.

Vilov plugged his headset into a panel at the forward bulkhead and transmitted, "Pilot, navigator, crew positions checked."

"Roger," came the reply. "Confirm oxygen flow."

Each crewmember flipped a lever on his oxygen panel, and feeling the cone-shaped masks pressurize, reported a positive flow.

On the flight deck, Dubronski leaned to his right over the throttle console between him and his copilot and pointed to the oxygen pressure indicator on the copilot's panel.

"That's indicating low," he said over the headset. Zharinov reached over and tapped the gauge. "Crew, remain on oxygen while we check something out," Dubronski said over the intercom.

"Yeah, and it's fluctuating," the flight engineer said, leaning forward from his seat aft of the pilots. "It was doing that yesterday too."

The Japanese pilot also leaned forward, peering at the instruments that Dubronski and Zharinov were studying. Dubronski slipped his left hand from the armrest down to the cabin pressurization panel. He felt the toggle switches, confirmed the position of each, and opened the guard protecting the emergency depressurization switch.

The pilot toggled the switch, and instantly there was a loud bang and a dense fog filled the cabin. A strident bell sounded and four lights on the instrument panel blinked urgently. The Japanese pilot was lost from view in the fog, but the flight engineer felt the man clawing at the air around him. In a fluid motion, the engineer seized a heavy flight manual from the leather case at his feet and swung it in an arc, smashing it into the Japanese man's head. He slumped in his shoulder restraints.

At the back of the flight deck, the Russian-speaking Japanese man was on his feet, pointing his machine pistol toward the pilots but unable to see through the mist. Suddenly the navigator was at his side, clubbing the man's skull with a fire extinguisher.

In the cargo compartment, the Russian crewmen grabbed tie-down straps, smashing the heavy metal buckles into their Japanese guards, who were disoriented in the fog and gasping for breath. In seconds, their captors lay on the floor, bleeding.

Dubronski pulled the throttles back to flight idle, switched off the transponder so that radar on the coast could no longer track them, and pushed the yoke forward, putting the huge transport into a steep turning dive. "Get that container open fast!" he yelled through the headset. The engineer grabbed the key from him and raced down to the mobile studio, opening the lock and throwing open the door. Two loadmasters ran in with portable oxygen bottles and masks, slamming open the door to the bedroom. They found Lenin and Gina unconscious on the floor and rolled the man and woman over on their backs. Their lips and eyelids were cyanotic blue. They clamped the oxygen masks on their faces and watched as the masks ballooned slightly with the pressure of the oxygen flow.

After several seconds, Gina's eyes fluttered open. She looked around in confusion at the man kneeling over her. Lenin began to cough harshly into his mask, his eyes glassy and unfocused. The loadmasters each gave a thumbs-up to the engineer in the doorway, who walked like a drunken man toward the ladder as g-forces alternately pressed him to the floor and made him nearly weightless in the tight spiraling dive. He struggled into his seat, put on his headset, and said, "They're okay."

"Good work, crew," Dubronski said. He watched as the altimeter unwound to one thousand feet, then pulled back the yoke and turned toward the shoreline.

"Remember when we did all that low-level flying in the mountains in Syria?" Dubronski asked. "I bet I still can do it."

"Yeah, I remember," Zharinov replied. "You were fifteen years younger then."

Dubronski laughed heartily as he banked the transport sharply toward a gap between two mountains, en route to the map coordinates of the abandoned airfield that Dennis Prinn's encoded message had designated as their destination.

*

Waro Moto sat at a simple but elegant desk, adjusting his reading glasses from time to time as he scanned the papers in front of him. Without looking up, he said to the young man who stood silently before him, "There is *nothing* noteworthy happening in the Philippines."

"That was our conclusion also, Moto-san," the man said.

"What did our people on board the aircraft say?"

"We have not heard from them since they called in to say they were aboard and ready for takeoff, with the aircraft under their control."

Moto grunted. "What else do you have?"

"The cargo manifest said the container was consigned to Dennis Prinn, care of P.K. Marcos Customs Agents, Manila," the man said. "Also, the flight plan was for a standard departure from San Juan Diego and then a direct flight to Manila."

"So you are prepared to let the matter rest at that?" Moto demanded, glaring at the young man.

"No, sir. We are trying to determine where, if he were to divert, Captain Dubronski would go."

"I have some ideas," Moto said.

CHAPTER TWENTY-FOUR

NICOLÁS IBARRA, DENNIS Prinn, and Alejandra Rojas hunched in the tall grass at the edge of the airfield. They looked anxiously into the clear sky, listening intently for the sound of approaching aircraft.

"How did you know of this place?" Nicolás asked Dennis.

"I did a piece on drug shipments for a television network in Hong Kong."

"I know it too," Nicolás said.

Dennis stared at him.

"Well," Nicolás said, "to do a revolution, you have to work with a lot of people."

Dennis smiled, then glanced at his phone. "I can't understand why Dubronski's late," he said.

"How reliable is this guy?" Nicolás asked. "Isn't he a kind of mercenary?"

"Mercenary. Revolutionary. I work with all kinds of vermin, don't I?"

Nicolás chuckled in response.

They heard a shrill whine in the distance. To the west, the silhouette of an enormous airplane banked with the left wing pointing straight at the ground, the right toward the sky, as it emerged from the narrow pass between two mountain peaks. Once out of the pass the Antonov 124 rolled its wings level and descended, hugging the treetops. The cargo craft roared over the valley floor, circling the airfield before touching down.

There was thunder as the thrust reversers slammed shut, decelerating the plane. It stopped at the far end of the runway, turned, and taxied back.

The engines spooled down and silence fell over the valley. When the door opened, Captain Dubronski lowered the entrance stairs, stepped out, and from behind him came Teodoro Lenin and Gina Ishikawa.

Nicolás, Dennis, and Alejandra emerged from the tall grass. Alejandra stopped in front of Lenin, looked him up and down, and asked, "Professor?'"

"Yes, Alejandra," Lenin said.

She smiled and reached out to shake Lenin's hand, but he leaned forward and kissed it instead.

"You have come a long way and endured much for my sake," he said. "For that, I thank you."

Alejandra's smile faded. "For Dave's sake, as well."

Lenin nodded solemnly. "Of course. Nico, Dennis—congratulations."

"Skittles and beer," Dennis said.

Nicolás rolled his eyes and spat at the ground. "All I've done is promote the cause of capitalism." His eyes, though, betrayed the satisfaction of a man who had achieved a job well done.

Lenin reached out and vigorously shook Nicolás's hand. "All the same, Nico, thank you."

"Professor, I have a great deal of information for you," Alejandra said.

Dubronski looked up and saw the contrails of a jet aircraft crossing the sky high above the field. "Plenty of time for that aboard the plane. Lenin, I hope you've figured out a destination to give me."

"Mexico City," Lenin replied.

Dubronski grunted and then cocked his thumb back toward the plane's cargo hold. "Happy to oblige. But first, could you guys give me a hand? We have some Japanese cargo that needs to be unloaded."

*

Waro Moto was finding it more and more difficult to center himself through meditation or the study of calligraphy. He sat at a low, highly polished wood table, calligraphy brushes and inkpot before him, his bulk wrapped in a white robe. Having considered the matter carefully, he had reached the conclusion that he had allied himself with inferior people, and that they were responsible for destroying his harmony.

From the beginning, he had harbored doubts about Takeshi Ishikawa, but had decided that since Ishikawa was racially pure—Japanese parents on both sides, emigrants from Japan to Brazil—and Ishikawa had married a woman equally racially pure, he could be relied upon as being Japanese. Now Moto knew the man was not capable of taking on the difficult decisions that were critical to properly execute a grand plan.

Moto looked down at the translation of the Torquemada document entitled "The Fourth Angel," which he had read twice in the past eight hours.

Incredible.

This man who had understood power so clearly was required to display a hypocritical humility in his life of service to the Christian god rather than showcase the honest arrogance that his ideas of power and control of inferior people justified. Torquemada's plan had operated in the shadows of Europe for more than five hundred years, unseen and undetected by emperors, monarchs, political philosophers, and academics. And then this enormous plan had rotated to the smallest degree on an axis of fate that handed a vital aspect of its resources to Waro Moto.

Of course, Moto had to remain in the background and allow the king of Spain and pope to prance and extol on the world's stage, pretending that they were realizing their Hapsburg destiny of world Christian dominion.

Let them think so.

The sun was setting on a world that had been dominated by those of European origin, and as fit the new millennium, it was going to rise on the Asian world. There was only one nation equal to the task of dominating the planet: Japan.

Waro Moto considered all of this and came to a decision on the question of Ishikawa. So many problems could have been so easily resolved if he had carried out the destruction of the airliner—either while it was flying or even better, after it had crash-landed. Nicolás Ibarra and his revolutionaries would have been blamed for the carnage. But Ishikawa's weakness had prevented this cleansing action.

Now only one other event could accomplish the same thing. Takeshi Ishikawa would have to die.

*

At Benito Juárez International Airport in Mexico City, Dubronski and Dennis Prinn went through seven levels of bureaucracy explaining why all their papers showed Manila to be the destination for the container, but here it was in Mexico.

Dennis called a friend at *El Excelsior*, a Mexico City newspaper, who called someone at the Ministry of Commerce, who spoke to the customs agents. Dozens of rubber stamps fulminated on pages of altered documents, and fifteen minutes later a drayage truck loaded Dennis's mobile communication center and drove out of the airport. Dennis led the way in his rental car, adjusting a small earpiece remotely connected to his phone.

"Can you hear me?" Dennis asked.

"Yes," Lenin answered, transmitting from inside the container.

"Where to?" Dennis asked.

Lenin had a map of Mexico City unfolded on the table in front of him.

Lenin directed Prinn to the Zócalo in the center of Mexico City, along the west side of the huge plaza, and then straight ahead on Tepeyac Street.

"You should see a slender steeple of a church ahead," Lenin said.

"Yes, I do," Dennis said.

"That's the church of Santo Domingo," Lenin said. "Across the street— that's looking east—you should see a building at the intersection that has a main entrance on a face that cuts diagonally across the corner. That's the *Casa Chata*, which means 'the barge,' named after that snub-nosed corner. The first home of the Spanish Inquisition in the New World. I think that's where we'll find Martín."

*

Dennis Prinn made another phone call, this time to a college friend who was the son of the owner of Latinovisa, the largest cable television system in Mexico and Central America. Dennis asked for a favor, the friend called his father, the father called a friend, and within a half-hour Dennis had a permit to set up his mobile ground station. Dennis had the drayage truck deposit his container onto the large patio of a building across the street from the Casa Chata.

Dennis bustled around the outside of his station erecting antennas and connecting power cables. He went inside and addressed the group.

"So, Professor, I think your best use of time right now is to hole up in my studio with Alejandra and pore through the documents. You need to be constructing your presentation on what is happening, who's behind it, how, and why. It had better be good, or we're just going to look like a bunch of silly buggers when this all breaks."

Lenin nodded. "Alejandra has already given me a good high-level summary of what she has in hard copy and on the drive, and during the flight we started cataloging everything. We will put something together for when the time comes."

"What will the rest of us do now?" Nicolás asked.

"Assuming Lenin's right about the site of the trial, we're just a hundred meters from the transmitter," Dennis replied. "They'll be using a narrow beam aimed straight at the satellite to avoid any interception. But, by being this close and using a few crude tools I have along, we can 'sniff' the beam's energy and we'll know for sure that this is where Marty's being held."

Dennis rummaged in an equipment cabinet, producing a dish antenna four inches in diameter as well as a small metal box. He put them on the table.

"I need someone to get a look at the roof of the Inquisition building to see if there's a dish antenna there. If there is, I need to attach mine to it. Let's see… who has the skills to help me pull off something like that?"

They all turned toward Nicolás.

*

Nicolás, wearing sunglasses and a Collingwood Magpies cap, came out of the container accompanied by Dennis. They crossed the street and walked along the south side of the building that Lenin had identified, noting its massive stone walls. At the street corner, they studied the angled facade and heavy wooden door with iron hardware, then turned the corner and walked the length of the east wall. Like the south side, there were many large windows overlooking the streets, but they had been painted a solid gray, making it impossible to see inside.

The two crossed the street and entered the empty Santo Domingo church. Nicolás and Dennis made their way past the alcoves along the sides of the nave. Behind a confessional, they saw an iron gate that led to spiral stairs rotating upward toward the bell tower. Nicolás tried the gate and found it locked. He removed a pick from his pocket, unlocked the gate, and swung it open with a loud squeak.

The two men jogged up the stone staircase, pushing cobwebs out of their path before arriving at the bright sunlight of the campanile. It was caked with years of dust, soot, and pigeon droppings. Both men hunkered down behind the waist-high wall and looked east toward the presumed Inquisition building. They could now see the entirety of the large square building that spanned an entire city block. A pyramidal roof tinted an opaque gray obscured their view of the courtyard in the center. A large parabolic antenna pointed straight upward from the roof.

"If we can put this dish close to that antenna," Dennis whispered, "we can tap into what they're sending."

"Show me how to place it, and I'll do it," Nicolás said.

*

It was after two in the morning, and the streets around Casa Chata were deserted. Nicolás had watched the building from the church bell tower across the street since five in the afternoon to get a feel for any movements in and out. Around seven, a dozen men and women had come out the front door, quickly dispersing into the pedestrian traffic on the sidewalk. At nine-thirty, two priests had arrived by car and disappeared inside. After that, there was no ingress or egress at all.

Nicolás crossed the street, looked for observers, and shinnied up the drainpipe to the roof. He withdrew a transmitter-receiver with a carrying belt, an earpiece, and a microphone from his backpack. He wrapped the belt around his waist, fastening the Velcro. Nicolás pushed the tiny earpiece deep into his ear and clipped the microphone to his shirt collar. Then he pulled out a tube the size of a pencil and held it up.

"Dennis, you read me?" he asked into the microphone on his shirt.

"I got you, Lima Charlie. Here comes video."

Nicolás saw a pinpoint of red light on the camera and pointed the lens end at his own face.

"You look like a wombat's arse, Nico," Dennis said.

Nicolás smiled.

*

A block away, Dennis sat at the control console with Gina. Nicolás's facial features on the monitor were clear but the image was jittery, with sporadic bursts of static and video noise.

"Why is it doing that?" Gina asked.

Dennis scowled. "You mean, why is the video feed from my tiny camera and makeshift relay not perfect? The one that I kludged together with parts I happened to have in my container studio that has been relocated thousands of miles without stopping to resupply with parts and gear that would be more fitting for an undercover operation, all while being chased by Japanese thugs and the reincarnated Spanish Inquisition? Next time I'll be sure to break out the higher end HD gear so as not to offend your videophile sensibilities."

"Sorry I asked," Gina said.

"Ah, no worries, Gina. I'm just cranky nervous as all hell. If you and Lenin are right, we're about to get a packet of video proof that the Inquisition is riding again." He put a flash drive into one of his recording devices and switched it on. They watched the jumpy picture as the view shifted.

"He's on the move," Dennis said.

They saw the tile roof and then the dish antenna came into view.

"I'm going to place your receiver antenna," Nicolás said.

"Bonzer," Dennis said. "See the horn in the center of the dish? Fasten my receiver to the side of that."

The picture blurred and spun as the camera swung freely from the lanyard around Nicolás's neck. After a minute the picture stabilized and Dennis saw the receiver being taped into place.

"Looks good, Nico. As always, duct tape is fair dinkum."

Moments later, the opaque plastic cover over the patio area loomed ahead. Lenin came in from the bedroom area and stood behind them, watching anxiously.

"I think that roof should be strong enough to support me," Nicolás said.

They watched as he stepped across the three-foot opening and laid down on the cover. The camera peered down inside the patio.

*

Nicolás watched two men with white clerical collars emerge from the building into the courtyard, talking quietly together and smoking. He looked for surveillance cameras or sentries. There were none, and the priests disappeared back inside after two cigarettes each.

"I'm going down," Nicolás whispered into the microphone.

"Whoa," came the reply in his ear. "This is way off-script, Nico. I was fine with getting in a little reconnaissance from above, but come on back to the container and let's discuss next steps before you... ah, shit Nico!"

Nicolás lowered himself to the ground using another drainpipe, ignoring the steady stream of profanities in his earpiece. He crouched and looked around. Straight ahead he saw a series of 21 doors, regularly spaced. Nicolás was sure that he was looking at the prisoners' cells.

"I'm going to check the cells to see if Martín is in one of them," he whispered into the microphone.

"Sure," came the sarcastic retort in his ear. "It's Nico's world and we're all just living in it, eh?"

Nicolás smiled to himself. It was good to be fully in charge of his own actions again. He started down the line of doors, seeing light streaming from each of the doorframes, indicating that the interiors of the cells themselves were brightly lit.

He pushed the miniature television camera through the space between the bottom of the first door and the stone floor.

"Tell me what you see," he whispered into the mic.

"Cell's about 4 meters by 4 meters, brightly lit, fluorescent tubes," Dennis said in a resigned but focused voice. "There's a bed opposite the door, a toilet and sink to the left. Point the camera up at the ceiling so I can see what's up there. Slow and careful, as I'm almost sure there will be a surveillance camera."

Nicolás worked his fingers under the door, holding the camera with his fingertips. He stood it up on end.

"Good on ya," Dennis said. "High ceiling, about three meters—there's the camera, upper right-hand corner in relation to the door. Stationary surveillance camera, wide angle—keeps the prisoner's bed in the center. We've got a problem, Nico. From down on the floor, I can't see who's in the bed."

"Shit," Nicolás muttered.

"Is there anywhere higher on the door that you can push the camera through?"

Nicolás looked over the doorframe and saw a space up at the top. He removed the lanyard from around his neck, lifted his arm, and pushed the camera part way in.

"Okay, I can see the guy on the bed," Dennis said. "It's not Marty."

Nicolás crawled to the next door, and they repeated the surveillance from the top of the door.

"Not him."

At the sixth door, Dennis said, "That's him! That's Martín. He's asleep, not moving."

"Can you do anything about the surveillance camera?" Nicolás asked.

"It's an old colonial mansion with massive, solid walls," Dennis said, "so all the wiring has to be on the outside. Can you see it?"

Nicolás scanned the wall and saw plastic conduit attached to it. At regular intervals there were wires going from the conduit into a hole drilled through the ancient mortar.

"I see it," Nicolás whispered.

"What do you want to do?" Dennis asked.

"Just cut that camera for a minute or so."

"Could set off alarms," Dennis said.

"For sure they'll send someone if it's off too long, but maybe if it's off for thirty seconds or so they'll just think it was a glitch."

"Then don't cut the wires," Dennis said. "Just strip back some insulation and touch two of them together. They'll still get a transmission from the camera, but it'll be distorted from the short."

Nicolás studied the wires into Martín's cell. He removed a knife from his pocket, reached up, and carefully peeled away the insulation from two wires. He flexed his hands several times, took a deep breath, and twisted the exposed wires together. There was no audible alarm. He removed the wooden bar and swung the door open. He stepped in, blinking in the brightness. His brother remained motionless, breathing slowly and deeply.

Drugged, Nicolás concluded, and walked quickly to the bed.

Dennis's voice came through the headset, full of alarm and urgency. "A light came on at the front of the building—they know something's up. Get out of there!"

Nicolás scanned the room. There was nothing he could use as a weapon.

"Another window lit up, and a yard light just came on," Dennis warned. "Get out!"

Nicolás watched Martín sleep. He wanted to just grab him and drag him out, but there was no time and no way he could get back up to the roof with the dead weight of his brother's limp body. But he had to do *something* to improve their odds. He hadn't come down here just to gawk at his sleeping brother without doing anything.

Nicolás jerked his earplug out of his ear, pulled the microphone off of his shirt, and ripped off the belt with the transmitter. He tucked all of them under Martín's pillow. The younger man groaned and his eyes opened momentarily, but they were glassy and unseeing.

Nicolás went to the door, listened, opened it as narrowly as possible, and stepped out. He replaced the wooden bar, then pulled the wires apart, restoring the normal transmission. He raced back into the shadows just as two men in dark uniforms burst out of a doorway. They sprinted to Martín's cell, tossed the bolt aside, and threw open the door. Standing in the doorway breathing hard, they gawked at the sleeping man. One looked up toward the surveillance camera. They made a call on a radio, backed out of the cell, and secured the door.

*

Nicolás burst into the communications trailer, pulling the cap from his head.

"What'd you do with the camera and voice transmitter?" Dennis demanded.

"I left them for my brother. We'll call him through the radio, wake him up, and he'll find the camera and microphone."

"And do what exactly? He is *drugged* and has no idea that we're here trying to help him! He'll be scared and disoriented and in all likelihood when he finds it he'll pull it out from under his pillow in full view of the surveillance camera."

"I couldn't think of anything else," Nicolás said with a shrug.

"Okay," Dennis said. "What's done is done. But can we please all try to stick to the fucking plan going forward? There's too much that can go wrong!"

Nicolás stared back, but didn't respond. His entire career as a revolutionary had been based upon improvisation, but now was not the time to argue the point.

Dennis shook his head. "We don't have much time. It's after three, and these religious nuts don't sleep in."

"Well, then," Nicolás said with a bit of a smirk. "Let's get to work."

CHAPTER TWENTY-FIVE

AS DAWN APPROACHED Dennis keyed his microphone. "Are you in position?" he asked.

"Yes," Nicolás said. "I found a good spot across the street. No activity so far."

Dennis looked at Gina, who nodded. He threw five switches and turned several knobs. Through the speakers Dennis and Gina could hear rhythmic breathing. The monitor in front of them was a dark gray.

Dennis adjusted the microphone in front of his mouth and cleared his throat. "Marty... wake up." They listened. The breathing didn't change.

They had debated whose voice should be used for the first contact. Gina wanted to do it, but Nicolás had argued that they should consider the potential for shock given that Martín believed she was dead. In his current state, Nicolás had said, Martín was likely to believe that Gina's voice was a hallucination generated by the drugs and exhaustion. The same was true for Lenin and even Nicolás.

"Marty," Dennis said again. He turned a knob, increasing the volume of the transmission. "Marty... Marty... Marty!"

They listened. The breathing changed ever so slightly, and sheets rustled. "Marty!" Dennis said.

There was no response, and the breathing resumed its steady, rhythmic pace.

"Marty!" Dennis repeated with a hint of exasperation.

For the next fifteen minutes Dennis periodically called out Marty's name, but mostly he sat and listened with a growing sense of dread and despair. He put his head in his hands and rubbed his exhausted eyes. He was about to ask Gina to pour him a cup of coffee while they waited when he heard a shrill tone come through his headset. Martín's breathing rate and depth increased dramatically.

"Marty, my name is Dennis Prinn. If you can hear my voice, don't move. Just pat your pillow twice."

They heard some incomprehensible muttering, and scratching as the pillowcase rustled against the microphone.

"Marty, can you hear me?" Dennis asked. "If you hear me, pat the pillow twice."

After a long silence, they heard two thumps. Gina squeezed Dennis's shoulder as the thumps echoed through the container's interior.

"Marty, I'm here in Mexico City to help get you out. We can hear the alarms going off inside the complex you are being held in. If you believe that the alarms mean that someone will be coming for you in less than five minutes, pat your pillow twice."

He and Gina again heard two thumps.

"Okay, I understand they'll be coming within the next five minutes," Dennis confirmed. "Listen carefully. There's a transmitter for a wireless television camera and earpiece under your pillow. Don't touch them for now—just leave them there. If anyone will be in your cell while you're out, and if you think they will do anything that might reveal the equipment, give me two pats now."

There was no sound. "Okay, I understand no one is likely to find the camera and microphone if we leave them where—"

There was a muffled sound of wood banging iron. A door hinge squeaked. "Come on, Ibarra," a man said. "Time for another session."

Prinn and Gina heard cloth rustle against the microphone, the door clang shut, and then silence.

*

Father Serrano looked at himself in the mirror as he slipped a fresh collar around his neck. He was satisfied that he had kept himself in excellent physical shape. The bruises where the peasant had bashed him with a rusted pipe were still visible, but apart from that—

His phone rang, interrupting his reverie.

"Yes?" he said, putting the phone to his ear.

"What is your update?" the Spanish cardinal asked.

"I expect the subject to be ready for trial tomorrow."

"You're cutting it very close," the cardinal complained.

"Why do you insist on telling me what I already know? Arbitrary time frames can't be imposed upon the process."

The voice from the phone was cold. "Tell it to the pope. Get your part done."

The line went dead.

Serrano cursed softly, then marched out of the room and down the colonnaded corridor overlooking the courtyard. From the darkness below he could hear movement from the prisoners. He enjoyed the cool morning air only momentarily before he was inside again, in a dark room with lockers and benches. He opened a locker, withdrew a pair of soft-soled shoes, and sat on the bench to put them on. He pulled on skin-tight gloves, donned night-vision goggles, and then made his way through an opaque revolving door, emerging into a pitch-black room.

Serrano's eardrums strained in the anechoic chamber that suppressed all sound to the point of causing his heartbeat and blood circulation to roar in his ears. He looked around in the darkness and pulled down his goggles. He could see the half-dozen kidney-shaped pods standing on end, each measuring two meters tall. They were supported by a series of hydraulic cylinders actuated by solenoids wired to the main console.

Serrano nodded at the man sitting at the control console and went to the pod with "1" painted on the side. There was a computer keyboard and small monitor on a plinth beside it. He touched the keyboard and the screen illuminated. The priest clicked "System Check" from the onscreen menu. At the top of the screen, it read, "Ibarra, Martin, male, age 31, education 18." He scanned the biofeedback data, seeing the heart rate was now less than 30 beats per minute and blood pressure less than 70 over 50. Something on the history chart caught his eye. Each morning when Ibarra had been connected to the bio monitors, his heart rate had been around 70 beats per minute, but this morning it had been up to 110. He wondered what had made today different. Dreams? He wasn't supposed to have any after getting his usual cocktail of drugs at the end of each session.

A graphic readout of the electroencephalogram showed the alpha waves associated with relaxation and creativity active within their low frequency seven to 12 hertz range. The beta waves, normally around 40 hertz during periods of alertness, concentration, and cognition were flat, indicating the narcotics were having their effect. The delta waves hovered around two hertz, and were being carefully monitored by the computer to be sure that Ibarra did not lapse into deep sleep, releasing hormones that would regenerate his body and refresh him. Ibarra was also on a chemical cocktail that activated theta waves whenever the delta waves were suppressed by normal sleep. This would move him into rapid eye movement sleep, and any images introduced to his mind would seem as real as a wakeful state.

The priest noted the history again, which also revealed an elevated state of wakeful brain waves when he was first hooked up this morning. Interesting, but not necessarily alarming.

Serrano marveled at the computer technology before him that in the next five hours would control every aspect of Ibarra's existence. From here Ibarra's body temperature could be regulated, as well as his states of consciousness. Even more impressively, Serrano could introduce visual, tactile, audio, olfactory, and taste stimuli at will. The pod delivered straight into Ibarra's ocular and auditory senses a lifelike but altered multimedia recreation of key moments of his life. It was a parallel version meticulously created from family photos, videotapes, CDs, digital files, and voice recordings purloined from the Ibarras' Miami home, online social media, Martín's apartment, and the public domain. Various additional media had been spliced into the narrative, including videos produced by the Inquisition during the last two years—all of it digitally mastered into a virtual reality that was now being transmitted directly into Martín's compromised brain. His memories were being reconstructed from data gleaned from three years of intensive research, with every detail corroborated and every sensation faithfully reproduced. His memories would be refreshed, reinforced, and sculpted, modifying them with variations so subtle that they would not awaken any dissonance between his conscious and subconscious memories.

Everything seemed to be on track, but Serrano still felt a faint anxiety. Was it because of the call from Spain? The odd readings from this morning? He couldn't pin it down. He walked to the control console outside the chamber. "Call security and have them double the guard, day and night."

*

Martín drifted on an elastic timeline that at times stretched out into infinity and at others compressed to a singularity. He was meeting Gina Ishikawa for the first time, sitting in a lecture hall at the University of Miami, feet shuffling around him, folding writing tables squeaking and clanking, whiffs of perfume mixed with mildew in the air-conditioned but humid air of a crowded room. He felt the slight movement of the chair next to him being occupied and turned his head. The girl was Asian, compact and slender. Every movement of her hands had drama and grace. Her dark eyes fixed on his and she spoke. What were the words she was saying? He could hear but not comprehend. She spoke for some time, smiling at first, but over time subtly changing her expression. Her face shaped into— forbearance was the best way to describe it. Her words were still incomprehensible, but her tone became clipped and increasingly harsh.

Suddenly Gina recoiled from him and put the palms of her hands out defensively. Her mouth had formed a contemptuous grimace. She whispered something. Martín reached for her hand, but she snatched it away.

Now he was dancing with Gina. He looked down at himself, seeing he was dressed in a tuxedo. She wore a simple, short black cocktail dress. He couldn't place the name of the song, but it was slow and tender and filled with warm memories. He stroked Gina's back. Her lips were close to his ear, murmuring. Her breath was minty and warm, but the words... he couldn't understand them. He drew his head back and smiled at her, but she was pulling away from him. Her face had contorted into a kind of snarl. She was saying a word over and over again, but he couldn't understand.

New sounds and smells crowded into his mind. He was lying down, and the surface was hard and smooth under his back and buttocks. He felt a slight rocking movement and heard water gently lapping against fiberglass. He smelled lemon oil, suntan lotion, damp canvas, salt, and diesel fuel.

Gina stood above him, gazing into his eyes. She was naked, and Martín looked and saw he was too. He was hard and she crouched down before him. But then her smile disappeared and her eyes became cold and her mouth showed teeth through a sneer. She spoke. What were her words? She stood back up and moved away from him, hands raised. Her mouth formed the same word again, just a single syllable, but he didn't understand.

Gina's voice rose to a shriek that vibrated his chest cavity. In his nakedness, he looked around and saw not the boat but a jury box packed with hundreds of people, laughing and jeering. Gina now sat in an impossibly high witness chair, looking down into his eyes and laughing with them. They intensified their taunts and whistles.

Gina pointed her index finger and abruptly all was silent. There were only the sounds of Martín's heartbeat and breathing. Gina's mouth slowly formed a word, shouting a shrill exclamation, its single syllable blaring with such force that it set off explosions of light in his head. The word blasted with a fervor rooted in the preceding centuries and rolling forward, gaining strength and hatred and breaking over him like an enormous wave:

"Jew!"

*

Father Serrano scanned the brain wave chart on Martín's capsule. He checked off the twentieth name on the list, Gina Ishikawa, and circled the twenty-first, Teodoro Lenin.

The next tranche of memory modifications would now begin.

*

Colonel Gustav Lavigne, commander of the infantry company of the French Foreign Legion billeted in French Guiana, peered down at the jungle below him. The Dauphin 2 helicopter skimmed over the thick canopy at five thousand feet to maximize horizontal visibility and minimize the risk of being hit by ground fire. Lavigne's gray hair under his maroon beret testified to his age and experience. His camouflage-mottled battle dress with infantry insignia covered a lean body. Major LaForge sat next to him, scanning a military map.

"This is useless," Lavigne said. "They could be directly under us and we still wouldn't see them. We couldn't defend this border with two full divisions."

LaForge clucked his tongue in sympathy. Lavigne stabbed his finger on the map. "This is the last place the Americans had acoustical contact, right?"

"Yes, sir, in Ciudad Bolívar, Venezuela."

"And there have been no updates on their position?"

"Negative, sir. Just small movements—individuals on the Orinoco River. No mass troop movements."

"And what does the Latino Union say?" Lavigne asked.

"Nothing, sir," LaForge said. "Their command post says it is a sovereign matter of the LU, and we are to respect their borders."

Lavigne shook his head. "I don't know who's worse. The LU, who don't give a shit that its revolutionaries are about to attack our space center, or our own politicians back in France. *One* helicopter to search all this." His arm swung in a wide arc toward the window. "No intelligence, no mobility. Unbelievable."

LaForge blankly gazed back at his commanding officer. He had heard this rant before.

Lavigne put on a headset and said, "Captain DuPont, patch me to the command post in Paris."

"Baton One, this is Chain Mail, go ahead."

"Chain Mail, this is Baton One Actual," Lavigne said into his microphone. "We have conducted a search along eight-zero-zero kilometers of border. Negative contact, negative intelligence update. I repeat my urgent, I say again, *urgent* requirement for reinforcements to be dispatched from France without further delay."

"Baton One, Chain Mail understands negative contact with enemy force. Return to base, maintain defensive alert, stand by for further orders."

Lavigne grunted in disgust and threw down his headset. LaForge kept his face down and stared at the map, trying to look busy.

*

A light began blinking at the Moto Electric world command center near Tokyo. The shift supervisor noted it immediately and swiftly coupled a high-capacity computer to the satellite downlink circuit. The flashing light signaled that this was a digital message, encrypted using a public and secret key—and highly compressed—which would be transmitted in its entirety in a nanosecond.

The technician intently watched his monitor, and the moment the word "Transmitted" appeared on the screen, he isolated the computer. He entered the commands to begin the decryption process, but large kanji appeared on the screen saying, "Eyes Only, Waro Moto."

Across the city, a laser printer in Moto's bedroom sighed and a page slipped into the tray. Moto picked it up and read, "Advance team is ashore in French Guiana. No resistance. Linked with friendlies. Main body of forces now moving from Venezuela, Guyana, and Suriname. Expect to be on land after midnight. Diversion force in Albina, Suriname, awaiting orders."

Moto checked his watch, calculated the time difference, and nodded. The final stage was now in progress, and it was time for him to depart for San Juan Diego.

*

Dennis Prinn, Nicolás Ibarra, and Gina Ishikawa were seated at the console in Dennis's control container. On screen, Martín stood in his yellow *sanbenito*, and above him a monk in his white hooded cassock sat on a velvet chair. As before, Martín's eyes were unfocused.

Another priest stood beside Martín. "The twentieth accuser of this suspected heretic, Martín Ibarra, is Miss Gina Ishikawa," he said, "a Christian of the Holy Catholic Church."

Gina let out a startled gasp, and Dennis reflexively turned the volume up. The camera closed in on the priest's face.

"On the second of January in this year of Our Lord, the accuser did say to you, 'You are a Jew and I am a Gentile.'"

Gina's hand flew to her mouth. "Oh, my God," she gasped. "I *did* say that. I remember that conversation. Martín had called me in Rome. But how could they know my exact words?"

"On the third of January in this year of Our Lord, the accuser did say to you, 'Martín, you raped me. You forced me to take you in my mouth—that circumcised penis of yours.'"

Gina rose to her feet and violently shook her head. "No!" she shouted.

"Also on the third of January in this year of Our Lord, you said to the accuser, 'I love to rape Christian women and I love to humiliate them and I love to have them on their knees in front of me and to tell them, let your Messiah save you now.'"

Gina clapped her hands over her ears and turned away.

Nicolás and Dennis watched as Martín stood, swaying slightly, his unfocused eyes glazed and staring straight ahead. The camera angle changed several times, ending with a static close-up that captured Martín's dazed look of confusion, doubt, and fear. Tears rolled down his cheeks. His head jerked back as if he had been struck each time the off-camera voice read another quotation.

Dennis finally turned the sound down. Gina had thrown herself back in her chair and put her face in her hands.

"Gina... did Martín say those things?" Nicolás asked.

"No," she said through sobs. "No! Well... yes... but not like that or in those words. And the context is all wrong. It was an intimate running joke between us—sexual role-playing. Who are these people? What are they doing?"

On the silent screen, the litany went on and on. The pain in Martín's face made it clear he was nearing a breaking point.

*

Father Serrano slapped the thick file on his ornate desk. "It has to happen tomorrow morning," he announced.

The physician sitting across the desk from him, also wearing a priest's collar, shook his head. "Impossible," he said.

Serrano brought his fingers to his temples and said in a reasonable tone, "Explain it to me, *Father* Silva."

"I note your emphasis on my role as a priest," Silva said. "But remember, for this Inquisitorial assignment, you have relied on me as a physician. To substitute memories of events that really happened to the patient with fabricated ones, I have to keep him in stage five rapid-eye-movement sleep.

But there are three sub-stages within REM sleep, and the balance among them is critical. The introduction of synthetic cortisol timed exactly with stress-provoking stimuli he is getting by visual, aural, tactile, and olfactory cues is a critical process. This keeps him aroused with high heart rate, blood pressure, and respiration—ready to run away from the frightening stimulus, if you will. It is such a high state of arousal that it reinforces the stimulus and drives it deeper into the subconscious memory. This makes the memory more easily retrievable, and therefore more believable than the true memory we're replacing.

"If you change the cycles of chemically induced sleep and true REM stage three sleep, two things could happen while you have him in the pod. The first: rather than staying in the cortisol-induced state of high readiness, he'll slip into another stage in which he is still ready to flee or fight, but with hydrocortisone, epinephrine, and norepinephrine blood levels at almost normal levels. Heart rate and brain wave activities will be reduced, and he will be able to sustain this state of physical readiness for a long time. The memories will not be as vivid—they won't be as strong in his subconscious memory. He'll figure out they are fake memories."

"And the other possibility?" Serrano asked.

"He'll move into the third mechanism, which is exhaustion."

"So he'll just sleep soundly?"

"No," Father Silva replied. "It rapidly brings on physical deterioration and psychosis." Silva gestured toward the file on the desk. "I'm already seeing some psychotic symptoms. Think of it as a car battery. When the battery goes dead, you can trickle charge it, which takes more time, but you'll get much longer service from the battery. Or you can give it a hot shot, which charges it instantly, but a short time later the battery won't hold a charge at all. You've been mixing hot shots and trickle charging, and your battery is already somewhat damaged."

"Doctor, it is you who doesn't understand," Serrano said. "Ibarra has to be repentant tomorrow morning so we can have the *auto-de-fé* tomorrow night. And he needs to be completely repelled by the sight of any of his friends or relatives. There is *no more time*."

"If you run him through another cycle in the pod, there's a good chance he'll be a vegetable when you remove him," the doctor declared.

"And that's unacceptable," Serrano replied. "It needs to look genuine. Not like coercion."

"But all of this mind alteration *has* been coercion. We all knew that from the beginning."

Serrano jumped to his feet and came around the desk. He bent over at the waist, putting his face in Silva's. "I don't care if I can't use this 'battery' anymore—he only needs to last another 24 hours. Tomorrow morning I want him coherent, compliant, and most of all, penitent."

"All right, *Father*," Silva said, rising to his feet and maintaining eye contact. "The only way for you to hope to achieve that is to take him back to his cell right now and let him sleep normally until you need him tomorrow night. No more time in the pod!"

Serrano stared at the other priest a long time. Finally he picked up his phone and gave an order.

*

Dennis and Nicolás stood under the arches at the front of the Municipal Palace, looking out into the expanse of the Central Plaza of Mexico City.

"There's no doubt about it," Dennis said. "They're setting up to televise live whatever is about to go down here."

The two men watched workers setting up a semicircle of steel grandstands with a platform in the center raised high above the stone paving. On the rooftops of each of the presidential palace on the east side, the main cathedral to the north, and the houses of Cabildo and Ayuntamiento to the south, workmen toiled with equipment and cables. Nicolás was lost in thought.

"Nico, what's happening here?" Dennis asked.

"Lenin said the Inquisition is remaining true to history. Martín's trial is going on right now—and probably for some other high-visibility 'heretics' at the same time. Of course, they'll all be convicted. And the sentence will be death by fire."

Prinn stared at him. "My God, man. This is the 21st century—people don't burn at the stake."

"No," Nicolás said, thoughtfully. "You're right about that. Everything they've done so far has been based on historical precedent, but with a modern, high tech twist. I imagine the 'bonfire' will be something new, but it'll be aimed at having the same cleansing effect. The purification by fire the Inquisition believed—believes—will bring on the Millennium of Christ's rule on Earth."

Dennis put binoculars to his eyes and looked again at the rooftop work. He studied each of the emplacements. When he lowered the binoculars, he said, "Lasers. High powered industrial lasers used to precision-cut very hard materials."

Nicolás nodded grimly and said, "You head back to the com center. I'll keep a watch here and call you with any updates."

*

Carolina mopped her forehead with a bandanna as she glared at the cell phone on the table. Her head ached from the echoing roar of the more than one-thousand men confined in the steel building—laughing, shouting, cursing, and bellowing. She snatched up the device and accepted the call the moment a tone sounded.

"Yes?" she said.

"Commander Delta?"

"Yes, tell me."

"We've lost Nico."

"*Lost* him?"

"We think he's gone from San Juan Diego."

"Did he know you were following?" she asked.

The man hesitated. "We don't know."

Carolina cursed loudly. "He was supposed to be back here by now with the television technician. We're supposed to have a global broadcast ready to go in Kourou when we invade!"

She was met with silence and she swore again.

"Fine. We go without him. I'm moving the Specter force to the river crossing—we'll be there in two hours. Make damned sure that colonel in Guiana knows it."

"Yes, Commander."

Carolina shuffled through papers on her desk until she found the schedule for reconnaissance satellites. She had 30 minutes until the next overflight. She removed a satellite phone in its original packaging from her backpack and walked outside where she turned it on and dialed.

"Yes?" a man asked over the phone.

"'Basque homeland and liberty.'"

There was a long silence. "Carolina?"

"Yes."

"How did you get this number?"

"I still know supporters."

"They must have also told you that I quit."

"I was a burnout too, but now I have an opportunity bigger than any we ever dreamed of in the ETA."

Another long pause. "Is anyone I know with you on this… opportunity?"

"Only me."

Carolina heard a long sigh over the phone line.

"Listen," the man said at last, "you were my best understudy. I wish… I wish I could recover our old fire and passion. But I have a nice quiet life here in Mexico. People respect me. I don't have to live in fear anymore."

"You don't understand," she said. "This is sure to bring Spain to its knees. We can gain true independence!"

Silence. Then, *"Bietan jarrai,* Carolina."

"'Keep up both,'" she repeated bitterly. "The snake and the axe. I was sure I could count on you."

"Good bye, Carolina."

The connection broke.

CHAPTER TWENTY-SIX

COLONEL LAVIGNE HAD a feeling. He had felt it before when the Legionnaires had been deployed overseas—once in Mauritania during the Western Sahara Conflict, again in Zaire while restoring order in Kinshasa, and a third time in Afghanistan. Outwardly Lavigne looked calm, but inside his diaphragm ached slightly and there was a tingling sensation around his hairline. Each time he had felt this way, an attack had come— swiftly and violently.

Below the helicopter he could see the sun glinting off a small river and shattering into points of light as the reflected beams hit the dense foliage. *Is that where the enemy is?* he asked himself for the hundredth time that day.

He answered his own question. If they were crossing that river right now, they would still have a one-week march through the jungle to get to the space center in Kourou. But he knew *something* was about to happen.

Where? And when?

*

Martín Ibarra felt closer to true consciousness than he had in quite some time.

A lifetime ago? A week? A day?

His existence had been a collage of gauzy, out-of-body sensations through which dreams of his family, friends, and lovers appeared and disappeared like a movie being streamed forcibly into his mind. All of the visions had ended with him being denounced as a Jew by those closest to him.

Gina.

His brother Nico.

Professor Lenin.

David Broch.

But now—was it day or night?—was a bit different. For the first time in what felt like eons he could manage thoughts about things other than the images and sounds that had been unspooling repeatedly within him.

He had a vague recollection that he had heard a voice—tinny and distant, but intelligible—that had come from under his pillow. Who had that been? His captors playing with his head? He recalled the voice being thick with a distinct accent.

British?

No.

Australian?

Yes. That was it.

Keeping his eyes shut and moving very slowly, he slid his hand under the pillow. There were objects there.

A tiny, rubbery, plug-shaped item.

A tube the size of a fountain pen.

A small metallic square.

A small package on a kind of strap.

They were real.

He heard the muffled voice again. "Marty, this is Dennis Prinn. Tap your pillow twice if you can hear me."

Martín considered the command. He scratched the pillowcase twice with his fingernail.

"Okay," the voice said. "Is there anyone in the room with you? Tap once if no, twice if yes."

Martín listened carefully and tapped once on the pillow.

"Okay. Marty, listen carefully. Take the earplug that's under your pillow and push it deep into one of your ears. Doesn't matter which one. You'll be able to hear me much more clearly, and it'll be hard for anyone to see it."

Thinking of the security camera, Martín slowly moved his hand under the pillow, seizing the plug in his fingers. He pulled it out and pushed it into the ear that was pressed against the pillow.

The Aussie drawl was now crystal clear. "Can you hear me? If the volume is set right, tap the pillow twice."

He tapped twice.

"Good," Dennis said. "There's also a microphone the size of a postage stamp. Hide it somewhere inside your clothes and as close to your head as possible so I can pick up your voice and the sounds around you. The cylinder is a television camera. Point the end with the lens and we'll be able to see what you're pointing at. Plug it into the battery pack for the camera—it goes around your waist and under your clothes."

Martín again put his hand under the pillow, felt the small square and pulled it out, keeping it hidden from the security camera. He felt a sticky substance on one side of the thin square, picked it up, and placed it inside his T-shirt at the collar.

He cleared his throat several times.

"Good on ya, Martín! I read you loud and clear. Don't take the camera and battery pack anywhere you might be searched. If they'll be taking you somewhere soon, tap once for no, twice for yes, and three times for 'don't know.'"

Martín thought a moment. He bumped the pillow three times.

Suddenly, out of the fog of troubled memories came a wave of clear thoughts.

The rocket at Kourou.

Satellite.

Nuclear weapon.

The rebel force sweeping east from Venezuela.

The expanse of jungle Martín had seen as Major Valencia flew him to Cunani, Brazil.

Impenetrable jungle, he had thought at the time.

Impenetrable, he thought now.

The rebels would not sweep into French Guiana through Suriname. The rebel forces Nicolás commanded were a feint—and somehow Martín was convinced his brother didn't know it. The attack would come by sea, straight to Kourou.

Nico was a pawn.

Martín almost leaped out of the bed, but fought to keep himself under control and motionless. He now had communication *from* the outside world, but how could he use it to talk *back* to the outside world? Speaking was impossible with the surveillance camera and microphone always listening and watching.

Code?

Morse code.

He had learned it during his CIA training, but had considered it useless. It had been so long ago. What were the letters?

He rolled over, facing away from the security camera, and moved his hand up his shirt to the collar area until it was just above the microphone that he had affixed to his skin. He scratched his fingernail along the shirt's fabric, and a long scraping noise emitted on the other end.

Methodically, he began.

*

Dennis had the speakers on and they all listened to the long scratching sound. There was silence, and then finally a short and a long scratch. A moment later there was another long scratch. The short and long sound again.

Dennis and Gina looked at each other.

"He's communicating," Dennis said. "Morse code, right?" he said into the microphone. "Tap twice." There were two distinct taps. "Go with it, Martín, I know it."

The first letter was A followed by T, another A, then a K.

"Attack?"

There were two taps.

"Okay, Martín. Next word."

Dennis listened intently. "K, O, R, O," he said into the microphone. The others shook their heads. "Koro? We don't know what that is, Marty. A place?" Two taps, followed by a series of fast scratches.

"You want to do that one over," Dennis said. "K, O, V, like Victor?"

Another series of scratches. "Start word again. K-O-U-R-O-U... end word. Kourou?"

"Attack Kourou," Dennis said, and got two taps back. "We heard about that—" Dennis stopped himself mid-sentence and winced. He had nearly said *from your brother*. "Um, you know something we don't?"

There were two taps and then the scratching began again. "A-T-A-K N-O-T F-R-O-M J-U-N-G-L-E B-U-T S-E-A."

*

Martín Ibarra had his arm draped across his eyes. He was still blind, but no longer to the point of total blackness. The fluorescent lights overhead produced a light gray haze through his eyelids. He thought about the coded messages he had just sent to Dennis Prinn, whoever he was.

If Prinn contacted President Ishikawa, the message would go nowhere. And would the French believe him? Or had they figured it out for themselves and reinforced the garrison?

His head ached from thinking this through. His thoughts during the last few hours had been convoluted and terrifying. When he pictured Gina Ishikawa's face, all he saw was a sneer. His memories of her body conjured up episodes of her looking at him with disgust at having been defiled by a Jew.

Martín shook his head, refusing to go further with that train of thought. Instead his mind splintered and branched and then settled upon Teodoro Lenin.

Lecturing, pontificating, denouncing.

What had he denounced?

Marranos.

New Christians.

Conversos.

Martín saw his professor vituperating loudly from his university lectern and then quietly, clandestinely, leading a fifth column from his home. A cadre of students—disciples of a learned professor.

All against Judaism.

Denouncing Jews.

Martín moaned out loud, and his thoughts splintered again and found a new focus: Nico.

There was Nico, a proud revolutionary—no! Instead he pictured his brother as haggard, bent, and broken.

His brother loathed himself.

Why?

Because his revolution was lost?

No, that wasn't it—that was an old memory. There was another memory, so clear now, but somehow faulty. Like one photographic image superimposed imperfectly over another.

His mind settled upon the vivid memory. It had to be true.

His brother loathed himself for being a Jew.

Martín's brain echoed with a guilt and self-detestation so deep and so wide… and all because he was Jewish. Where were these thoughts coming from? He tried to recall having ever felt this way about his heritage.

He wasn't religious—he had only a superficial knowledge of Judaism and never went to temple. But he also seemed to recall, faintly, that he had once felt pride about his heritage—that the diversity his history represented was honorable and strong.

But these new feelings were so clear and overwhelming.

Martín wrapped his arms around his head and squeezed as tightly as he could, trying to exorcise the demons that possessed him.

*

The lieutenant from the signal corps verified that the voice encryption on King Carlos's phone was working correctly, saluted, and left the room. Carlos keyed a number in Burgos, and on the third ring a voice said, "Yes, Your Majesty."

"When will we have the confession and *auto-de-fé*?" Carlos asked without preamble.

"Uh… yes, Your Majesty, we believe the confession will be forthcoming soon."

"When, damn it?" he demanded. "There are other events predicated on this."

"Your Majesty, we're doing the best—"

"Get him on video *now*."

"Yes, Your Majesty."

*

Father Serrano's cell phone rang once, and he answered immediately.

"Yes?" he said.

"Get him on video now."

"Not yet, he's having to assimilate—"

"Father, this is the cardinal, and I order you to get the video confession *now*."

The line was broken before Serrano could reply.

*

Guards threw open the door to Martín Ibarra's cell and descended upon him before he could react. A nurse followed behind, producing a syringe from a leather bag. He quickly swabbed Martín's arm and administered an injection.

One guard held Martín down while the other yanked Martín's pants off and then pulled the yellow and green *sanbenito* over his head, roughly tugging it down over his T-shirt. Martín was hauled into a sitting position and the pointed *sanbenito* hat was placed on his head. Each guard took hold of an arm and hoisted Martín to his feet.

Martín's mind raced. His earpiece and the microphone remained in place, undiscovered. But the television camera and battery pack were still under the pillow.

Martín was propelled toward the door.

*

"Marty, this is Dennis. If you hear me okay, cough."

In a moment Dennis heard two raspy coughs.

"Okay. I've got your confirmation. From the sounds I'm getting, you're on the move. A quick update for you: another bloke and I were out in the Zócalo earlier today, and we saw preparations for a big event that's going to happen soon. We think the Inquisition is going to run an *auto-de-fé* and you'll be one of the convicted penitents. I just want to tell you we've got people working on this, and we're going to get you out of there some way. I don't know how or when, but I promise you, we will get you out."

At that moment through his headset Dennis heard a loud voice saying, "Martín Ibarra Paz, stand in judgment of the ecclesiastical court of the Holy Office of the Inquisition!"

*

The revolutionaries were exuberant as they were finally released from the steel hell of the warehouse where they had been quartered for nearly a week. Their officers moved up and down the column, threatening and cajoling them into silence. By the time they had moved three miles from Albina following the Maroni River toward the southwest through dense forest, their initial enthusiasm had given way to grim determination. No more cheers and exclamations—only grunts of exertion and the muffled clinking of military hardware taped and tied to web gear.

Carolina, known to the revolutionary band as Commander Delta, marched at the head of the column. From this point position she could scan the blackness of the night sky, judging the moment when she would make her move.

*

Martín turned his head toward the source of lights that he could vaguely detect through his chemically induced blindness. The amplified voice was also coming from that direction.

"Martín Ibarra Paz, do you accept the jurisdiction of this court reviewing your heresy?" the voice asked.

Martín shook his head, trying to clear the storm that raged in his brain. The voice had told him someone would get him out. But... did he deserve to be freed? His memories reverberated with guilt and self-hatred for violating the covenant his forbearers had made with God. He needed to accept that he was unworthy of God's grace.

"Do you accept the jurisdiction of this court?"

Martín had to try his voice several times before he finally croaked, "I do."

"Martín Ibarra Paz, you are charged with heresy—an affront to

God and all His saints. You have heard the charges against you and you have heard the evidence from men and women who witnessed your heresy firsthand."

Martín hated his friends and relatives for denouncing him by providing this court with words that he had spoken in private moments, but most of all he hated himself for what he was: a Jew.

"Martín Ibarra Paz, will you now elect to save your immortal soul by admitting your heresy?"

Martín's head dropped to his chest. The revulsion to his Judaism was so strong, and yet part of his mind sought to counter that revulsion—the undercurrent of pride in his heritage tried to make its way again to the forefront of his thoughts. His mind reached out but couldn't quite reach the source of that pride. He was too exhausted to try to piece together what was true and what wasn't. Maybe if he just told them what they wanted to hear they would let him sleep.

"Yes," Martín croaked, as loudly as he could. "I admit my heresy."

He began to sob.

"Martín Ibarra Paz, do you now renounce Judaism and embrace the one true faith, the one true religion, the one true God, the one true Messiah?"

Martín moved his head, stretching his coiled neck muscles. He heard himself saying, "Yes."

"Martín Ibarra Paz, you have admitted your heresy and embraced the true faith. Now you must atone for your sins and heresy. The court directs that on this night, two hours before midnight, you shall appear in an *auto-de-fé* to publicly admit and atone for your heresy. Your temporal being will be cleansed by fire and you will go to Purgatory where you will be judged by God. You will be shown the torment of your forbearers, who were all heretics and are now burning in hell forever. If you truly cleanse yourself of sin, and if it is God's will and judgment, you will ascend to heaven.

"God have mercy on your soul, Martín Ibarra Paz."

*

Tears ran freely down her face as Gina watched the video. As the inquisitor asked whether Martín admitted to his heresy, the container door opened and Nicolás came in.

"What the hell?" he yelled when he saw the screen.

Gina faced him. She said, "The Inquisition has condemned him as a heretic, and Martín admitted his guilt."

Nico's body tensed with rage.

Dennis put his hand on Nico's shoulder. "Keep calm," Dennis said. "We need your help to get him out of there. I have an idea."

*

Takeshi Ishikawa strode rapidly down the corridor of the presidential palace. A military aide walked beside him.

"Sir, the latest photos and acoustical pick-ups indicate a column of about a thousand troops moving south from Albina. They are believed to be seeking a crossing of the Maroni River to enter French Guiana. And our intelligence confirms that the French do not have sufficient military assets in place to defend their border."

They stopped in front of the door to the president's office. "So they are currently violating LU territory, and threatening French Guiana," Ishikawa stated.

"Yes, sir."

"Very well," Ishikawa said. "We must uphold the sovereignty of the Latino Union and lend assistance to France and their department. Contact General Mello and tell him to dispatch aircraft to interdict them. Tell General Mello he is not to use force unless directly fired upon. I want him to use any means available short of attacking them to stop their movement and get them to surrender. Is that clear?"

The major drew to attention and saluted. "Yes, Mr. President."

"You'll have my written orders within the next hour," said Ishikawa, who then waved his hand to dismiss the aide.

The aide double-timed to his office, closed the door, and punched a button on his phone.

"Yes?" said the answering voice.

"General Mello, we have to act quickly. Ishikawa will have new orders delivered to you within an hour."

"I understand," Mello replied, and the line went dead.

*

General João Mello lurched out of his chair. He opened a metal door and strode into the darkened operations center. The duty officer stood and saluted as the general approached. Mello read the man's nametag, then spoke in a low voice audible only to the officer.

"Captain Moreno, I authenticate X-ray-Sierra-Papa."

Moreno picked up a large black notebook from his workstation and broke the seal. He opened it, ran his finger down a column, and then across two rows.

"Authentication valid, sir."

"Stop voice and video recorders," Mello said, and the officer hit a series of keys on his console.

"All stopped, General."

"I now issue a verbal order to Task Force Thirty-One operating in the vicinity of the French Guiana border. This is a violation of the sovereign space of the Latino Union. The Latino Union is required to counter this insurgency by orders of the president. The task force is to attack and destroy the rebel force with all available resources. The lead aircraft will receive a ground-based K-band beacon signal five minutes before the attack commences. Transfer the image to all task force aircraft to establish the axis of attack and initiate action. Are my orders clear?"

"Yes, General," Captain Moreno said.

"Get me Colonel Lavigne of the French Foreign Legion in Cayenne," Mello ordered.

Moreno picked up his phone and relayed the call request to the communications officer. That completed, he sat at his desk rapidly keying the attack orders into the command computer.

"Orders transmitted to, and acknowledged by, Task Force Thirty-One. Attack to commence in six minutes, K-band beacon broadcast to begin in 55 seconds."

"Very well," Mello said. "Put this call through to my office."

Mello climbed the amphitheater steps two at a time, went into his office, closed the door, and picked up his phone. "Colonel Lavigne?"

"Yes, General. I'm in my helicopter, please excuse the background noise."

"No problem, Colonel. We have an airborne task force that has been shadowing the rebel force moving south from Albina. The revolutionaries are looking for a river crossing into your department, avoiding the main highway to Cayenne by staying in the jungle. While they are still in LU territory we will commence fire because our task force has been fired upon. We're starting an attack in a few minutes. I suggest that if you have rapid deployment capabilities you move your forces into that area in case survivors cross your border."

"Thank you for the warning, General. I've had a feeling all day that the shit was about to hit the fan. Also, thanks for the military assistance—our troops are spread pretty thin here. I'm moving my men immediately."

"Good," Mello said. "Out." He hung up the phone.

*

As Carolina trudged beneath the dense jungle foliage with her troops, she felt the slight vibration of her beacon receiver against her waist. "I've gotta take a leak," she said to the nearest soldier. "Keep the column moving."

The man nodded and gestured to the string of soldiers behind him. Carolina waited until they passed her, then clicked a button on the beacon and dropped it in the thick grass by the trail. Then she turned and sprinted into the dense forest. Branches tore at her face and torso as she raced ahead, struggling with her footing amid logs and tree roots. She continued to run until she came to a ravine. She slid down until the bottom arrested her descent.

Carolina checked her watch again and dropped to one knee, gasping for breath.

She pulled out a flare gun and shoved a flare into the breech.

*

The radar screen in front of Lieutenant Ramirez cast a shadowy green glow onto his face.

"Pilot, F-C-O, turn left heading zero-zero four."

"Roger," came the response over the interphone from the pilot of the AC-130 gunship.

A pulsing light appeared on Ramirez's screen. "Task Force Commander, F-C-O, K-band beacon zero-two-four at nine kilometers."

"Roger," came the response from the flight deck. "That beacon is your target point, the axis of attack is a line extending two-zero kilometers north to two-zero kilometers south of the beacon at headings zero-three-zero, break, two-one-zero."

Ramirez checked two other monitors. "Sir, I confirm the presence of target forces on infrared sensors and low-light-level video."

"Wait for the signal to begin firing," Lieutenant Colonel Branco, the Task Force Thirty-One commander, responded from behind Ramirez.

"Roger, sir," Ramirez responded, and turned a disk on his communications panel. "Task Force Thirty-One, Lead F-C-O, putting target axis and kill zone on your repeater screens now. Commence attack upon your visual confirmation of the signal."

*

Carolina heard the sound of the turboprop engines and checked her watch. As the second hand moved toward 12 she raised the flare pistol over her head and looked for an opening in the jungle canopy. She found one, aimed carefully, and squeezed the trigger. The flare shot upward on a flaming tail through the vegetation and up into the black sky.

*

Lieutenant Colonel Branco stood behind the copilot's seat looking out the side windows of the C-130 cockpit. He saw a phosphorescent red ball rise abruptly from the canopy and arc through the sky beneath him. "F-C-O, I have visual on ground fire tracer rounds two o'clock, two kilometers. We are under attack by hostile ground forces. Certify that in the combat action report. Commence fire, commence fire."

Through his headset he heard the F-C-O repeat over the radio, "Task Force, commence fire, commence fire!"

Branco watched as tracer rounds formed glowing tubes extending from 10 AC-130s flying in formation, dull red hoses streaking to the ground and performing a leisurely, undulating lightshow. From the rear of his command aircraft he could hear the whine of the electric motors rotating the multiple barrels on the two 20-millimeter and two 40-milli-meter Vulcan cannons, spewing a steel hail of bullets at a combined rate of 12,000 rounds per minute. Chemical clouds wafted up from the aft cargo compartment.

The carnage on the ground was unthinkable.

*

Colonel Lavigne watched through the open door of his helicopter, look-ing across the river into Suriname. The navigation lights of a formation of aircraft were easily visible in the moonless night until the lead airplane banked to the left and turned off its lights. Each successive gunship did the same as they established a wide elliptical orbit. All 10 ships opened fire at the same moment, their cannons unleashing tracer rounds that looked like magenta-colored ropes extending from the black early-morning sky to the ground. Explosive rounds glittered against the black velvet of the jungle.

From his time in the infantry Lavigne knew what it was like on the ground under the gunships. The rebel soldiers had been hiking in the dark-ness, careless and confident that they were hidden and unnoticed. They may have heard the engines of the approaching aircraft, but probably not. The men and women in the column, nearly blind on a night like this, were suddenly surrounded by the din of death: grunts, groans, and screams as their comrades were ripped apart by the bullets. Headshots mostly, because the fire was coming from above. The lucky ones would have their brains disintegrated instantly, never feeling any pain. Others would topple to the ground and scream for help that would never come.

Lavigne tore his eyes away from the terrible strike to check his watch. By the time he looked up again, the firing had stopped. He knew it was unlikely anyone had survived the shooting, but in less than a half-hour from now two C-47 transports—aircraft from the 1930s, Lavigne thought ruefully—would land his forces in Saint-Laurent-du-Maroni. Lavigne had left just a single platoon back in Kourou after bringing most of his com-mand here. The command post back in Paris had ordered Lavigne to tem-porarily fortify the border opposite Albina to block any surviving revolu-tionaries from entering French Guiana.

Colonel Lavigne leaned back in the web seat, expecting to feel relief now that the waiting was over. Instead he felt the familiar ache in his diaphragm and tingling around his hairline.

*

Carolina felt the ground impacts before hearing the sounds. Hunkered down in the ravine, she sensed a vibration from the dank clay under her knees and heard the dull crunching of heavy rounds thudding into the earth a short distance away.

Men and women howled and shrieked as they were caught in the fusillade from the sky. Carolina looked toward the top of the ravine and saw the lights strobing from the blackness overhead. She knew the 10 AC-130s were flying in an ellipse using the beacon she had dropped to establish the target offset, all firing relentlessly into the kill zone.

After five minutes elapsed on her watch, the shooting stopped. There was a long period of eerie silence, and then the animals of the jungle resumed their cacophony. Carolina pulled a second beacon from her pocket and activated it. Ten minutes later she heard the whumps of a helicopter arriving to pick her up.

CHAPTER TWENTY-SEVEN

WARO MOTO WAS awakened when his private jet was 30 minutes out of San Juan Diego. He slipped on a robe and opened the cabin door, admitting an aide who had been sitting outside with a briefcase on his lap. The young man entered, bowed, and handed a pot of hot tea to Moto.

"Moto-san, the Inquisition broadcast from Mexico City will begin airing live in a half-hour, and the *auto-de-fé* is scheduled for 10 p.m. The decoy force in French Guiana was attacked and destroyed just after nightfall, and the French moved most of their legionnaires to the northwest corner of the country, at least an hour by air transport from Cayenne. Commander Delta was extracted and will lead the main attack force beginning at midnight."

"And President Ishikawa?"

"General Mello had to advance the attack time on the rebel decoy force to avoid contradicting a direct order that was forthcoming from the president."

Moto nodded thoughtfully. For once, everything seemed to be falling into place as planned.

"Anything on Gina Ishikawa, Lenin, or that television technician?"

"No, sir, nothing. They have disappeared."

Moto's short-lived contentment evaporated. "Use your powers of deduction, Fujimoto-san," he growled. "Lenin and Gina Ishikawa have affection for Martín Ibarra. I believe they will attempt a rescue."

"The priests assure me that will be impossible."

"The priests?" Moto scoffed. "They are children in such matters. Send more of our men there, and tell them to be on the lookout."

*

General Mello stood in front of President Ishikawa's desk, making no attempt to hide the disdain he felt toward his commander-in-chief.

"You disobeyed a direct order from me," Ishikawa said quietly.

"I had received no written order from you."

"You know I issued a verbal order that was to be confirmed in writing."

"It was a military decision," the general responded. "Our task force was fired upon, and we had to launch a protective reaction strike. If you doubt that, feel free to question the task force commander or any of the crewmen."

"I do not doubt you have them well-rehearsed by now," the president snapped. "Just as you eliminated the audio and video feed from the command post."

"Equipment malfunction, sir."

Ishikawa studied the general's face for a moment. "It was an unnecessary slaughter."

"It was a *necessary* military operation to stop a violation of Brazilian sovereignty."

"Of Latino Union sovereignty, you mean, General."

Mello's look of disdain hardened. "Of course, that's what I meant... sir."

"I want a full report on my desk by five o'clock," Ishikawa said. "Dismissed."

The general saluted, executed an about-face, and left the office.

*

Martín Ibarra sat on his bed with his head hanging. It would be a matter of minutes before the guards came to take him to the *auto-de-fé*. His mind reeled with confused images of heresy, jumbled with glimpses of a time past when he was at peace with himself and his heritage.

Martín threw himself down on his bed, trying to get control of his runaway thoughts. When his head hit the pillow, he felt the lump of the camera and battery pack under it.

What had the voice in his ear said?

To put the belt on when he knew he wouldn't be searched. Martín had no idea whether he would be searched, but since he was to die at the *auto-de-fé*, it didn't matter.

For the thousandth time, he asked himself: who was trying to rescue him? The voice had said "we." Who were they? Did he even want to be rescued? Or was it better to accept the verdict of the Inquisition and the release of death?

Martín searched his will and found that his survival instincts had not been fully extinguished yet.

Martín grabbed his pillow and the camera belt under it. Keeping his body between the camera and the equipment, he moved over to the toilet. There, he dropped the pillow, pulled up the front of the *sanbenito*, and quickly threw the belt around his waist, fastening the Velcro tabs. He tucked the slender television camera into the belt. Once it was in place, he dropped the front of the *sanbenito*, flushed the toilet, and washed his hands. Then he returned to his bed to await his fate.

*

"Martín, if you're wearing the battery pack and camera, tap the microphone twice," Dennis said.

Two tapping sounds came from the speakers.

"Okay, great," Dennis said into his microphone. "We're going to be improvising from here on out, Marty, so you'll have to just listen and trust us. You'll hear from me again when you begin to move."

Dennis toggled a switch, muting the microphone.

Gina reached up and tapped her finger on a monitor that displayed a BBC broadcast showing a map of northeastern South America. An arrow marked a spot near the French Guiana border.

"Turn the sound up for that," she said to Dennis.

He did, just as the announcer was saying, "… and the Latino Union air force reported that its gunships struck a rebel force nearing the Maroni River. The spokesman for the LU general staff estimates that at least one thousand rebel soldiers were in the military unit. The spokesman said he believed that rebel casualties were one hundred percent, but that confirmation would not be possible until daylight arrives."

"Oh, my God!" Gina exclaimed. "That's Nico's army."

Dennis shrugged. He had too much to deal with here in Mexico City. He looked Gina in the eye. "No word of this to Nico yet. Okay?"

Gina nodded and Dennis threw some switches. "Okay," he said into his microphone. "Nico, you need to move up to the entrance of the Inquisition building and be my eyes. We think they're going to move Marty real soon."

*

Martín heard the bar being lifted from his door and the hinges squeaking as the door opened. "Come on, Ibarra," a voice called to him. He stood and two guards entered, with one taking each of his arms.

"Okay, let's go," a guard said.

Through the earphone Martín heard the unknown yet now familiar voice saying, "Okay, Marty, I know they're moving you again. As soon as we know what's up, we'll work something out."

Martín made the usual walk across the courtyard, but instead of turning right toward the courtroom, the guards turned him to the left. A heavy door squeaked and the guards pushed him forward. The air felt cooler, and the city sounds were more distinct. He could hear the murmur of a large number of people milling around.

*

"They're going to a live broadcast!" Dennis shouted. He, Alejandra, and Gina watched the monitor as a coat of arms appeared on the screen. It depicted a small tree surrounded by a Latin phrase.

"The seal of the Holy Office of the Inquisition," Gina said.

The image faded, and was replaced by a priest dressed in formal vestments standing in front of an ornate life-sized cross.

"For too long, we have allowed sin to spread unchecked across the earth," he intoned to the camera. "Even worse, sin has been normalized by its acceptance. That cannot continue! This historical broadcast is a momentous leap forward for true Christians of the One True Church to reclaim the quest toward righteousness that will lead to the realization of our common goal: Christ's second coming and his rightful place ruling Earth!"

The camera shot changed to the outside of the Inquisition building across the street. A crowd had gathered around a door centered in the screen. The door opened and two priests came out followed by masked men wearing gray uniforms and Kevlar helmets. They carried riot batons, and they swung them in front of them as they walked, pushing people back to clear a path. A man in a tall conical hat and a green and yellow long shirt came out next with a guard gripping each of his arms.

"Martín!" Gina exclaimed.

His eyes had the blank look they had seen before. Behind Martín another man emerged wearing the pointed hat and *sanbenito*. He was middle-aged and heavyset and blinked rapidly as his eyes stared straight ahead. His face depicted sheer terror.

A woman was next, young and pretty. She also shook with fear as her eyes flickered around. At the end of the small procession a guard held up a kind of stick figure with a *sanbenito* draped on it. A cardboard name card hung from the neck of the figure, and in the bright television lighting the name MANUEL ORTIZ was written in heavy black ink.

"What the hell is that?" Dennis asked.

"An effigy," Gina said. "I'm guessing they had to try someone in absentia."

Alejandra turned and left the control room, letting herself into the studio where she and Lenin had been working on their presentation. Her eyes brimmed with tears. She shut the door behind her, turned off the one monitor in the studio, and sat down. She began going through the presentation again, line by line.

"Okay mates," Dennis said into his microphone. "They're on the move, heading toward the plaza on Tacuba. There's people along both sides of the street—at least twenty guards walking, ten on each side of the procession."

"Are the guards armed?" Nicolás asked.

"Billy clubs for sure, but we can't tell if they've got firearms," Dennis said.

"Does the crowd look hostile to the Inquisition?" Lenin asked.

"Not hostile," Dennis said. "But they sure aren't thrilled about what they're seeing, either. From what I can tell, they look scared shitless."

"Lenin, meet them at the corner and shadow Martín as they move him," Nicolás said. "Just stay back in the crowd."

Dennis flipped from one audio channel to another. "Marty, we've got a guy in the crowd near you," Dennis said. "I'm watching you on TV. If you hear me, shake your head. Okay, great. Hang in there, mate. They've got you well-guarded right now so we can't do anything yet, but we're with you every step, okay?"

Martín shook his head again.

*

The television feed begun airing live on a Mexican state-owned channel—little more than Mexico's equivalent of CSPAN—but the Inquisition had timed an email and internet blast to news producers and social media outlets around the globe, offering up a live feed of the first Church-sanctioned *auto-de-fé* in centuries. The audience leaped into the millions in the span of less than thirty minutes.

Simultaneously with the beginning of the broadcast, hundreds of thousands of previously dormant social media accounts sprang into life. All of them bore the names and photographs of church congregants whose identities had been stolen by Moto Electric. The accounts began churning out posts and content that had been pre-loaded, and algorithms run by the supercomputer in Burgos, Spain assessed people's responses and reactions to the posts in real time, formulating and composing replies. Anyone who posted negative comments regarding the broadcast was flagged by the computer, and those persons' profiles were crosschecked against its massive database. If the supercomputer located incriminating audio, video, or texts relating to those persons, a message was sent to them with a link. It was a simple statement: stand down, or the link would be published publicly and disseminated to the Inquisition for review and possible prosecution.

During the course of the broadcast, social media platforms across all of the Spanish-speaking countries of the world initially surged with outrage and horror, but very quickly the initial tidal wave of dissent was turned into a mere trickle.

The Inquisition's propaganda accounts ran rampant through the internet with a singular message: what was happening now in front of the eyes of the world was righteous and good, and anyone who said otherwise was a traitor to Christianity.

*

King Carlos sat on a sofa with Pope Pius next to him in the opulent visiting dignitaries wing of the Latino Union's presidential mansion. The cardinal of Spain sat nearby in a chair, leaning forward and peering wide-eyed at the screen in front of them. They watched together as the television feed showed the solemn procession in Mexico City.

An aide to the king came into the room. "Your Majesty, a call from President Ishikawa."

Carlos waved dismissively without looking up. "Tell the president I am indisposed, and that I will call him at my earliest opportunity." The aide withdrew from the room.

"Ishikawa is seeing this now," King Carlos said. "He's trying to find out what's going on."

"He knew nothing of the trial, I presume?" the cardinal asked. The contemptuous look he received from the others answered his question.

"Look at the expressions of the people lining the street," the king said. "They are awed by the power of the Church! Threatening them with an *auto-de-fé* of their own was as effective as we could have hoped."

On the television, the Inquisition prisoners plodded in procession through the crowd. A voiceover gave background information on the arrest and trials of each of the prisoners, and stated that all of them had made verbal confessions of heresy followed by signed statements. A photo of Martín Ibarra appeared on screen and the voiceover summarized his life and work. The program showed excerpts from the trial, with sound bites from each of the lawyers, as well as Ibarra himself, culminating in his admission of heresy.

"Do you think that this will convince the Americans that Ibarra had due process of law?" Pope Pius asked.

"It doesn't matter," King Carlos said. "By the time they figure anything out, Ibarra will be dead and we will be on our way to asserting dominion over Spain and the Latino Union—with the full and unwavering support of our constituents."

Television coverage moved on to each of the other prisoners, showing their pictures and reciting their lives and sins, each time finishing with their admissions of heresies.

"What about the President of Mexico?" asked the pope.

"Dealt with," said the king. "The Mexican army has blockaded a four-block radius around the plaza. He found the Inquisition's evidence of his past transgressions… convincing. The *auto-de-fé* will proceed undisturbed, and all participants will be granted immunity from prosecution in Mexico."

The pope nodded with satisfaction.

"Where is Mr. Moto?" the cardinal asked.

"On his way from the airport," Carlos answered. "He's going directly to Ishikawa's office to remind him of his personal liabilities if he tries to interfere with the *auto-de-fé*."

"Is everything ready in Kourou?" the cardinal asked.

"It's underway right now. Nico Ibarra's decoy force from Venezuela was destroyed, and now the real invasion is moving in. Tomorrow morning I will assume power as the head of the Latino Union and Spain—with the full support of His Holiness. By tomorrow afternoon, I will have 'negotiated' the end of the rebels' insurrection and they will agree to stand down, with me granting them immunity for doing so. The LU military will immediately annex French Guiana, making the LU, under me, a nuclear power."

King Carlos raised his glass of wine toward the cardinal and beamed the radiant, confident smile of a man who had never seen, or even contemplated the possible existence of, meaningful adversity.

The cardinal nodded, a smile tugging at his mouth. It was an astounding privilege to be at the end of the long line of Guardians. An unbroken succession that had, through their loyalty and faith, brought about this glorious day. For more than five hundred years, the Guardians had done what was required. And now the Millennium was about to arrive.

*

Colonel Lavigne had established a base camp along the Maroni River, set up perimeter defenses, and deployed patrols to look for rebel survivors who might have crossed the river. His helicopter was twenty minutes out of Kourou when a radio call came in.

"Colonel Lavigne, this is Lieutenant Beloit. Sir, First Squad reports engagement on the northern perimeter of the launch complex."

"Say again?" Lavigne asked. "Armed engagement?"

"Affirmative, sir. Small arms fire. They landed on the beach, and the squad commander reports that there are other boats offshore."

Lavigne wiped his forehead. This couldn't be happening. The command center in Paris had fallen for the feint—the oldest trick in military tactics. Almost all of his troops were more than two hundred kilometers from Kourou.

"Lieutenant, call the Shore Patrol immediately. Have them dispatch their two boats to intercept the landing forces and—"

"Colonel, sir, I already called them. Both of their boats were at the refueling pier when there was a sapper attack. One is sunk, and the other is on fire."

"Goddamn it!" Lavigne shouted. "Forget that, call the Gendarmerie and—"

"All their vehicles have been sabotaged and their communications lines were cut. We can only reach them with a citizens-band radio. Armed civilians have surrounded the barracks. They're not letting anyone in or out and they're monitoring all C-B channels."

Lavigne swore again, cursing the military command back in France for ignoring his warnings of the growing separatist civilian movement. "Call Major Fayette at the forward base camp and tell him to get the men ready to redeploy back to Cayenne tonight. Next, call the airfield and get those C-47s headed back to airlift them."

"Sir… I called the airfield… the planes. Well, sir—"

"Sappers there too?"

"Yes, sir."

Lavigne covered his microphone and let loose a long string of profanities. "Pilot, tie the lieutenant and me into a call to Chain Mail."

In a moment, the duty officer at the military command center in Paris was on the radio.

"Chain Mail," Lavigne said, "we must have reinforcements sent here immediately. My forces are divided and it will be at least 24 hours before I can get the main body to Kourou. We need an airlift from France of at least a division with armored vehicles. What ETA can I expect?"

There was a long period of crackling static, and finally the voice from

Chain Mail said, "Colonel, it will be at least 72 hours before we can get the logistics organized to begin any troop movement from here."

"All right. I'm going to call the Latino Union and request immediate military assistance."

"Colonel, that's a negative. Do not request Latino Union assistance."

"What? All I have is one platoon of light infantry in Kourou! We cannot hold our position without reinforcements. The LU can have a force here in a couple hours."

There was no response for a full minute. Then a different voice came over the radio.

"Colonel, you are ordered to use French forces to the best of your ability. You are ordered not to request any foreign forces."

"What the fuck is the matter with you?" Lavigne roared.

"Colonel, there are important sovereignty issues. If any of the Latino Union's forces set foot in the country, they won't leave."

"Then call the Americans! They can be here in less than a day. The civilian population is already siding with the rebels. We must have help or Guiana is lost anyway!"

"Colonel, this is Chain Mail. You have your orders—carry them out."

*

The lights around the Zócalo were dazzling. The metal grandstands set up on three sides of the square were full of people who sat quietly, watching the procession of penitents filing into the central plaza. A crowd lined Tacuba Street, forming a human corridor ushering the two men and one woman in *sanbenitos* to the raised platform in the center of the plaza. In the center of the platform was a 15-foot tall, ornately decorated metal stake. A cross sat atop it, and straps protruded from it near its base. The procession climbed the steps and one of the priests produced a microphone.

"Let us pray. Oh, God, our Father, we are here with three sinners *in corpus*, and one *in absentia*, who have appeared before a court of the Holy Office of the Inquisition. They, under Your guidance and in the presence of Your beneficence, have admitted their heresy. Now they stand before You, having received their temporal sentences, and await Your judgment."

*

Nicolás Ibarra and Teodoro Lenin stood at the foot of the grandstand, among the gawking mob, looking around frantically.

"Do you see anything?" Lenin demanded. "Something, anything to use to get him out of here?"

Nicolás's eyes scanned the area, looking for a usable escape route. He pointed toward the ground next to one of the stage's legs that supported the corner of the platform. "Ventilation for the Zócalo metro station," Nicolás said into his microphone.

"If you're going underground," Dennis said, "I won't have radio contact with you. And we really gotta stay in touch to get Marty out of there once things get chaotic."

"You're the communications expert," Nicolás said, grabbing Lenin's arm and steering him toward the entrance to the Zócalo metro station. "Think of something."

Dennis angrily flicked off his microphone. "Goddamnit! This guy does *not* stay on script!"

"Isn't that why you got into this business, Dennis? No scripts?" Gina asked.

Dennis glared at her.

Gina put her hand on Dennis's shoulder. "There's no more planning from here on out. Marty's life depends on our actions over the next minutes. We've got to work the problems as they come."

Dennis looked at his friend and nodded. "No pressure, eh? Well, as I told you before, I'm a hell of a lot better than you print journalists at meeting deadlines."

Gina smiled. "Prove it. Save Marty and give me a 20,000 word feature I can offer to the highest bidder while you're at it."

Dennis smirked and then his smile faded as he rubbed his head. "Gotta get a comm circuit... anything!"

"So, what's the specific problem we're working through here? Talk it out and maybe I can help."

"Our radios can't penetrate all that concrete and steel above the metro. We've gotta have a way to relay or amplify the signal."

Gina thought. "Dennis, does Mexico City's metro have an underground cellular network? Something you can tap into?"

"I like your thinking," Dennis said as he pulled up Google and typed in a few phrases. The search results popped up, and after scanning for a few seconds, Dennis groaned. "Nothing in service yet. TeleMexico said they'd have one installed and operational two years ago, but you know how that shit goes. It's still at least a year away."

"Any chance that the infrastructure already put in place as part of the build would be useful?" Gina asked.

"Probably not. If it's down there and not active and powered up, there's no way for me to— wait a second! The New York subway has an emergency communications system that relays radio transmissions from above ground and rebroadcasts them underground, and it works both ways. Maybe they have that system here too. What the hell was the frequency?" He pulled up an app and started spinning through the frequencies. After a minute they heard the abrupt cadence of two-way radio transmissions.

"What are they saying?" Dennis asked.

"One guy is asking for a visual check for vagrants on a station platform," Gina said. "The other guy said he's on his way."

"That's got to be it. Now I need to tie our TV camera as a sideband to that frequency… we may need visuals."

Dennis worked furiously for several seconds.

"Nico, are you at the station?" Dennis asked into his microphone.

"Yeah, we're waiting for you," Nicolás said.

"Go down the stairs, and keep talking as you go."

"Okay, I'm walking… one… two… three… four… five… six…"

Nicolás and Lenin walked quickly down the steps, taking them two at a time, and stopped in the lobby.

"We're in the station," Nicolás announced.

"Hot damn," Dennis said. "I've got you loud and clear. You'll hear other calls on this frequency though. With any luck they've got enough to deal with right now and won't come looking for us while we're intruding on their band."

Nicolás vaulted over the turnstiles and kept running. Lenin stood at the stainless-steel gate, puffing hard. Finally he crawled under the metal arm and trotted after Nicolás.

*

Dennis turned up the sound and stared at the video transmission he was receiving. Clergymen walked around the platform swinging incense burners while an ornately dressed priest chanted a long prayer in Latin. The camera scanned the crowd in the grandstands, panning in on the faces of the men and women in attendance. They all sat in sullen silence, watching intently.

Through Martín's microphone they could hear his rapid breathing, and in the background, the booming amplified voice of the priest.

"Don't worry, Marty," Dennis said. "We're working on something right now, mate."

*

"Here!" a voiced hissed at Lenin.

He looked to his left and saw Nicolás standing inside a steel door. Lenin stepped into a space thrumming with electric motors and rapidly moving air. They walked quickly up a flight of stairs to another door. Inside was a large sheet-metal cabinet bristling with ducts headed out in every direction.

Nicolás knocked on the sheet metal with his knuckles. He was answered each time with a clang, until at one location the sound that reported back was muffled. He got down on his knees and felt around with his hands. Nicolás twisted some butterfly-shaped tabs and a panel gave way. He laid it on the concrete floor and looked inside.

The cubical cabinet was an air plenum with an enormous fan—10 meters in diameter—horizontally mounted at the top. The fan drew air from various areas of the station and siphoned it through the ducts and into the plenum, where it was expelled through the grating at the top.

Nicolás cupped his hands around Lenin's ear and shouted through the noise generated by the fan and rushing air. "Got to shut it off! Find a switch!"

They both looked around the inside of the plenum but saw nothing.

Lenin ducked out the door and found a control box mounted on a wall. He grasped the lever on the side and pulled it down. The roar of air tapered off as the electric fan wound down. After a few seconds there was silence.

When Lenin went back into the room, Nicolás pointed upward at the bottom of the grate next to the stage. The glow of bright lights shone through the steel slits, and they heard an amplified voice fulminating against religions that were contrary to God's laws.

Nicolás climbed the metal rungs welded to the sides of the plenum and made his way between the now-stationary blades. Through the grate he could see the leg of the platform standing on top of one of the steel panels. He studied the clamps used to secure the panels and began to work one of them. Lenin saw what Nicolás was doing, climbed the rungs on the opposite end of the plenum, and began to loosen a clamp at his end.

"Dennis, we're directly under the west side of the platform," Nicolás said. "There's a steel grate, and we're going to get it open. We'll have to get Martín off the platform and into the opening. Once he's down here, we can disappear into the maze of subway tunnels and figure out a place to rendezvous on the fly."

"Got it," Dennis said. He turned to Gina. "So how do we get Marty off that platform and through that grate?"

*

Father Serrano took over the ceremony and announced with great flourish the name of the first heretic.

In the fog within Martín's mind, something sounded oddly familiar. Of course, the priest's voice was familiar, but... something else.

Then he heard Father Serrano's voice intone the name once again, and Martín's blood ran cold. "No," he said softly.

"Sister Maria Trinidad," Father Serrano said. "Her sins, among many, include her failed and blasphemous attempt to aid a Jew and heretic!"

Martín bolted forward in a wild attempt to bull rush Father Serrano, but was quickly grabbed by two pairs of muscular hands that effortlessly pulled him back. Ahead of him, he heard the soft, heartbreaking sound of a young female voice crying in terror.

"Sister!" he cried out.

"Mr. Ibarra," Maria sobbed. "They told me all the terrible things you have done! Why did you do this to me?"

"No, Sister!" Martín wailed, but his feelings betrayed him. He was a sinner and a heretic who had admitted to his horrible crimes against God, and he had brought this woman into his profane plot. By doing so, he had desecrated her. This was his fault, and his fault alone.

Father Serrano began reading from Revelation.

"You monster!" Martín bellowed. "She's innocent! She didn't know!"

"Spoken from a fellow heretic!" Serrano sneered. "Your words carry no weight, and your turn will come."

He returned to the ceremony, intoning that God would now purify this heretic by cleansing her with fire that symbolized the flame brought to Earth by the Fourth Angel and that resulted from the Fourth Angel's vial being poured upon the sun. As he spoke, Sister Trinidad was strapped to the stake.

"Do you sincerely repent your heresy?" Serrano asked.

The question reverberated throughout the plaza as the crowd gawked.

There was no audible reply. The crowd had gone utterly silent. All Martín heard were Sister Trinidad's choked sobs, and all he could see in the darkness behind his blinded eyes was her sweet, innocent face and how she had trusted him and believed that it was God's will to help him. And he had allowed her—no, *encouraged* her—to do so. His attempt to escape had been a failure, and this was the result. Nothing had changed other than that this innocent woman was going to die. All because of him.

"You are no longer Sister Maria Trinidad," Father Serrano said. "You have desecrated your vows to your order and they are hereby annulled. I excommunicate you and banish you from the bosom of the One True Faith and the One True Church. You, Maria Anita Perez Moreno, are cast out, anathema. As written in Revelation, you blasphemed the name of God by your actions and repented not. You shall now be scorched by the vial of the Fourth Angel, in the name of the Father, the Son, and the Holy Spirit."

*

Dennis and Gina watched the monitors in horror. They didn't understand why Martín had charged the priest, but for a few terrifying moments they thought that he was going to destroy any chance they had of saving him.

One of the cameras zoomed in on Sister Trinidad's face. A wide band of red light emanating from each of the triangulated lasers played across her head as their operators swiveled them into place. One of the bright red lights flashed into the sister's wide eyes and she jerked her head around wildly. There was a murmur from the crowd in the grandstands. Sister Trinidad shrieked and then yelled something incoherent, struggling against the restraints on her arms and legs.

The three laser beams locked on the nun's head and immediately smoke began to emanate from her skin. She jerked her head, but the beams remained on her, scorching her face. She began crying hysterically and yelling in desperation, "No! No! No! I repent! I repent!" Her howls were nearly inhuman.

The priests prayed, clutching their Bibles close. Sister Trinidad shrieked and turned crimson as her face contorted and burned. Her eyes rolled wildly and spasms wracked her body. She screamed again and again until blood sprayed from her mouth, choking off her wails into a weak gurgle. Finally, with a cough, she slumped forward. In the cool night air, steam rose from her motionless and unrecognizable head. A small flicker of flame lingered in her hair.

From Martín's audio feed, Dennis and Gina heard soft, whimpering cries. They were the sounds of a man whose mental collapse was complete.

Two guards stepped forward with the priest, who held out a crucifix toward the body as the guards untied the still smoldering prisoner.

Dennis concentrated on his work in an attempt to mentally push past the atrocity he had just witnessed, adjusting the gain from his antenna and clearing the pictures on the monitors. "How's it coming?" he asked Nicolás through his microphone.

"We've got five more grate locks to remove. Tell him that in a few minutes we'll need for him to get to the west side of the platform—um, his... left—and be ready to jump."

Dennis relayed the information to Martín, but was unable to tell whether it registered. All he could hear was weeping.

CHAPTER TWENTY-EIGHT

DENNIS HAD THE raw feeds from four different television cameras in the Zócalo giving him various views and close-ups. Several times the cameras had captured Martín Ibarra's face and he and Gina could see the muscles of his neck and jaw corded and working. They watched the guards and priests while trying to devise a means to move Martín down to ground level where he could get to the steel grate.

"The fastest way is for him to just step off the side of the platform and drop straight down through the grate and you two get him out of there," Dennis transmitted to Nicolás.

"It's a good five-meter drop and he can't even see!" Nicolás said. "He could easily break a leg blindly falling that far. We'd never be able to escape with him hobbled. Once we get him through the grate, we're already going to have our hands full negotiating him through fan blades and then getting him down a two-meter ladder. We need him fully mobile."

"There's four guards up on the platform and at least ten surrounding it," Dennis said. "But they never closed off the gap that the processional up the stairs created. His best bet will be to make a break for it and run down the platform stairs and then jump into the grate opening."

The radio crackled back with barely controlled rage. "Dennis, he's blind! He can't make that on his own! Someone's got to get out there and help my brother... now!"

"But Marty's used to hearing my voice," Dennis said. "If we change—"

"No time!" Nicolás hissed. "Do it now!"

Dennis looked at Gina. "He's right," she said. "We'll have to take a chance. Get out there, Dennis, do something." She moved his hands aside and nodded at the control panel. "These are the switches I use to talk to Marty and Nico, right?"

"Yeah," Dennis said as he grabbed an earpiece from a table next to the console and jammed it into his ear. A wireless microphone was hurriedly affixed to his shirt collar as well. "You've got me now, too. The switch to the right of Nico's will let you talk to me, and my audio is on the third slider."

"Got it," Gina said.

Dennis stuck two pistols into his belt, went to the door, looked back at Gina with wide, frightened eyes, and then disappeared through it at a run.

Gina turned around and studied the monitors. The male prisoner preceding Martín was now being strapped onto the stake. The feed cut to a tight shot of Martín's face. She took two deep breaths and keyed the microphone.

"Martín, this is Gina. Tap twice over the mic if you hear me."

*

Nicolás and Lenin sweated heavily as they worked to unscrew the clamps holding the grate in position. They each had one more clamp to remove. Nicolás's wrist trembled from the exertion as he gripped the locking ring and twisted. It started to rotate.

Lenin did the same, but the ring on his side didn't move. He flexed his hand several times and gripped it again, grimacing in pain as he tried to turn it.

Nothing. He looked desperately at Nicolás. The revolutionary scrambled down the ladder rungs and climbed up next to Lenin. He gripped the side of the locking ring opposite Lenin's hand and they both pulled with everything they had. The ring refused to move.

Lenin looked down at his watch. From the noise directly above, he knew that another prisoner's execution had just commenced. Martín would be next.

*

From the tumult around him, Martín knew that the second prisoner was dead. In a few seconds they would begin leading him to his fate.

He heard a voice in his earpiece, but this time it was a woman's voice. The voice of a dead woman. The voice of the woman he loved. The voice that had whispered so many intimacies in his ear—but also the voice that had shouted "Jew!" at him with loathing and hatred.

His head spun with dizziness and he sank to one knee. The dreamlike memory washed back over him—Gina leaning from her towering witness stand and accusing him over and over: "Jew, Jew, Jew, Jew!"

But now the dream was slightly different. This time, underneath the voice that was spewing hatred at him from above, there was another version of Gina's voice. This one was soothing, quiet, and urgently pleading. It was saying something about... tapping? And unlike the dream voice, this voice had the feeling of immediacy. It was happening now, through the same earpiece he had been receiving instructions from.

It was impossible.

Was this somehow a trick orchestrated to make his final moments even more horrific? His inner voice shouted a warning: "Don't listen!" It drowned out Gina's voice in his ear. His mind flashed through a series of images with Gina demonstrating her loathing of him.

But there it was, still... Gina's faint voice in his ear saying, "Martín, you've got to listen to me. We don't have any time."

Martín began to sob.

*

Dennis pushed through the crowd toward the grandstands. He wondered what the hell he would do when he got there. He strained as hard as he could to move forward, but his feet felt sluggish and heavy—bogged in the pavement. Sweat poured off of his face and his lungs burned in the thin air of the seven-thousand-foot-high, smog-choked city.

*

Gina watched as Martín's head snapped back and his limbs splayed out as though he had been jolted by a cattle prod. His vacant eyes rolled in their sockets and he dropped down on one knee. She heard his anguished voice coming through the speakers crying, "No, Gina, no, not you! You're dead. Why so much hate, Gina? Why the hate?"

Gina swallowed hard, and steeled her resolve. "Martín, you've got to believe me. Your brother Nico and Teodoro Lenin and a man named Dennis Prinn—they're all trying to save you from these fanatics. You have to do what I tell you."

In the monitor she could see him clamping his hands over his ears. From the speakers, she heard him moaning, "Lenin hates me… Nico, they've broken him… Gina hates me… and I have killed a nun!"

"No, Martín, I love you. You have to believe that! I never stopped loving you. Listen to me now, and do what I say so that I can tell you that in person."

She saw him doubled over with his hands squeezing his ears, tears streaming down his face. On the main feed they were broadcasting Martín's admission of heresy. He was begging for forgiveness before the Inquisition court. Gina wondered what she could possibly say to bring any sense of reality back to the man she loved.

*

Dennis slumped against a leg of the bleachers. "Lenin, Nico, I'm at the grandstand. Do you have the grate open yet?"

Nico's voice sounded strained. "Not yet," he said.

Well, fuck, thought Dennis. His hand instinctively reached down and palmed the grip of one of his pistols. He was out of time.

*

Gina saw the guards grabbing Martín under each armpit, yanking him to his feet, and shoving him forward. The red lights from the lasers teased the empty stake that awaited him.

"Gina, I'm going to try to take out the lasers," Dennis said. "I probably won't get all three—do what you can to get Marty moving off that platform."

"Nico, is the grate open?" Gina asked.

She heard a couple of grunts and then a satisfied yelp. "Yeah, we're ready here! Get Martín to it and we'll pull him in."

"Dennis," she said, "see if you can do something to clear the way for Martín after you take out the lasers."

From the speakers Gina heard Dennis's high-pitched, hysterical laugh. "Yeah, mate," he said. "I'll get right on that!"

*

Dennis watched the platform. Martín was slowly being led to his execution. The lasers were flitting over the stake—ready to lock onto Martín's head once he was in place.

Dennis pushed back through the crowd and ran a hundred meters beyond the grandstands to a small opening in the throng. He could see laser emplacements to the east and west. The technicians were focused on the platform below them. He looked around, saw that no one was paying attention to him, and slipped one of the machine pistols out of his belt. He raised the gun and squeezed the trigger.

There was a rattle and a bright muzzle flash from the gun, and Dennis saw the laser burst into a shower of sparks. The technician operating it dropped to the floor of the platform, covering his head with his hands. Ignoring the screams and commotion around him as the people in the crowd began to panic and flee from the sound of gunfire, Dennis turned to the west and pulled the trigger again. There were a series of electrical arcs from the equipment, and the laser went dark. Emboldened, Dennis fired wildly at the remaining laser, but his line-of-sight was blocked by a stanchion of lights.

People around him were scrambling to get away. "Run," he shouted maniacally, "or I'll kill you all!"

They ran.

His path now cleared, he turned and raced back toward the platform.

*

Martín felt himself being dragged. Strobe-like images flashed in his brain of Gina, Lenin, his brother, and Sister Trinidad. Everyone hated him for being a Jew and wanted to kill him, and yet Gina's voice was saying into his ear that she loved him and that people were trying to save him.

He didn't know who or what to believe.

"Martín," Gina pleaded, "if you ever loved me, listen to me now and remember when we were on your boat in the ocean and I didn't know where we were or where we were going, and you showed me how the compass and the compass rose on the map worked together. You told me that those would always guide us to where we needed to go. I'm your compass now. Let me guide you. We can work together to get you where you need to go. Do this for me—because it's the last chance we've got, Martín. Listen to me closely and don't think—just act." Gina paused, took a last, deep breath, and then shouted into the microphone with everything she had. "Turn to your left ninety degrees and run... now!"

She watched the monitor as the guards led him forward. Martín's head jerked and then he twisted his torso to the left and lunged. The guards' grips on Martín's arms were wrenched free by the sudden, unexpected movement, and one of the guards took an unsteady step backward.

"Run forward—go!" Gina shouted. She watched as Martín accelerated blindly forward, running on pure faith and instinct.

Dennis Prinn appeared on screen at the top of the platform stairs, running toward Martín. He was shouting something when a luminous red dot appeared on his shoulder. She saw a wisp of smoke ascend from his shirt and dissipate into the night air. Dennis whirled around and slapped his hand against the smoldering fabric. The speakers emitted a loud yelp of pain and a curse.

Dennis looked off screen and shouted at Martín to run toward his voice. A red dot moved to Martín's head, trying to remain fixed as he sprinted forward. A guard lunged at Martín from behind, baton cocked and ready to strike. But as he did so, he ran between the laser and its target. Smoke rose off the guard's back in tight ringlets and the man threw his arms up in pain and surprise. He collapsed to the platform.

"Turn ten degrees more to the left and keep going!" Gina shouted.

On the monitor she saw Martín turn slightly and dash ahead. Dennis leaped forward as Martín arrived at the top of the stairs and he grabbed Martín by the arm. Martín started to wrest himself away from his unknown assailant. Dennis shouted something into Martín's ear.

"Martín," Gina said, "you're four paces from the stairs. Just let Prinn be your eyes!"

Dennis released Martín for a moment to slug an oncoming guard, and Martín staggered forward a few steps, suddenly unmoored and directionless. He bumped into the wooden handrail and grabbed it. The red dot glowed briefly just above Martín's hand on the top of the post, which burst into flames and sailed off. Martín recoiled from the heat and then began to try to find the edge of the stairs with his foot. Dennis was suddenly beside him again and helped him forward to the top of the stairs. As the laser moved upward toward Martín's face, a priest seized him by his *sanbenito* and caught the crimson beam across his eyes for his troubles. The priest's mouth opened into a wide 'O,' and his hands clutched his smoldering eyes as he fell.

"One pace forward, and the next step will be the first step down," Gina called through the microphone. "I don't know how many stairs there are, but just keep going until you get to the bottom."

Martín obeyed and disappeared off the screen. Dennis saw that Martín had his footing and turned around at the top of the stairs. He raised his gun and fired a sequence of shots into the air. The priests and guards on the platform flattened themselves upon the wooden planks.

The searching scarlet point of light fell on Dennis's breastbone. Dennis grunted, spun around, and disappeared down the stairs.

*

Dennis ran down the steps to Martín and caught the blind man's arm. "Come on! Your brother is waiting for you!" Dennis turned him to his left and saw the laser beam sweep past them, searching back and forth. As it flashed over Martín's head and down toward his face, Dennis shoved him aside. The beam settled on the metal leg of the grandstand instead, setting off a shower of sparks. As the sparks arced over the two fugitives, the beam moved on, illuminating a wooden post that quickly burst into flames.

"Keep running!" Dennis shouted. "Lenin and your brother have an escape hatch ready—I can see it six meters ahead!"

Dennis saw Nicolás and Lenin emerge from the hatch, crawling onto the pavement. He yelled in their direction and they turned to see the onrushing men. The laser beam cut into a steel strut beside Nicolás, burning him with flying molten metal as the strut melted. He dropped prone on the ground and the beam swung toward Lenin. Nicolás grabbed the professor by the ankle and yanked him to the ground.

Dennis dragged Martín toward the open grate. Suddenly there was a sharp pain in his leg and he pitched forward to the pavement. "Go, go straight ahead!" he shouted to Martín.

"Dennis!" Nicolás bellowed. "The gun, the gun!"

Dennis could barely see Nicolás as the pain blurred his vision. He tossed one of the machine pistols, sending it scraping across the concrete into Nicolás's hand. As the revolutionary brought the gun up, the red dot traced across his chest. He rolled, and chips of concrete flew amid crackling sparks beside him. He pointed the gun in the direction of the laser emplacement and repeatedly hammered the trigger, letting loose a stream of fire. The red dot skittered across his forearm. Nicolás rolled to his left, aimed, and squeezed again, firing another dozen rounds. Bright flashes erupted from the laser emplacement.

Martín sprinted five more paces straight ahead until there was nothing under his feet. His stomach fluttered with the sudden downward acceleration as he dropped. Sharp metal jammed under his armpits, arresting his fall and causing searing pain. He let out a cry as his feet dangled in the air below him. Martín extended his hands, feeling around to get oriented. There was a round hub with steel paddles extending out from it—a large ventilator fan, he guessed—and he had fallen between two of the blades.

Shots rang out, and screams erupted above him. There were thuds as bodies fell to the pavement. "Martín, drop down!" his brother shouted. "Drop down before they kill you!"

Martín lifted himself off the blades, turned his body, and let go, dropping straight down through the gap and crashing onto a metal floor. He heard a voice shouting in English from the opening above him, "Pull out the camera, pull out the camera!"

Martín lay stunned for a moment. Then he remembered the camera and battery pack under his *sanbenito*.

*

For several seconds, Gina could only see people lying dazed, dead, or wounded on the platform.

Dennis's voice came over her headset, strained and muffled. "Gina, throw the G-eight sliding switch and tie in the Delta receptor."

She looked around the console, found a sliding switch marked "G-8," and moved it from zero up to the maximum position. She then searched the console until she found a switch labeled "D" and toggled it to the opposite position.

Gina looked up at the bank of monitors and saw that one of them had stripes flashing across it, but no picture. She checked the intercom switch settings and said into the microphone, "Martín, do you have the camera out now?"

She heard heavy breathing. "Yeah, it's out," Martín finally said. "But what the hell good will it do?"

"It'll give me a picture and I'll be your eyes."

Gina looked at the monitor again. There was still nothing on the screen but wild patterns. She ran her hand through her hair and looked over the console. What did she have to do to get his camera turned on? Then it occurred to her that the problem might not be on her end.

"Martín, have you connected the camera to the battery pack?"

"Shit. No," he said back through the headset. There was a pause. "Okay… I found a wire… you getting anything now?"

The stripes on the monitor changed, rolled, and suddenly she was seeing a picture of a corner formed by a wall and a floor.

"I see something, Martín!" she exclaimed. "Pan the camera around you."

"He's down here!" a voice off camera called.

Gina saw a wall with vertical seams and metal rungs attached to it. The camera moved on and she saw a series of black squares down at floor level. "Martín, there's an opening down by the floor. Get down on all fours, turn ten degrees right, and crawl forward. Hold the camera in front of you as you go."

The view on the monitor changed as he dropped to the floor and the dark squares straight ahead became larger as he crawled to them.

"That's it, keep going… keep going… okay, it's a pipe or a duct or something."

"Which way?" Martín croaked.

Another voice barked in the distance, "Get some men down here, now! *Now!*"

There was a loud clash of metal. "Shit!" Martín said.

"You're at the wall, Martín—turn the camera to the left." The screen was blank. "Turn it right," she said. Blank.

"Point it down."

On the monitor she could see the dim outline of a square.

"Martín, the duct turns ninety degrees downward. I can't tell how far. Ease yourself forward, use your hands, and try to brace yourself on the sides. Let yourself down slowly."

Martín crawled forward, feeling with his hands. He felt the precipice and stopped. Behind him he heard boots thudding onto sheet metal. Voices echoed through the duct.

"Martín, someone's close behind you, I can see the light of a flashlight shining on the metal. Get down that duct fast!"

"Wait, I think I see someone up ahead!" a voice called.

Martín shoved his legs down the opening and let himself slide. His hands burned against the metal as he slid downward for what seemed like an impossibly long time until his feet hit something solid. He held the camera out, turning his body at ninety-degree intervals until he had scanned a full circle with the camera.

"The duct splits four ways," Gina said. "I don't know where any of them go," she added with a slight tone of resignation.

There were metallic thuds ringing nearby.

"Someone's crawling into the duct behind me," Martín whispered into his microphone. "Guess!"

"Turn all the way around from where you are now, get down on all fours, and move straight ahead."

He did as she said, holding the camera out ahead of him.

*

Dennis rolled over on his back and looked up. A circle of grim faces glared down at him. Three pistols and a rifle were inches away from his face.

"*A pie!*"

"Uh, I don't speak Spanish," Dennis said.

Hands gripped him under his armpits and jerked him to his feet. A searing pain shot up his calf and he slumped back down to his knees. He was pulled upright again and his captors shoved him forward toward the open grate.

"*Donde está tu compañero? A donde escapó Ibarra?*"

Dennis shrugged in mock ignorance. Someone shouted up from below and the guards shoved Dennis to the opening in the grate.

"No way!" Dennis said. "I can't go down there! What if that bloody fan turns on?"

He heard the pistol under his ear being cocked. "Yeah... I'll give it a go, *amigo*."

Dennis gave a wan smile and thrust his legs between the fan blades, slowly letting his body slide into the flashlight-illuminated chamber below.

*

Nicolás and Lenin stood outside the plenum. As they replaced the removable panel to seal off their escape route they heard men climbing down from the open grate. They heard Dennis saying, "No way! I can't go down there! What if that bloody fan turns on?"

Nicolás walked quickly to the fan control switch on the wall. He checked his watch, then put a hand on the lever. After ten seconds he threw the switch.

The howl of a large electric motor energizing mixed with a cry of surprise and distress. The motor caught for a moment as the blades found resistance, then they gained speed again and screams echoed around the plenum. The fan turned faster, the screams were abruptly cut off, and multiple thuds reverberated against the floor. The fan accelerated to full speed creating an impenetrable barrier between the surface and their location.

Nicolás went to the removable panel and listened. There was silence other than the rumbling of the enormous fan. Then, much closer to the metal door, a voice pleaded in English, "Let me in!"

Nicolás got down on his knees, twisted the butterfly screws holding the panel, and slid it aside. He crawled in until only his feet were visible to Lenin, who waited with apprehension. Nicolás backed his way out a few seconds later, and Lenin watched as Nicolás reappeared, dragging Dennis by his shirt collar.

Dennis was covered with blood but was intact. Nicolás pulled him clear of the access panel, put it back in place, and secured the screws.

"Son of a bitch," Dennis said. "I could have been killed in that fucking fan!" He looked back and saw that there was no line of sight from the panel to the fan blades. "How did you know when I cleared it?"

Nicolás gave a dry chuckle and shrugged. "*Buena suerte?*"

"*Good luck?*"

"And here I thought you didn't speak any Spanish," Nicolás said.

*

Martín crawled as fast as he could, holding the camera out in front of him.

"There's a turn coming up," Gina said. "To the right."

He felt ahead with his hand and made the turn. He stopped a moment to listen. He could hear thudding in the ducts above and behind him.

"I can't tell how close they are," he whispered.

"Turn the camera behind you." He did. "I don't see any light—they must not be too close."

Martín crawled on until Gina said, "I see a T-intersection going left and right. Go left."

He turned and steadily moved forward.

"Slow down, slow down!" Gina said. "Show me what's ahead."

Martín held out the camera.

"Point the camera down," Gina instructed. "Okay, it turns straight down. There's a blue light below, and it looks like there's a grate or something. Let yourself down easy—it's maybe three or four meters—but keep a hold if you can in case the grate can't support your weight."

Martín felt around the square duct, trying to find something to grasp. The duct was smooth except for the sheet metal seams. The echoing thuds were getting louder behind him. He pushed his feet down into the duct and let himself down. He extended his arms, letting his body hang down as far as he could.

Martín hung on one hand and put the other out to push against the duct to act as a brake, but it was awkward while clutching the small camera. He couldn't get as much purchase against the sides as he wanted to, but he needed to act quickly. He let go of the ledge above and started dropping. He accelerated much faster than he intended and he jammed both hands out against the metal, slowing his fall until his left hand slid over a metal seam, slicing his skin. Martín yelped in pain and his hand involuntarily released. He fell several meters until his feet slammed onto something solid. Before he could get oriented he heard the groan of steel bending and felt a snap as the metal gave way beneath him.

*

Gina heard the loud crash and watched as the picture on the monitor turned at crazy angles, finally stopping dead. There was no sound.

"Martín?" she said into her microphone.

Silence.

"Martín?"

She threw a switch on the console.

"Nico, can you hear me?" Gina asked.

"I hear you, Gina. What's happening?"

"Martín fell down a duct, and I think he's unconscious."

"Do you have a picture? Can you tell anything from it?"

Gina studied the dim picture before her. There were no features visible except for a light source on the left side that was some distance away, glowing blue. There were two parallel lines coming from behind the camera and converging near the light source. She spoke into the microphone describing what she saw.

"We just got Dennis away from the Inquisition," Nicholás said, "but he's badly hurt. It'll be a few minutes before we can go looking for Martín."

Gina looked at the monitor and called Martín's name. As she studied the televised picture, she realized what she was seeing. Martín had fallen from a ventilation grill above the subway tunnel. The converging lines were the tops of the steel rails illuminated by a blue-tinted work light. The camera had fallen between the tracks and was pointed down the tunnel.

From the perspective of the light and the shiny steel rails, Gina knew that Martín was lying on or between the subway tracks.

CHAPTER TWENTY-NINE

PRESIDENT ISHIKAWA PACED as he watched the *auto-de-fé* on television and waited for King Carlos to call him back. The door to his office opened and Waro Moto swaggered in, seating himself without being asked to do so.

"Were you aware that this—this—travesty would take place?" the president demanded.

Moto gave a dismissive wave of his hand. "It is of no consequence. It is among the *gaijin*."

Ishikawa glared. "I will not tolerate such an outrageous act of religious fanaticism." He walked to his telephone, picked it up, and hit a button. "Minister Luz, come to my office at once."

"Do not get your minister of justice involved," Moto said when Ishikawa had hung up the phone. "You don't seem to understand—or won't allow yourself to understand—what is required to seize, and more importantly, *hold* power in the world."

"You *knew* of this?" Ishikawa asked.

"Of course," Moto said. "Why must I continually explain these things to you? It is like talking to a child."

"*You* delivered Martín Ibarra to them."

Moto laughed. "Actually, to all appearances, you did. One of your military planes took him to a small airfield and he boarded a plane operated by the Inquisition. We have the exchange on video, of course."

"That was supposed to be a French military plane taking him to the launch complex."

"No one but you knows that," Moto replied.

Justice Minister Ernesto Luz, standing in the doorway to Ishikawa's office, cleared his throat. The president looked at Moto, then walked to his desk. He sank into the leather chair.

"Excuse me, Minister Luz," he said, looking out the windows at the mountains. "I was mistaken. You are dismissed."

*

Lieutenant Colonel Lavigne jumped out of a camouflage-painted vehicle, crouched, and ran to three Legionnaires, throwing himself down beside them.

"Sir, automatic weapons fire one click to the right," a corporal said.

Colonel Lavigne's radio erupted into life with a report of another contact two kilometers away—small arms automatic weapons fire reinforced with mortars. Bullets cracked over the ditch as heavy automatic weapons rattled close by.

Another call came in to Colonel Lavigne. A squad had engaged three kilometers to the east and was encountering mortar and rifle fire.

"Alpha One, this is Echo One."

"Go ahead, Echo One," Lavigne said.

"Sir, there are… locals advancing with the invaders. Civilians."

"Are you sure?"

"Yes, sir. One of them is Guillerme Portier—"

"Cease fire, cease fire!" He held the radio away from his mouth and swore violently. He hit several keys and said, "Chain Mail, Chain Mail, this is Alpha One."

"Go ahead, Alpha One, this is Chain Mail."

"There are French civilians mixed in with the invading forces and they are moving off the beach toward the launch complex perimeter. We cannot hold them off without returning fire. Awaiting your orders."

"This is Chain Mail. Stand by, Alpha One."

"Chain Mail, we have very little time. The enemy has already engaged my forces and they are at the perimeter!"

The responding voice, sounding bored, said, "Chain Mail copies, Alpha One. Stand by for orders."

Lavigne watched the seconds counting off on his digital watch and silently seethed.

*

Standing on the beach under the clear night sky, Carolina peered at her map with a red-tinted flashlight. The man next to her, Guiana's representative to the Chamber of Deputies in France, was listening to a handheld radio. He hooked it back on his belt.

"Commander," he said, "it looks like we have at least four French soldiers pinned down here and eight more a bit further west. From this morning's military briefing I know that there is only one squad here in Kourou—the rest are at the Suriname border. Lavigne has called his commander in Paris, telling him that there are civilians mixed in with your men. The military will have to consult with civilian politicians and that will paralyze them for a good while. Move your troops in quickly."

"I'm ordering one of my reinforced squads to increase the rate of fire with mortars so Lavigne thinks that's the main body," Carolina said. "We'll keep flanking until we string them all the way out and they run out of men."

A soldier ran up, out of breath. "Commander Delta," he gasped, "the scientists are very nervous hearing the gunfire."

"Keep them back on the beach, but away from the barge and the boats. Just tell them to keep their heads down and they'll be okay."

Carolina excused herself and walked swiftly down the beach, passing the huge rusted dredging barge they had used to move most of their forces, equipment, and scientists from Point Delta in Guyana, where a sympathetic government and population had hidden them as they had massed their forces. The cavernous hull of the barge had been loaded with two hundred of her men along with the scientists, engineers, and their tools. Another fifty of her men and their equipment were hidden below deck in the tugboat that pulled the barge.

They had sailed slowly down the coast of Suriname. A patrol boat looked them over, but its bored-looking captain decided the barge was heading somewhere to dredge. As they came into French waters off the coast of Guiana, another patrol boat had concluded the same thing, waving amicably to the ragged men in the tiny wheelhouse of the tugboat. The mast of the dragline concealed an antenna that they used to communicate with support locations all over South America via sophisticated encryption gear obtained in North America and Europe. They had arrived unopposed and now had an established beachhead where they joined up with the local independence forces. Carolina's plan to mix the Guianese civilians among her own forces was working perfectly, paralyzing the French military and civilian command structure.

Carolina quickly covered the four kilometers to where a platoon was firing into the launch complex perimeter. There was still no return fire coming from the Legionnaires. Some of the best fighters in the world were being rendered impotent by men six time zones away—men who were being called from the beds of their wives and mistresses to deal with an inconvenient problem in an overseas department that they frankly didn't care about.

*

"Martín," Gina called into the microphone. "You've got to wake up. Please, Martín."

Only a few minutes had passed, but there had been no sound from the speakers and no movement of the camera. She looked at the other monitors and saw pandemonium in the Zócalo. More gray-clad armed guards had marched into the plaza while Mexico City police and army units milled around, looking unsure of what to do. Bodies were being hoisted out of the open grate at the base of the raised platform. The priests on the platform stood in a tight group, their leader gesticulating broadly and pointing toward the steel grate.

Nicolás's voice came through Gina's headset. "Gina, we've got Prinn's bleeding stopped, but Serrano's got his guards reorganized and they're everywhere in this station. What's happening with Martín?"

"He's unconscious and he's lying on the subway tracks…"

The picture on her monitor moved slightly, and she heard a groan.

"Hold on," she said, then clicked over her mic to Martín's channel.

"Martín!" she called.

"Wha... who?"

"Martín, this is Gina. You've got to move! You're on the subway tracks!"

"Dream...'nother dream. What's happening to me? I can't think... I can't..."

The background noise coming from the speaker increased—a deep vibration.

"Martín," Gina said, trying to stave off her rising panic. "Can you move?"

"Leg... head... can't think."

"Pick up the camera and point it around you," she said.

There was another groan and the picture on the monitor moved. She saw shadowy shapes, a curving wall, and a signal light. "Keep the camera moving, Martín," she pleaded. The picture rotated again, and in the dim light she could make out the tunnel stretching away. The noise through the speaker was growing.

"Point it the other way," she said and the picture swung. A point of light appeared in the center.

"Wind," Martín said.

Gina looked at the monitor again. The point of light was growing.

"Martín, listen," Gina said. "There is a subway train coming. You have to move off the tracks. Do you hear me? You have to move off of the tracks, now."

All she heard in response was a weak groan.

*

Voices squawked over Lavigne's radio, all of them raised several octaves by the adrenaline surge of combat. They called out casualties, demanded combat medics, and reported enemy positions fewer than fifteen meters away. Lavigne calmly passed out assurances and issued battle orders. All squads had reported casualties—a total of three men dead, twelve seriously wounded, and twenty-one walking wounded. The squad leaders couldn't be sure, but they thought there had been at least ten Guianese casualties, and an unknown number of revolutionaries were down.

Lavigne knew that his order from Chain Mail, which he had just passed on to his junior officers and non-coms, was impossible to obey. Command had ordered Lavigne to use lethal force only against the invading revolutionaries, and not against the Guianese citizens. They were outmanned, outgunned, and paralyzed by a ridiculous order.

The colonel had tried the citizens band radio once to establish direct communications with the Gendarmerie, but from the occasional blasts and the glow of firelight from the direction of Kourou, Lavigne knew they had their own problems. The latent independence movement that had been smoldering for years had exploded into open violence against French rule.

"Alpha One, this is Juliet One."

Lavigne put his radio to his mouth. "Go ahead, Juliet One."

"Sir, we're at coordinates five point two four six one nine eight break negative five two point seven six three six zero two. There are about two hundred civilians coming toward the wire, many of them armed. They are heading straight for us. Am I authorized to fire?"

Lavigne wiped his face with his hands. The non-stop adrenaline buzz that had been ratcheting up his senses for the past three hours was taking its toll.

"Juliet One, at what distance are they?"

"Their point man—and woman—are less than a click from my position."

"Alpha One, this is Hotel One."

"Juliet One, standby, break, break, Hotel One, this is Alpha One."

"Hotel One has approximately two hundred civilians coming toward our position. They are armed and less than a click from the wire. What do you want me to do?"

"Alpha One, Alpha One, this is Kilo One, I've got civilians coming at me too. Sir, I've got to open fire if I'm going to be able to repel them. Do I have permission?"

Lavigne clicked off his radio. "Goddamn son of a bitch! Shit! What the hell do they expect me to do?"

His driver, a young enlisted man from Greece, looked back him with wide eyes, but said nothing.

Lavigne squeezed his eyes shut. "Chain Mail, Chain Mail, this is Alpha One. Our position—" His voice broke. He tried again to speak, and made only a hoarse croak. He cleared his throat. "Chain Mail, this is Alpha One. Our position is untenable and indefensible. If we defend our positions, there will be hundreds of French civilian casualties. I have carried out your orders to the best of my abilities. You decide what to do about the missile. I say it should be destroyed right now by an air strike, and we will just have to accept the Japanese civilian casualties against the many more that will result if these rebels carry out their plan. Alpha One out."

Lavigne turned off the frequency linking him to the general staff and switched to tactical frequency. "All units, all units, this is Alpha One, authenticating Delta-Bravo-Mike-November-X-ray-Lima. I order all units to cease fire. I say again, you are ordered to cease fire. Report immediately to company HQ, where we will surrender. Alpha One out."

*

Martín felt the wind blowing on his face and a sense of nostalgia swept over him. He remembered traveling on the São Paulo metro trains with Gina. They waited in stations talking, hugging, and kissing, and when a train approached they would feel the breeze first. Martín had explained how a subway train in a tunnel was just like a piston in a cylinder. As it moved, it pushed a wave of compressed air ahead of it signaling its imminent arrival. Then he had made a lewd joke about a piston pumping in a cylinder.

Gina's voice was calling to him now, reaching him through his reverie. He felt a terrible pain in his right leg and he couldn't remember whether Gina hated him or loved him. Both seemed equally possible. Either way, her voice in his ear was imploring him to move, and a train was coming… if it came, he—*they*, he corrected himself, if Gina was still with him— would just get on it and ride it to… wherever.

He was vaguely aware of an object resting in his hand. Oh, yes, the camera. The one that felt like a pencil and allowed him to "see" because he would point it and Gina's voice would talk in his head, telling him to go left or go right or up or down. And now she was telling him to move, and her voice pleaded the way he wished she had pleaded with him so long ago not to leave her in Brazil. If she had, he was sure that he would have relented, and they could have been together. Instead he was just laying here in a state of confusion and pain. His leg hurt so much. He didn't want to move.

But there was her voice, in his ear, telling him urgently to move, over and over and over.

He reached out and felt the steel rail. It was smooth on top and vibrating. And surely that meant a train was coming. At least that's what Gina kept saying.

He pulled himself toward the rail but, God, his leg hurt so badly! *How about that*, he thought. *I can see stars of pain even with my blind eyes.* And the noise—now a roar—was getting louder. More and more the wind pushed against his body. He strained again, pulling himself, but his leg hurt and the wind and the vibration and the noise and Gina's voice and the train were all crashing together...

*

The noise of the approaching subway train thundered from the speakers. Gina watched the light growing until it filled the screen—a white fireball that washed everything out. There was a flash, then darkness, and then a receding roar. She squeezed her hands against her ears and looked away. In ten seconds, it was gone.

Silence.

Gina slowly relaxed her hands on her ears. She raised her head, reluctantly looking at the monitor. Half the screen was black, but on the other half she could see a stationary light. Another signal, she guessed. There was a moan of wind, and nothing more.

Gina pounded the control console with her fists as tears welled in her eyes.

*

Father Serrano had discarded his miter and vestments in favor of a gray jacket. Behind him, armed guards trotted in his wake as the priest hurried through the subway station.

"So, when Nicolás Ibarra... overpowered you," Serrano sneered, "you last saw them in this part of the station, right?"

"Yes... Father," one of the men said.

Serrano led the guards to the train platform. He stood looking both ways into the tunnel, shining a powerful flashlight.

"They'll be in this tunnel somewhere," he said. "He couldn't have made it very far. Divide up. The two of you—that way… I'll go this way. Stay in touch by radio."

They climbed down onto the tunnel floor, walking quickly along the concrete pads supporting the rails. Serrano called out as he gestured to a shrouded rail running parallel to the pads, "And stay clear of that third rail, gentlemen. It'll do even more damage to you than Nicolás Ibarra did."

The guards broke into a jog and disappeared into the tunnel.

*

The dying wind gave way to another sound.

A tone.

Then another.

They were going up and down slightly in pitch. "Doo, doo, doo, da-doo."

Gina looked up at the monitor and was greeted with the same view of… nothing. The tones continued, a little faster now. A melody.

Humming!

"Martín?" she asked quietly into the microphone. The humming stopped.

"Martín?" she asked again, louder this time.

The humming resumed, rising and falling without a recognizable melody. "Cam-er-a, cam-er-a, T-V, T-V-cam-er-a," the voice sang.

"That's right, Martín! Pick up the camera. Pick it up so I can be your eyes again."

"Be my eyes, beeee my eyeeees… ag-ain!"

Gina watched the monitor. The picture rolled crazily, and the signal light spun and disappeared off the screen. Then it stabilized, looking down the tunnel. The rails were shining from below, and the tunnel structure was arcing overhead in a graceful curve. A line of small lights, glistening like shining beads, stretched away into blackness.

"Martín, listen. Listen to me. There will be another train coming. You have to get moving. Walk the way you have the camera pointed."

The picture on the monitor started moving. The string of lights moved toward the camera, dropping off screen one at a time as Martín passed them.

"That's it," she said. "Keep moving! Something will turn up. Just keep moving."

*

Nicolás Ibarra peered through the ventilator grate. "We're at the subway tunnel, southbound," he said into his microphone. "How's my brother?"

"He's down in that tunnel," Gina replied. "He's delirious—maybe from the fall, maybe from the drugs—but he's walking now. I can't tell whether it's north or south."

"Has he come to any stations?" Nicolás asked.

"No. Just a long line of lights in the tunnel."

Nicolás felt wind blowing on his face. "Train coming," he said.

He listened as Gina said, "Martín, listen to me. Get over against the side of the tunnel. That's it. Turn ninety degrees… now, straight ahead. Now, step up over the rail! Go ahead… two feet, one foot, put your hand out. There, that's the wall. Turn the camera to your left. Get flat, get flat against the wall!"

Through his earpiece Nicolás heard the train thundering, and a few seconds later it flashed past the grate. He turned to Dennis Prinn and Teodoro Lenin.

"He's in this tunnel and he's close. This way!"

*

Pope Pius picked up the phone on the first ring. He glanced at the television where the live broadcast from Mexico City had been hastily superseded by a prerecorded program about the Inquisition's role as a bulwark of the holy faith and underwriter of political power.

"Yes?" he demanded.

"Your Grace, I—"

"I don't want to hear excuses! There are none for that, that…" The pope sputtered as he gestured toward the television.

"We're doing the best we can to find Ibarra and—"

"What do you mean, your best? Your incompetence has cost us much of the momentum we needed for the next phase."

"Of course, Your Grace. We will find him and capture him so that we can carry out the sentence on tele—"

"There's no time for that. Just kill him and we'll show the body afterward."

King Carlos nodded as he nervously listened to the conversation. His ascension to power was, to put it mildly, experiencing some bumps in the road. He reminded himself that while the dog-and-pony show in Mexico City was symbolically important, the truly crucial element was what was happening right now in Kourou. Even with the *auto-de-fé* ending in a fiasco, the eyes of the world were still all focused on one city block in Mexico City. And like a good magician, the Inquisition would utilize that diverted attention until it was ready to dazzle its audience with what had really been going on all along.

*

Colonel Lavigne heard the voices of a multitude singing and chanting all around him, the combined volume vibrating his chest. His staff vehicle stopped and he was lifted to a standing position.

With a sharp tug, the blindfold was ripped off his head. He blinked rapidly as his eyes accommodated the stunning white lights. Lavigne looked around and saw that he stood between two revolutionary soldiers.

He twisted his head around. Behind him his men lay or sat in the back of French army trucks, all of them blindfolded with their hands hand-cuffed behind their backs.

He looked to the other side and saw the Ariane Six rocket, shiny and graceful, poised for launch. The red-painted gantry tower stood next to the rocket, embracing it protectively with structural steel arms. Metal towers stood in a circle around the pad holding banks of sodium vapor lights that turned the night into day. The festive crowd around them stretched out into the surrounding darkness.

A young woman in camouflage military fatigues rose from the front seat of Colonel Lavigne's staff car and put a bullhorn to her mouth. Her left arm shot straight up and her hand clenched into a fist.

"*Vive la liberté Guianaise!*" she shouted through the bullhorn.

A roar came back: "*Vive la liberté Guianaise!*"

Commander Delta swept her eyes across the crowd, seeming to make eye contact with every one of the thousands who were now surging close to the army trucks. She dropped her left arm and said into the bullhorn, "Tonight, I have witnessed a death. Tonight, I have witnessed a birth."

An earth-shaking shout came back: "*Vive la liberté!*"

"Tonight, I have witnessed the death of a colonial anachronism—the death of French rule. Tonight, the dead hand of Eurocentric white rule has dropped away from the throat of the people of Guiana."

"*Vive la liberté!*"

"Tonight," Commander Delta went on, "after painful hours of labor, came the birth of a new free nation, of a new free people. Tonight, I humble myself before the citizens of free Guiana."

"*Vive la liberté Guianaise,*" the crowd roared, and guns were fired into the air.

When the firing stopped, Commander Delta again scanned the multitude, looking into the faces of the men, women, and children. She smiled. "I hope I will not be presumptuous to say that I was the midwife in this birth."

The crowd roared its approval. Carolina waited for the cheers to dissipate, relishing the expectant silence that followed it. Her voice dropped to a dramatic whisper.

"The man who we can all agree is the godfather to this birth of freedom… is not here tonight." She stopped speaking and swallowed several times, letting the drama of the moment grow. "Nicolás Ibarra would have walked barefoot through broken glass, would have crawled through burning coals, would have broken down the gates of hell, to be here with you this night."

The thousands around her hung on the pause, not daring to breathe.

"The man who fought for you, sweated for you, and bled for you cannot be here this night—this magic night, this birth night—" She spun around and slashed her index finger into the chest of Colonel Lavigne. "Because of this officer, this relic of colonialism, this dead hand of the old tyranny!"

The thousands roared, and a chant went up. *"Mort, mort, mort!"*
Carolina's voice rose again.

"You, who have suffered so long, deserve to shed his blood. But he is only a lackey in the power structure, and I believe you should be magnanimous toward him. For it was not this particular officer who killed Nicolás Ibarra—it was those of his reactionary military fraternity in the Latino Union who killed him."

She again muted her voice to a prayerlike susurration.

"Live with me, now, tonight, the horror. My companion, my compatriot Nico, leading brave men and women through the dense forests in the Latino Union. Their dream: to be with you tonight for this moment. They endured unspeakable hardships for weeks and months. They were near their goal, looking across the river from Suriname into your land. But that river was to become their River Styx! Fire and steel rained from the sky, and after an eternity for those brave men and women, they were transformed into martyrs to the cause of freedom."

Shrieks and howls of grief ripped from the crowd.

"But," she said, raising her voice, "on this night of freedom, I say we show our higher purpose by forgiving these agents of death." Carolina waved broadly toward Colonel Lavigne and the French soldiers in the trucks. "I say we spare them even though they would not have done the same for us. I say we use them as shields for this magnificent engine of struggle."

Commander Delta gestured grandly toward the Ariane rocket.

"This is now our prize of war and we will use it to protect our freedom from the vicious despot Ishikawa and the Latino Union that will surely try to crush our free state and annex it into the imperialist union."

The crowd roared its approval and again the cracking of gunfire filled the air.

"I ask you tonight to stand with me, to shield me and my friends for a few hours, and we will give you the instrument to preserve your freedom. Now, this night, this moment, chain the French mercenaries to the rocket! Then, I want you—all of you—to take your place on the gantry tower. Take your place with your children, with your elders, with your friends, and give us a bulwark against a strike from the air by the same cowardly dictator who murdered Nicolás Ibarra and the magnificent revolutionary men and women with him!

"I call on the spirits of hell to claim Ishikawa as one of their own and take him from this world. I call on the Prince of Peace, Pope Pius, and his temporal brother in Christ, King Carlos of Spain, to deliver us from Ishikawa's tyranny into their warm embrace of freedom and Godliness. Do it now, my brothers and sisters! Take your places now—be my aegis—and in return I will give you the weapon to protect your freedom forever!"

The thousands of men and women cheered and surged forward, with small children riding on their shoulders and infants in their arms. They led the French soldiers from the trucks and snapped their handcuffs to the gantry structure at the base of the Ariane rocket. The people formed a joyous line, singing freedom songs and dancing as their column undulated in serpentine-fashion up the gantry steps, level after level, until the entire structure rang with a vibrant festival.

*

Lenin stumbled yet again as he supported Dennis, who limped while transferring as much weight as possible to the professor. Nicolás moved ahead of them, impatiently pushing the pace.

"Come on, come on," he hissed at Lenin and Dennis behind him.

"We're doing the best we can," Lenin said, gasping for breath.

Dennis clenched his jaw against the pain in his leg where the laser had cut into his skin. Gritting his teeth, he turned to the professor and said, "Come on, prof. I can push the pace a little more. Nothing like a little searing pain to get the adrenaline going."

Lenin looked at Dennis skeptically, then nodded and dutifully increased his speed.

*

Gina's eyes watered with the strain of studying every visible detail on the monitor. The seemingly endless string of lights was interrupted occasionally by other light sources. Another metro train had approached and she had guided Martín off the tracks and up against the tunnel wall. She turned him and started him on his way—toward what, she had no idea.

As she swept her eyes back and forth on the monitor, she saw one light black out momentarily, then shine again.

"Martín, stop!"

The swaying movement on her monitor halted. She watched the lights and saw two of them blink out at the same moment.

"Someone's up ahead," she whispered. "Turn to your right. Now, two steps, up over the rail. Two more steps. Put out your other hand."

On the monitor, she could see some details of the concrete tunnel wall.

"Now, Martín, lie down along the wall and point the camera the way you were walking."

She watched the monitor, seeing the line of lights. From the very low angle they seemed to merge into one large luminous blob. There was an interruption of the lights, then another, and then another.

"Stay down and stay quiet," Gina warned. "Keep the camera pointed."

On the television she saw a human form in the dim light. It was moving forward with stealth, head turning from side to side. It paused, moved ahead a few paces, and paused again. Behind it were more figures, close together, matching the leader's starts and stops—implacable, searching, advancing.

From the camera angle looking up from the floor of the tunnel, the figure suddenly loomed, towering above Martín. It stopped and looked directly into the camera. Gina could see no features except for the two dark orbs of the eyes.

Then the face zoomed up close.

*

Martín stopped breathing. He heard the footsteps approaching him pause. He realized he was still holding the television camera out from where he lay, but there was no longer any narration from Gina—his eyes and conscience for the last several hours.

Martín could feel, as well as hear, shoes planting firmly beside him. Hands spaded under his armpits and he was propelled to a standing position. Strong arms encircled his shoulders and constricted him, forcing the air out of his lungs.

"Martín!"

It was Nico, and relief flooded Martín as he returned the embrace.

*

After the subway train raced past, Father Serrano called on the radio to the guards who had gone the other way. No, they responded, they hadn't found anything yet.

Serrano put on night-vision goggles, giving him an eerie green-tinted view of the tunnel. The line of work lights were hot spots washing out the features around them, and the rest of the panorama showed the concrete ties, the steel rails, and the third rail.

Serrano rechecked his pistol, making sure a round was in the firing chamber and ready to shoot. He held it up in front of him.

The priest moved carefully but relentlessly, scanning up and down and side to side to ensure that he missed nothing. Rounding a gradual curve, Serrano saw four figures standing to the side of the tunnel. Two were embracing, with two more standing behind them.

Serrano dropped to one knee and studied the scene before him. His grip on the pistol tensed. From here in the darkness he would have the element of surprise and could take out one of them for sure—maybe two—before the rest scattered or returned fire. He would have to get off a few rounds and then retreat further into the darkness where his goggles would give him the advantage.

He would have to make these shots count, and his top priority was to make sure that Martín Ibarra, the heretic, was taken out for good.

Serrano crouched in the darkness, moved forward to get the best shots possible, and listened for Martín's voice.

*

Gina listened to Nicolás's voice cracking as he said "My brother, my brother, my brother" over and over. On the monitor, the picture was a blur. It stabilized as the two brothers talked.

Behind the reunited brothers, she thought she picked up some sort of movement, but once again the picture veered wildly. Gina tried to relax. Between the three men who still had their vision, one of them would be able to see anyone approaching much better than she would on her feed.

"They're not going to hurt you anymore," Nicolás said. "By God, no more."

Martín sounded weepy. "Nico, you came for me. You weren't broken."

"Me, broken? What are you talking about?"

Martín's voice filled with joy and relief. "You have come so far, Nico! Don't you have men to order around in the jungle?"

Nicolás chuckled. "For you, my brother, I am willing to leave the comforts of the jungle and come to... a rat-infested underground tunnel! The sacrifices I make for my family!"

Martín smiled broadly, and then the smile faded and he grabbed Nico's shoulder. "Where's Gina?" Martín asked. "She's alive, see, she's alive! She's in my head."

"Ah, yes! Your girlfriend—the living embodiment of all I hate in this world? Power, privilege, inherited class! Her? Yes, you will get to see her soon. Like you, she has quite the story to tell! Come, let us get you out of here."

Nicolás squeezed his brother's neck affectionately and began to lead them slowly down the tunnel. Reflexively, Martín pointed the camera in his hand forward as they began to walk.

*

Gina listened with tears welling up in her eyes. Was it possible that she would soon be reunited with Martín? It seemed too far-fetched to actually happen, and there was still work to be done. Her friends were still being pursued, and she needed to focus on helping in any way that she could to get them out of the subway and to safety.

On her screen the picture swung back and forth lazily as the two men turned and walked. She was about to ask Martín to give her a steady look down the tunnel when the picture stabilized, as if Martín had already heard her unspoken command.

Gina now had a clear shot down the tunnel—and her blood went cold. Through the darkness she could now see some movement—a human form moving toward them in a low crouch.

"Martín, Nicolás, look out!" she shouted. "Just in front of you! Someone is approaching!"

Nicolás let out an explosive breath and the camera angle dropped as he threw Martín to the ground.

"The priest," Nicolás hissed.

"Serrano," Martín said, certain of it, though he couldn't see the figure's face.

"This persecution ends now," she heard Nicolás say. "The justice you administer is from hell, not from God!"

The picture stabilized, and Gina watched Nicolás running down the tunnel toward the shadowy figure, his back to the camera. The crouched figure in the shadows raised his arms, one supporting the other.

"Gun!" Gina shouted. "Gun!"

There was a bright flash on the screen and a popping sound from the speakers, and then another flash and pop. Nicolás spun completely around and stopped. He doubled over but then straightened up, turned around, and resumed his sprint.

Nicolás's image merged with the priest's as a new series of flashes and pops punctuated the video and audio. The two men toppled backward, locked in an embrace, and then the images on the monitor's screen were completely washed out by a brilliant flash of light. When the glare died down, Gina could see sparks arcing gracefully into the air and drifting to the ground.

The speakers above the console where she sat vibrated to the point of distortion with a chorus of screams.

CHAPTER THIRTY

PRESIDENT ISHIKAWA SAT staring, unblinking, at the large television screen in the Latino Union's military command center. The rocket gantry at Launch Pad Three in Kourou appeared as a living thing, teeming with humanity.

Major Soto consulted several sheets of paper on the conference table before him, then stood. "Mr. President, these images came to us fifteen minutes ago. Paris has not confirmed it, but it appears that the French Foreign Legion company and the gendarmerie in Guiana have surrendered. For now, French rule in Guiana has effectively ceased. From these images we estimate there are more than two thousand civilians on the gantry: babies, the elderly, women, and children. The Japanese technicians from Moto Electric are being held here—" the major paused the video and touched the screen with a metal pointer— "in this clean room around the nose cone, and a platoon of French Legionnaires are chained here, at the base of the Ariane booster."

Major Soto took a sip of water and adjusted his glasses. "From earlier intelligence, we know there were Russian and Iranian nuclear weapons scientists and engineers under the employ of this revolutionary group. There does not appear to be any way to destroy the missile without extensive civilian collateral casualties."

"'Extensive civilian collateral casualties,'" Ishikawa recited, mocking the dry delivery of the officer. "How long until it is nuclear capable?"

"All they have to do is remove the communications satellite and replace it with the warhead. Two hours."

President Ishikawa steepled his fingers and looked up at the fluorescent lights. He thought of the last twenty-four hours, and how many times the Japanese ambassador and foreign minister had called him to demand that no air strike be launched against the missile. The opportunity for a strike was now lost, of course. Ishikawa saw clearly in this moment that it had always been Waro Moto, manipulating him and his government.

The president reflected on his audiences with Pope Pius and King Carlos during the past day and night, when they had also appealed to him for restraint and inaction. Their complicity was clear now too. Professor Lenin and Gina had been right from the beginning. Ishikawa had been duped into delivering a political union and its people to the conspiracy of a dead monarchy, a theocracy, and a technocracy.

Ishikawa sensed the dead silence around him. General Mello stared down at a pad of paper before him. The other officers looked anywhere except into the president's eyes.

"General Mello," the president said. "Prepare as many fighters as are available with the best pilots from the combined Union air forces for a strike against the missile if it launches."

"Impossible, sir," the general replied.

"We are dealing with the impossible now. We will not strike it on the ground, but if the rebels decide to launch, we will at least have a chance to destroy it in the air."

Mello looked agitated. "Sir, I cannot—"

"You're fired, General Mello," Ishikawa said evenly. "General Hidalgo, you are now chairman of the Joint Chiefs. You have your orders."

The army general looked at each of the other service chiefs and at General Mello. They gave no response.

Ishikawa stood. "I see." He adjusted his coat, walked out of the operations building, and stepped into his limousine. As the car pulled away, heading for the executive complex, he pulled out his phone and thumbed a number.

"Colonel Kobe," a voice answered.

"Colonel, this is the president. I want Captain Fujiwara to report to the presidential aircraft in fifteen minutes and to prepare the aircraft for flight."

"Yes, sir."

*

The first slug had slammed into Nicolás's chest, spattering his face with his own blood and nearly dropping him. The priest's eyes glowed red with the light reflected from a trackside signal. Nicolás's vision blurred, and he knew that his life was about to end right here in a Mexico City subway tunnel. Everything he had ever been, and would ever be, was now coming down to these last seconds. He would not be denied this final act.

Nicolás willed the energy that came from the sum of all the hatred, love, nightmares, and dreams of his life into his leg muscles. From his genuflected stance only a meter from the priest, he lunged toward the outstretched gun. His peal of laughter echoed in the confines of the tunnel and grew into a roar as he crashed into the priest and threw his arms around the inquisitor.

Nicolás felt hot breath on his cheek as his face touched the priest's, smearing the holy man with his blood. He heard the deafening roar of the gun and was distantly aware that his body was being torn apart by bullets fired at point-blank range. But Nicolás's momentum continued to carry into Serrano, and he felt the moment that Serrano's feet lost their purchase on the ground and he began to fall backward.

Nicolás's laughter turned into a shriek of triumph as they toppled toward the third rail. As they fell, Nicolás stared into Serrano's horrified eyes and relished this final moment of victory.

Then the blinding flash washed everything away.

*

"What, what?" Martín cried out.

He had heard a snap like the sound of a whip, followed an instant later by the crackle of raw meat being dropped into a searing-hot skillet. His nostrils filled with a stench.

The work lights and signals went dark. Dennis and Lenin staggered to their feet.

"What's happening?" Martín shouted again.

"That short on the third rail tripped the current to this block section of the tunnel," Dennis said. "The third rail is cold now. We have to get those bodies off the tracks."

"Bodies? Is Nico—?"

"I am so sorry, Martín, but Nico is gone," Lenin said. "He died to protect you and to try and end this madness."

Lenin looked around and saw a hatch to a maintenance access. He opened it and helped Dennis carry the two smoldering corpses into it.

Lenin helped Martín to his feet and said, "I am sorry I can't do more for your brother right now, but we have to get out of here. All hell is breaking loose, and we need to see what we can do to stop it."

Dennis lifted his microphone. "Gina, both Marty and I are a bit worse for wear, so we need all the help we can get. Do you have a safe path between here and the next subway station?"

The voice that came back was grave but resolute. "If there isn't one, Alejandra and I will make one."

Dennis managed a wan smile. "That's what I wanted to hear."

*

Lenin, Alejandra, and Gina supported Dennis and Martín as they struggled along the subway tunnel. The trains were running with additional frequency now and they constantly had to flatten against the wall to let them pass. Eventually they saw the fluorescent lighting of a station ahead.

There were only a few people in Piño Suárez station. They watched with silent, wide-eyed amazement as three relatively healthy people climbed up from the tracks and then hoisted two injured, bedraggled men to the platform. Without acknowledging their audience, they staggered through the station and up to street level. Gina hailed a cab, and once she had pulled its right-side doors open, the others crowded in with Dennis taking the front passenger seat.

"Get us to the airport," Dennis told the driver. "There's a little extra in it for you if it's a quick trip."

The cab driver looked puzzled, and Alejandra translated for him. He grinned at the beautiful woman in his back seat, slammed the car's transmission into drive, and bolted away from the curb.

Gina watched the opposite lanes and saw a black Lexus shoot by at high speed, brake hard, and make a fishtailing U-turn into their lane. She elbowed Alejandra, who turned around and watched in dismay as the Lexus accelerated, quickly shortening the gap on their cab.

"Driver, five hundred U.S. dollars if you lose that Lexus!" Alejandra said. She reached into her bag and found what remained of the cash that Gallego had given to Lenin. She pulled a handful out and waved the bills in the air.

The driver cut the wheel hard to the right. The cab streaked down a narrow side street. Trashcans flew as the car smashed into them and a pedestrian dove out of the way. The car came to another wide street, turned onto it, and cut left and through the traffic. Dennis craned his neck around and still saw the Lexus several cars back. It was gaining, and they heard muffled pops as men fired guns from the windows. Bullets thunked into the cab.

"Make it a thousand!" Lenin shouted, and Alejandra dipped her hand back into the bag for another handful of bills. The cabbie and Lenin's eyes met in the rearview mirror and Lenin was startled to see nothing short of unbridled exuberance. The cabbie flattened the accelerator and the cab lurched forward.

Another Lexus passed from the opposite direction. It made a violent U-turn and joined the first one, zigzagging between cars to catch up.

Dennis pulled his phone out and tapped the screen.

"Dubronski," he said. "We're on our way to the airport. I'm hurt bad, we got one blind guy, three are okay."

He listened to the response and looked at Gina. "Tell him to take us to something that sounds like 'hangers avian.'"

"Hangares de Aviación," Gina said to the driver. "Hurry!"

The car jerked left and slid sideways through an intersection as another Lexus tried to cut it off from a side street. The driver laughed maniacally and the taxi roared ahead. He turned left, jumping the curb and speeding the car across a small grassy park and into another narrow street.

Dennis shouted, "Dubronski better have the plane ready to go!"

The cab's rear window shattered, showering the backseat with safety glass pellets. Three Lexuses pursued. The cabbie steered onto the sidewalk, drove a full block there, and then thundered out into a large intersection just as the light changed. Behind them, the lead Lexus screeched to a halt as traffic flowed in front of it.

Gina saw the speedometer reach one hundred fifty kilometers on the wide boulevard, and the driver only slightly reduced the speed to make a careering turn onto a side street. They crashed over speed bumps that bottomed the suspension. A Lexus flashed from a side street and caught the rear fender of the taxi with its front bumper, spinning the cab three hundred and sixty degrees. Bullets smashed into the windows, blowing them all out as the cab's occupants ducked. The driver reoriented himself and sped off again. "Two thousand American, don't you think?" he shouted over the roar of the wind rushing through the shattered windows.

"Yes!" Lenin called, bracing himself as they streaked between a tanker truck and a city bus.

The car made a series of turns at full speed and suddenly braked hard. The passengers looked out through the glass-free windows and saw aircraft hangers and a long cyclone fence. On a taxiway a hundred meters from the road a lumbering Antonov 124 rolled along at low speed. Lenin looked up and down the fence but didn't see a gate.

"That's our plane!" Lenin shouted, leaning forward. "Smash through that fence and we'll give you another five hundred American!"

"With pleasure," the driver replied, smiling as he shifted gears. He cut the wheel hard to the right and smashed into the cyclone fence. It bowed ahead like elastic and the car's rear tires spun until they smoked. Finally, the fence gave way. The car rolled over it and onto the grass. The cab accelerated, heading straight for the giant aircraft. In the distance they saw the flashing lights of official vehicles racing across the airport's maze of runways and taxiways. Behind them, two of the Lexus automobiles drove across the flattened fence.

"Martín, be ready to run," Gina yelled. "We'll have to break for it!"

Bullets snapped through the passenger compartment, wiping out the windshield, the only remaining glass. A Lexus was twenty meters behind and police cars were several hundred meters down the taxiway and coming fast.

Dennis's phone rang. "Yeah?" he answered.

"This is Dubronski," the voice barked. "Mexican officials have a problem with me leaving without a flight plan or tower clearance, so get behind me. We have the ramp down—get your asses on board!"

Dennis told Lenin what Dubronski had said and he relayed it in Spanish to the driver, with yet another five-hundred-dollar sweetener. The man grinned, skidded into a ninety-degree turn, and accelerated to match the increasing speed of the mammoth transport aircraft. The two Lexuses were gaining and the pistol fire continued unabated. The police cars were 30 meters behind the Lexuses, sirens bawling. The Antonov turned from the taxiway onto the active runway where it began to slowly gain speed.

"Are you guys out for a Sunday drive or do you want to get the hell out of here?" Dubronski roared through the phone. "Punch it!"

The driver floored the accelerator and the car covered the last few meters separating it from the transport's steel ramp, which was kicking up a rooster-tail of sparks as it dragged on the asphalt. The front tires of the taxi climbed up the ramp. Bullets raked the back of the car and one rear tire exploded, sending a hubcap pinwheeling away. The taxi fell back off the ramp. The driver goosed the pedal and the front wheels again climbed upward. The smell of smoke filled the air as the flapping, punctured tire heated to the point of combustion. Inch by inch the cab moved up the ramp until the rear wheels spun onto the steel ramp, gained traction, and the car shot forward into the cargo hold.

As Gina looked out, she saw two Russians with fire extinguishers spraying a dense fog onto the smoldering tire. Another team jumped forward and locked the disintegrating cab into place with huge hooks and chains. The loadmaster sprinted around the vehicle, checked the restraints, and then barked into his headset while giving a thumbs-up to the other crewmembers around him. The giant doors closed and the taxi's occupants could feel the 124 vibrate all around them as it accelerated down the runway and lifted off. The plane banked into a hard-left turn, then finally rolled its wings level.

Inside the cargo hold, the occupants of the taxicab regained their breath, and silence filled the interior of the car. The driver let out a shriek of pure exultation, pounding his hands against the steering wheel and whooping joyfully. No one joined in the celebration, and after composing himself the driver looked around at the remains of his vehicle. His manic grin faded just a bit. He made eye contact with Lenin, who shrugged apologetically.

The driver beamed again. "I'll leave the meter running, no?"

*

Waro Moto sat on an easy chair, speaking in Japanese on the telephone while King Carlos and Pope Pius talked quietly to each other. The industrialist savagely sucked air into the corners of his tightly closed mouth. He slammed the phone down, causing Carlos and Pius to jump.

"I am surrounded by idiots!" he barked.

"What happened?" Carlos asked.

"Your damned fool Inquisition guards let Ibarra and Ishikawa get out of the subway tunnel. They made a break for the airport. My people had to intervene—" He again stopped to suck in air. "But they also failed. Ibarra and the others are airborne in that damned Russian transport plane."

Carlos clicked on his phone and demanded to be put through to the president of Mexico. The two conversed, and the king hung up. He rose and began pacing a different part of the room.

"The Mexican air force will immediately scramble fighters to intercept the transport," the king said. "But he did say that they haven't picked the plane up on radar. They don't know where it is."

"More incompetence!" Moto cried. "How can they miss the world's largest airplane?"

*

Dubronski squinted, his face glistening with a sheen of sweat. He gingerly worked the control yoke as his copilot locked his eyes on the radar altimeter. The tops of trees were a mere foot or two below the belly of the Antonov as it hugged the ground while flying at three hundred and fifty knots.

The navigator had his face buried in the visor of the radar screen.

"I see the coast," he said by intercom to the Dubronski. "Feet wet in two minutes."

A new voice came over the radio, saying in accented English, "Antonov transport, this is Mexican Air Force Inca-Zero-One on guard channel. Reduce airspeed and fall into my six o'clock or you will be shot down."

"*Góvno!*" the copilot exclaimed, looking out of his windows. "I don't see the son of a bitch."

"Antonov transport, do you copy?"

"Don't answer," Dubronski said. "Engineer, get ready."

"Thirty seconds to coast," the navigator said.

"Antonov, I will commence firing in five seconds if you do not comply."

"Ready defensive systems," Dubronski said on intercom.

"Antonov, Inca-Zero-One has command clearance, commencing fire."

"Flares now!" Dubronski said.

The flight engineer threw a toggle switch, ejecting two blazing phosphorous flares from the rear of the plane. At that same instant Dubronski hauled back on the control yoke and, after a moment's climb, snap-rolled the aircraft violently to the right.

The copilot twisted his neck and looked out the window. "First missile's following the flare—clear!"

Dubronski rolled back to the left, held a fast climb, and then dumped the control yoke forward, dropping the nose into a dive.

"Chaff and flares!" he called. He looked toward the left wing and saw a missile streak past, turning wide of the transport.

"Number two followed the chaff cloud. Flares!"

The Antonov's fuselage creaked as the aircraft porpoised rapidly, with the nose alternating between snapping up toward the sky and then back down to earth.

"Feet wet!" the navigator called.

The Mexican fighter plane flew past, taking a position off the nose of the 124. Dubronski gently pushed the bank of throttles forward, dropping the nose to gain airspeed, and then gently pulled back up until his wings were level and the transport plane was just aft of and below the fighter. The jet filled the windscreen, causing the flight engineer to look away. Dubronski eased the transport forward under the fighter's elevators.

Suddenly the fighter plane seemed to lose control and rolled onto its right wing. The fighter's nose tucked under and the plane ripped away, disappearing aft.

"Twelve-mile limit, international waters!" the navigator called.

Dubronski and the copilot scanned ahead and as far aft as their side windows permitted.

"Nothing here, chief," the copilot said.

"Clear here," Dubronski said.

"I got streaks in my shorts," the flight engineer said. "What'd you do to that guy?"

"Bow wave," the copilot said, looking at Dubronski with admiration. "A huge rush of air three meters out in front of this big motherfucker. Threw that fighter off like the wake of a supertanker wiping out a rowboat."

Dubronski turned his head and saw a white-faced Dennis Prinn standing behind the flight engineer, held up by Gina Ishikawa, whose lower lip was trembling.

"Thanks for flying ass-buster airlines—we look forward to you flying with us again," Dubronski said, grinning broadly.

*

Takashi Ishikawa returned the salutes of Captain Roberto Fujiwara and Lieutenant Jorge Flores.

"Thank you for coming on short notice," the president said. "Is the aircraft ready?"

"Yes, sir," the pilot said.

"Are you both fully briefed on the situation in Kourou?"

"Yes, sir," Fujiwara replied.

"Captain Fujiwara," the president said, changing from Portuguese to Japanese, "I knew your father—we were classmates together."

"Yes, sir, he speaks of you often," Fujiwara replied, executing a bow from the waist.

"Your father is a very good man," the president said. "He is, like me, a man of the past in many respects. A man who understands the customs of Japan."

"Yes, Ishikawa-san. My father taught me many things about... the old ways."

"Did he talk about *bushido*?"

"Of course, Ishikawa-san."

"Then you know what must happen when a man dishonors himself and his cause?"

"Yes."

"And you understand that sometimes, in order to expiate shame, a man must have another act in concert with him—doing together with him that which he cannot do by himself—so that he may take the honorable course of action?"

"Perfectly, Ishikawa-san."

"I will see you on board in five minutes, Captain Fujiwara," the president said, bowing slightly. He ascended the roll-up stairs, entered the presidential Boeing 737, and took his seat.

Four minutes later Captain Fujiwara came through the door and bowed to the president.

"It will not be a problem flying the aircraft by yourself?" the president asked.

"I am fully trained and qualified," the young captain answered. "Lieutenant Flores will regain consciousness in about twenty minutes. He was not seriously harmed."

"Your father will be proud, Fujiwara-chan," the president said, using the familiar form of address.

"Yes, Ishikawa-san," Fujiwara replied. He bowed once more, turned, and let himself through the cockpit door.

CHAPTER THIRTY-ONE

DUBRONSKI STOOD IN the cargo compartment looking at the wrecked taxi. He turned to the taxi driver and said in English, "Nice driving, my man," and gave him a high five.

Lenin translated what he said and the driver grinned broadly, then replied, "*Pensé que el avión se iba a estrellar!*"

Lenin chuckled wearily. "He thought you were going crash the plane." Lenin paused. "To be honest, I did too."

Dubronski laughed wryly and gestured back at the taxi. "Maybe so, *amigo*, but my plane still looks a hell of a lot better than his cab!" Dubronski didn't bother to wait for Lenin to translate, turning the conversation back to the task at hand. The cabbie peered back at his taxi, his grin slightly dampened as he tried to figure out whether he had just been insulted.

"Professor, we are heading directly for San Juan Diego," Dubronski said. "Are we going to get the same warm reception there?"

"I'm hoping that if Gina Ishikawa talks over the radio the Latino Union won't shoot us down," Lenin said.

"Yes, that would ruin our whole day," Dubronski said. The pilot climbed back up the steps to the cockpit.

Gina sat on the web seat next to Martín. She studied him as he stared blankly ahead. She struggled to think of anything to say to him now that they were alone with each other.

He shook his head several times and then turned toward her. Using only his fingertips, he touched her, beginning with her forehead and then moving his fingertips slowly down over her eyelids, then her nose, and around her cheeks. He touched her lips and stroked them gently. Finally, he traced her chin and neck.

"It really is you," he said, tears filling his vacant eyes.

"Yes."

There was a long silence.

"I recognized your voice right away," he said, and after a pause, "But I couldn't believe it… I couldn't trust it. There were so many memories one on top of another. So hateful, so crushing, so…"

"But you did what I told you to do."

"Yes."

"Why?"

"Because you remembered the compass rose."

Gina smiled, but looked at him with a questioning expression. Then she realized he couldn't see her facial features. She took his hand.

He sighed. "I've been through hours—days—of pictures, words, videos, nonstop… about you, by you, directed at me. They were true… but not quite. Accurate… but not quite. Believable… but not quite. Still, I was sliding in that direction, beginning to believe that you hated me. All those scenes seemed completely real and were pulled directly from our life together. But only you were with me that night on my boat. Only you could have known about when we talked about the compass and the compass rose, and how together they would keep us safe."

Gina touched a finger to his lips.

"I think I'm getting some of my vision back," he said, squinting fiercely. "No features at all, but I can see light much better than before."

"I'm glad for you," she said. "What do you think we should do now?"

"Go to your father and get him to join us in exposing Carlos and Pius."

Gina considered that. "He's such a proud man. He'll lose a lot of face doing that. His career and legacy will be in shambles."

"He's also a responsible man, and an intelligent one. He'll know that's the only reasonable thing left to do," Martín said.

Gina remained silent for a moment. "Martín, I'm so sorry about Nico—"

"There are many things we will have to mourn…" Martín interrupted, "when we have time. But I do need to know something, Gina. Did you mean what you said to me through the earpiece when you were guiding me?"

"Yes."

"Even after I didn't take you with me from Brazil?"

"You can't know how much that hurt me," Gina said.

"Gina, that was my evil twin," Martín said weakly. She let out a small, wounded, laugh. "I couldn't seem to make myself move—to say to you what I wanted, what I felt. But I've thought about nothing else since the night I saw you at Lenin's house, and I know I want us to be together—if you'll still have me."

Gina smiled. "I believe you."

Martín realized that her answer was non-committal, but he responded only by squeezing her hands. Right now, it was more than he could have ever hoped for.

*

The Russian radio operator sat Gina Ishikawa at the console and put his headset on her, and she made a radio transmission to the Latino Union Command Center. She identified herself and suggested they check her voice against the computer voiceprints that were maintained in an electronic database. The command center accepted her authenticity. She asked to speak to her father.

After thirty seconds of silence, her father was on the radio.

"Father," she said without preamble, "I'm with Doctor Lenin, Dennis Prinn, Alejandra Rojas, and Martín Ibarra. We require safe passage to San Juan Diego to meet with you, and to bear witness."

"I am not in San Juan Diego right now," her father replied. "Stand by for a moment."

A minute passed, and then the president rejoined the line.

"Gina, I have made arrangements with a trusted friend in the military, and he will assure your safe passage to land in San Juan Diego. From there, he will make sure you are protected and that you are brought to help deal with the persons responsible for this madness."

"Father, where are you?"

His voice came back with a dreamy quality. "You and Lenin were right—I know it now. It is up to me to expunge this threat to the world. I am responsible, so I must act."

Gina was speechless for a moment. "I don't understand what you're talking about."

"You may not be aware, but the rocket in Kourou appears to have been fitted with a nuclear warhead."

"No!" Gina exclaimed. "Father—"

"Please, my daughter," the president said quietly. "I have enough information to believe that this threat is real, and that I am at least partially responsible for its existence. You must understand that though I do not believe the rebels will actually launch the rocket—it has far too much value as a symbolic threat—I cannot let them terrorize the world and jeopardize millions of lives."

A long silence followed while Gina collected her thoughts and emotions. "Yes, I understand," she said.

Gina heard her father sigh over the radio. "You have made me very proud, my daughter... my Gina. I love you." There was an almost imperceptible click on the line as the connection was terminated.

*

Colonel Celso Kobe looked up at the large screen where the image from the radarscope on the Latino Union EC-10 airborne combat control center was projected. He saw a square around the Guiana Space Centre at Kourou, and crosshairs on what the colonel knew to be the Ariane rocket. Bright blips circled lazily off the coast of Guiana—radar transponder signals from two Brazilian R-5 Relâmpago fighters. Colonel Kobe had repeatedly queried the joint chiefs, requesting the codes needed to validate his orders to guide the fighters in to attack the rocket on the launch pad. Each time the joint chiefs had told him to stand by.

The communications officer turned to Kobe. "Encrypted transmission from President Ishikawa." Kobe watched the officer isolate the circuit so that Kobe was the only one hearing the conversation.

"Mr. President, this is Colonel Kobe speaking."

"Colonel, I need you to leave the command center to complete a special assignment for me. My daughter is critical to the destiny of the Latino Union. She is flying toward San Juan Diego in a chartered transport aircraft, and if you don't prevent it, the plane may be destroyed by conspirators within the military and the government. You cannot let that happen. Arrange for loyal fighter escorts to protect that plane as it arrives, and then you and only your most trusted military policemen must escort Gina and her companions to safety. Can I count on you?"

"Yes, sir," Colonel Kobe said. He ordered Lieutenant Colonel Lisboa to take over as duty officer and left the command center.

*

Waro Moto raged over the phone.

"How is it possible that such a large airplane arrived undetected, landed without the knowledge of your defense control system, and now the passengers have already disappeared into the city?"

He listened for a moment, and then continued. "And what about President Ishikawa? You let him walk out of the palace and get on his plane, and now you don't even know where his plane is or where it is headed?"

Another pause.

"Mello, you are the stupidest…"

He cut the call off, then dialed another extension.

"Do you have a transcript of that encrypted call you detected?"

"No, sir," was the reply. "It was directed onto a special circuit, bypassing the command center's recorders. I heard the live transmission, but because of the encryption, it was unintelligible."

Moto threw the phone across the room. His panic-stricken aide scurried over to retrieve it.

Pope Pius wrung his hands as he watched Moto storm back and forth. "Things are not going as planned," he said to Carlos. "Perhaps we should call off—"

Heavy vibrations thudded in the air. Moto went to a window and pushed the curtain aside. "Our helicopter is here. It's time to leave," he said.

The king's neck snapped around. "Leave? What are you talking about? As of tonight, this palace belongs to me! The imposter president has already abandoned it, and we have the head of the LU military in our pocket. I am not going to leave in my moment of triumph! My address—"

"Will go on as planned," Moto grunted. "I ask you though, Your Highness, whether you would rather be here in San Juan Diego with rebels and their unstable leader holding a nuclear weapon and delivery system, or thirty thousand feet in the air, ready to land as soon as the situation in Kourou has been resolved in our favor? I, for one, prefer to be cautious while variables I cannot control play out. Particularly after seeing how that debacle you called an *auto-de-fé* went. And that's without considering that there may be factions here in San Juan Diego that are still loyal to the president and might try to imprison us here."

"But," the king protested, "we paid the rebels and the joint chiefs of the Union an enormous—"

"And you can either take comfort in that while you are sitting here, at what is potentially ground zero, or from the safety of my plane. Your choice. I am leaving now."

Moto strode from the room without looking back, his aide trailing behind him. The wide-eyed pope watched the Japanese industrialist depart, looked at the king apologetically, and then followed Moto with the Spanish cardinal in tow.

Exasperated, the king stood up and took in his surroundings. The palace and its furnishings gleamed with its newness. He patted the edge of the sofa. *So be it*, he thought. *When I return, it will be the world's heads of state who will sit in this room, waiting for me to grant them an audience.*

The thought gave him great satisfaction.

King Carlos strode defiantly from the room and headed to the helicopter pad, where he boarded with the others and departed for Moto's private airplane.

*

The presidential jet skimmed over the Amazon River basin at treetop level, with Captain Fujiwara gently handling the yoke. The president sat strapped into the copilot's seat looking out into the blackness, scarcely sensing the dense forest rushing beneath the plane.

"We will have no problem avoiding radar detection at this altitude,"

Fujiwara said. "When we get within twenty miles of Kourou, I'll ascend to thirty thousand feet, put us into a holding pattern, and await your instructions. My only comment, Ishikawa-san, is that we have the civilians to consider."

The president remained silent, once again contemplating the calculus of the lives of the few, weighed against the many.

*

Colonel Celso Kobe, surrounded by a president's daughter, a professor, a television technician, an architect, and a law student, sat in darkness inside the armored personnel carrier that rumbled along the boulevards of San Juan Diego.

"Nice ride," Dennis said, gesturing to their steel surroundings.

"It gets you there and back," Kobe said. "Bad gas mileage, though."

"When we get there, how do we get in?" Gina asked.

Kobe smiled back at her. "Special delivery," he said, and banged his fist on the metal wall of the transport.

Colonel Kobe left the group of civilians and walked to the front of the vehicle, a radio pressed to one ear, talking to the APC driver. The personnel carrier had slowed, but still clanked its way toward the presidential complex. Kobe came back and said to the others, "We're almost there. Make sure those harnesses are tight."

The APC slowed to a crawl. They all leaned into a sharp turn. The interior clanged with reverberations that sounded like tin cans bouncing off the skin of the armored vehicle, and it accelerated. There was a sharp impact, and the passengers lurched toward the front. The APC crawled forward, tilting at a crazy angle. Colonel Kobe pulled a sidearm from his holster, threw open the rear hatch and looked out.

"We're inside the palace!" Gina said.

Kobe listened intently to his radio. Two shots were fired, and then there was silence. "Okay," he said. "Let's go."

Lenin, Alejandra, and Gina helped Dennis and Martín climb out the rear hatch and down to the marble floor. Soldiers in full battle dress lined the stairway while others went room to room, kicking doors open. The four followed Kobe up a staircase, where three soldiers were leading away a small contingent of soldiers who had their hands placed on top of their heads.

"Where are we within the palace?" Martín asked as he was led along.

"In one of the state guest quarters," Gina said.

The group walked ahead, with Gina leading Martín. Dennis limped, leaning heavily on Lenin. They came into a living room where a butler stood wringing his hands. Dennis eased himself onto a couch, grimacing. Lenin sat next to him, catching his breath.

"Where are they?" Colonel Kobe asked.

"Gone. They simply left," the man answered with a high-pitched voice.

"With Moto?" Kobe asked.

"Yes," the man answered.

"Now what do we do?" Lenin asked.

Gina looked thoughtful, and turned to Dennis. "There's a communications center for use by visiting heads of state. I think it's about time to let the world know what's going on. Alejandra, Professor, how long will it take you two to get set up?"

Lenin looked pensive. "We did some preparation in Mexico City, but it will take a while to piece everything together in a methodical way that will endure the burden of proof required. As my fellow academician Carl Sagan once said, 'extraordinary claims require extraordinary evidence.'"

Alejandra unshouldered her bag and produced a thumb drive. She tossed it to Dennis, who reached up from his seat on the couch and caught it.

"On there is a PowerPoint presentation I finished putting together while you all were busy playing with guns and lasers in Mexico City. Give me and the professor an hour with Gina and Martín and we'll have a rundown of all the high points we'll want to hit for the initial broadcast. The rest we can improvise."

Dennis beamed. "Fair dinkum! Just get me to the studio and we'll get you set up and ready to air!"

Lenin looked around at the group with mounting panic in his eyes. "Improvise? But we've got to ensure our citations to the documents will pass muster, and…"

For the first time in her life, Gina ignored her mentor. "Follow me, everyone. Let's get ready to talk to the world."

The professor looked down at himself in abject horror. "For the love of all that is holy, I need a new suit!"

*

Carolina stood outside the Kourou space center and marveled at her accomplishment. Looking at the teeming gantry, her heart pounded. Never before, and certainly never again, would she have this amount of power at her disposal. She inhaled deeply and basked in the moment. The men who had financed this operation were likely sitting in San Juan Diego and drinking champagne, congratulating themselves on what a fine job *they* had done. Perhaps they were even discussing the next phase of their plan, where the bastard king would air his broadcast and "convince" the rebels to relinquish the nuclear weapon to his control, making him a hero to the people of Spain and the Latino Union.

Further strengthened by the partnership that the king had formed—an unholy alliance with the head of the godforsaken Catholic Church and the ill-gotten capitalistic might of Waro Moto—Carlos VII would be just short of a god.

She could never let that happen.

With one act, Carolina could destroy the tyranny of the Latino Union, cripple the Catholic Church, and behead one of the largest corporations in the world. The people of South America would be freed, and the resulting chaos would allow true revolution to take hold and spread among the poor and the oppressed. As the catalyst of the revolution, she would lead the people as they united and went forth to cleanse the continent of the power structures that had kept them down for so long.

She breathed in deeply again and smiled.

It was time to make history.

*

Carolina burst into the space center's control room, followed by twenty revolutionary soldiers who fanned out around the space. The foreign scientists and engineers working at their consoles looked up, startled.

"Get the rocket ready for immediate launch," Carolina ordered the chief engineer.

"What?" the Russian demanded, yanking off his reading glasses.

"We're launching it."

"It is meant to be a credible threat, not an actual launch. I have to consult with—"

"Launch the fucking rocket!" she shrieked. The ring of soldiers around the walls of the room clicked off the safeties on their weapons and glared at the engineers.

The chief engineer slowly stood, trembling. "All right, people," he said, voice shaking. "Let's get it done. Checklist for a hot start and quick launch. Clear the gantry."

A Klaxon began to bleat. The engineers scrambled to their designated consoles, throwing open manuals, consulting tablets of handwritten notes, and punching lighted buttons. Through the large windows facing Launch Pad Three, they could see warning lights flashing and vehicles racing out to the missile. The gantry tower suddenly looked like an overturned anthill, seething with frenetic movement.

A door into the control room flew open. Carolina turned to face Guillerme Portier, the president *pro temp* of Free Guiana.

"Commander, is this some kind of drill?" Portier demanded. "My people are still on that gantry!"

"No, this is a launch," she replied, turning back to the engineer.

Portier grabbed her shoulder and spun her back around. "That was to be our shield of protection against reactionary forces."

"Yeah, well, things have changed," she said, flicking her eyes down to his hand on her shoulder. "Now get out of my way and do not *ever* touch me again."

"There are thousands of people on that tower!" Portier cried. "I need time to get them off."

Carolina glanced at her watch. "Fifteen minutes tops," she said.

Panic flooded the man's eyes, and he raced out the door.

"How long?" Carolina demanded.

"Thirty minutes, maybe more," the engineer responded, throwing a stack of papers on the floor.

"Fourteen," she said. "Get it off in fourteen minutes."

The engineer stared at her.

"Move!" she yelled in his face. Carolina turned to look out the blockhouse windows. She saw a car speeding to the base of the gantry tower. Portier got out and started climbing the steel stairs three at a time. There was a silent tableau on each level of the gantry as people gathered around Portier, listened intently to what he said, and then began streaming down the gantry stairs.

*

The Japanese scientific team and the Russian missile engineer toiling in the clean room at the top of the gantry froze when the alarms began blaring. They were perspiring in spite of the air conditioning pumping into the space.

After an initial burst of puzzled and fearful chatter, their leader pulled a phone from his pocket and gestured for everyone to calm down. He dialed a number, and after a few moments his call was answered.

After a brief introductory exchange and confirmatory passwords, the team leader held his phone up over his head, letting the alarms speak on his behalf. He brought the phone back to his ear and politely asked for his superior at Moto Electric to please confirm that what they were hearing was some sort of drill or test of the alarm system.

He was placed on hold.

While he waited, he smiled anxiously at his underlings, trying to project confidence. *I've got this all under control,* his beaming face conveyed while his stomach churned. His team looked up at him, their eyes never leaving his face as they awaited his report.

After an eternity, he heard a series of clicks. A sterner voice came onto the line.

"Hold for Waro Moto," it said.

The team leader straightened up, almost to attention, and his eyes widened. His team exchanged nervous glances.

Moments later, Waro Moto's sharp, familiar voice cut through the surrounding noise with the clarity of a dog whistle that only the team leader could hear. "From the sounds I am hearing, things have gotten out of hand in Kourou. Disable the rocket."

"What?" the scientist whined.

"Disable it! Make sure it can't launch."

"Launch? Is that what the alarms are about?"

Moto's voice boomed from the tiny speaker. "Stop talking and get that rocket disabled in the next thirty seconds!" There was a pause. "But make sure we can still repair it."

The scientist stood gaping at the men in white coats around him. Like a flock of startled birds simultaneously fluttering into the air, the scientists scrambled for the gantry staircase. The discarded cellular phone lay on the floor with Moto's voice bleating, "Hello? Hello? Disable that damned rocket, do you hear me?"

*

Pope Pius strode rapidly up and down the aircraft's small aisle, murmuring prayers of supplication. King Carlos watched Moto, his own anxiety mounting.

"Are we far enough from San Juan Diego?" he asked.

Moto looked at him with disdain. "Yes, king, your royal ass is very safe. It's a small warhead that will only destroy the Latino Union's federal zone and the immediate city. Nothing else."

"But this part wasn't planned," the pope whimpered.

Moto shrugged. "In a lot of ways, this is better. The warhead's destruction will leave a power vacuum. The Spanish king will be alive and well, and will take up the fallen reins of government. Yes. I think that works well."

"What about Ishikawa?" Carlos asked.

"We need to find him and kill him," Moto answered.

"And what about the reaction of the rest of the world when I take over?" King Carlos demanded. "The nuclear weapon was to be my trump card."

Moto was lost in thought for several seconds. "While making the Latino Union a nuclear power would have been a good thing, a single warhead wasn't going to deter the superpowers from interfering for very long. Instead we will have worldwide sympathy as your acts of kindness stabilize a third of the world and prevent it from descending into utter chaos. The

Americans will only care that economic stability is reestablished so that its precious financial markets are able to regain the ground that will be lost in the initial aftermath of the nuclear attack. All the while, we will work to tighten your grip on the continent using the tools and infrastructure that are already in place, as well as the vast fortune you have at your disposal."

He looked up at the fearful pope.

"Your Holiness, you will have a terrified populace looking to you for spiritual guidance and leadership. I trust that this will provide a great opportunity for you to spread the influence of the Inquisition and usher in the new rule of God on earth."

The pontiff stared at Moto and then slowly nodded as he pondered the possibilities.

"Yes," Moto said confidently to his co-conspirators, "I believe that this will all work out just fine."

*

Carolina turned to the Russian chief engineer. "How long?" she demanded.

"We can't—look, there are interface problems with the guidance computers, a warning light on the—"

"Ten minutes," she said. Carolina gestured nonchalantly at the soldiers surrounding them. "My friends with the rifles want it off in ten minutes."

The Russian ran from console to console, frantically exhorting his colleagues to keep moving.

The steel door crashed open and Guillerme Portier sprinted back in. He reached out as if to grab Carolina's shoulders, thought better of it, and retreated a step. "More time, Commander, please give me more time to get my people off the gantry!"

Carolina casually looked at her watch. "Oh... yikes. Less than eight minutes. You'd better hurry."

"Stop the launch, for God's sake! Just a few more minutes, that's all we need!"

"You have the same amount of time as the rest of us have," she said, shrugging and turning to check the launch sequence status on the display board.

Portier grabbed her and spun her back around to face him. "Children, old people—*you* put them there, *you*! Stop the launch—"

Commander Delta smoothly put her pistol to the politician's head and pulled the trigger. The blast brought an anguished, startled cry from the technicians in the command center. They stopped their work and stared at Carolina and the dead man at her feet.

"I'll kill every one of you!" she shrieked. "Launch it!"

Pandemonium ensued. Men were crying as they threw switches and cut off blinking warning lights while Carolina periodically checked her watch. She glanced at a monitor and saw that the French soldiers had been freed from the base of the rocket and were helping civilians get off the gantry.

She rolled her eyes at the absurdity of their efforts and glanced back down at her watch.

"Five minutes!" she shouted.

*

"What the hell is going on?" General Mello demanded. His command post buzzed around him and he held his cellphone to his ear. First, forces loyal to President Ishikawa had gained control of an entire wing of the presidential complex, and then that disaster had been quickly followed by reports he was getting from French Guiana that the rocket in Kourou was about to be launched, with San Juan Diego as the target.

Waro Moto's voice dripped with calm condescension. "General, the reports you are panicking about are untrue. King Carlos and I have been in recent contact with both Commander Delta and my own people, and nothing is happening in Kourou other than the implementation of the plan as scheduled. You are reacting to wild rumors. I thought you were better than that."

Mello seethed. "Even so, I am going to order the LU fighters in the area to—"

Moto's voice rose to a shout, "General, you make damned sure those fighters don't go anywhere near the rocket! It's too important for the cause! One rogue act of stupidity by your men and it will all be for nothing! We've already had one of your idiot fighter pilots refuse to take a direct order from his president to shoot down the Iberia plane. We cannot have men taking matters into their own hands! Do not send the fighters!"

As Mello listened to Moto rant, a wide-eyed intelligence officer handed the general a photograph. Mello processed it for a few moments, then shouted into the phone. "I just got handed confirmation, Moto! She's going to launch, goddamn it, and I'm at ground zero!"

"No, she's not," Waro retorted. "I paid for her tin pot revolution."

"Moto, I'm in the crosshairs and you're somewhere safe! The fighters are going in!"

Mello cut off the connection.

*

On the monitor she saw the last of the civilians and freed Foreign Legion soldiers running away from the base of the rocket.

"Fifty seconds," Carolina announced. Men traded shouts. One collapsed, clutching his chest, apparently suffering a heart attack.

The chief engineer was everywhere at once, issuing orders, resetting switches on panels, and yelling at technicians.

"Twenty seconds!" Commander Delta called. The stench of sweat and fear permeated the control room.

"Ten seconds!" she cried. Someone ran toward the blockhouse door in a desperate attempt to flee but was casually shot by a revolutionary soldier.

Carolina stood over the Russian chief engineer, who was slumped over his console. His right hand shook as though palsied while he punched a bank of status lights for the scores of systems activating the Ariane 6. His index finger flipped up the guard covering the toggle switch labeled FEU, the switch that would deliver the electric charge to the solid fuel motors, light the rocket engines, and send the missile into the sky on a ballistic arc, briefly into space, and then falling under power to deliver a nuclear holocaust to the people of San Juan Diego.

"Time's up," Carolina said. "Fire it!"

"I can't—there's an anomaly of the—"

"Fire it!" she demanded.

"Don't you see, there's—"

Carolina put her gun against his temple. "Launch it! Launch the fucking rocket! Fire it! Fire it!"

The engineer let out a long shriek and threw the toggle switch. Carolina looked through the window and saw smoke and flame pouring out of the nozzles of the rocket engines. She smiled.

Through the thick blockhouse windows Carolina could hear the roar of millions of pounds of thrust. One by one the gantry arms swung aside and the giant steel clamps holding the rocket to the pad released. First slowly, then accelerating rapidly, the gleaming white spear shot upward on a plume of fire and smoke.

The first nuclear weapon fired on a civilian populace since Fat Man was falling through the skies toward Nagasaki was on its way to its target.

*

The duty executive at the Moto Electric control center near Tokyo said, "Yes, Moto-san," when the special encrypted circuit directly from Waro Moto activated.

"Make sure nothing interferes with that rocket. It must hit its target."

"Yes, Moto-san."

The controller broke the seal on a checklist in front of him and opened it. "Satellite?" he barked into his headset microphone.

"Primary, secondary, and backup links to all three satellites are viable," came the crisp reply.

"Radar?"

"Repeaters activated, control circuits established."

"Radio comm?"

"All transmitters and receivers are under our control."

"Weapon systems?"

"Intercept and override circuits viable."

"Aircraft simulator?"

"Manned, intercept, and override circuits viable."

"Checklist complete," the executive said.

CHAPTER THIRTY-TWO

LIGHTS ON THE electronic countermeasures panel of the Latino Union EC-10 airborne command post blinked crimson and alarms sounded. Hawk Leader, the pilot in command of a formation of two R-5 Relâmpago fighters, called through the radio, "North Star, we have visual of launch, visual of launch. Are we clear to strike?"

High-pitched voices screeched back and forth from the command post aircraft to LU satellites to antenna arrays in San Juan Diego. There was a babble of demands, retorts, arguments, and curses—and suddenly the satellite link, controlled by a bank of microprocessors manufactured by Moto Electric, disconnected. Radar screens on the EC-10 and the repeaters back at the situation room in San Juan Diego went blank, and the earphones went silent.

The command and control element was out of the loop.

Major Vega, Hawk Leader, had already turned toward the rising flame clearly visible below him. His air-to-air missile head-up display on the canopy showed green lines undulating back and forth, then snapping into a cross as a tone sounded through the pilot's helmet, indicating that the missile was locked in his sights.

"North Star, Hawk Leader, am I cleared to fire?"

"Hawk Leader, North Star has lost radar and satellite com with the Situation Room. Stand by one."

Vega considered the communications procedures dictated by the positive command and control doctrine, which required him to wait for orders.

On the other hand, he was also trained to think and to take initiative. "Hawk Leader is locked on. Locked on and going for the kill."

"Hawk Two, I'm right behind you, Hawk Leader."

The Relâmpago jets, with their autopilots now linked with the missile fire control system, banked steeply and nosed over, dropping straight toward the rising plume. Hawk Leader tightened his grip on the joystick, moving his thumb to the weapons launch button. The tone continued and the crossed lines remained fixed.

"Hawk Leader has tone, firing one, firing one. Now firing two."

His thumb moved slightly, and the electronic signal shot from the fire control computer to the missiles mounted on rails under each wing. In a nanosecond, the computer transferred data to the guidance system, telling the air-to-air missile the relative speed and distance of the target, the wind, the air temperature and density, and the initial intercept course to the Ariane 6. During that same nanosecond, the computer microprocessor, a product of Moto Electric, queried the navigation positioning satellites overhead—three satellites that had been manufactured under the strictest Japanese industrial standards relentlessly applied to all products of Moto Electric. Those satellites were simultaneously receiving a speed-of-light radio transmission that had originated from Tokyo and now transferred a code embedded in the position data to Hawk Leader's fire control computer. The computer flashed the positioning data through its redundant Moto Electric microprocessors that converted the binary bits to updated position information and decoded the additional data. These last few bytes overrode the program sequence that was holding the air-to-air missile firing until the latest target and launch platform position information was reconciled, jumped ahead in the sequence to the program step that directed an electrical impulse to the missile warheads, and detonated the high explosives.

Hawk Leader vaporized in mid-air.

"North Star, this is Hawk Two, Hawk Leader is splashed. Missiles blew on the rails. I'm going in."

Hawk Two, piloted by Lieutenant Marco Otaki Albuquerque of Recife, Brazil, watched the Ariane 6 rocket rise toward the flight level of his R-5 Relâmpago fighter. The jets had been delivered only one month before from the São Paulo plant of EMOSA, a joint venture of Embraer, the Brazilian national aircraft company, and Moto Aviation of Japan. The fighter was the newest and best in the world, combining aircraft and avionics design that Moto Electric and Moto Aviation had acquired in a joint venture with American aircraft companies, and which had then been further refined by Moto, working in concert with other Japanese electronics companies.

Otaki had watched Hawk Leader's rockets explode on the rails and suspected a fault in the computerized missile arm and launch system. He focused on the flame of the armed nuclear rocket, and his targeting system automatically locked on, using the latest Moto Electric ocular target acquisition system, commanded by the pilot's eyes. The attack computer calculated the rapidly closing distance between the fighter and the Ariane 6.

The canopy displayed the intercept speed and the necessary heading data flashed to the flight control system. The five stage afterburners automatically went to attack power. The sleek fighter rolled and smoothly accelerated. Lieutenant Otaki scanned the status board and saw that his fighter would arrive within firing range in five seconds and the air-to-air missiles mounted on his aircraft were armed, locked on target, and ready to launch. He thought about Major Vega and switched off the computer, maneuvering for a manual intercept.

*

A cloud of cigarette smoke hung at eye level in the darkened room at Moto Electric headquarters outside of Tokyo. Tightly controlled voices spoke in clipped sentences and eyes were glued to high-definition tactical displays and radar repeater screens. To one side was an exact replica of the cockpit of the EMOSA Relâmpago fighter, its interior dark and occupied by a single pilot whose displays duplicated those of the fighter diving after the Ariane 6 rocket.

A man in a gray jacket sat at a console overlooking the simulator.

The simulator pilot's voice came over the commander's headset saying, "Intercept alignment valid." The commander knew this meant Flight Lieutenant Otaki, half a world away, was closing on the Ariane 6 rocket, perfectly aligned to destroy it.

"Terminate Hawk Two," the controller said.

The pilot in the simulator transmitted back to the controller, "Executing dive." As he spoke, he shoved the control stick full forward. Repeater gauges and instruments in the simulator confirmed that the aircraft was diving with its nose straight down, the vertical velocity indicator pegged at the maximum, the altitude scroll unwinding in an unreadable blur.

Then all gauges zeroed.

The simulator pilot stood and bowed toward the master technician. "Hawk Two terminated," he said.

*

General Roble on the North Star airborne command post heard his pilots yell "Holy shit!" over the intercom.

"Pilot, Command, what happened?"

"The Relâmpago went into a vertical dive with full burners and crashed!" he cried. "The missile's still flying, passing fourteen thousand feet!"

"How are we gonna stop that bastard?" Roble demanded over the intercom. As he asked the question, he already knew they were out of answers.

*

Captain Fujiwara, piloting President Ishikawa's 737 aircraft, pulled one earphone muff aside. "The two fighters are down," he said to President Ishikawa. "I can see the flames of the rising missile."

"Do it, then," Ishikawa said.

"Yes, sir," Fujiwara responded, shoving the throttles forward and dropping the nose.

*

The darkened radarscopes suddenly lit up and images appeared.

"Give me the picture," General Roble called to the airman beside him.

"Sir, I confirm two fighters down. Missile is climbing through seventeen thousand feet. Shall I call for more fighters, sir?"

"No time. Any armaments on this aircraft? Anything at all?"

"Negative, sir, and—what the *hell*?"

"What?" Roble demanded.

The airman was concentrating on his radar screen. "Skin paint on an unknown aircraft passing flight level two-one-zero, rate of descent five thousand feet per minute, heading vector… straight for the Ariane rocket!"

Roble stared at his repeater scope, watching the blip with disbelief. The radar computer painted a vector based on the aircraft's heading, a glowing arrow straight to the image of the rocket.

"Range two thousand meters, closing fast."

Roble keyed his microphone. "Aircraft descending, passing flight level two-zero-zero, heading zero-eight-zero, say identity and intentions."

He released the key and listened.

Nothing.

"Unknown aircraft, say identity," Roble radioed again.

The blip crept closer and closer to the missile's image.

"Who are you, and what are you doing?" Roble demanded, dispensing with radio procedure.

"One thousand meters, closing," the airman said.

Through his headset, the general heard only static.

"Five hundred meters."

"Turn, turn away!" Roble broadcast.

He heard transmission feedback, followed by a quiet voice saying, "With this, I restore my honor."

The image of the unknown aircraft and the missile merged on the radar screen.

*

Waro Moto frowned fiercely as he pressed the headset muff to his ear. He had listened to the calls to and from Hawk Leader and Hawk Two until each of them had fallen silent. Now he listened to North Star repeatedly transmitting to the unknown aircraft. There was no response. After two minutes, Moto heard, "This is North Star transmitting in the blind to anyone listening—the Ariane 6 missile has been destroyed. It was intercepted in midair by what we have now identified as Latino Union One… we believe the president was on board."

Moto put the headset down and flexed his large hands open and closed. King Carlos and the pope watched him closely.

"Ishikawa's dead. Unfortunately, the missile will not strike San Juan Diego. The government is still viable, but it's headless. We have to move quickly."

Moto rose from his seat and went forward to the cockpit. He talked to the pilots for a moment and came back to his seat. "I'm going to make a broadcast," he said, pulling on his headset. "My communications center is making sure I will be heard on all radio and television stations in the Latino Union with a simultaneous translation into Spanish and Portuguese."

Moto adjusted the microphone as King Carlos also pulled on a headset to listen. The industrialist composed himself and pushed the transmit key.

"Ladies and gentlemen, all citizens of the Latino Union, this is an official announcement from your government. A very serious threat to the security of our member countries has just been averted, thanks to the courage and decisiveness of one man: King Carlos of Spain. In brief, a group of revolutionaries commandeered a missile in Guiana—a missile that they then modified by attaching and arming a nuclear warhead. That missile was launched with the intention of destroying the city of San Juan Diego and the Latino Union government.

"President Ishikawa, head of state of the Latino Union and commander in chief of the armed forces, became incapacitated by the stress of the crisis and committed suicide. King Carlos, backed by the rock of moral courage, Pope Pius, stepped into the leadership vacuum, and in the face of disloyal factions of the military, made the difficult decisions and caused the missile to be destroyed.

"These two great leaders saved the Latino Union, prevented the loss of millions of civilian lives, and took leadership from Ishikawa, a cowardly incompetent.

"A cabal led by General Manuel Roble and Colonel Celso Kobe, and abetted by Ms. Gina Ishikawa, the president's daughter, and other foreign elements, is now brazenly attempting to assert control over the Latino Union through a military coup. I appeal to the disloyal officers and their followers to lay down their arms, and for General Mello, a loyal officer and head of the joint chiefs of staff, to secure the airfield so we may bring King

Carlos to San Juan Diego where we will beg him to accept the scepter of state for the Latino Union, with the full support and backing of the pope and the Catholic Church.

"I urge all citizens of the Union to remain calm, to be vigilant for the disloyal cabal, and to help us bring them into custody. Please support our leaders until Carlos's benevolent rule is assured. To all citizens, good night."

*

Dennis, Gina, Martín, Alejandra, and Lenin sat in stunned silence as static crackled from the communication center speakers.

The door opened and Colonel Kobe quickly walked in.

"Did you hear that?" he asked. They nodded.

"What about your constitution?" Lenin asked. "What's supposed to be the succession?"

"The vice president," Kobe said. He unhooked a military radio from his web belt, keyed it and said, "Task Force Echo, this is Echo Lead. Form up and we're headed for Daisy on the double. Move out!" He looked at Gina's group. "You all better stay put—there could be some shooting."

"What's 'Daisy,'?" Lenin asked.

"Vice President Saavedra," he said. "The VP residence is just across the compound from here, and we need to protect her. Sounds like Mello's going to try to keep her from taking over. The door into this comm center's heavy and should protect you. I'll try to keep you up to speed by radio."

They watched as the colonel closed the door behind him.

Gina sat with her arms tightly wrapped around herself, tears forming in her eyes. "My father," she said. Martín held her closely to him.

"Gina, we have no idea if anything he said is true," Alejandra said.

"I know. But in the meantime, we can't just sit here."

"I agree," Lenin said. "Although it's still sooner than I would like, I think it's time for our own broadcast. We need to counter the propaganda immediately."

That made Dennis perk up. "Watch my dust, Doc."

*

Dennis had two television cameras set up and adjusted to capture Alejandra,

Lenin, and Gina. As he attached small microphones to their shirts, he said, "The control panel has a network override to tie big-time visitors into the Latin American television network, preempting normal broadcasts. It all goes through the Moto Electric communications satellites, so I figure we'll have five minutes, ten tops, before Moto reprograms the transponders on the satellites to block us. I'm counting on a few of the bigs like CNN and Star to pick up the story by the time we're cut off so that we can keep broadcasting through one of their birds. I'll also be streaming this over the internet, but I'm also worried about that link staying active, given Moto's fingerprints are all over the whole goddamned system here. Get your best points across early."

Lenin nodded.

Dennis moved back behind the cameras, checked the console setting, and counted them down with his fingers from five to zero.

Lenin saw the red light on the camera illuminate. "Citizens of the Latino Union, good morning. I am Teodoro Lenin, professor emeritus from the University of Buenos Aires, and most recently, the University of Miami. I am considered an authority on Latin American history and government. With me this morning is Ms. Gina Ishikawa, daughter of the late president of the Latino Union, and Ms. Alejandra Rojas Deza, a law student and legal assistant whose importance in our story will become clear in a few minutes. We are here to talk to you about an injustice that is about to be perpetrated on all of you.

"About fifteen minutes ago there was a radio broadcast that has since been rebroadcast every few minutes claiming that president Ishikawa was a coward, King Carlos is a hero, and asking all of you to accept the king of Spain as your leader. All of this is contrary to the truth and tramples on the constitution that all of you voted upon and that protects your rights. What that broadcast is proposing is nothing more than turning the clock back two hundred years and making the Latino Union a colony of Spain."

Dennis watched the signals from the satellite, which was still receiving and retransmitting his broadcast.

"It was further stated in that broadcast that 'disloyal' elements of the Latino Union, Ms. Ishikawa included, were trying to usurp the Latino Union's proper line of succession," Lenin continued. "This is also a lie, and

I intend to prove it in the next few minutes. Colonel Celso Kobe is trying to protect your rights and your constitution as I speak. The man you heard pronouncing all these lies is Waro Moto, a Japanese citizen whose industrial empire is part of the conspiracy to make you the subjects of foreign powers."

*

Waro Moto put the headset on when the pilot motioned from the cockpit door that Moto needed to hear something. Moto heard a man's voice, calm and reasonable, talking in a conversational voice about the Fourth Angel document and the underlying conspiracy.

He ripped off the headset. "Get my control room on the radio!"

When the supervisor was on, Moto ordered, "Reprogram those transponders right now!" He picked up his plane's phone and dialed the Latino Union Military command post.

"Mello," he demanded, "get your troops over to that studio and shut it down!"

General Mello sounded strained. "Mr. Moto, Colonel Kobe has set up a perimeter around the compound. He has my troops pinned down. We're moving up armor, but it will take some time."

"For god's sake, you idiot, call in an air strike!" Moto exclaimed.

"Mr. Moto, there are some air force units siding with Kobe, and they're flying combat air patrol overhead."

"Get them off the air!" Moto shouted. "Blow up the power lines to the complex!"

*

Dennis's eyes never left the signal monitoring equipment that tracked the strength of the satellite uplink. The stack meters glowed brightly, rising and falling with variations of the transmission. Suddenly they all collapsed to zero.

"He cut us," Dennis called out. "Hold up a minute until another network picks us up."

He watched the dedicated phone lines marked with the names of various well-known networks. "Come on, come on," he muttered, "Pick up the goddamned story of the century."

The light for the BBC lit and blinked. Dennis snatched up the phone. "Prinn here."

"Dennis?" asked the voice with a plum British accent. "What's going on there?"

"You want the story?" Dennis asked.

"If it's for real."

"It's fair dinkum, mate. Give me your code and coordinates."

Dennis wrote down the numbers the man gave him. He hung up, attacked his computer keyboard, slewing the dish antenna around to new coordinates and entering the transponder code. He threw a bank of switches and stared at the signal monitors. Suddenly they jumped and filled the readout blocks.

"We're up again," he called to Lenin and Ishikawa. Lenin began ticking points off from his fingers, citing the deaths of persons who had been caught up in the net of the conspiracy, beginning with Father Croix in France.

*

"They're broadcasting again, on the fucking BBC," Moto shouted. His voice had roughened considerably over the day.

"We have the signal corps looking into it," General Mello said, "trying to cut—"

"The antenna, you imbecile, take out the antenna! It's up on the roof of that residence compound."

*

"When did you first meet David Broch's employer?" Lenin asked Alejandra.

"It was during the second week of David's research in Sevilla. The man's name was Julio Vargas, and he showed me his identification cards that said he was an official of the crown, the Office of Special Projects."

"Did you ever see Mr. Vargas with Mr. Waro Moto?" Lenin asked.

"Yes. I came to Vargas's office with David because David didn't speak Spanish and Vargas spoke very little English. As we were waiting in the reception area, a secretary came out, and while the door was open, I saw Mr. Moto sitting in the chair in front of Mr. Vargas's desk."

"Do you have documents signed by King Carlos, proving it was he who commissioned Mr. Broch's work on Latin American sovereignty?"

"Yes, I do."

Alejandra clicked the remote in her hand, Dennis punched buttons on his console, and the screen filled with an electronic scan of the retention letter between Broch and the king. Carlos VII's dynamic signature was unmistakable.

"Do you have documents signed by King Carlos and Mr. Waro Moto proving that they worked together?"

"Yes, I do."

Alejandra clicked the remote again, and the presentation she put together flicked to the next slide.

*

"General, I do not understand," Waro Moto said into his airborne telephone. "You have given orders for your air force to bomb the presidential compound, but your orders have not been carried out?"

"Units closest to San Juan Diego have refused to carry out the order," Mello responded. "And they have launched aircraft to intercept other units that are willing to carry it out."

"It sounds to me like you have a mutiny on your hands. And the penalty for mutiny is death."

"Yes, Mr. Moto, that's true—but you have to have soldiers willing to carry out the order."

"General, it seems I put my confidence in the wrong man."

There was a long silence, finally broken by Mello.

"Mr. Moto, you are welcome to try to find someone else."

The circuit was broken.

CHAPTER THIRTY-THREE

GINA METHODICALLY INTERVIEWED Lenin and Alejandra until they all heard the high-pitched scream of a jet fighter, followed by a muffled blast as a bomb exploded on the roof of the palace. As plaster showered down from the ceiling Dennis looked at the panel and saw all the signal monitors at zero.

"Shit!" he shouted. "They got the dish."

Dennis looked around the room. He spotted an aluminum case the size of a coffin, threw open the lid, and began rummaging through the contents.

"Get Kobe on the horn," he called to Lenin. "Tell him we need his APC. We're going mobile."

*

The armored personnel carrier rumbled along the street, shaking its occupants as it lurched around corners and bashed up and over curbs. Gina held tight to Martín. Vice President Saavedra sat next to her, looking disheveled but resolute. Lenin, Alejandra, and Colonel Kobe sat on the troop seats opposite them. Between them were two mobile television cameras on tripods and a stack of audio and video control units. Dennis climbed down the steel ladder from the vehicle's turret, unrolling heavy cables as he descended.

"I got the flyaway set up topside, but with all this driving, I'll never be able to keep it on the bird."

"What's a flyaway?" Gina asked.

"A small dish used by camera crews broadcasting from fifty k's south of Woop Woop—they're aimed manually to transmit directly to the satellite. Colonel Kobe, can you get us to a park or some open space so we can stop and aim the dish? I need to be clear of these tall buildings to get line of sight on a satellite."

Kobe thought. "Union Park," he said. "It's risky, though. We'll be in the open and susceptible to an air strike. The vice president is my security priority right now."

Vice President Saavedra, a tough-looking woman in her mid-fifties, shook her head. "Without getting the truth out, I'm just ballast in this damned tin can. Do what you have to do, Colonel."

Kobe went forward to talk to the driver.

*

All over San Juan Diego people tuned their televisions to BBC cable news. A few had been watching it when Colin Blackwater, the news anchor in London, told viewers they were picking up a remarkable broadcast from the capital of the Latino Union. Those few who were watching saw the familiar face of their president's daughter, and were stunned by the story she, an Argentine professor, and a Spanish law student told from a studio in the presidential compound. The viewers called and texted friends and relatives, telling them to turn on the BBC.

Then the BBC had lost the video signal. Blackwater assured viewers that the BBC was working to restore the link to continue the remarkable story alleging treachery and deceit at the highest levels of the Latino Union government, even involving Pope Pius and King Carlos of Spain.

Word spread quickly. Soon thousands of homes, bars, coffee houses, and restaurants were tuned to the BBC. As Colin Blackwater recapped the story and replayed the digital recording made while the satellite link was still operating, a Spanish language voiceover was added to translate for viewers in South America. People listened in dumbfounded silence to the allegations about leaders who had been considered gods and heroes only hours before. The sounds of jet aircraft streaking over the capital and explosions rocking the quiet city called to mind too many military coups, too many despots, and too much palace intrigue from years past.

People became angry.

With millions of Latin American viewers now tuned in, Colin Blackwater announced, "I'm told we're again receiving that broadcast from San Juan Diego in South America, this time from the inside of an armored personnel carrier."

The video broadcast cut from Blackwater to a dim picture that frequently broke up. The faces of Gina Ishikawa and Teodoro Lenin emerged from the obscurity.

"I am continuing the broadcast that Mr. Waro Moto and King Carlos are trying desperately to keep you from hearing," Gina said into a handheld microphone. "I have with me Architect Martín Ibarra Paz, who served with distinction on the managing board of the San Juan Diego construction project. Architect Ibarra, please tell me in your own words about these past few days when you were in the custody of the New Spanish Inquisition."

"Thank you, Ms. Ishikawa," Martín said. "I have been a victim of the culmination of centuries of mind control technology amassed by this demonic institution. Let me explain…"

*

Waro Moto called the command center. "You damned idiot, they're broadcasting again!"

"Yes, they're in an armored personnel carrier."

"You know where it is?" Moto demanded.

There was a pause before Mello answered. "Yes."

"Then blow it up!"

"Mr. Moto… there is citizen support growing for those people… and for Vice President Saavedra."

"I don't give a bag of shit for their support."

"Mr. Moto, people have taken to the streets. They're riding on top of the APC and forming a human shield. If we strike the target, there will be thousands of civilians killed."

"I don't care about civilians, General, I care about protecting a very large investment. Do what you have to do!"

Colin Blackwater's face looked out from millions of television screens all over the Latino Union. "You have been listening to Ms. Gina Ishikawa's extraordinary broadcast indicting King Carlos of Spain, Pope Pius, and industrialist Waro Moto. You have heard a firsthand account of a victim of a modern Spanish Inquisition employing horrifying techniques of mind control and mind alternation. While the stories Ms. Ishikawa, Doctor Lenin, and Mr. Ibarra have presented have been compelling, there had been no independent corroboration.

"Now, however, I have made telephone contact with BBC news correspondent Russell MacMillan, who is in San Juan Diego to cover what was to be the inauguration of the new capital city. Russell, what can you tell us about the situation in San Juan Diego?"

A photograph of a mid-thirties balding man with a bushy beard appeared over Blackwater's shoulder.

"Colin, I'm in the Sheraton Hotel near the center of San Juan Diego. Things were pretty much business as usual until about an hour ago when I could hear small arms fire and then the detonation of heavier ordnance around the city. From my window I could see military vehicles moving, so I went to the lobby to leave the hotel. There I ran into a cordon of soldiers who refused to let me out.

"Just five minutes ago I had a call from a highly placed source at the Ministry of Defense who claimed to have a recording of an encrypted radio transmission between Waro Moto, who has been cited by Ms. Ishikawa in the conspiracy, and General João Mello, who we all heard Mr. Moto describe as a loyal army officer. Let me play that recording now."

*

"My men tell me there are more than fifty thousand people here in the park," Colonel Kobe shouted over the diesel engine, "and we're right at the center of them."

Loudspeakers had been jury-rigged throughout Union Park, and the BBC audio echoed everywhere. People gathered in tight knots around smartphones to see the video. Through questions and answers, Gina,

Alejandra, and Lenin listed all events starting with the Fourth Angel document written by Torquemada up through the people killed to keep the conspiracy secret. This, on top of the intercepted radio transmission from Waro Moto to General Mello, stirred the crowd into a low-grade fury. Citizen leaders were emerging and calling their compatriots to action.

*

Deep in the steel belly of the APC Gina and the others felt the air vibrate with the whump-whump-whump of heavy helicopter rotors. Kobe pulled himself up to the turret and looked out of the hatch.

"Gunships!" he called down to the others.

A voice electronically amplified to ear-blasting proportions intoned, "Citizens of San Juan Diego, the Latino Union Joint Military Command is declaring martial law. Until further notice, no public gatherings are allowed! You are all in violation of the law."

"Tanks are moving into position around the park!" someone on top of the APC cried.

"Clear the park immediately. If you do not comply, our helicopters and tanks will open fire in ten seconds."

*

"Russell, we're hearing a loudspeaker announcement in Spanish. What are they saying?"

MacMillan's voice sounded strained and he puffed loudly as he said, "It says the army's going to open fire on men, women, and children in ten seconds if they don't clear the park. I'm with a camera crew on our way to the roof so we can look down into the park and give you video... Okay, we've got the door open, but the ten seconds are already up. I have a very bad feeling about what we're about to see."

Colin Blackwater said nothing while he listened to MacMillan huffing over the telephone.

"We're running to the other side of the roof... fifty meters to go... almost there."

Blackwater's face, pinched with concentration as he strained to listen to the phone patch, filled millions of television screens.

"Russell?" Blackwater asked. "Russell, what do you see?"

"I don't believe it," MacMillan wheezed, trying desperately to catch his breath. "I don't believe it."

"What do you see?" Blackwater repeated more urgently.

"I see… Mardi Gras, Carnival, New Years in Time Square, and a World Cup victory party all rolled into one big celebration. Military units have broken ranks and the crews have come out of their tanks! They're singing and dancing with the civilians in Union Park!"

*

The thundering rotors of the helicopter gunships beat the air above the APC so hard that Martín could feel his rib cage vibrating. He stared blankly while holding Gina against him. Lenin, Dennis, Alejandra, and the vice president looked up at the open hatch. Suddenly the rhythm changed and the roar died away, replaced by a different reverberating cacophony— the distorted blasts of amplified music and the combined bellow of thousands of human voices.

*

"Russell, your video's coming through now," Colin Blackwater said.

The television screen filled with human tumult as seen from above at a high angle. The camera lens zoomed in on the APC.

"Russell, it looks like people are being pulled out of the armored vehicle."

"Yes, Colin, they are being pulled out and put on the shoulders of the people in the crowd around it and carried as heroes. There's Vice President Saavedra, who will be sworn in as president as soon as the death of President Ishikawa has been confirmed."

"Speaking of the broadcasts," Colin chimed in, "there's Dennis Prinn now. Our satellite television links are thanks to Prinn, an Australian freelance technician."

"That's right, Colin, and believe me, I'll thank him and the others properly when I get a chance," Russell MacMillan said. "I guarantee that none of this lot will have to buy a drink in this town for a long time. Right now, we're hearing a huge round of cheers for Gina Ishikawa, daughter of the president, as she's being lifted off the APC and onto shoulders of admirers."

"Russell," Blackwater said, "from your close-up, it looks like some of the well-wishers around her are crying."

"Yes, Colin, that's what I'm seeing through my binoculars. This is a celebration of the defeat of despotism, but it's also an outpouring of condolence for Miss Ishikawa over the presumed death of her father, who apparently gave his life to destroy that nuclear missile. He was always an admired man, and now he'll forever be a hero to the people of San Juan Diego."

MacMillan continued, "That young man you see coming through the hatch now is Martín Ibarra, the Cuban-American architect who headed up the project to design and build this capital city that has seen some destruction today by the military action. I think we were all spellbound when we saw this young man on that shocking television broadcast of the *auto-de-fé* conducted by the Inquisition."

Blackwater said, "Yes, Russell, that was chilling to see such a thing happening in the twenty-first century, and until now no one really knew if Mr. Ibarra was alive or dead. I'm hearing reports that Ms. Ishikawa was instrumental in saving Ibarra's life. What do you know about that?"

MacMillan said, "I'm hearing those same stories and here in Union Park in San Juan Diego they are the Romeo and Juliet of this crowd of thousands. At this moment you can see that he and Gina Ishikawa are being carried by the crowd, side by side."

Colin said, "It looks like the crowd is forming a long line, Russell."

"Yes, Colin, and if my experience at other world class celebrations serves, that's a conga line. The music we're hearing here in Union Park is grabbing everyone, and they're dancing. We've zoomed in on the attractive young woman out in front leading it—it's the Spanish law student who helped describe the conspiracy on the broadcast that has held our attention for the past hour. And I'd have to say she's one of the best dancers I've ever seen! Onscreen you can see the crowd is carrying Martín Ibarra and Gina Ishikawa in a victory lap around the park. What a hold Ibarra has on her! It doesn't look to me like he's *ever* going to let her go."

EPILOGUE

Waro Moto slowly pulled the headset from his ears and laid it on the seat beside him. King Carlos and Pope Pius each did the same, their faces ashen.

"Five hundred years of planning," Carlos murmured. "Five hundred years of careful execution. Five hundred years of waiting to realize Christ's rule on Earth."

Moto's face filled with contempt.

"Don't waste even a second of my time trying to make me think you really believed that religious rubbish. You were in this for the power—not for the 'glory forever, amen.'"

Carlos stood and pulled himself up to his maximum height.

"You are a crude barbarian, Moto, and you have squandered my opportunity to correct a grave historical error!"

The industrialist laughed crudely. "Listen to yourself. You call me a barbarian? What about that mass execution you staged in Mexico City? For television, no less. That's the 'bread and circuses' of your European 'civilization.'"

The two men glared at each other. The pontiff was slouched over in his seat, head buried in his hands. As he rocked back and forth, a muffled whimper of anguished torment burbled forth.

"Over!" he cried out. "It's all over!"

Moto and Carlos exchanged a glance, their mutual contempt overshadowed for the moment by their disgust for the pathetic, naked emotion on display in front of them.

Moto's satellite phone rang, startling both men. The pope continued to quietly sob. Moto looked into the king's eyes, then over at the phone, and then back again.

Carlos nodded, and Moto picked up the phone. His thumb clicked on the speaker, and he grunted at the handset.

From the phone emerged a language that neither of them spoke, but both recognized immediately. The thick accent was all-business, but carried with it the unmistakable air of barely disguised amusement. Carlos had just enough time to share a shrug with Moto before another voice cut in—female and in English. It droned without emotion as it translated.

"Are you done with your childish games now?" the female voice intoned. "Did you really think that it would be so easy to establish a new world power, just because you had piles of money at your disposal and some religious zealotry to use as a catalyst?"

The male voice cut through with laughter, and then resumed speaking, followed a few moments later by the translator.

"Gentlemen, do not get me wrong. I very much admire your audacity, but watching you play this out over the last two days made me somewhat sad for you—like watching a puppy slowly drown after falling into a toilet bowl."

Moto's fists balled, and his face reddened. "How dare you reach me on my private line to insult me like—"

"*Nyet!*" the male voice shouted. A few beats later the female voice chimed in neutrally with "no." Moto and Carlos stared down at the handset in silence, Moto stewing and the king wide-eyed in anticipation as to where this conversation was going. The Russian resumed speaking, his voice once again calm, yet commanding attention. The female voice followed.

"We do not have much time. Or, rather, I should say that *you* do not have much time. If I am correctly understanding everything I have heard in the public domain—and what my intelligence sources are busy confirming—at this moment the men aboard your private jet still have access to an enormous fortune. Enough of a fortune to retire a superpower's worth of debt and still have plenty left over to assert global financial domination. If this is true, then it is your only opportunity to survive.

"Your access to this fortune is now in grave jeopardy. The nations of the world—once they are able to ascertain the veracity of the impossible things that they have now been told—will begin the process of freezing the assets that you have access to, and for the next five hundred years they will wrangle impotently over what to do with the money. Some of it will simply disappear, but most of it will waste away, doing nothing for anyone. I am here to give you a final opportunity to rescue your colossal failure from the ashes of history—to give meaning to the remainder of your lives instead of spending years in prison.

"Instruct your pilot to turn off your plane's transponder. I will send coordinates to you. They are for a remote airfield in the Cayman Islands— you should have enough fuel to get there, I believe. Land there and then board the unmarked plane waiting for you. Once aboard, you will immediately begin working with us to secure as many of the accounts as we can. You also have a great deal of technological infrastructure in place that we could make very good use of. There will be so much to discuss."

Moto and King Carlos looked into each other's eyes, searching, and the two men immediately and wordlessly found common ground.

They would do this. They had no other choice.

"Yes," Moto said. "We agree."

A shrill shriek cut through the plane's cabin. The pope had lifted his head and was looking in horror at the handset in Moto's hands. Tears streamed from his bloodshot eyes, and his chest heaved as he tried to speak, but only more shrieks emerged. Mucus and saliva poured from his nose and mouth unabated.

The Russian voice began again—now upbeat—followed by the monotone, emotionless translation.

"That is very good, Moto-san. Very good. But please, unless that person I hear sniveling in the background is absolutely necessary in order to gain access to the accounts, I see no need for you to bring them along. It's… unseemly."

Pope Pius's breathing hitched, and he looked up at his two co-conspirators, his face a frozen mask of fear. Moto reached under his seat and pulled out a pistol.

"Yes, comrade," Moto said as Carlos stepped behind the pope, grabbing him by the shoulders and pinning him against his seat. "It does seem that not everyone has the stomach for world politics."

Thirty thousand feet above South America, the reign of the 267th pontiff—and *de jure* leader of the short-lived New Spanish Inquisition—abruptly ended.

ACKNOWLEDGEMENTS

My thanks to my mother—and Craig's grandmother—Elsie Codlin for teaching me that writing was not about putting words on paper, but rather about putting exactly the right words on paper. Thanks also to my father, James B. Codlin, for drilling me night after night on my high school Spanish homework until I suddenly got it and became fluent. My wife Terri has been my critic-in-chief for years, always pointing out shortcomings, but also always encouraging me to write more. My daughter Meredith helped me through extensive rewrites, correcting errors and suggesting more expressive writing. To the many men and women with whom I had business and friendly (in most cases one in the same) relations in Latin America and Spain and who were my windows to the culture and history of the Spanish-speaking world—not just as an observer but also as a participant. And thanks to Geoff Smith, editor extraordinaire, who helped us rip apart and reassemble the original manuscript, and polish it into a coherent, streamlined story.

The idea of *A Vial Upon the Sun* emanated from a banker I met in Austria during a business trip. We had dinner and I was absorbed by this middle-aged man who was an active officer in the Austrian army reserve. He spoke nostalgically of an Austrian princess who was exiled from her country during World War II, and to whom he and his fellow officers had secretly pledged their fealty. He knew businessmen in Hungary who also harbored that fealty and who would genuinely be happier under her righteous rule. I listened and mused—but jolted when I realized he was implying military restoration of the Austro-Hungarian Empire. From the seeds of that conversation germinated the question: What if the Spanish Inquisition, born in 1487 but moribund by the nineteenth century, rose from the shadows to launch Dark Age repression with twenty-first century tools? My efforts to flesh out and fictionalize the answer to that question resulted in this novel.

Finally, my gratitude to Joseph P. Lawler, my high school Spanish teacher. Tests had shown I had no aptitude for foreign languages, but he opened the Hispanic language, culture, and history to me. I built a forty-five-year business career on that inspiration.

—James Codlin (May 2019)

ABOUT THE AUTHORS

James Codlin received a Master's degree in Latin American Studies from the University of Minnesota and served five years as a navigator in the Air Force. He retired from a 42-year career in international business having traveled extensively in Latin America, Europe, and Asia. He was active with the Atlanta District Export Council and served on an international panel to advise the railroad transit system of Hong Kong. He speaks fluent Spanish and has a working knowledge of Portuguese, Italian and French.

Craig Codlin graduated from Syracuse University's S.I. Newhouse School of Public Communications as a broadcast journalism major before heading to law school at the University of Georgia in Athens, Georgia. He has practiced as a lawyer in the telecommunications industry for more than twenty years and currently lives near Seattle, Washington.